GRAYLING CROSS

To Marcia

Thanks so much for the support

– Gayleen Froese

Gayleen *Froese*

GRAYLING CROSS

NeWest Press

Library and Archives Canada Cataloguing in Publication

Froese, Gayleen, 1972 –
Grayling Cross / Gayleen Froese.

ISBN 978-1-897126-73-8

I. Title.

PS8611.R634G73 2011 C813'.6 C2010-906765-7

Editor: Leslie Vermeer
Copy editor: Andrew Wilmot
Cover and interior design: Natalie Olsen, Kisscut Design
Author photo: Sebastian Hanlon

 Canada Council for the Arts Conseil des Arts du Canada  Canadian Heritage Patrimoine canadien 

NeWest Press acknowledges the support of the Canada Council for the Arts, the Alberta Foundation for the Arts, and the Edmonton Arts Council for our publishing program. We acknowledge the financial support of the Government of Canada through the Canada Book Fund for our publishing activities.

NeWest Press

201, 8540 – 109 Street
Edmonton, Alberta T6G 1E6
780.432.9427
www.newestpress.com

No bison were harmed in the making of this book.

printed and bound in Canada 1 2 3 4 5 13 12 11 10

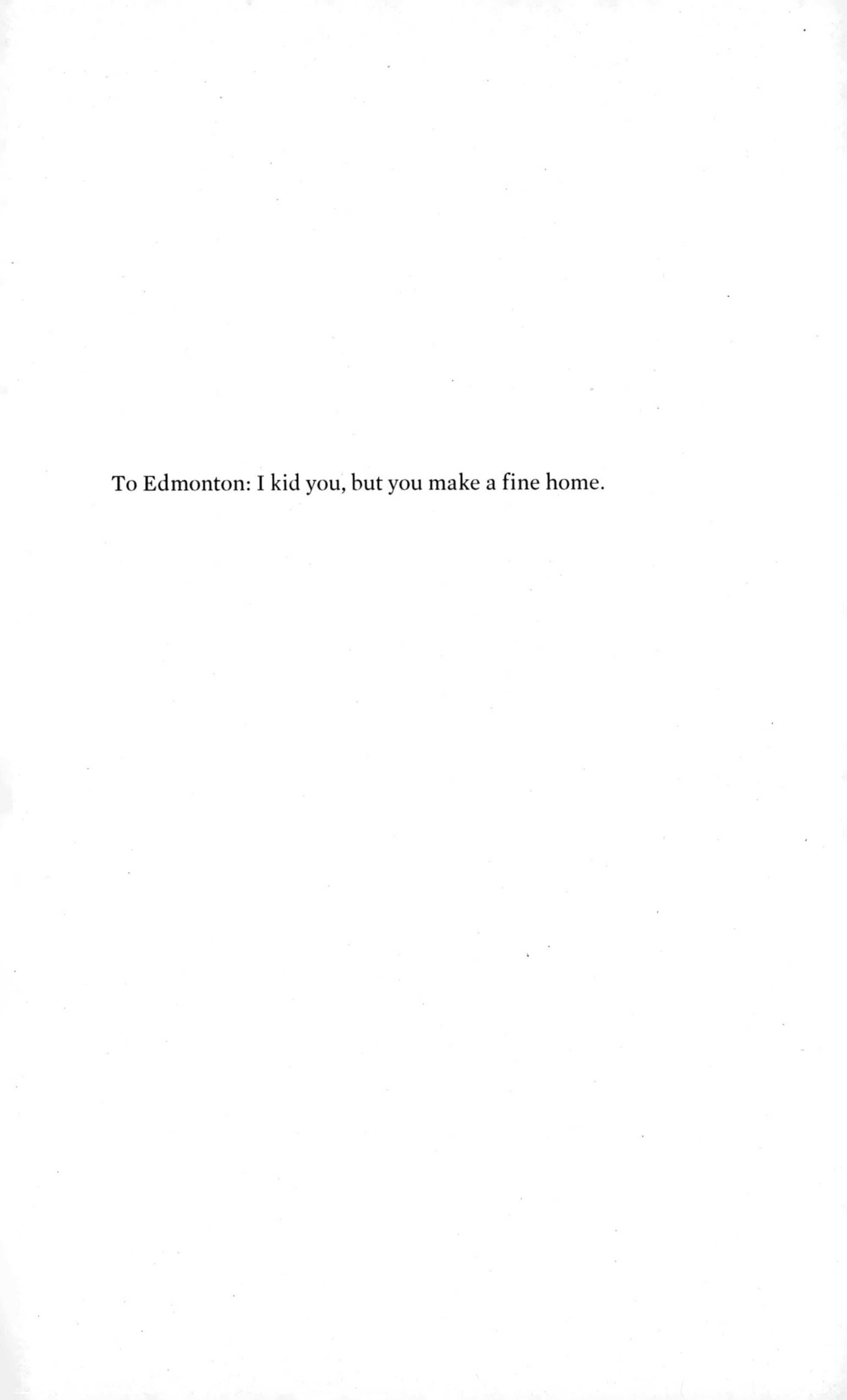

To Edmonton: I kid you, but you make a fine home.

Wann wann nich wäa,wäa Koohschiet Botta.

— Mennonite adage

"IF YOU THINK I'M STUPID, why would you want to hire me?"

The office door was stuck open again, hung up on a bump under the short grey carpet. Anna could see that from the bottom of the stairs, as clearly as she could hear Collie's voice.

She took the stairs two at a time, not that it mattered. She was already late.

From the landing, she could see the client. Prospective client, anyway. He looked young, late teens or early twenties, with long dark hair and sharp features.

"I... don't? Why —"

He stopped because Anna had reached the doorway. He gave her a curious look and she answered it with a guilty smile, then turned the contrition to Collie.

"Sorry. There was a... thing."

"Gotta hate things," Collie said cheerfully. So she wasn't pissed about the lateness. Anna made her way to her desk, careful not to bump the client's arm as she went past.

"This is Anna Gareau," Collie told the prospect. "We work together. You don't think I'm stupid, or you don't want to hire me?"

The prospect twisted in his seat and looked at Anna as if trying to place her, then faced Collie again.

"I don't think you're stupid."

Collie was tapping one key on her laptop, too lightly to actually depress it. It was her latest fidget.

"Then let's try this again. Your name is..."

The client, who had been slouching in a youthful way, sat up straight.

"Rowan Oake."

Collie smiled. She wasn't even pretending to mean it.

"One more strike and you're out of here, kiddo."

Anna felt a little sorry for the guy, who seemed to have decided words weren't working out for him and was now trying a shrug. His hair moved when he did it and Anna saw thin braids woven into it. Not many, just a few on each side. It would probably have looked ridiculous on most guys, but this one had natural good looks that saved him from that fate.

"Maybe I'm overreacting," Collie said. "Anna, if someone asked you to find their mother, how helpful do you think it would be to know that someone's real last name?"

"It's not Oake?" Anna asked. Collie gave her the same nasty smile she'd used on the prospect.

"It is not."

"It might as well be," the kid said. "I don't know my real last name. Or hers."

Collie leaned back in her chair. One click back. The chair had three positions, one upright and two slanted. When Collie was good and fed up with someone, the chair went two clicks back. Apparently Rowan Whoever still had her attention.

"There are channels," she said, "for adopted kids who want to find their parents. There are also agencies that specialize in it."

"I know. This is different. Ian said I should talk to you."

"Ian..." Collie said. As if there could be more than one answer.

"Ian McLaren."

Anna let her head drop to her desk . From that position, she heard Collie's response.

"Mandrake."

"Uh... I don't think he likes being called Mandrake," the prospect said.

"I don't think we liked the last four clients Mandrake sent us," Collie countered. Reluctantly, Anna lifted her head.

"What exactly did Mandrake say about us?" she asked.

The prospect turned to her with undisguised relief. Apparently he was tired of talking to Collie.

"He said you were a retrocognitive clairsentient."

"And do you know what that means?" Anna asked. "Because I don't."

Collie made a choking sound, which alarmed Anna until she realized it was the start of a laughing fit.

"Did Mandrake tell you that we specialized in anything?" Anna asked.

"He said to ignore the sign on your door."

Anna glanced at the door. Maybe it had changed since her arrival five minutes earlier.

Nope. It still read, "Colette Kostyna, Public Relations."

"Most people ignore it," Anna said. She glared at Collie, who had more or less finished laughing. "Please step in anytime."

"We're, uh, not well-qualified detectives," Collie said. "We just have some specialized knowledge and, because of that, we're able to work within a certain community. I really am a PR person most of the time."

"Huh." The kid tried to lean back. His chair didn't do that, so he gave it up and settled for resting one leg on the other, right ankle over his left knee. "I would have figured a retrocognitive clairsentient would be more broadly useful than that."

"Regardless," Collie said, "the situation is as I described it. So Ian was probably wrong to point you in our direction."

"He told me what you did in Victoria," the kid said. Anna was surprised to hear herself snort.

"And you took that as a recommendation?"

He looked at her, emotion seeming to push his sharp features forward.

"*Yes,*" he said. "I told you I was in kind of a different situation."

"Look," Anna said, "Rowan... is it actually Rowan?"

The kid smiled. Something about the smile made Anna feel bad for him again.

"Ever since I can remember."

"Rowan, Colette and I have one, ah, skill in this detective thing. One. You can call us if you have a problem you can't explain to the police or to a real detective without sounding like you're crazy. That's it. If you can explain it to a normal person, or if you don't care that you sound nuts, we are not for you. I mean... unless you're pretty sure things can't get much worse, I would question hiring us for any reason at all. Except PR. Collie knows how to do that."

Collie raised her travel mug to Anna.

"We have got to get you on tape, make some infomercials."

"I'm just saying," Anna said, looking Rowan in the eye, "we can't guarantee that we will not screw up and cause trouble. Unless you need our... unique point of view... you're better off with professionals."

Rowan shook his head and Anna got the sense her little speech had meant nothing to him. He had the look of a guy in the midst of a downpour who'd been threatened with a squirt gun.

"You have another skill."

So that was what retrowhatsis meant. She'd figured as much. Fucking Mandrake.

"That's not on the table," she said, as evenly as she could manage. It wasn't the kid's fault Mandrake had been out of line.

His eyes seemed to widen and narrow at once. Anna had been able to do that, too, when she was a teenager. One of the few gifts of adolescence.

"Why the –"

He stopped.

"I'm sorry. None of my business."

From the look on Collie's face, she was as gobsmacked by that as Anna was.

"Wow," Collie said. "I didn't think anyone your age knew those words."

"Not with those pronouns," Anna agreed.

The kid didn't smile. Fair enough, since he was the one getting ripped on.

"Sorry," Anna added.

That made the kid smile, just a little.

"Even if you don't want to –" he stopped again, but this time it was different. His eyes had lost focus and he'd turned his head toward the door before freezing in place. Anna looked at Collie, who was looking at her.

"What..."

Anna shook her head.

"I don't –"

Rowan shook his head, sharply. The thin braids flew. His eyes focused and he smiled at them as he got to his feet and grabbed a worn leather jacket from the back of his chair.

"Gotta go. I'm sorry. Can I come back tomorrow? Same time? I really do have my reasons for wanting to hire you guys."

"Uh..." Collie looked at Anna. "When are you off?"

"I can be here by seven," Anna said.

"Seven's good," the kid said. "Thanks."

And he was gone, out the door and down the stairs at a run. He did not shut the door behind him.

"Wanna follow him?" Collie asked brightly.

Anna gave Collie a look that she hoped would convey her

deep love for asinine suggestions.

"That would be one of the many detective skills we do not have."

"True," Collie said. "I guess you could feel up the sidewalk and figure out where he went."

"Thank you," Anna said. "For a moment, I'd forgotten that I was going to kill Mandrake."

"Oh, yeah," Collie said. "That's right. No time like the present."

Before Anna could say anything, Collie had the phone in her hand and was dialing. Anna remembered, suddenly, that she had a headache. She'd had one since about noon. She dug in her purse for Advil as Collie spoke.

"Mandrake! We just spoke with a friend of yours... yes. Rowan. He was charming, but he had this notion that one of us was a psychometrist for hire. Where would he have gotten an idea like that, Mandrake?"

Anna made her way to the kitchenette, which was what Collie insisted on calling the stand where they kept their kettle, microwave and coffee pot. As she grabbed a bottle of water from beneath the table, Collie spoke again.

"He did, yeah. But... no. I don't. I... what?"

Anna swallowed the pills, finished the water and tossed the bottle into the recycling box. As she went back to her desk, Collie was still talking.

"We can do that. The usual place?"

Were they meeting Ian? Anna raised her eyebrows at Collie, who offered a completely unhelpful shrug.

"Okay. See you in ten."

Apparently they were meeting Ian.

"You decide to make it a fair fight?" Anna inquired. "Face to face, fair warning?"

Collie was rooting around under her desk, probably looking for the purse she'd left beside the kitchenette.

"Sure, because that would make a fight with Mandrake fair." She shrugged. "He sounds contrite. He wants to talk. At Katja's."

No surprise. Ian was probably getting kickbacks from the place. Not that Anna minded.

"Your purse is over there," Anna said. Collie nodded.

"I was just testing to see if you'd spotted it," she said.

They were on the street a minute later, weaving through packs of underdressed students on their way to Whyte Avenue. This early in September, it still felt like summer, at least until the sun went down. Collie was dressed for it. Slight of build, she was suited to sundresses and strappy shoes. She hated having to shove her long red curls under a wool hat or bury her narrow shoulders under enough material to keep her vaguely warm. Anna, being a thousand feet tall and wide as a barn, switched to sturdy fall clothes the moment the first leaf turned. Boots and sweaters and heavy jeans. She was regretting that decision today.

About a block along, Anna remembered something.

"Col?"

"Yeah?"

"Why wasn't his last name Oake?"

Collie was looking at her, paying no attention to where she was walking and still managing, somehow, to avoid hitting anyone. And she thought Anna was the one with a mysterious power.

"Rowan Oake? That doesn't ring a bell? Vanished colony? One of the great mysteries of the last two hundred years?"

Anna shook her head. Collie grinned.

"And you an occult detective. You crack me up."

"I'm a riot," Anna said. "Watch where you're going. I am not an occult detective."

"Well..." Collie paused, then had to scramble to catch up. "To be fair to us, we did solve that case in Victoria. I mean, we figured out who did it and we put a stop to it, right? Technically, we —"

"Bitched it up," Anna said. "We just kept shaking the jar until the murderer got nervous. What do nervous murderers do again? Refresh my memory."

Collie glared at her.

"Give themselves away," she said.

"By murdering," Anna said.

"I get that," Collie said. "But it's not as if we knew what we were doing. And you were the one who pretended to be a real detective. I was just trying to find out who killed my friend."

"You knew damned well I was not a real detective," Anna reminded her. "Look, you can't argue that we're pros because we did such a good job in Victoria and then argue it wasn't our fault the body count went up because, hey, we didn't know what we were doing."

Collie said nothing for many more steps. Just heels clicking, quick and hard on the sidewalk.

"Apparently," she said, as they crossed at Whyte, "I can. Argue that."

Anna nodded.

"Not convincingly."

Katja's was less loud than usual, if no less crowded. The tiny coffee shop insisted on hosting live musicians, from solo acts to small jazz combos, on a stage not much bigger than a manhole cover. The acts were usually pretty good, and geared to an old enough crowd that the U of A freshmen stayed away. The food wasn't bad either. On the other hand, having a conversation within two feet of three other tables and three feet of a double bass was challenging at best.

"There," Collie said. At least, she said something and pointed toward a table at the back, where Ian was enjoying a beer. One of those microbrew things he liked, thick enough to stand a spoon in.

Anna nodded and took the lead, clearing a path to Ian's table. If she kept her eyes on where she was going and moved without hesitation, she found that most people got out of her way.

"Ladies." Ian raised his beer in salute. He was holding it in his normal hand. The other was gloved and hanging at his side, a faint orange glow slipping out between his glove and shirt. He still hadn't told them how he'd come to have a glowing orange hand, and Anna didn't suspect he ever would.

Anna nodded and took a seat. Collie scooted past her and sat next to Ian. He'd parked himself near the stage, as usual, but it was just a guitarist and not a particularly loud one. Talking, and not screaming, was a definite possibility.

"Mandrake," Collie said brightly. Ian shook his head.

"You make it difficult to do favours for you."

"You know, that's —" Collie stopped. "Just a sec. Anna, have you eaten?"

Anna hadn't, but this conversation could go in any direction and she didn't think it would be smart to commit to a meal.

"I'm okay," she said. "I'll get something later."

Collie turned to Ian.

"Where were we?"

"Favours," he said.

"Right." Her expression softened. "Ian. I'm not gonna say don't do us any favours, because we all know you throw us most of the work we get."

"Not me," Ian said. "The Embassy."

Collie waved a hand.

"Whatever. It comes through you. But telling normal people about Anna is not a favour."

Ian looked at his fingers, which were covered in condensation from his beer bottle, and rubbed them lightly against the wooden tabletop.

"Normal?"

He sounded as if he wasn't so much questioning her word

choice as asking her to define a word he'd never heard before. Collie gave him a disgusted look.

"You know what I mean."

Ian responded with his most beatific smile.

"You are what you do."

"I also eat, sleep, and watch TV." Anna said. "Nobody shows up at our office spouting those fun facts."

"Hire them," Collie said in a passable impression of Ian's thin voice. "The dark-haired one watches reruns of Barney Miller."

"Is what I'm saying," Anna confirmed. "The kid –"

"Operative word here," Collie put in. "Kid. Child."

"Was looking for his mother," Anna went on. "Nothing weird about that. Plenty of trained professionals could handle that competently."

"And without collateral damage," Collie added. "Did you mention our body count?"

Predictably, that was when the waitress appeared. Rain, Anna reminded herself. After being served by the same person at least once a week for six months, Anna had decided to check the bill for the woman's name. Not knowing had seemed rude, somehow.

Tonight, Rain had gelled her black hair into spikes, put a blood red stud through her nose and donned a t-shirt that read, "I ate my twin." There probably wasn't much reason to worry about what she might overhear.

"'Nother one?" she asked Ian. She had a knack for pitching her voice so she could be hear without yelling. Ian smiled and nodded. Rain raised her eyebrows at Collie and Anna. "Ladies?"

"Iced coffee," Collie said.

"Iced tea," Anna said. Rain nodded.

"You guys should make that your regular thing and stick with it. Then you could be all, 'the usual'... or I could just get it for you when you walked in."

"Our moods shift like wind-blown sands," Collie said. "Sorry."

Rain nodded again and moved on to the next table.

"You didn't kill Stella," Ian said. "Or that other friend of yours."

"No," Collie agreed. "We just poked a crazy guy until he felt obligated to do it himself. Seriously, man, people who do not need us do not need to be hiring us. And Anna has made it pretty clear about the touching thing. That is not our USP. That's strictly a second line tactic."

"Yeah, and what did you even say to that kid?" Anna added. "Retro something or other?"

Ian looked lost. Collie laughed.

"Your buddy called Anna a retrocognitive clairsentient." She turned to Anna. "It just means that, when you touch things, the information you get is from the past."

Why these people couldn't just say that, Anna would never know.

"Look," she told Ian. "I don't care if the people in this crowd know what I do... but telling this kid we were a good bet to find his mother because I could get touchy feely with his keep-sakes was way over the line."

Ian looked from one to the other. He seemed to be studying their faces, looking past the skin and bone. It was a look so profound and searching that it seemed impossible that anyone else would ever know them so well. After a few moments, he took a slow, deep breath and spoke.

"What's a USP?"

Anna looked at Collie, hoping it would cue Ian to do the same.

"Unique selling point," Collie said. "It means... okay, say you had a detective agency, and you wanted to advertise it. You wanted to tell people why they should hire you instead of all the other detective agencies out there. You might do that by saying, 'Whatever crazy-ass story you bring us involving the supernatural, we will believe you.' See, because no one else in town offers that. So, if that's what you're looking for, we're your agency. Or, you know, you could tell people 'We have a psychic lady who can feel up stuff and have visions and get clues that way' and, hey, no one else has that either. And it's an even better USP, really, because it could be of use to almost anyone, rather than just to people whose problems involve the supernatural. Where was I going with this?"

Yeah. No wonder Ian didn't believe what he'd done was a problem. Anna leaned back a little, hoping it would widen her glare enough to spread it over both of them.

"You were going to say," she said, "that it wasn't our USP, because the psychic lady doesn't like touching other people's crappy memories and she doesn't like being called the psychic lady either."

"Right," Collie said, looking at Ian. "I was going to say that."

"Again," Anna said. "Because we have told you this many, many times. And Collie didn't mean it any of those times, but I did."

Collie's head turned so fast, her hair swatted Anna's face. Anna swiped at it to clear the last few strands before looking Collie in the eye.

"Wanna deny it?"

Collie cocked her head.

"You gonna poke me to see if I'm lying?"

"Don't need to," Anna said. "I know what you think about this. Changes nothing."

"I've noticed" Collie answered. She leaned back in her chair. It was less satisfying for her, by necessity, as anything more than a few millimetres would have blocked Rain's path. "So, Ian, you can see where sending that kid to us was folly at best."

Ian was tapping lightly on the table, keeping time to something that was not the music.

"He's cagey. He needs your USP. He wanted your measure. He'll tell you more the second time."

"What huh?" Collie asked sweetly. Anna laughed.

"Let me guess. This Rowan is involved with something supernatural. He didn't want to tell us because he doesn't share his business with just anyone. He probably faked that little fit as an excuse to leave so he can sleep on the idea of confiding in us. How'm I doing, Ian?"

"You're denying your soul," he said. Anna had to unclench her teeth to respond.

"And my analysis of Rowan?"

"He isn't a nephew."

Anna tapped Collie's arm.

"Tag," she said. Collie bit her lip, then nodded.

"Okay. He's saying the last four people he sent to us were relatives or whatever. They didn't know Ian was... you know... Mandrake. No offence."

Ian spread his hands and smiled. It was a funny effect, the one hand gloved, the orange peeping out as the cloth shifted.

"But this guy," Collie said, "knows Ian in a professional capacity."

"He's my friend," Ian said. "But he knows what I am."

"What you do," Collie corrected absently.

"Same thing," Ian said, and Anna mouthed it along with him.

"Okay," Collie said, "So Rowan's a supernormal paranatural whatever. I guess we can sort this out tomorrow, if your buddy decides to show up. Anything your employers need from us in the meantime?"

Ian shook his head.

"They're good. The cheque for last time is in your purse."

Collie rolled her eyes but said nothing. Anna looked at Ian.

"Showoff," she said mildly.

"I didn't put it there," Ian said. "Anything I port, I port with it."

Anna couldn't remember if he'd told her that or not. Every teleporter in town seemed to have their own style and she couldn't keep them all straight.

"They couldn't have just given it to you to give to me?" Collie asked. "Like only slightly abnormal people?"

"They have their ways," Ian said placidly. Anna could see Collie's teeth gritting at that, but she could see the sense in it. That was probably exactly the attitude that working at the Embassy required.

Even Collie, working at arm's length from them, made small concessions. With any other client, she would have pulled the cheque from her purse and made sure everything was in order. With these guys, she didn't count her money while sitting at the table. Anna would have asked why, but she had a feeling Collie didn't actually know. Just an instinct.

Their drinks arrived and Ian paid, as always. At first Anna had thought it charity – they'd been jobless upon their arrival in Edmonton. Now she figured it was simply Someone Else's Money... and a well-off someone, at that. If the Embassy wanted to ply her with iced tea, she wasn't going to object.

"They're very happy with you," Ian said. It was as if he were reading Anna's mind.

Collie snorted and grabbed the spoon jutting from her iced coffee.

"We're pretty happy with them. Rent's paid up."

"It always was, before. And you quit. If putting out one cigarette can be called quitting."

Collie stopped swirling coffee and condensed milk and stared at him.

"I could ask you what you think you know about my old job, or what you're trying to say about your bosses, but I don't think I'd like your answers. So how about I just tell you to drop it?"

He did, with his usual shrug. Collie dropped it as well.

Collie's old job had been, supposedly, doing publicity for a successful nonfiction author. Actually, Anna had learned, Collie had been the author's partner in blackmail. She'd never told anyone, as far as Anna knew. She'd never even told Anna in so many words. That meant there was no way she's told Mandrake.

And yet, he seemed to know.

Collie did not ask him how. She chatted with him about inconsequential things as Anna sipped her iced tea and pretended to care. She wasn't sure if she'd been angrier when she thought Ian didn't get it about her position on the psychometry thing, or if she was madder now that she knew he got it and didn't care. A toss-up, she supposed. Both paled in the face of how pissed she was at Collie for not fucking well leaving it alone.

The party broke up early and amicably. Anna let Collie's good mood persist until they nearly back to the office, then said, "How's the Tercel?"

"Grr," Collie said. For a moment, Anna thought she might not elaborate. Just as she was about to ask for details, Collie went on. "They don't have the part yet. They have to order it in from... Mars."

"Oh," Anna said. "The delay is understandable then."

"That's how I look at it."

"Office?" Anna inquired as they reached the downstairs door. Collie shook her head and they proceeded toward the Jeep parked across the street.

Not for the first time, Anna was grateful that they were living just over the bridge from the office. She was getting hungrier by the minute.

"Work sucked?" Collie said as Anna pulled away from the curb.

"If anyone ever tells you," Anna replied, "that a sugar glider is a sweet-natured animal, they are a damned liar."

Collie perked up.

"You had a sugar glider at the clinic? Really? They're adorable."

"No. They are not."

Collie grinned.

"Maybe it just didn't like you."

"It liked no one. And it got out the back door."

Anna hit the brakes as someone cut her off. Or didn't. She still didn't have the hang of traffic circles.

"If you went the other way," Collie pointed out, "you wouldn't hit the circle."

Anna said nothing. She kept saying it until Collie shifted uncomfortably beside her.

"So. An escape. That's exciting. Did you get it back?"

"Yes."

"Oooookay."

As they approached the bridge, Anna said, "The number of times I have told Ian is nothing to the number of times I have told you. And the very idea that you need to be told..."

Collie was looking at the skyline as hard as she possibly could.

"I think it scares you and upsets you because you've never gotten comfortable with it. Which may be why you tend have unpleasant visions. I know you've had a few good ones when you weren't anxious."

Anna jammed the Jeep into second, preparing to climb the bank. She shoved a little harder than was necessary.

"Someday you'll find a rattlesnake in your purse with a note tied to it saying you just need to get fucking comfortable with it."

They climbed the bank in silence, Anna taking the curves with practiced ease. They'd thrown her, at first, but she'd found a rhythm in them and almost loved them now.

As they waited to turn onto their street, Collie said, "Moms."

"What?" Anna asked mildly.

"You know. This Rowan kid is looking for his mom. You were looking for your mom."

Anna shook her head.

"Mothers aren't rare, Colette. Guy comes in missing a first edition of... whatever that book was you lost last month... that would be a coincidence worth mentioning."

"*Something Wicked This Way Comes,*" Collie said. "Joce gave it to me, by the way. The topic, Anna, is not odd coincidences. It's empathy. I thought maybe you'd feel a connection."

Anna snorted. Twice in one night. Once more and she'd be three times a lady.

"The day I do, Kostyna, I will let you know."

6:45, RUSHING AROUND the corner with a wrap in her hand, Anna nearly bumped into a coffee-toting Collie heading for the door to their office building.

"You eat?" Anna asked. Collie shook her head.

"Had a PR client who would not go. There's a cookie in my pocket."

"I'm sure there's innuendo in that somewhere," Anna said.

"I'm too hungry to think of any," Collie said. "We have got to start booking dinner."

On the face of it, that was absurd. Who had to put supper in their day timer, unless it was a meeting or something? But, then again, she couldn't argue with the fact that a Bad Ass wrap was currently dripping down her sleeve to the elbow and that she hadn't really sat down to eat anything in weeks.

"It's a thought," she admitted.

They went up the stairs and Anna took Collie's coffee while Collie unlocked the office door. She regretted that a moment later when Collie yelped and jumped back into her.

"Hey," Anna said. She meant to follow that up with something brilliant, but was stopped by the sight of a dark-haired man sitting in their client chair. In their office. Which had been locked.

Anna dropped the coffee and the wrap, grabbed Collie's arm, and yanked her back into the hallway. They pressed against the wall beside the open door.

"What the *shit*?" Collie hissed. "The door was locked."

"I don't know," Anna said from between clenched teeth.

"Do we call the cops?" Collie asked, cell phone already in her hand.

"I don't know."

"Do we run for it?"

Anna considered that.

"We'd have to go past the door."

"So... cops?"

It was probably the smart thing to do, but Anna couldn't bring herself to okay it. It was like calling someone to boost her car – she couldn't help thinking she ought to take care of it herself.

"Maybe we could –"

Anna was rescued from having to think of an end to that sentence by the wall shaking behind her. She jumped and heard Collie squeak. After a second of terror, Anna realized their office door had slammed shut.

"Was that the door?"

Anna looked at Collie. What else did she think It might have been?

"Probably not by itself. I bet it was that guy."

Collie's eyes narrowed.

"But seriously, folks... why the fuck would – excuse me."

She was asking to be excused, not for her French, but for her ringing cell phone. She took it from her pocket and glanced at the display, then held it up for Anna to see. It showed their office phone number.

Anna pinched the bridge of her nose. Beside her, she heard Collie's voice.

"Care to explain yourself?"

A minute or so passed with no sound from Collie, apart from the occasional "uh-huh." Then Collie said, "Okay, I appreciate that, but breaking into our office isn't just rude. It's creepy. If we go in there, you could shoot us both dead and step over our bodies on your way out and no one would ever — what? You what? Why —"

More silence. Anna looked at the ceiling. It had water damage. Maybe it would cave in and kill her.

"I can't say that does make me feel better about you. It's more that it makes me feel worse about everyone else. But we'll confer and I'll get back to you."

Anna looked down in time to see Collie putting her phone away. Collie looked at her.

"He says there's no point worrying about him shooting us because he searched our desks and we don't have guns, so anyone could just walk in and shoot us anytime without breaking in or lying in wait."

"Could we not be carrying guns?"

Collie shrugged.

"He seems to think we could not."

"Did he say why he broke in?"

"He didn't want to be seen waiting outside."

Huh. Anna leaned against the wall and shut her eyes.

"Leaving aside the whole issue of, you know, seen by who —"

"— m," Collie finished. Anna ignored her.

"He obviously knows how to use a phone. He couldn't have called?"

Anna could feel Collie's next shrug against her arm.

"That is kind of weird. But I don't think he's here to kill us or anything. I mean, if someone came here to kill us, I doubt we'd have time to talk about it. Not if they were halfway competent."

"We'd be dead." Anna agreed.

"So we might as well go inside."

There seemed to be a gap in that logic, somewhere, but Anna didn't feel like analyzing it. Without moving from her spot on the wall, she stretched out one arm and knocked on the door.

"It's open."

It was a low voice, without any suggestion of humour. Collie responded to it by pushing forward from the wall, walking past Anna and entering their office. After a heartbeat, Anna followed.

The man was sitting in the client chair, not seeming to have moved an inch since they'd first spotted him.

Viewed dispassionately, he was probably an appealing sight. Anna wasn't feeling all that dispassionate about the jerk, so she couldn't be certain, but she thought he might have the looks of a big-screen action star. Handsome, strong, generic. He had thick black hair, just a bit longer than a brushcut, and broad shoulders beneath a black leather coat. Black jeans, too. Black crewneck sweater. Black boots. He was Collie's dream date circa 1992, or would have been with the addition of some heavy eyeliner and without the Y chromosome.

Collie wasn't eyeing him the way she would eye a dream date. She was glaring at him from behind her desk, where she had dropped into her seat with a thud.

"I'm sorry," she said. "Did we forget to close the door?"

Their guest kept his eyes on Collie as he spoke. They were a dark blue, almost navy. They probably made chicks swoon.

"You should take this seriously. It's for your protection."

Anna didn't care for the paternalism, but he did seem serious and he probably knew something they didn't. Maybe a few things. She shut the door and glanced to Collie to see if that was okay by her. Collie didn't glance back. She was still looking at their client as if trying to activate the heat vision she wished she had.

"If it's so dangerous for us to be around you," Collie said, "and you really care about our protection, have you considered not being here?"

"I have business with you," he said, seemingly unfazed by Collie's attitude. Collie, not used to someone being unfazed by her attitude, looked bewildered. She turned to Anna.

"You want this one?"

Anna shrugged.

"Sure."

She went to her desk. By the time was she seated and settled, their guest had turned his chair to face her. She gave him a nod.

"We do have business with someone, shortly. So you have about ten minutes to say whatever you came here to say."

He breathed in through his nose, his chest puffing out visibly as he did so. He said, "How do you know Rowan Bell?"

"We don't know anyone with that name," Colette said. Which was accurate enough, Anna supposed. It was also churlish, but Anna had some sympathy for that stance. Breaking into their office to await one of their clients... well, almost clients... did not impress her.

"Can't help you," she told the man in black.

"I think you can." He reached into his coat and Anna sat up straighter, for no reason that made sense. Was she trying to give him more torso to shoot if he suddenly pulled a gun?

Instead of a gun, he produced an index card. Even from a few feet away, Anna recognized Mandrake's handwriting. Colette Kostyna, it said. Anna Gareau. And a few details, including their office address and Collie's cell phone number. Beneath that, an unfamiliar hand had noted their second appointment. Ten minutes in the future. In theory. Except Anna was starting to think it might have been cancelled.

"I found this at Mr. Bell's apartment," he said, handing the card to Anna. "Also, your colleague recognized his name."

"I did not," Collie protested. "I don't know a Rowan Bell."

He swivelled to look at Collie.

"The way your desks are placed, someone is always behind me."

"It's not ergonomic," Collie allowed. "But the feng shui is amazing."

"You're paranoid. Defensive."

"There is also that," Collie said mildly. She seemed to have cooled off some, though Anna couldn't think why. "I sincerely do not know anyone by that name. Now, some people, for reasons of their own, use fake names. So maybe I've met this guy. But I'm not going to puzzle out who he might have been so I can talk about him to a stranger. Surely you can understand."

"I can. Let's look at this another way. What if I were your client?"

Collie cocked her head.

"I couldn't quite hear you," she said. "It sounded as if you said, 'what if I offered you a bribe.'"

The man in black actually smiled a little.

"Incorrect. I'm investigating Rowan Bell's disappearance."

Anna had been expecting it, but somehow it still surprised her.

"He's missing?" she said, just the way a big idiot would. "Since when?"

Their guest didn't even bother to turn her way.

"I came here to talk with him and couldn't find him. I did find your card in his apartment."

"It's a big city," Collie said. "Physically. It sprawls. Also, we have many fine highways. And a couple of airports. And buses. And a trai —"

"I know," their guest interrupted, "that he has disappeared."

"Okay," Collie said. "A teenager isn't where you think he should be for, like, an afternoon, and you feel confident in declaring him 'missing.' Cops wait, like, forty-eight hours, but not you."

"He has his habits," the man said. Collie nodded.

"Obviously you're very comfortable with your detective skills and you feel you have a handle on this situation. So... besides the information you claim you're not trying to buy, I can't imagine what you'd need us for."

"The sign on your door says Public Relations. I'm told you act as liaisons with the local psionic community. Rowan was involved with that community. They're hostile toward outsiders and I need their cooperation. This is the capacity in which I would like to hire you."

Unbelievable. Anna stared at him.

"Why are you looking for him?"

"That's not relevant to the job," he said.

"Sure it is," Collie protested. "You show up here with something of his, something he might have even kept on his person, and you break into our office, and we're supposed to happily accept that you're his friend and you're looking for him? What if you killed him? Or you want us to help you find him so you can kill him? After introducing you around town, we would feel a mite foolish."

"I'm surprised to hear that concerns you," the man said mildly. Anna heard the squeak of Collie's chair pushing back from her desk and raised a hand to still her. She didn't take her eyes off their guest, but the noise stopped, so she assumed Collie had stopped as well.

"Why are you looking for him?"

"He's a friend," the man said. "And you're a fool to ask. What kind of answer do you expect?"

Anna opened her mouth, but he cut her off.

"I could attempt to prove he's my friend, but many people have been murdered by people they considered friends. Anything I tell you is meaningless."

Anna looked at Collie, who rolled her eyes. The guy was right, but that had never in the history of the world made anyone less irritating. Anna stretched a hand toward him.

"Do you have anything at all to back up your story?" she asked. "A photo, maybe?"

He tilted his head. Apparently it was possible to surprise him.

"I just explained to you –"

"Yeah," Anna said. "I remember it fondly. If you had nothing, you'd have said so by now. What have you got?"

He was watching her with interest now. He was probably arrogant enough to think that someone who was capable of surprising him was capable of anything. Anna tried to look as if that were so.

He reached into an inside jacket pocket, still staring at Anna, and pulled out a packet. It was a piece of leather, folded and bound with leather ties. It looked like something Jacques Cartier would have carried his important papers in.

From the packet, he took a photograph. A printout, really, on photo paper. He hesitated, looked at it for a moment before holding it out for her.

Not wanting to see Collie's "what the hell are you doing" expression, Anna didn't look at her. She just took the picture.

It showed the kid they knew as Rowan not-really-Oake, maybe a year or two younger than he was now. It was black and white, grainy, time-stamped with a code she didn't understand. A security camera shot, showing a plain bedroom with bare walls, no window, and the kid asleep in bed.

Collie was half-standing behind her desk, leaning forward to see it. Anna rode out on the sound of Collie's voice as she turned to the client and said,

"Dude..."

She has her back against something sharp and cold. Given the racks of computer equipment and control units surrounding her, it's a good bet that computer equipment is behind her as well.

She's flattened into the far corner of the room because there isn't much space. It's six by six, maybe, designed to hold one person at a time, and she is far from alone. The man in black is pressing buttons on a console to her right and the kid is standing in front of her, watching him.

"Can I help you with something?"

Anna can see Rowan's face, so she isn't surprised when he speaks. The man in black, on the other hand, twitches. His shoulders tense and he whirls around, hands up and ready for a fight. Anna gets the sense that, for him, it's the equivalent of fainting from shock.

"Jesus," the man mutters.

"I think he has a beard," the kid says. "Can I help you?"

The man in black is studying Rowan, his face in particular. Rowan looks the same as in the photograph, down to the sleep-scattered hair. He's even wearing a t-shirt and boxers, the kind a person would wear to bed.

"You live here," the man says.

"Sad but true," Rowan says.

"You're supposed to be in your room. Locked down."

"I bet you're not supposed to be here at all."

"I can stop you before you scream," the man says. It's chilling, both in content and delivery, but the kid just laughs.

"Ooh, tough guy," he says. "Are you in the security system? Can you unlock rooms? You got in here somehow."

"Maybe it was magic," the man in black says. His face stays impassive, but he has wrapped a sneer around the words. The kid stops smiling. He has the same troubled expression that bothered Anna so much the night before.

"Magicians never get in here. Or out of here."

He turns to Anna and she jumps a little. She has almost

forgotten she's there.

"Except for you."

He grows, changes before her eyes to the teenager she's met, and gives her a rueful smile.

"I was one smug little jerk at that age, wasn't I?"

ANNA SHUT HER EYES and opened them again. She was in the office, still holding the picture. Collie was still railing at the man in black. Neither seemed to have noticed that Anna had checked out.

"...ask you to supply something that backs up your story and you hand over a *security camera* photo of the kid *sleeping*? Do you not see how that does not help you? Or how creepy it is? Are you, like, retarded? Should I feel sorry for you because you can't help being this way?"

"My mind is exceptionally strong," the man in black said. He held his hand out toward Anna. "If you're finished looking at that..."

Anna returned it, deliberately touching his hand as she did so. Maybe he'd given it to her because he thought she'd get something off it. Maybe he knew what she did. But he didn't flinch from her touch and, when they knew about her, most people did.

"Are you some kind of stalker?" Collie asked. "Not to denigrate you, because you have that index card and you either got that from his place or from him, so you're clearly a very good stalker."

"I am not a stalker. Rowan walked into a dangerous situation and he should have known better. There are people looking for him. I had hoped I'd find him first."

"What was that place?" Anna asked. "From the photo? It looked... institutional."

"You don't need to know that," the man said. "He once lived

there and I suspect he's in a similar place now." He checked his watch. "It's 7:05. Rowan is punctual. I suppose, on some level, I hoped he'd show up for your appointment. But I knew he wouldn't and, as you can see, he hasn't. We've discussed this and you're wasting my time."

"Somebody's wasting somebody's time," Collie said, almost amiably. She looked at Anna. "Thoughts?"

"We should talk about it," Anna said. "And talk to someone. Just, one thing... uh, I'm sorry, your name?"

His eyes narrowed, but he came out with it.

"Eric Quinlan."

Anna glanced at the closed door.

"Why are you so worried about being seen?"

"The people who most likely have him are not very nice," Eric said.

"Okay," Anna said. Not that it was okay, but she didn't see the sense in discussing it. "Leave us some contact information, and... leave. We'll let you know tomorrow if we're willing to work for you."

"Fine," Eric said. He took a pen and notepad from his pocket, wrote down a few words and handed the sheet to Collie. Eric pocketed the pen, the notepad and his leather packet, and left without another word.

"THAT," Collie said, "was one weird-ass piece of work."

She was coming back into the office as she spoke, having gone to the hall window to assure herself that Eric had really gone.

"I think he's telling the truth, though," Anna said. Collie shoved the door shut and sat on the corner of her desk.

"How was your vision?"

Anna shrugged. She hated describing them.

"It went to support his story."

"How so?"

"It was the two of them in a computer room in that institution. Eric had broken in, I think, and Rowan surprised him. Rowan seemed… I think he was angling for Eric to help him leave. And he said something about how magicians couldn't get in or out of the place, which… I don't know. He could have meant he was a magician, and that's why he was stuck there. He does know Mandrake as… Mandrake."

Collie sighed.

"Do you think that kid really is in trouble?"

"I thought so last night," Anna said. "I just don't know if Eric is it."

"Vision says no," Collie said. "At least, from how you described it. And… I don't know. It's dumb."

"Share it anyway," Anna said. "Dumb is our specialty."

"We should put that on business cards," Collie said. "It would be like 'Murder Is My Business'. Only dumb."

Anna nodded.

"A fine plan, and also a way to distract me from the thing you're embarrassed to say to me."

"Okay. I just… he had a way of handling that photo before giving it to you. Like he didn't want to let go of it. And not because it made him look creeptacular. He seemed… this is stupid, considering the picture, but… sentimental." She placed her hands on the desk, palms flat, as if she needed them for balance. "Just me being dumb, I'm sure."

"No," Anna said. "I saw that, too. And the vision didn't feel… it wasn't a bad memory for him. I think… maybe we should go to Katja's and talk to Mandrake. I don't know how well he knows Rowan, but he's all we've got. Maybe he even knows where the kid is. Maybe he put the kid where the kid is."

Collie looked pained.

"Sure, maybe. If I were on the run, I'd ask Mandrake for a favour or two. But do you honestly think we'll learn anything useful by speaking to that guy?"

Anna pushed her chair back and stood.

"Our usual problem with Ian is that we have no idea what he's talking about, so we're lost from the start. In this case, we want to know if Rowan has told him anything about Eric Quinlan, or if he knows what their relationship is like. Or, I guess, if he knows anything that's prejudicial about Eric, either way. I'll take any other information he can give us, but that's all we really need to know. Even Ian can't make that confusing."

"I believe he can," Collie said as she lay back on her desk and reached an arm down to blindly grope for her purse. "I bet, after talking to him, we'll realize we should have asked a fortune cookie instead. Oh, and by the way — I told you so."

"Probably," Anna allowed. "You talk all the time, so the odds are with you. What do you mean, specifically?"

"You can have good visions, too. Miss 'Can I See That Photograph?' Miss Grabby-Pants."

Anna nodded, giving that statement the careful consideration it deserved.

"Hmm," she said thoughtfully. "Shut up."

COLLIE RANG THE BUZZER with one hand and knocked with the other. Anna never quite managed to believe it when Collie did that. It seemed ruder than was even possible.

"He might not be home," Anna pointed out. "When people don't answer their phone, it doesn't mean they're home."

"Doesn't mean they're not home, either," Collie said. "It's late and he's not at Katja's. Where else is he gonna be? On a hot date?"

"Maybe he brought his hot date home," Anna suggested. "And he doesn't want to be disturbed."

Collie grinned.

"Picture it," she said. "With the hand glowing in the dark… the romance of it all."

She raised her hands to knock and ring again. She hit the buzzer okay, but missed the door as it slid open to reveal an empty hall.

"Ian?" Anna said softly, half calling for him and half asking Collie if she thought he'd opened the door. Collie pursed her lips.

"Not his style," she said, her voice low.

"We going in?" Anna asked. Collie leaned against the iron railing for a second, then quickly straightened as it started to pull loose from the crumbling concrete steps.

"Could just be some friend of his getting cute with us," she said. "We'd never hear the end of it if we ran away like whipped dogs."

"I don't like what this line of work is doing to our instincts," Anna said, extending a hand to usher Collie inside.

Ian lived in a basement suite in Calder, just above the rail yards. It was an assortment of tiny rooms with low ceilings and pipes jutting from the walls. The first time they'd been inside, Collie had commented on the musty odour of the place and suggested, not seriously, that Ian should teleport somewhere and take the smell with him. Which he did, and damned if it hadn't worked, though Anna's nose had bled and Collie's migraine had lasted for two days. The party they'd been attending at the time had broken up quickly.

Collie walked easily though the narrow hall, her hair picking up static as it brushed the water stained ceiling panels. They were old yellowing squares, the kind with holes you counted when you couldn't sleep. Anna pulled her head down and shoulders in and bent her back a little for good measure. At least she didn't have to worry about breaking anything in this place, since Ian hadn't decorated and it was pretty much a dump.

Collie stopped.

"What the fuck is that smell?"

Anna brought her hand up to her nose, as if covering it would help.

"Col?"

"Yeah?"

"Don't touch anything."

Collie turned to give her a nervous look.

"This from you?"

Anna ignored it and pushed past her, which would have been impossible if Collie hadn't pressed herself back against the wall.

Her days working in vet clinics meant Anna had spent some time around death. She'd come to feel that death itself didn't have a smell, per se. But blood and feces and rotting did, and when you combined them in just the right way, they represented death pretty well.

The main room was to her right. She didn't have to enter to see what she was looking for. Ian was on the floor, face down, blood at the back of his head and pooled beneath him in front. One shot, execution style. Of course you'd have to do it that way with a guy who could teleport. It was vital that he not see you coming.

He'd knocked over a table as he fell. Well, not really a table. A stack of stolen milk crates. Anna leaned against the doorframe. How fair was it to die when you had milk crates for furniture? Shouldn't you at least get the chance to trade up to something from the Sally Ann?

"But we didn't even decide to take the case," Collie said. It was a hell of a thing to say, but she sounded about as stable as Anna felt, so Anna decided not to take offence.

"Could have been a coincidence," she said.

"Please."

They stood like that for a while. Anna leaning against the door frame, Collie standing in the doorway. Anna had a hazy idea that there was a fire burning somewhere in the room.

There wasn't, though. Just Mandrake's hand glowing softly, giving an orange tint to the room. And a faint odour of smoke beneath the other, more aggressive smells. The place had always smelled of cigarettes, though, and there were sub wrappers on the floor and toasted subs smelled burnt. To Anna, at least. Collie always said Anna was imagining things and should just shut up and eat.

Imagining things. She wished.

"Yesterday, maybe?" Anna said. "Or... early today? I'm not...animals are smaller and we don't keep them around for –"

"Should we call the cops?" Collie asked, giving Anna a dizzying attack of déjà vu.

"I don't know," she said. She was pretty sure that was her line. "His hand is still glowing."

"Yeah. I thought maybe it would stop. Guess not."

They stood a while longer. Anna couldn't take her eyes off that hand. She wasn't sure why it bothered her so much now. It never had before.

"Do you think we should call the Embassy?" Collie asked.

"Maybe. Yes."

Collie took out her cell and nudged Anna's arm. Anna shivered.

"Sorry."

"No, it's... can you just hold the phone for a sec? I need my address book."

Right. Because it wasn't a number Collie would have in her Contacts. Because they'd always called Mandrake instead. Anna took the phone and held it loosely in her right hand, waiting for Collie to find the number and take it back. There was a black jacket draped over Ian's dumpster salvage couch. Tough to be certain, because black leather jackets weren't rare, but it looked a hell of a lot like Rowan's.

"Col," she started.

"Just a sec," Collie said. Anna felt the phone leave her hand, a brush of icy fingertips. Just what she needed.

"Uh... hi. This is Colette Kostyna. I'm... yeah. I know. Normally I would, except we're in his apartment and he's... somebody shot him."

She winced and switched the phone to her other ear.

"He was... it was too late when we got here. I... no. Did you say... back of the head? Because that seems to be what... uh-huh. What? Who's... oh. Anna. Me and Anna."

She looked at Anna and mouthed "sorry." Anna wasn't sure what she was sorry for. Dragging her into the conversation, probably. As if it mattered.

Anna pointed at the jacket. Collie looked at it and her eyes widened.

"The door was open," Collie told the phone. Not exactly the whole truth, but Anna wouldn't have wanted to get into it either. "We could leave it... yeah. No, we haven't."

Collie stepped into the room and moved around the jacket, staring at it intently.

"We'll go now. You know how to... well, yeah. I guess you would. Okay then."

She hung up and turned to Anna.

"They're coming. They want us to get out."

"I got that, "Anna said. "Is that Rowan's jacket?"

"I think so," Collie said. She hesitated, then grabbed the jacket and pulled it on over her fleece. "Let's go."

If Anna had harboured any desire to stick around and wait for the Embassy's forensics crew, Collie's little stunt would have taken care of it.

She took a last look at Ian, thinking she should. She'd be sorry later if she didn't, wouldn't she? Last chance to look at a friend, even if he looked... well, like that?

Truth was, though, she didn't want to look at him for another moment. She headed out, barely even listening for the click of Collie's boots in the hall behind her.

IN THEIR LIVING ROOM, they pulled the curtains, took chairs and, together, stared at the coffee table. Anna wondered if it were possible to stare for a living. They both did it so well.

"Why did we take the jacket?" Anna asked. Collie looked up. The dim light glinted on her hair.

"That was a 'we' thing?"

"I could have stopped you," Anna told her.

"Not without touching it."

"Oh." Anna didn't say anything else, but apparently her tone said it for her, because Collie was glaring at her.

"What? You don't like the taste of that? Then chew on this – is everything I do your responsibility because you can physically stop me?"

Anna didn't want to chew on anything. She shut her eyes and leaned back in her chair, the leather one she'd picked out for herself. No one else got to sit there.

"There might not be anything on that jacket," she said. "Unless he was touching it when... you know. And even then, there might not be."

"I think the Embassy thinks someone ported in," Collie said. "They said something about someone popping up behind him, and they were kind of 'meh' about the door being open. They just wanted us to leave it open for them."

"They gonna debrief us? Or something?"

Collie shrugged. The jacket slipped off her shoulders a little. "I guess."

"You gonna tell them about the door opening like that?"

"Dunno."

This, like the theft of the jacket, was strange territory for Anna. It didn't make sense to keep things from Ian's employers, but she too felt the impulse. Maybe it was just her old dislike of authority stopping in to say hello.

"There wasn't a struggle in there," Collie said. "Apart from the table."

"So someone ported in, shot Ian, took the kid?"

"Hard to shoot a guy who teleports," Collie said. "You'd have to completely surprise him."

"I was thinking something similar," Anna admitted.

"What do we say to Eric?"

Anna thought about that.

"What you're really asking is, did Eric do this."

"No. I'm asking what we tell him. But I guess we do have to answer your question first. And we don't really know what happened there."

"I know," Anna said.

"Hell, Rowan could have shot Mandrake. And left his jacket. And left town."

Anna looked at her.

"You think?"

"Of course not. But we don't know."

They sat in silence for a few minutes. The neighbours' Siamese was complaining a few doors down, probably angry that it wasn't being let in and out on its preferred ten-minute rotation.

"Killing Ian was not cool," Collie said finally.

"Nope," Anna agreed.

"Someone has to do something about that."

"Someone will," Anna said. "The Embassy. And possibly Eric, if the killer also took off with the kid."

"So, we tell the Embassy what happened," Collie said. "And we tell Eric what we found. He'll either still want to hire us, or he won't. And if he still wants to hire us, we... have no idea what to do."

"The rational thing," Anna said, feeling a doomed urge to speak up on behalf of reason, "would be to tell everyone everything, turn down Eric's job, if it's still on offer, which I'm sure it will be... and walk away."

"Why do we turn down the job?" Collie asked. Anna opened her eyes.

"Are you kidding?"

"Yeah. I'm in a jolly mood. Why do we have to turn down the job? This is the sort of thing we do."

"If you mean insinuate ourselves into murder investigations where we don't belong and get more people killed, yes, that is what we do. Where were you when we were explaining this to Mandrake just last night?"

"I –"

"Didn't mean it?"

Collie glared at her.

"We don't have to screw up. All this Eric guy wants is for us to help him ask people questions. I'm betting those are questions that will help us figure out who shot Ian, so I'm interested in the answers. Besides, honestly, why come to us for help finding Rowan if you shot Ian and kidnapped the kid?"

Anna shrugged.

"Misdirect –"

"–tion?" Collie finished. "I knew you were going to say that. You could say that about anything anyone does ever, but it goes against most people's instincts and that gives it a high cost in terms of energy and effort. Why would he bother misdirecting the likes of us? Breaking into our office to misdirect us?"

"I don't know, Sigmund," Anna said, "I don't have your deep insight into human behaviour, but I'm thinking it could be because he knew Rowan was talking to us and he wanted to know what Rowan said or – oh, here's a wild thought – what Rowan might have wanted to hire us for."

Collie shifted a little in her seat. Anna could hear the leather jacket creaking.

"Fair."

"Yep."

"However," Collie said slowly, "if he did do it... and, let's face it, we're going to need more time and observation to figure that one out... if he did do it, wouldn't the best thing be to work for him? Stay close?"

"Right," Anna said. "Keep your friends close and your enemies right behind you with a switchblade."

"Oh, like that guy would use a switchblade. But you know what I think?"

"Rarely," Anna admitted.

"I think this whole situation will look better once we've had Vietnamese food."

Anna started at her.

"You want to eat? Now? After... that?"

"Yes. I'm a monster. I'm a monster who hasn't eaten since noon."

"What about the cookie in your pocket?" Anna pointed out. Collie made a face.

"I had it on me wh... I don't want it. We'll have to drive. No one in this city will deliver Vietnamese."

It was true. Anna stood.

"You may want to ditch the jacket before we go."

"YOU KNOW, they don't call it Badass Jack's in PA," Anna said. Collie eyed her suspiciously.

"Are we having a Royale with Cheese conversation?"

Anna spooned chilli sauce onto a spring roll.

"Not exactly. I'm saying, they call it Badass in Edmonton and Saskatoon. In PA, it's Wrapper Jack's. They must have done some market research and decided the people of Prince Albert weren't prepared for that kind of shocking language."

"Don't the people of Prince Albert have no bus service after seven PM because they kept shooting at the buses?"

"Yes."

"Huh," Collie said, pouring fish sauce over her rice noodles. "You know, if somebody in Edmonton decided to home-deliver Vietnamese food, they could write their ticket. It would be a license to print money. And other clichés." She stirred the sauce, gave the bowl a critical look, poured more sauce. It didn't matter how many times she did that in the course of a meal. It always went to the bottom of the bowl anyway. And yet she kept on.

"There's probably some reason for it that we don't understand," Anna offered. "Maybe travel disrupts the delicate texture of the... something."

Collie pointed a chopstick at her.

"Did they deliver Vietnamese food in Prince Albert?

"Yes."

"Then shut up. You know, the thing that really gets me is, I have no idea why we're so scared of them. Do you?"

Anna took a moment with that. To the casual listener, it would have sounded as if Collie had conceived a mortal terror of Vietnamese food delivery people. But Anna was pretty sure she hadn't, so she was talking about...

Ah. The Embassy.

"We're scared of them?"

"Yes," Collie said. "Reference any of the times we asked people at occult shops, or people at Ian's parties, about the Embassy, and they all, without exception, told us to shut up and drop it. Or the fact that Ian recommended we always go through him because it wasn't a good idea to get too involved with the Embassy. He did say that."

"Yeah, I remember," Anna said. "Seems to me we're scared of them because everyone else is."

"Speak for yourself," a man's voice said. It came from behind and above her. Anna didn't bother to turn her head, just scanned Collie's face, which might as well have had "BUSTED" spraypainted across it.

"Kieran," she said. "Is there something we can do for you?"

Oh, for fuck's fucking sake. Speak of the devil. Kieran wasn't Embassy staff, exactly, but she was pretty sure the Embassy bankrolled the domestic violence shelter he ran in old Strathcona. Whenever she and Collie had been hired to troubleshoot for him, the money had come from the Embassy. Through Ian.

The tall blond slipped into the chair beside Anna, jeans making the vinyl seat squeak.

"Not for me, exactly," he said. "Do you, uh, mind if we cut in here?"

Anna was about to question the "we" when a slight, pale, black-haired man took the chair beside Collie. He didn't look any happier to be there than Anna was to suffer a dinner invasion.

"I don't know," Anna said. "Do you mind if we keep talking about how you freak us out?"

Kieran looked at the table. Anna followed his gaze. Someone had spilled pepper on the scuffed Formica surface. There was no pepper shaker in sight. With a nervous flick of his fingers, Kieran brushed the grains to the floor.

"We're not the Embassy. But they did ask us to extend an invitation to meet with them this evening. Have you met Joel, by the way?"

Collie glanced at the man beside her. He did not glance back. He was looking somewhere over Anna's shoulder, green eyes unfocused. He looked young, not much older than Rowan.

"I don't think so," Collie said. She looked as if she were resisting the urge to poke him.

"Okay, well, that's Joel," Kieran said. He looked up from the table and Anna saw that his eyes were red. Apparently he'd heard the news. "He's not talking these days. I'm sorry about intruding, honestly. They just... want to get on this. As do we all."

Collie sighed and looked at her food. It was probably irritating her, since it had shredded carrots on top and Collie preferred to shred her meals herself.

"Sure. Us, too. But they could have called."

Kieran nodded.

"I know it seems that way to you, and to me, but to them this is actually more natural and straightforward than making a phone call. And... uh... not rude."

"Kieran," Collie began, "you seem like a nice enough guy..."

He did. It was the main reason Kieran grated on Anna.

The shelter he ran leaned toward a peculiar brand of domestic violence. Less throwing hot coffee on one's spouse and more making one's spouse's arms turn into snakes... to name one example Kieran had shyly and politely trotted out during their first meeting.

Anna figured if she ran a place like that, she'd never sleep. She'd probably be snake-armed or dead within a week. Kieran seemed to handle his job just fine, which made her wonder what he had up his shy and polite sleeve.

"Nice enough guy, but?" Kieran asked, half-smiling and tilting his head a little as he did it. He was young, too. Gawky. Endearing. Anna wanted to throw her bowl at him.

"I think you've been working for the Embassy for too long. Do you seriously expect us to leave our meal and go meet with your employers because they, with extreme creepiness, sent you to track us down? And, presumably, drag us? Upset though we all are about Ian, do you really think that's reasonable?"

"Wow," Kieran said softly. "It's amazing how reluctant people are to use his nickname all of a sudden. As if it's worse now that he's not around to hear it. Pretty dumb."

"Fair enough," Collie said. "But not what I asked you."

A movement caught Anna's attention and she realized that it was Joel. He'd blinked. She'd noticed because he hadn't so far. Now he was staring again, motionless. Anna looked at Collie. Collie stared at Kieran.

"They aren't our employers," Kieran said. "They just fund us. And we socialize with them."

Collie flapped her hand as if it were a puppet's mouth.

"Them, them, them. We don't even know what that means, you know? I got back to town a few months ago and bumped into Ian and he started throwing us work on behalf of something called the Embassy and, seriously, no one will tell us who they are. How many of them there are, where they live, what they want... nothing. I have a phone number and Ian told me not to use it. Which I didn't. Until tonight."

Anna heard Collie's speech, but part of her brain was stuck on the idea of this Joel character socializing at all. Did they stand him up in a corner and set drink trays on his head?

"They're exceptional types," Kieran said softly, leaning in a bit. "No big mystery. They just want to live quiet lives and they want their people to be left alone. What happened to Ian... they take that very seriously. They don't want to wait to see you."

"Would it be okay if we ate first?" Collie asked.

Anna considered throwing her bowl at Collie instead. When did they decide they were going to go to this meeting at all? How the hell had Kieran known where they were eating? Had he followed them, perhaps, from Ian's house to their townhouse to the restaurant? And why did Kieran keep saying "we" as if that petrified wood he was dragging around had participated in the decision?

For a lesbian, Collie was pretty sappy around college boys with floppy haircuts.

"They didn't specify," Kieran said, "but I think it's only fair to let you finish your meal."

Anna considered all the questions she wanted to ask, opened her mouth and was surprised when another question came out instead.

"Why the Embassy?"

Kieran looked at her in surprise, as if he had forgotten she could speak. Right. Because she was the local aphasic.

"What do you mean?"

"Why do they call it that? It's just a bunch of... let's say people. Right? A family or something? So why not call themselves the Smith family or whatever their name is? It's good enough for the Mafia."

Kieran laughed. Not loud. Nothing that might disturb the tables around them. He probably apologized when other people bumped into him.

"I don't know. I never asked. Maybe one of them thought it was funny."

Something about that made Anna's stomach twist. She glanced away from Kieran, landed on Joel, and dropped her head so her field of vision took in the table and her food. Tables and food she could deal with.

"More and more," Collie said, "I get the sense that I don't know what funny is. Did you guys want to order? Since you're here anyway?"

Anna loved that idea. Let the waitress have a shot at the catatonic guy.

"No," Kieran said, breaking her heart a tiny bit. "Thanks. We ate at home. Is there a minimum here? We can wait outside. Or we can just pay it."

Albertans. Anna couldn't conceive of someone paying the minimum just to sit in a restaurant and not even order anything. At home, people would at least have asked for something to put in a doggie bag.

"I think it's okay," Collie said. "I just thought you might be hungry."

"And it's rude to eat in front of people who aren't eating," Anna added. Kieran looked at her as if he couldn't figure out whether she'd meant to be bitchy. She kept her face neutral. Let him guess.

"I will have dessert," he said. "Do they have green tea ice cream, do you think? Or... is that Vietnamese?"

"They have pad thai and chao fen here," Collie said. "I don't think they're hung up on geography."

On went the meal. Kieran and Collie had dessert. Anna did not. Kieran and Collie talked about the impossibility of Vietnamese food delivery and various road construction projects that were pissing them off and how they'd enjoyed the folk festival a few weeks earlier. Kieran agreed with everything Collie said, in the way that got sociopaths a reputation for being easy to talk to.

Anna stared at Joel, trying to figure out how often he blinked. About once a minute, on average. Once she had that, she tried to figure out how often was normal, but counting her own blinks skewed the results and Collie and Kieran would probably notice if she started staring at their eyes. Probably.

At quarter to ten, Kieran dropped money on the table.

"The least I can do is pay," he said. "It's their money anyhow. Did you want a lift?"

What Anna wanted was to go home and try to sleep. She didn't think she would sleep, all things considered, but she had to work the next morning and she wanted to give it a try. It didn't seem, though, as if she'd be getting her chance anytime soon.

Collie fished in her purse and came up with an index card. Collie, somehow, always had index cards. Anna had never seen her write a phone number on a gum wrapper.

"If you just give me their address, we can drive. You can follow us, if you have to, but it would be more convenient for us to have our own vehicle when we're ready to leave."

"All right," Kieran said. "We do have to follow you. I think it's mainly to keep an eye on you, what with you being witnesses of a sort and things being violent as they are."

He pulled a pen from his jacket pocket, wrote down an address, and gave Collie the card. She looked at it.

"Your place is, like, three blocks away. You would have had to drive us there, drive us back here to get the Jeep, and go home."

"Not a problem," Kieran said.

"They're on the clock," Anna said. Collie looked at her and shrugged. Anna turned to Kieran.

"I drive a twenty-year-old blue Cherokee. I'm having trouble getting into fifth these days, so if we decide to make a break for Red Deer, you should be able to keep up."

"I really do think they're more concerned about your welfare than about you making a break."

"I'm sure the possibilities are endless," Anna said. She pointed left, past Kieran, then pointed to the wall on her right.

"Oh, right," Kieran said. "My getting up would make this easier."

He stood and moved away from the table, allowing Anna to do the same.

"Joel," he said. He said it casually, but Joel immediately got up and stood beside him. Collie watched them warily, then got up, moved past them and out the door.

"You need us to wait for you?" Anna asked. Kieran looked puzzled for a moment, then shook his head.

"We'll be fine."

Anna had no trouble believing that. She went to the door and stepped out into Chinatown.

ANNA HAD HEARD A LOT of Edmonton people apologize for their Chinatown, saying it was just a stretch of road and scattered buildings in the blocks nearby. Since she knew people who'd grown up in whole towns no larger than that, Anna figured Chinatown was fine. Dim sum, jade Buddhas, Asian pears, onion-domed churches mysteriously scattered between herbalists and grocery stores. She wasn't sure what else she was supposed to want.

Collie wasn't in sight, so Anna stepped on it. The surrounding streets weren't Disneyland in daylight and the daylight was gone now.

Anna shook her head at requests for change and tried to ignore the drug deals going on in the alley. She'd often wondered where people got off glaring at her when she saw them dealing drugs. It wasn't as if she wanted to see them. The problem wasn't that she was being nosy. The problem was that they weren't being discreet.

When she got to the Jeep, she saw Collie hunched in the passenger seat, seemingly attempting to disappear inside her coat. Not that it was remotely cold, but Collie seemed to think winter had rolled in whenever the sun went down.

Anna banged on the window, startling Collie, who unfurled it and leaned over to flick open the lock on the driver's side. Anna was happy to crawl inside, slam the door, and pull away from the curb.

"I would never park here," Collie said. "You're lucky no one would ever want your vehicle."

Anna could have taken offence at that, but why? It wasn't in any way untrue.

"What's even better is that no one would look at this thing and think I own anything of value," she said.

"This is why I like for you to park out front of the house," Collie admitted. "It's a burglar deterrent."

Anna swung the Jeep around, bouncing over a curb and in and out of a parking lot, interrupting a business transaction along the way. As she turned toward the river, she hooked at thumb at the street behind them.

"Why is it always Chinatown and Ukrainian churches, mixed together? It's like that in Saskatoon, too."

Collie shook her head.

"I don't know. Why do you dislike Kieran so much?"

"Ah." Anna cut into the leftmost lane. "Let me turn that around and ask you, why did you run out of the restaurant as if your ex-boyfriend had just walked in?"

"That shit with that Joel guy was greebly," Collie admitted.

Anna smiled.

"Correct. Kieran is greebly."

"I didn't say that," Collie said. "It was just the whole zombie vibe. Kieran doesn't seem greebly."

"Which makes him greeblier," Anna said.

"I don't think so. He runs a shelter. He just gets funding from them."

"He told us almost nothing about them," Anna said. "Actually, no, that's wrong. He told us absolutely nothing about them. Nothing he said had any weight to it. Yeah, he runs a shelter, but do you ever wonder how? Would you like to try running that place?"

Anna's eyes were on the road, but she could feel Collie's eye roll without having to turn her head for it.

"It's probably, I don't know, warded or something. I think he's just a guy. They give him information, like about where we were eating. And sometimes they ask him to do stuff for them."

"Would you say," Anna said. "if associating with someone or some organization makes us sound like paranoid schizophrenics, that maybe it's a crazy thing to do?"

"Are you proposing a break for Red Deer?"

"No," Anna said. "I just don't like being summoned and I would have preferred to stay under the radar with these people. You can tell me the address anytime."

"Just a sec..."

Collie flipped on the interior light and grappled with the contents of her purse. After more than a second, she produced the index card and read off an address.

Weaving through the one-way streets, Anna peered at the houses, trying to pick out addresses.

"Would it kill people to put visible addresses on their houses?"

"Maybe," Collie said. "It never happens, so there's no way of knowing what the consequences might be. Oh — I think that's it on the left. With the columns."

Anna looked where Collie was pointing and saw the columns, thick white borders to a small porch. The house behind the porch was huge, the kind of 1920s house that would normally be divided into apartments. This place, though, had just the one address by the door. Anna couldn't be sure, but she thought there was just one mailbox.

"Imagine vacuuming that place," Collie murmured. Anna smiled. Rambling houses always drew a similar reaction from her. Not that it was the kind of thing Collie needed to worry about, since she never vacuumed anyway.

"They probably have a maid," Anna said. "Or maybe a roommate who gets stuck cleaning everything."

"Maybe," Collie said pleasantly. She unsnapped her seat belt and got out of the Jeep, slamming the door just a little harder than was necessary. Anna followed her, checking twice to be certain she'd turned off the lights.

Collie had stopped at the steps and was running her foot over the bottom one. The stone was worn away in the centre, half a narrow oval.

"How many times does something have to be stepped on before that happens?" she asked.

"A lot," Anna said, helpfully. "We going in?"

Collie looked up at the front door.

"Guess so."

There was nothing scary about the door. It was painted white, no windows, one peephole. "Abandon all hope" was not written on or above it. Anna tapped the doorbell and it lit up as it rang.

"Did you see Kieran behind us on the way here?" Collie said.

"No," Anna said. "I assume he took the Embassy's invisible jet."

"Do we want to talk to Eric first?"

Anna kept her eyes on the door.

"Sure. Call him and ask him to meet us here. Tell him he has about thirty seconds."

It was on the word "seconds" that the door opened to reveal a pair of small children looking at them with wide green eyes.

Anna figured them as school-aged, but barely. They had the serious demeanour of kids who had begun their studies only recently, and who were starting to see themselves as having responsibilities in the world. They were the same height, one boy and one girl, not much taller than the doorknob. The girl, who had opened the door and was still holding the doorknob as she eyed them, was wearing jeans and a candy pink Powerpuff Girls t-shirt that clashed with her dark red hair. The boy was more subdued, with mousy hair and a navy t-shirt that read "Property of Miskatonic University". Even his stare was subdued, edgewise and flickering.

"May we help you?" the girl said.

Collie knelt in front of her. Anna looked at their hair, all those red curls. But a daughter of Collie's would look different. Her hair would be lighter. Hair almost always got darker with age.

"Sweetie, you shouldn't open the door for strangers."

The girl looked amused. It was an adult expression, wrong on that round face.

"You're Colette Kostyna. You're supposed to go to the office."

She stepped aside and Anna saw the living room for a moment, a warmly lit space centring on a pale yellow couch. Then her focus sharpened and her viewpoint dropped, making her stomach lurch. What she saw changed as if she were in motion, charging impatiently through the house on short, sturdy legs. A red haze fell before one eye for a moment before being clumsily swiped away. Right turn at the far end of the room, straight to the end of the hall, then left. An old wooden door faced her, tarnished brass doorknob even with her gaze.

And she was back, tall again, standing on the front porch and staring at a framed print on the far wall of the living room. It was a movie poster from *The Long Goodbye*. "Nothing says goodbye like a bullet," it declared.

"Thanks," Collie said. Her voice was shaky. Anna looked down and saw that Collie, still crouching before the girl, had put a hand on the floor to steady herself.

"Sure," the girl said. She spun on the heel of a scuffed blue sneaker and walked away. The boy hesitated, looked at Collie as if he might say something, then shook his head and went after the girl.

Collie stood, stepped into the house and turned to look at Anna.

"Did you see that?"

Anna considered asking which "that" Collie meant, but it was good bet she was talking about the travelogue.

"Yeah. I can't come in if you don't move."

Collie took a few more steps into the house, backwards.

"Is that what it's like when you… you know…"

Anna stepped into the house and pulled the door shut behind her. Should she lock it? It was always awkward, being left in charge of the door at someone else's house. Hell with it. She was pretty sure home invasion wasn't a worry in this place.

"No," she told Collie. "I'm taller. Can we do this now and talk it to death later?"

"Probably," Collie allowed. She started toward the office with the confidence of long practice. Anna followed. Straight. Right. Straight. Left. And there was the door.

"Come in," a voice said from the other side. It was a male voice, strong and low.

Collie turned the doorknob and shoved the door open, moving nothing but her arm. Anna looked over her shoulder at the dimly lit room.

It was an office all right, the kind of office Philip Marlowe would have kept if he'd had money and an interest in interior design. Dark, heavy furniture, leather chairs, a green-shaded banker's lamp the only light in the room.

A tall blond was sitting behind the desk. He had straight, even features, close-cropped hair and shoulders broad enough that lesser furniture would have been dwarfed by him. He didn't seem any particular age, just iconically adult.

"I don't want to raise my voice," he said. Collie went into the room and stepped to one side. Anna followed her.

"Please sit," the man said.

"You prefer eyes at a level?" Collie asked. For some reason, the blond smiled a bit.

"I'm not the detective." He pointed to the two chairs facing the desk. Collie took the one on the right. Anna took the other. The leather was thick and stiff.

"You may be wondering why I've asked you here," he said, that slight smile still on his face. His eyes didn't know anything about it.

"I hope you're not about to say that one of us is a murderer," Collie said. She'd probably hoped to sound casually witty, but Anna heard nervousness. The blond raised his eyebrows. His forehead, somehow, stayed smooth.

"At least two of us are," he said. "But that's old news."

Meaning, presumably, himself plus one of them. Anna let it roll off her. There were only two deaths he might be talking about and she didn't own either of them.

"I know you didn't kill Ian," he went on. "That's all I care about. I – hold on."

There was a blur, a rush of air, a closing door, a seat creaking on a swivel. He sat in front of them as if nothing had happened. Anna looked over her shoulder and saw the door she'd left open, now shut. He spoke softly. She turned toward the sound.

"You found Ian tonight."

"Yeah," Collie said. She was still looking at the door. Not very cool, but Anna couldn't blame her. She took a breath and faced the blond. "We did. We arrived just before eight PM and —"

"Not necessary," the blond said. "We have that information. Why were you there?"

"How would you have that information?" Collie asked. She was probably dying to know if he knew about Rowan's jacket, but of course she couldn't ask that. "Did Mandr — Ian have security cameras in that place?"

"We have a psychometrist on staff," he said, then looked at Anna. "I don't mean to devalue the work you do for us. Our psychometrist can't be everywhere. And you have other skills."

Did he just apologize for what she thought he'd apologized for? Anna tried to keep from gawking at him.

"*De rien*," she said evenly.

"Your psychometrist gets time-date stamps?" Collie asked, leaning forward a little. Anna wondered how hard a shove it would take to propel her right out of her chair.

"Sometimes," the blond said. "Now. You were about to tell me why you were at Ian's suite this evening."

Anna didn't know if Collie intended to lie, but it was possible. Collie would try to lie to almost anyone. Maybe even to this guy, which would likely be a waste of time. At best. She jumped in before Collie could open her mouth.

"We were trying to decide whether to take on a client. We thought Ian might know something about him."

He nodded. Anna got the sense she'd passed a test.

"Why did you think that?"

"Ian knows everybody," Collie said. The blond's eyes narrowed. Anna ran her fingertips over the worn leather arms of her chair.

"They had a friend in common," she said.

"Ian and the client."

"Potential client," Collie said, a little too quickly. "Yes."

"You're still deciding?"

"Yes," Collie said. "We don't work for just anybody."

"We should feel honoured, then," the blond said. "Here's what you're going to do. You'll tell the client you'll work for him. Really, you'll be working for us. The job is finding out who killed Ian. You," he nodded at Anna, "will quit your day job. You," a nod to Collie, "will turn away all other clients. Money won't be a problem. That's an understatement. We'll put you on the payroll. Of course we'll cover expenses. You'll start tomorrow morning."

What made him think he could say all of that? His reputation? Or something more? Anna stared at him, as if his face would give it away. In the corner of her eye, she could see Collie vibrating.

"Or," Collie said, her throat tight and her voice high, "we might do none of those things."

"You might do none of those things," the blond agreed. "But then you'd have to leave town. You would be escorted out and you wouldn't be allowed back."

Anna looked at Collie, a little concerned about what might come out of her mouth. She quickly saw she had no reason to be concerned. Collie was far too angry to speak.

"Look," the blond said. "I don't like to play games. I get the impression you don't like games, either. You know we're running this place. The ugliness you experienced in Victoria would not have happened here. The price for that is us keeping a handle on things." He paused. For the first time, Anna could see lines in his face. "Stay and do this. I need to fuck up whoever killed Ian. I need you to find out who I am supposed to fuck up."

"So," Anna said, "exile is your standard punishment for insubordination?"

He snorted a laugh.

"Insubordination. We just want peace and quiet. If the only mages and witches and psionics in town are people who work with us toward that end, perfect. If there are a few who don't work with us but we never hear from or about them, fine. Up to a week ago, you guys could have stopped working for us and we would have forgotten you existed. But now you're connected with the death of one of our people. Policy says you help us or get out."

"And you would have to stay out."

Anna's fingers dug into leather as she shifted in her chair to see who owned that soft, melodic voice.

It had come from a redheaded woman with dark green slanted eyes. Her face was pretty enough, objectively, and her hair and eyes were vivid even in the dark room, but there was something about the ghostly skin and sharp features that made her look cold. Like plastic poured into a cheap mould, the kind that left seam marks.

Anna was so busy studying that face that it took her a moment to realize there was no way that woman should be there. There was no way Anna could have missed seeing her when she'd turned to look at the closed door, and she didn't believe anyone could have opened and closed the door so quietly that she wouldn't have heard. Nor did she see anyplace the redhead could have been hiding, Still, there she was, impossibly and gracefully leaning into the corner behind the door. Another teleporter, maybe? Or just someone who was as quiet as the blond was fast?

"Jesus," Collie breathed. Anna wasn't sure if that was in honour of the woman's sudden appearance or her appearance in general.

"Where did you come from?" Anna asked. The woman shrugged, gracefully, and smiled.

"Nowhere. Look, we don't mean to be rude. But we have a lot invested in this place. We've put in a lot of effort making it safe. It's as quiet as it is because we removed a lot of bad elements when we got here. Now, people who might cause trouble tend to stay away. If we let you tell us to go fly a kite, how would that look? Ms. Kostyna, you're in public relations. You must understand."

Collie's mouth was hanging open, which didn't really say "competent professional." Anna was tempted to reach over and shut it for her.

"I... guess... it would also be bad PR if you threw us out and we told people you'd tossed us so you'd seem like badasses. Ms...."

The redhead smiled more broadly and it warmed her face a little. Her hair was a darker red than Collie's, and it hung straight to her shoulders. It had to be a dye job. Damned good one, though.

"We are badasses," the woman said, not bothering to drop her name. "In the internet age, isn't sincerity the first rule of information management?"

Anna heard the blond moving papers on his desk and couldn't decide which of them to look at. They were equally scary, in their own ways. She flashed back to her own office, to Eric the Half a Client telling them only paranoids would set their desks so that someone was always watching the guest from behind.

"I'd rather talk about Ian," the redhead told them. "I think it's interesting that he was friends with Rowan Bell, who now seems to be missing."

Collie said nothing. The tiny crow's feet gathered around her eyes said she was painfully tense.

"That's their client," the blond said. "Not Bell. A friend of his."

Collie looked at the blond. Anna kept her eyes on the redhead, who was raising an eyebrow at Collie.

"Friend? Do you mean that head case who's trying to bring down Varanus?"

"Later," the blond said sharply.

Collie's eyes were so wide, Anna thought they might break her face. She kept her voice admirably calm.

"Would 'head case who's trying to bring down Varanus' in fact be another way of saying 'our client'?" she asked.

"Technically," the blond said, "the Embassy would be your client."

"*So* not the point," Collie said. She whirled on the redhead. "Are you talking about Eric Quinlan? And what the hell is Varanus?"

Anna wasn't certain in that light, but she thought the redhead might be blushing a little.

"I probably shouldn't have said anything. For all I know, Eric Quinlan may have a legitimate point. It's just that the man is insanely quixotic."

"Well, we can't all be sensibly quixotic," Collie said, in the tone she used when she was mere seconds away from throwing a bottle of white-out at someone's head. Not that Anna would have reason to recognize that tone. "We were at Ian's place tonight because we thought he might know the score on this Eric Quinlan. We think the guy might have kidnapped Rowan Bell himself. Please. Ditch this enigmatic shtick and tell us what's going on."

That brought out what Anna figured was the redhead's real smile. This one was a tiny bit too wide and it made the skin look about to crack.

"I doubt he would have done anything to hurt that kid. Adam, may I?"

To Anna's surprise, the blond – Adam, she supposed – beat Collie to the flinging of office supplies. He threw a pencil in the air in what looked, from the corner of her eye, to be a casual gesture. It hit the wall and broke, fell to the ground in at least three pieces.

"Sure," Adam said. "Why not. And since we're using names here tonight, did you want to give them my birth certificate?"

"Did you have one made up?" the redhead answered, then stopped smiling as Adam pushed his chair back, ready to stand. The redhead put her hands up. "Peace. I'm sorry."

Adam stared at the redhead for a good long time, much longer than Anna would have liked to be stared at by those cold blue eyes.

"Fine," he said at last. He turned his attention to Anna and Collie. "It's not a long story. Have you heard of a town called Grayling Cross?"

Anna looked at Collie, who was shaking her head.

"No," Anna told him. Adam nodded.

"It was never much of a town. On the north shore of Lake Athabasca, near Fort Chip. At its peak, it had maybe two hundred residents. About twenty years ago, the town was destroyed in a fire."

"Forest fire?" Collie asked.

"No," Adam said. "There were none in the area at the time. Could have been anything. The houses were wood and there was no fire department, obviously, and the houses were all built pretty close together. I would say it was waiting to happen."

"So someone was smoking in bed and the whole town went up?" Anna asked. Adam smiled a little.

"That's one theory."

"Another," the redhead put in, "is that a fire-breathing dragon flew into town and burned it to the ground."

Collie rolled her eyes.

"Remember ditching the shtick?"

"Believe it or not," Adam said, "she was being direct. That dragon rumour has been circulating since shortly after the town burned. A bush pilot claimed to have seen it. No one's seen or heard from that guy in a while, though, so there's no verification."

Anna stared at the corner of the desk. It was solid, unremarkable. It came together well. She decided she liked it.

Beside her, for some insane reason, Collie was probing for details.

"What do the survivors say? From the town? Some of them must have seen it."

"There was only one survivor," Adam said. "A ten-year-old boy named Eric Quinlan."

"And now you know," Anna muttered, "the rest of the story."

"You need more of a gap between 'rest' and 'of the story'," the redhead said.

Anna looked at her, not smiling, until the redhead's little grin went away.

"In the interests of getting this conversation over with," Anna said, "could you just tell us what Quinlan thinks he saw and what it has to do with this... Varonus?"

"Varanus," the redhead corrected, her tone gentle. "I can't tell you what Quinlan thinks he saw because I don't know. He does say it wasn't a dragon. He also says Varanus destroyed the town, which I assume is what started his grudge."

"You've talked to him about this?" Collie asked. The redhead laughed. It was a little stagy.

"No. I don't think I'd like to, from what I've heard. Did you enjoy talking to Quinlan?"

"He was to the point," Anna said. The redhead looked at her.

"He's been on this for a long time. Anyone who's in the know knows about it. If you know what I mean."

"Uh-huh," Collie said. "And Varanus is?"

"You can think of them," Adam said, "as a multinational. Lots of money. Branch offices. Letterhead. But they deal in the paranormal, so you don't hear about them unless you're in that line yourself..."

"...or they approach you with an offer," the redhead finished. "Say they have information – maybe predictions about the future that could be useful to you or your company. They'll share that information, for a price. They don't advertise. If they think you have money and that you might be interested, they call you. If you're their client, they might do other work for you."

"Such as?" Anna asked.

"They use an unusual blend of magic and psionics. There's a remote viewing team, and they have some other people who do more intense remote work. I'm pretty sure they have teleporters. You're looking at a lot of espionage, corporate and otherwise. I think they have some weather control. And other, miscellaneous..."

"It would not be out of scope for them to raze a town," Adam said. "These are not nice people. Quinlan may or may not be delusional, but either way he's hit upon a deserving target. He most likely believes that Varanus is behind Rowan Bell's disappearance."

"If so, it would be tit for tat," the redhead put in, "since Rowan was, in a sense, the property of Varanus until he was sixteen years old. At least, according to our sources. Our sources also say that Quinlan broke him out of whatever compound he was in."

Did she say "property of"? Anna checked Collie's face, saw horror, and felt a little better. The way these people talked, it was easy to get the sense that she was either hearing things or vastly overreacting.

"What did you say?" Collie asked. "Property?"

"We said they weren't nice," Adam said. "I didn't want to tell you any of this because Quinlan will tell you himself and now you're going to have to act as if it's news."

"We could just say you told us," Anna pointed out. "We don't have to say you hired us."

"No," Adam said. "If you want to let on that you know his story, fine, but don't mention us. We want no direct contact with your client. If he wants to come sniffing around here, we need you to redirect him."

"Why?" Anna asked. "I mean, you sound as if you have some

theories in common. Why not just work with him? Or ignore him and do this yourself? You too scared of Varanus?"

"We need you as our proxies because we believe Eric Quinlan is one of the good guys," Adam said. Before Anna could protest that complete lack of answer, the redhead spoke.

"He hates the paranormal, so he will hate us on principle, no matter what we have in common. If we're on this case, either with him or alongside him, that's going to rankle. He'll react in ways we might not be able to tolerate."

Collie leaned forward and pinched the bridge of her nose. She was down long enough that Anna thought she might have a weird, stress-related nosebleed or something. She was about to ask when Collie finally raised her head.

"I want to be sure I have this right. You want Anna and I to investigate a murder and a kidnapping that may or may not have been perpetrated by the International House of Evil Sorcery... which is nowhere near as good as pancakes... and, while doing this, you want us to pretend to a paranoid man that we're working for him... *and* you want us to keep this paranoid pseudo-client away from you so that you won't have to whack him. Is that accurate?"

"We're only interested in the murder," Adam said. "The kidnapping is incidental. This isn't as complicated as you're making it out to be. If you need anything, a teleporter, clairvoyant, whatever, ask Kieran. As soon as you've found the murderer, let us know and we'll step in. There's no need to put yourselves in any real danger."

Anna looked at Collie, who seemed to have shrunk a size or two. Her shoulders were pulled in and her hair had fallen forward to hide her face.

"They say," Anna said to Adam, "when someone is doing a hard sell on you, you should remove yourself from the situation and give it some thought."

Adam's mouth twitched.

"It is a truly fine set of encyclopedias," he said. Anna couldn't help returning the aborted smile.

"Be that as it may," she said. "We're going. We'll call you tomorrow."

"Call Kieran," he said. "From here out, until you have the murderer's name for me."

"For us," the redhead put in. For the first time, Anna heard unvarnished emotion in that voice. She sounded genuinely sad.

"You want us to be specific about which goon did it?" Collie asked. "Instead of just proving it was that company?"

Yes," Adam said. "I'm not sure we're up to punishing the whole company. We might have to be specific in our retribution. We'll see."

Anna stood and grabbed Collie's arm, trying to get as little hair as possible in her grasp.

"Col."

Collie got up, shook her arm free and left without a word to their hosts, though she stole a glance at the redhead as she went through the door. Anna followed.

They left the same way they'd come in and Collic didn't hesitate in the winding hall. It really did seem to Anna as if they'd both had the route implanted in them as surely as if they'd walked it a hundred times. Or as many times as that little girl had walked it, she supposed.

They didn't see the little girl again. They let themselves out and Anna was once again left with the question of what to do about the door. This time, she locked it.

Collie's head was still down and Anna suspected she couldn't really see where she was going — a suspicion that was soon confirmed as Collie went down the stairs, turned to head up the street to the Jeep and barrelled directly into Kieran's silent partner.

He was by himself, standing on the sidewalk in a way that made the hair rise on the back of Anna's neck. It reminded her of an image she'd seen in some cheesy haunted house documentary, a supposed ghost just casually wandering down a hall. It wasn't trying to scare anyone, not hurrying or rushing the camera, and that somehow was what had terrified her. She couldn't have said why, anymore than she could have said why Joel put her in mind of it.

"Sorry," Collie said. Joel said his usual nothing. He hadn't even made a sound when Collie had collided with him.

He looked at Collie steadily, his eyes moving once to take in Anna, then going back to Collie's face. He looked like something that had been cut out and pasted into the scene. Slowly, he reached into the pocket of his long dark coat and pulled out a notepad. He flipped a few pages over, tore one off, and handed it to Collie. After she took it, he gave her a nod, turned, and walked up the street.

Collie looked at the paper in her hand, then called after Joel.

"Do you want a lift?"

He didn't respond. A few more steps, then he'd turned the corner and was gone.

"He lives close, anyway," Collie said as Anna stopped beside her. She held the note up for Anna to see. It was Joel's name, just the first name, and a phone number.

"It would be like a reverse obscene phone call," Collie said. "We'd call him and he'd breathe at us."

She folded the paper and tucked it into her purse. Anna made a bet with herself that the number would be transferred to an index card before the night was out. Maybe Collie wouldn't even have to physically do it. Maybe, in that purse, the index card thing just happened.

Collie looked at Anna.

"Here sucks," she said. "I mean, this street. Let's go."

THEY DIDN'T GET FAR, not more than a few blocks, before Collie crawled out from under her hair.

"Would you mind pulling over?"

They were along the river, next to the University. Anna found a spot and parked.

"Forgot to pick up a degree?"

Collie smiled absently.

"I just wanted to talk."

"And we can't do this in our living room because?"

Collie just shrugged. Anna waited, looking at the city skyline through the trees. Broken up that way, it looked like a string of Christmas lights. After a minute or so of silence, Anna spoke.

"Does it ever get cold here? It's like summer never ends. I swear I remember coming here one time and seeing white stuff."

"Was it the eighties?" Collie asked. "Might have been cocaine."

"Seriously, doesn't it bother you that it's September and it's still, like, twenty-two degrees? After sunset?"

Collie nodded.

"This country is going to hell. We don't know who we are anymore."

Anna had left the Jeep running and the radio was playing softly, some rolling piano thing with a deep voiced singer. The sound was sad and... something else. Almost threatening. Anna turned it off.

"I can't believe you just have a radio in your vehicle," Collie said. Anna snorted.

"This from the chick with a tape deck in her late nineties car. I bet you had to pull that deck at Pick Your Part. I bet you can't even buy them in regular stores."

"I told you," Collie said. "I like music. I like car windows. It seemed like a way to have both."

They contemplated that in silence. Collie broke it, finally, with, "I was going to make this whole speech about how, really, truly, we can take this case or not. No matter what the Embassy says. We can do whatever we want. And then we had the meeting."

"Well, I guess we could do whatever we want," Anna said. "Elsewhere."

"Let's go to Edmonton," Collie said, her voice a nasty high-pitched parody of itself. "We can have a weird little detective agency. I can do PR until it's making money. You'll find work, easy. It'll be fun."

"Some of that was true," Anna allowed. Collie shut her eyes and tipped her head back against the seat.

"I'm sorry."

It wasn't her usual kind of apology, the shield she used to deflect criticism while she did whatever she wanted to do. It was, instead, a simple statement of fact.

"I'm not," Anna said. "Edmonton's fine. I don't think coming here was a mistake."

"That's funny," Collie said. "You have the air of 'sorry' about you."

"I don't know what you mean," Anna said. "I'm not thrilled that we seem, once again, to be in the shit. Bottom line, though, it's about Ian. I liked the guy. I'm sorry this happened to him. I know you are, too."

"Much though I bitched about him," Collie said. "Would we be in this position, though, if it weren't for the agency? Because I did kind of twist your arm about that one."

"I have issues and concerns," Anna said. "Mostly about touching things, which I will not do unless I damned well feel like it, no matter how hard you push. But the detective thing, in general, does beat the hell out of sluicing urine from cages."

"Ah," Collie said. "I thought so. I thought you didn't like your day job."

"It's a job, Col. If it were fun, they wouldn't have to pay people to do it."

Collie shook her head. Her hair took on some static from the seat cover, floated up and back.

"Considering the amount of time people spend at work, don't you think you should do something you want to do?"

Anna laughed. She didn't mean to, because Collie looked so serious, but it really was funny.

"When did I ever give you the impression that there was anything I wanted to do?"

Collie opened her eyes and looked at Anna. It took Anna a second to recognize her expression, because she saw it so rarely. Collie looked hurt.

"What?" Anna said.

"I didn't mean to drag you," Collie said.

"You didn't," Anna told her. "That's the point. I didn't have anywhere in particular I wanted to be. You did. I like hanging out with you, so here I am. I'm just... not a cheerleader."

At that, Collie laughed.

"Wow. I totally thought you were. Little pink skirts and pompoms are so you."

A jogger went by, armbands flashing in the Jeep's headlights. Anna turned the lights off. No sense killing the battery.

"At least we got that second opinion on Eric Quinlan."

Collie smiled.

"Pretty good match for your vision, hey?"

"It was in line," Anna agreed.

"I don't feel too bad about taking him on as a client. It's all the rest of this I'm not loving. Although, I suppose our interests and Quinlan's interests and the Embassy's interests are currently well-matched. As long as whoever took Rowan is the same person who killed Ian. And as long as that person isn't one of our clients."

"Sounds simple," Anna said. "It must *be* simple."

Collie was looking at the trees, but her eyes were unfocused. The lights were probably a blur to her.

"When we first saw Ian here, so soon after we arrived, I thought it was weird. Remember? And you said it probably wasn't weird to see a guy who could teleport in any particular place."

"I stand by that. Also, you already knew this was a hotbed for supernatural screwballs. Why are we dredging this up, Col?"

Collie turned her head, not lifting it from the seat. Strands of hair fanned out behind her.

"I don't know. Maybe I'm just trying to figure out where we went wrong."

"Maybe nowhere yet," Anna said. "But I'm sure we can change that if we sit here all night and wind up having to call the client on no sleep."

"And by client you mean Eric?"

"Yeah," Anna said. "Until further notice, he is our client in my heart. The Embassy can be the fuckers in my heart."

"You have room in your heart for a client and a whole Embassy's worth of fuckers?" Collie asked.

"May we proceed homeward?" Anna sighed.

"Have we decided to do this? So there's no confusion about it later?"

"We have decided to do what we're being forced into doing," Anna said. Collie nodded.

"You put it that way, I feel worlds better. As if my fate were in my hands."

"Whatever lets me sleep at night," Anna said. Collie was silent as they pulled from the curb. Then, softly: "That chick was pretty hot."

"Which chick?"

"The only one we came in contact with tonight who wasn't a waitress," Collie said, "is who I guess I might mean. Otherwise known as the incredible hottie."

"The redhead?" Anna asked. "You thought she was attractive?"

"Good god, yes," Collie said. "Who wouldn't?"

"Me, apparently," Anna said.

Collie didn't look at her. She kept looking at the river. After a moment, Anna did the same.

"Everyone's younger than us," Collie said. "Have you noticed? Rowan and Kieran. And the hottie."

"She could be eighty for all we know. She was an obvious product of plastic surgery. Possibly with real plastic. She looked like Tupperware."

"Oh, come on," Collie said. "I saw no signs of that."

She didn't sound happy about it. Collie's reactions to attractive women – attractive in her eyes, anyway – were always unpredictable. She seemed, at times, not to know whether she was captivated, jealous, or both. Anna didn't figure Collie had much reason to get jealous, being a trim and stylish little redhead in her own right, but women were funny that way.

Anna had long ago given up on fixing her straight coffee-coloured hair or disguising her unfashionably large frame with a perfectly-cut coat. All the little makeup tricks that were supposed to make her face softer never seemed to work. The whole thing was a game she was better off not playing, as she could never win. But it bothered her sometimes, all the same.

"Oh, hey," Collie said, with the brightness of someone who had found a much more agreeable subject, "Quinlan will pay us, won't he? And the Embassy will pay us. We'll rake it in. If we live."

"And there's every reason to think we will," Anna said. "Baddest people in town sticking us with a client who wants to fight them and, for a prime suspect, a corporation that seems to intimidate the hell out of them."

"Noticed that too, did you? And how much do you love it that our client wants us to liaise for him because he thinks magicians hate him and the magicians want us to liaise for them because they think our client hates them?"

"I'd say it's all a big misunderstanding," Anna said. "Except, in this case, I think everybody is probably right."

"Good thing you and I are so damned affable," Collie observed as the steel-floored bridge buzzed beneath them.

"A damned good thing," Anna agreed.

The floor must be filthy, considering how many feet cross it in a day, but Rowan seems not to mind. He is sitting on it anyway, his back to the glass wall, watching teenagers and couples and parents draped in shrieking children as the lot of them push and push toward the theatres. Anna wonders if they'll stop once they get inside, or push their way right through the screens and out the other side.

Anna sits beside him, beneath a surfing Batman that hangs from the ceiling, and breathes deep. Theatre popcorn. Still strong enough to block the nacho cheese and ice cream, the smells that aren't from the theatres of her childhood. Complications. They dilute everything.

"What's wrong with a bag of popcorn?" she asks.

"Ssh," Rowan answers.

Music is playing, barely audible above the hiss and rumble of human voices. It's some new ager's idea of traditional Chinese music, all synthesized flutes and washes that even Jon Anderson would consider cheesy.

Smoke begins to drift downward. Heavier than air. Isn't smoke supposed to rise? She turns to Rowan to ask and finds him rapt, eyes on the theatre's centrepiece — a mechanical dragon that hangs above the ticket desks, tail curving toward the concession booth.

"Show's starting," Rowan explains, but Anna knows that. It's an old show.

Above them, the dragon stirs. His eyes glow orange and the smoke thickens. A little boy starts to cry.

"That's a ghost dragon," Rowan says. Anna nods. Cursed to hang there forever, repeating its sad routine, breathing fire into empty air. Scaring a few children, if it's lucky.

The dragon swings its head around and begins to breathe out fire. In the sudden orange light, the pipes in its mouth can be seen. The illusion betrays itself.

Some people watch. Most keep talking, uninterested. The crying child is picked up by his mother, whisked away somewhere. Anna's face feels warm.

"That guy has a hell of a job," Rowan says and Anna looks where he's pointing, across the room. As if by collusion, the crowd has parted just enough to create a clear line of sight between her and Eric. He's standing, perfectly still, staring at the dragon as it coughs out a last cloud of smoke and pulls its head back again, to wait half-hidden in the shadows between the metal stars.

"He been here all day?" Anna asks. Behind Eric, the theatre wall is hazy. Squinting, she thinks she might see water stretching out to nowhere.

"Gotta keep an eye on the dragon," Rowan says. "If no one's watching him, he might turn real someday."

A phone rings, startling them both. Eric is staring at the dragon. He doesn't seem to hear, even though the crowd has gone silent and it's just the three of them, woods on three sides, a lake on the other. Metal stars in the sky.

"I have to take that," Rowan says.

And disappears.

AND IT WAS SEVEN in the morning and the fucking phone was ringing and ringing because someone thought that was an okay time to make a call. Anna rolled over, face down on her pillow. If she couldn't see the world, maybe it couldn't see her.

Collie was downstairs. Anna could hear her talking to the bastard on the other end of the phone. She wasn't raising her voice enough, so Anna couldn't make out what she was saying. After a minute or so, the phone beside the bed let out a muffled ding. Collie had hung up.

"Col?"

Anna yelled it, but the pillow was in her way. Goddamn. She rolled over again.

"Colette? Who the fuck was that?"

"What?"

The obvious solution, as Anna saw it, was for Collie to come upstairs and start talking. She didn't figure Collie would see it that way, though.

Anna rolled out of bed, pulled a sweatshirt over her t-shirt and stumbled into the bathroom. Couple of quick stabs with the toothbrush. Swipes with the deodorant. Good enough. She'd deal with the rest later.

Collie was at the kitchen table, eating a bagel and giving the newspaper her usual disgusted once over. Anna didn't know why Collie kept her subscription. Maybe it was like black coffee, a little bitterness to kick start her day.

"That was the clinic," Collie said, brushing bagel crumbs off her shirt. "Wanting you to come in early. I said you were in the shower."

Where did Colette imagine bagel crumbs went when she brushed them off like that? Just... away? To Narnia? Anna pointedly grabbed the broom and swept them into the dustpan.

"How do they expect me to do that? I'm scheduled for eight as it is. What time did they say?"

Collie grinned.

"You're forgetting that it doesn't matter. The Embassy said to quit your day job. If you liked your day job, I'd say to ask for a leave of absence. But you don't, so blow it off. You're still under your three months. You don't have to give notice. Just walk."

"I guess I could," Anna conceded. She pulled out the other chair and straddled it, amazed as always that it didn't crumple beneath her. A scrap of bent metal with a little bit of plastic glued to it did not equal furniture where Anna came from. "I just don't want to burn a bridge."

"Sure you do," Collie said cheerfully. "There are always more jobs. Teach them not to harass people about coming in early, like, an hour before their shift starts. It'll be a public service."

Anna glanced at the front page of the paper. No mention of the murder. Not that the death of someone like Ian would necessarily be front page news. Or that anyone in the media would have had any way of knowing. And it had been late. The newspaper had probably already been printed for the next day.

"Okay. I'll call. And then you can call the client."

Collie reached into her purse, retrieved her cell phone and held it up.

"Two phones. No waiting. I'll be in the living room."

Anna made her phone call, scooped the remains of Collie's bagel off the table and rounded the corner to the living room.

"So," Collie said. "They give you leave?"

"Did you hear me ask for leave?" Anna asked. Collie laughed.

"No. But you did anyway."

No point hiding it. Anna shrugged.

"They insisted. However long I need. Did I ever tell you how hard it was to find work back home?"

Collie nodded.

"Yes, but only a thousand times, so I might not have caught all the details. I talked to Eric."

"You wake him up?" Anna asked.

"Not that he would admit. He'll meet us at the office in an hour."

"Okay," Anna said. "I'll meet you there. I have to swing by the clinic and get some food out of the break room. Or… do you need a lift?"

Collie shook her head.

"I can take the bus. It'll give me time to think about what I'm going to do to my mechanic if I don't get my car back soon."

"That sounds nice," Anna said. She grabbed her purse, decided against her coat, and glanced at the leather jacket still lying on their couch.

"You gonna take that to the meeting?"

"I was considering that," Collie said. "I've decided no. I'm going to put it in the linen closet, under some sheets. And no, I do not know why."

"Good enough," Anna said. "Catch you later. Don't start lying to the paranoid loner without me."

ANNA WAS SURPRISED to hear Collie's voice as she started up the stairs to their office. Not because it would ever surprise her that Collie was talking, but because hearing her voice meant the office door was open, which meant their client had loosened up considerably overnight.

At the top of the stairs, she skirted her abandoned coffee and wrap from the night before. She was tempted to turn around and go home, since she'd already solved her mystery for the day. She'd been wondering for months if the janitors came in every night. Evidently not.

As she entered, the client was sitting with his arms folded, listening. He looked reasonably relaxed, but Anna noticed he had angled his chair a bit toward the door.

"…and the town was not called Michael's Landing," Collie

was saying. "It was called Grayling Cross. Did I get everything?"

"What about the dragon?" the client asked as Anna slipped past him to her desk. Collie shrugged.

"We're not here to judge your sanity. You have the rest of the world to do that for you."

"Did your sources tell you it was a dragon?" the client asked.

"They told me you thought it was," Collie said. "Anna... let me catch you up."

So, Collie had decided to let Eric know that they knew a thing or two about him. Anna hoped she'd managed to do that without bringing the Embassy into it. She reached into her jacket pocket and retrieved one of the cans of Pepsi she'd rescued from her former workplace's fridge.

"Go hard," she said, flipping the tab.

"Well, Mr. Quinlan here... can we call you Eric?"

"I don't care what you call me," the client said.

"I doubt you mean that," Collie said. "We can test it later. Anyway, Eric told me about his background this morning. Nothing we didn't already know, but some details were at variance with what we'd discovered. I assumed he was measuring our detective skills, so I pointed those details out."

"Huh," Anna said. She drank some Pepsi and set the can down on her desk. No coaster, but shellac didn't get water rings, did it? "Maybe he was testing your ability to keep your mouth shut even when someone's insulting your intelligence."

Collie blushed at that, but said nothing. She was lucky she had all that hair, really, because it was tough to tell when she was blushing. You had to look carefully.

"I wanted to know that you'd done your due diligence," Eric said, looking at Anna. With his chair angled, he only had to turn his head a little. It was probably a better placement for the chair, in general. Maybe they'd leave it that way.

"We looked into you," Anna said. "We said we would."

"And you have received accurate information," Eric said. "So you're competent. Your partner will never be a poker player, but I don't need you to bluff on my behalf."

"In her defence," Anna said, "there's no sense bluffing around people who can read your mind, which is the sort of thing we're used to."

That was an exaggeration. Hardly anyone in town, as far as Anna knew, could actually read minds. But the client had no way of knowing that.

"Mind reading is rare," he said. "Scientifically, it's been difficult to document. Unlike remote viewing – that's what Rowan does. I doubt you know as many telepaths as you believe you do. Considering the circles you run in, I hope you aren't easily convinced by claims of magical powers and spells and the rest of that bunk."

"Bunk?" Collie sounded not so much offended as pleased by the choice of word. "Really?"

Anna shot her a warning look. Do not offer to have me demonstrate. Do not. Do. Not.

Eric looked at Collie.

"Bunk. At best. I did not think it was a dragon."

"Don't believe in them?" Collie asked.

"Dragons? No. Nor unicorns, nor mermaids. I told you it was a dragon to find out what you'd been told. I'm aware of the rumours. It wasn't a living creature. When I first saw it, I was momentarily convinced, but then I realized it must be some kind of animatronic device."

"I thought you were out of town when the attack happened," Anna said.

"I was on the water," Eric told her. "I saw everything. By the time I got into the town, it was almost over. The machine turned toward me and was likely about to shoot fire at me, but it was poorly made and fell apart as I watched – probably due to the surrounding heat."

"You're saying," Collie said slowly, "that this machine looked like a dragon, flew into your town, breathed fire until the whole place had burned up, and then fell apart in front of you. And this happened about twenty years ago."

"I realize it sounds beyond the scope of current technology, let alone the technology of twenty years ago," Eric said, "but certain corporations hoard advancements. The government does as well. I need no further proof of what happened than that it happened to me."

"Our policy is to believe our clients until they're proven wrong," Anna said.

"Sometimes even after they're proven wrong," Collie added. "So, if you say it was a big ol' flying robot with a flamethrower for a mouth... okay. That's what it was."

Anna blinked, remembering her dream. Though she doubted the local movie theatre's dragon could burn up a whole town, or fly.

"But," Collie went on, "can I ask why no one found this thing lying in the middle of Main Street?"

"1st Street," Eric corrected. "I don't know for certain. There was a lot of smoke and I passed out. When I came to, I was in a hospital. By the time I got back to the town, the machine was gone. From the way people talk, I assume it vanished before the rescue crews arrived."

"Big ol' vanishing robot?" Anna inquired.

"I've always assumed its owners retrieved the parts before anyone could see them. They must have thought I was dead, like the rest of the town, and left me there. No witnesses. No evidence. Except this."

He opened his left hand and Anna realized for the first time that he had been holding it in a loose fist since she'd arrived. She tilted her head for a better look and saw a piece of polished silver metal, about the size of a doorknob, with a hole in one end.

"I found it in the street when I got back to the town," Eric informed them. "It's part of an artificial joint. A ball and socket joint. That type of joint is more common in reptiles than in humans."

"Slithery," Collie said. "Anna?"

In other words, Anna, would you like to touch the weird artefact and see if you wind up facing down a robot dragon in a town filled with smoke and charred corpses?

She held out her hand.

"May I see it?"

Eric gave her an odd look, one that passed so quickly she thought she might have imagined it.

"Yes."

He placed the ball in her hand, his fingers brushing her palm. His skin was cold and dry.

Anna bounced it a little in her hand, getting the heft. It felt like a bigger version of the steelie marbles she'd played with when she was little. Ball bearings, she'd later found out.

"Stainless steel?" she asked. Eric nodded.

And that was it. No vision. Not even a sense of anything unusual. Just a piece of steel in her hand. She turned it over, saw a symbol and some numbers carved just inside the hole.

"What's this?" she asked, pointing it out to Eric.

"It's how I tracked them down. The manufacturer of the joint put their mark on it. I traced it, found out who made it, got a customer list. Eventually that led me to Varanus."

"You did that when you were ten?" Collie asked, holding her hand out for the ball. Apparently she had figured out no vision would be forthcoming. Anna dropped the ball into her hand.

"No. I was in my twenties. I was already watching Varanus by that point, because one of their holdings established a uranium mine where Grayling Cross used to be."

"So," Anna said, "you think they burned your town to the ground because they wanted to put in a uranium mine?

Wouldn't it have been easier to put the mine nearby and use the town for infrastructure?"

"If they wanted a mine," Eric said, "yes. But they never operated that mine. Just dug it and let it sit."

"You think they were looking for something else," Collie said.

"Obviously," Eric answered, snappishly. "Not that it matters. They ruined the land, got what they were looking for and left. Or they didn't find what they were looking for and left. No different from any other mining company in the area. Varanus just took less time to do it."

"And used a fake dragon," Anna said. "That's a little different."

"You want to know why they would do that," Eric said. He leaned forward a little and plucked the steel ball from Collie's hand. "You want to know why they would draw attention to themselves, when they could have destroyed that town by other means. Or just bought up the land."

Anna's line of thinking hadn't gone that far, but she didn't see any reason to admit it.

"All good questions," she said.

"I don't have good answers. But I'll find them." He placed his hands on his knees in a way that suggested he was about to stand. "First priority is to find Rowan. I need you to get out there and start asking questions. How long has he been in Edmonton? Who has he talked to? What did he talk about? Was he working for anyone here? Most importantly, has anyone else been asking questions about him?"

"Aside from you?" Anna asked.

"Obviously."

"Before you go," Collie said, "I've been wondering... if you just got into town and no one would talk to you, how did you know where Rowan's apartment was? And what convinced you that he was missing instead of just... staying with a friend or something?"

"I found his apartment with the help of a remote viewer," Eric said. "That's all I'm going to say about that."

Anna wasn't certain what a remote viewer was, but she had a feeling it has something in common with clairvoyance. Going into a trance and seeing far away lands. Gazing into a crystal ball.

This from a guy who, according to the Embassy, hated the paranormal. Anna glanced at Collie. Her face was calm, curious but not surprised.

"Okay," she said. "And you knew he was in trouble because?"

Eric took one hand off his knees and slipped it into his jacket pocket, the same one he'd used for the packet of photos and papers. For a moment, Anna pictured his hand sliding into darkness, a space as cavernous as an abandoned mine, containing anything and everything he might want to produce for them.

He took his hand out and showed them a plastic duck, yellow dulled by scuffs, eyes blank where paint had been rubbed away. A child's toy, worn by being handled for years.

"He uses this to focus. Every day at noon, he does a meditative exercise. He uses the toy for that. I was in his apartment at noon yesterday. The duck was there. He was not."

Collie was blinking furiously, as if she hoped the duck would disappear while her eyes were closed. No such luck.

"*Quod erat duckonstrandum*?" she asked. Eric glared at her.

"He spent most of his life in a structured environment. His habits are important to him. Possibly even vital to his mental well-being."

Anna said nothing. She was picturing her grandmother, in a rare fit of optimism, pinning a dreamcatcher to her bedroom's window frame. It hadn't helped, but for years Anna had thought that it must be helping. Figured that, without it, things would have been even worse.

"Okay," she said. "He wouldn't leave the duck. When you find him, you can give it back to him."

Eric stood.

"I will. I'm going to leave the initial investigation in your hands, since you know the community. Once you've spoken to the key players and reported to me, I'll be able to direct you further. Tomorrow, this office, eight AM."

"Make it ten," Collie said. "Some of these key players aren't real sociable before midnight."

"Fine," Eric said. He pocketed the duck and left. They sat and listened as he went down the stairs and out the door.

"You get anything off his thingama?" Collie asked. "The dragon part?"

Anna shook her head.

"It's like that sometimes. You know that."

"I'm surprised," Collie said. "It seemed like the kind of thing that would set you off."

"Never can tell," Anna said.

"Maybe he threw you off," Collie suggested. "Saying magic was bunk."

That wasn't worth a response, so Anna didn't give it one.

"That woman at the Embassy said Eric hated paranormal stuff," said Anna, "not that he didn't believe in it. I thought it was strange that he would say that."

"The Embassy is a skosh paranoid," Collie said. "I'm not surprised that they would interpret any response other than deference as hate. Besides, Eric probably does dislike people who, to his mind, *pretend* to be magical types. Bunch of fakers. Like you."

"I'm desperate for attention," Anna said. "It's sad."

Collie took out her cell and dialed.

"Kieran? It's Colette."

Oh. Right. They hadn't officially taken the case yet. Not for the other client.

"No, everything's fine… the Embassy just asked us to talk to you instead of them. I guess you're the new Mandrake."

For the first time, Anna was sorry Kieran wasn't in the room with them. She would have liked to have seen his face when he heard that.

"Well," Collie said, "you know what I mean. Anyway, can you just tell them we're taking the case? No, that's it. Great. Thanks."

She dropped the phone into her purse.

"Done."

Anna nodded.

"You know, you have a phone right in front of you. You pay a monthly charge for it and then you get all the local calls you want. Free."

"Yeah," Collie said. "I don't know. It just feels clunky. Why do you care, anyway? You think the client's outside the building picking up my signal?"

How terrific was it that Anna couldn't completely discount the possibility?

"I didn't think of that," she said, "but why not? On the other hand, he could have bugged the office. Or tapped our phone. Or maybe the other client has done those things. Or maybe one or both of our clients are watching us right now, through a remote viewer. Since remote viewing isn't bunk."

"That's what I hear," Collie said.

They looked at each other for a moment. In the silence, the microwave beeped. Five times. Shave and a haircut. Collie kept staring at Anna, but she raised her fist and lightly rapped her desk. Two bits. The microwave's door popped open. Collie pushed back off the desk, her chair rolling until it hit the wall beside the door. Anna watched Collie out of the corner of her eye, her face turned toward the microwave.

"Mandrake?" Collie said. "Is that you?"

"I think it's a microwave," Anna said. Collie stood and went to the microwave, pulled the door all the way open and peered inside. Anna couldn't see past her, but from the dejected way

Collie crouched in front of the stand, she assumed Collie hadn't found anything more than the food splatter they both kept saying they'd clean.

"What?" Collie said, not turning. "You think that was just a fluke, that it shave and a haircutted us?"

"That reminds me," Anna said. "You got a letter from the Canadian Noun Association. All it said was 'quit it'. I assume you know what that's about."

"Ian?" Collie said, still looking into the microwave as if she expected drops of squash soup to rearrange themselves into a message. It was risible, but mostly it was sad. Anna didn't have the heart to keep hassling her.

"I don't know what that was," Anna admitted, "but I think the show's over."

Collie turned, without standing. Just slowly spun around, as if she were on a turntable. How she did that sort of thing, Anna would never know.

"Remember," Collie said, "how the door opened? At his house?"

"Yeah," Anna said. "But let's not jump to conclusions about what caused either of these things."

Collie rolled her eyes.

"I can't believe you're proposing a scientific explanation."

"Did I say that?" Anna asked. "All I said was, we don't know what it was."

To Anna's surprise, tears came to Collie's eyes at that. Whether they were tears of sorrow or anger, or both, Anna couldn't say.

"He's trying to communicate," Collie said, then stood and briskly returned to her desk. End of conversation.

Fortunately, they had an obvious new topic.

"What now?" Anna asked. "You must have some people in mind, since you said we'd have to talk to them after midnight."

"Oh," Collie said. "That... I mean, do you like getting up in the morning?"

"No," Anna said. "As you well know."

"So? Ten AM sounded good to me. That's all that was. Anyway... I've been thinking. Though you're not going to like this..."

"Kieran," Anna said, taking a swig of Pepsi to wash the taste away. Collie nodded.

"Sorry."

Anna crushed the empty can and set it at the corner of her desk.

"No, you're right. You want to ask him to meet us somewhere, or..."

Collie grinned.

"You don't want to go to the house."

"It's a shelter," Anna said. "Those people deserve their space."

"Those people scare you."

"Those people's spouses," Anna corrected, "scare me. But less than Kieran does. So, wherever."

"Let's drop in on him," Collie said, getting to her feet. "It's folksy. And sometimes illuminating."

Anna stood and hesitated for a moment, looking at the Pepsi can. The thing to do was rinse it out and put it in the plastic bin Collie had bought for just that purpose.

"You coming?" Collie asked.

The hell with the can. Maybe they'd get ants and the next guy who broke into their office would be so disgusted, he'd turn around and leave.

"Right behind you."

KIERAN'S HOUSE WAS, as Collie had mentioned the night before, just a few blocks from the Embassy. The neighbourhood was certainly nice, lined with mature trees and filled with well-tended character homes. It was close to the university and to the bars and shops of Whyte Avenue, which some people considered a positive. Anna considered the area extortionate and overhyped. Nothing but noise and drunks spilling into the surrounding streets, and even the smallest houses priced for the wealthy or the reckless. She was pretty sure it was Collie's dream to live there someday.

Like the Embassy, Kieran's house was three storeys tall and had just one mailbox. It housed up to ten guests, who each had their own bedrooms but shared the rest of the place. It was usually full, which made Anna wonder what the deal was with Joel. If he'd earned a bed in the shelter, was he some kind of domestic abuse victim, or survivor, or whatever the term was supposed to be? Or was he there for some other reason?

Collie went to the door with a spring in her step. Whether it was because she liked Kieran or whether she enjoyed ambushing people, Anna couldn't say. Each was equally likely.

The door, as always, was unlocked. Anna shook her head and Collie glanced at her, amused.

"Like I said," Collie told her, "it's got to be warded."

They moved carefully through the foyer, which was large but crowded by racks of coats and shoes. To their right, in the living room, a woman's voice was rising with agitation.

"...and *he* cursed *me!* So you tell me why he's living in our condo and I'm here sleeping on a foldout couch!"

"I'm sorry about the couch," Kieran's voice told her. "Normally we give that room to kids, but we're full right now and everyone's an adult."

"The couch is not the *point!*"

Collie stopped just outside the living room. If she had been anyone else, Anna would have thought she didn't want to intrude. Over the top of the curly head, Anna could see a thin blonde in a skirt suit pointing a long red fingernail at Kieran. He looked uncomfortable enough that Anna almost, *almost* felt sorry for him.

"Mrs. Karr, the Embassy agrees that his behaviour was out of line and they're working on a solution. This is a safe place for you to wait that out, but you're free to go home anytime you like."

She shuddered with anger, a move that made the suit jacket shake around her shoulders. Anna realized it was the wrong size, too large for her. Something scrounged from the house's communal wardrobe, most likely. It was impressive that she looked as put together as she did.

"Of course I am not."

Kieran sighed.

"No. Of course you're not. That's not your fault, but it's not our fault, either. The Embassy are not the police. They can and will do something about this. They just have to investigate first and decide what's appropriate. What if your husband is possessed, for example? What if he opened the wrong box and something got into him? You wouldn't want to throw away a good marriage over something like that."

"Yes," Mrs. Karr said, squaring her shoulders so the jacket sat right again. "I would. He's always doing that sort of thing and I'm sick of it."

"Well," Kieran said, a hint of impatience in his tone. "That's between you and your husband and maybe a counsellor. Or a lawyer."

His eyes flickered in Collie's direction and Anna realized they'd be spotted. He was subtle about it though, enough so that Mrs. Karr didn't notice.

"Is there anything else," Kieran said, "that I can do for you?"

"I suppose not," Mrs. Karr said, stomping on the word "not" with her cultured voice. She rose, with dignity, and swanned out of the room. Kieran shut his eyes and leaned back against the sofa.

"Hello," he said, eyes still shut. "And what can I do for *you*?"

The room held four couches, all long, all covered in

mismatched blankets and throw pillows. The look, overall, worked well enough that Anna suspected it wasn't as random as it pretended to be.

"We have questions," Collie said. She moved forward and seated herself on the couch where Mrs. Karr had been. Anna took the couch across from her.

"About Mandrake," Kieran said, opening his eyes.

"And a kid named Rowan Bell," Collie added. Kieran's eyes widened a little.

"Really."

"Yes. Did the Embassy tell you to cooperate with us?"

Kieran smiled.

"No, but after last night I assume any questions you're asking are on their behalf."

"Don't assume that," Anna told him. "We actually have a different client. Do you know of anyone who would have wanted to kill Ian?"

Kieran sat up straighter.

"A different client?"

"Whose identity is confidential," Collie said. "Again: do you know of anyone who would have wanted to kill Ian?"

Kieran shook his head.

"I've thought about it. He was a hired gun. I don't mean gun in the sense that he was a hitman, but just that he did what the Embassy told him to do. Getting mad at him would be like getting mad at the car someone was driving when they cut you off."

"Which people manage to do," Collie pointed out.

"True," Kieran conceded, "but they don't destroy those cars. They just key them or spit on the windshield. The other thing is, someone must have teleported in behind him in order to do the job. Getting a teleporter to kill another teleporter that way... I wouldn't even know where to start hiring for that job. I can't imagine it being too attractive to the prospective employees, you know? It would take a lot of work just to find someone who both *could* kill Ian and was *willing* to kill Ian. That's not something you'd arrange on a whim."

Collie frowned.

"Couldn't someone he trusted have walked into the room, stood behind him and pulled a gun?"

"No."

The sound of breaking glass came from the kitchen. Collie jumped and Anna felt her own heart race. Kieran didn't seem to react at all.

"Sorry," a young man's voice called from the direction of the sound.

"It's okay," Kieran called back. "Broom's in the hall closet."

"That happen a lot?" Collie asked.

"Our guests are a little distracted. About Ian... he had a subconscious instinct about danger. If a car was about to hit him, even if he didn't see it, he'd teleport out of the way. Involuntarily. The only way you could get the drop on Ian would be to port in behind him, shoot and port out. Just... not give him any time to react. Not any time at all."

"Or you could disable his ability to teleport," Anna said. Kieran gave her a strange look.

"Why would you say that?" he asked. Anna returned the look.

"Seemed like an option. Why would you think it was odd for me to say it?"

Kieran blinked a few too many times.

"Sounds like a long shot," he said. "Unless you know of someone who could do that. I certainly don't."

"Oookay," Collie said. "Do you have any thoughts about why Ian was killed?"

"It had occurred to me that he'd been hanging around with that new kid. Bell."

"Any particular reason why you'd latch onto that?" Collie asked.

Kieran shrugged.

"For starters, it was the only thing that was new or different in Ian's life. That I knew of, anyway. And the kid was mysterious. Said he was an astral projector and that he had a lot of professional experience, but no one aside from Ian had ever heard of him and he wouldn't say where he'd been working. He seemed nervous, too."

"You think he might have been responsible for this?" Anna asked.

"Depends what you mean by responsible," Kieran said. "I met him a few times, with Ian, and I never got the impression that he was a bad kid. But I did think he was in trouble and that could have followed him here."

"Did you have any particular reason to think he was in trouble?" Collie asked. "Did he say anything? Or did Ian?" Kieran's mouth twitched and Anna realized he was smothering a laugh.

"Ian said a lot of things. He never said much about Bell, though. Just that he was a friend and an astral projector. Honestly, it was just an impression, because the kid was twitchy and he wouldn't give out any information."

"Did you see Ian and Rowan together a lot?" Collie asked. Kieran thought about that, picking idly at a loose thread on one of the throw blankets surrounding him.

"I guess... yeah. Not that I saw them a lot, but whenever I saw Ian, Bell was usually with him. From about the beginning of August. I don't know the exact date when I first saw them together."

"I'd be looking at you funny if you did," Collie assured him.

"I'd be thinking you did it," Anna said mildly. "But I'm a suspicious person."

Kieran gave her a look she was starting to think he kept in stock just for her, the one that said he wasn't sure whether she was kidding and, further, didn't know if he'd be more offended if she were joking or if she were serious. Collie, not bothered by such fine points, just stared daggers at her.

"We don't think that," she told Anna.

"It was a conditional statement," Anna said, then gave Kieran a wide smile. He gave her a tight smile in response.

"What I think," he said, "is that Ian was the only person in town that Rowan Bell knew. I think Ian put him up when he got here, found him some work through the Embassy, and found him an apartment. I can't say for certain whether I think these things because Ian said as much to me, or if this was just the impression I got, because I never gave it that much thought. Until now. Okay?"

"Speaking of Rowan's apartment," Collie said, "would you happen to know where it is?"

She said it with such perfect "in over my head again" ruefulness that Anna wanted to applaud. Never would Kieran have guessed that they could find out Rowan's address with one phone call to their client. Either of their clients, most likely.

"Sorry. All I know is that Ian was looking through the paper one day and I asked him if he was finally moving out of that hole he lived in and he said no, he was looking for a place for Rowan. And I said... I don't know. If he's going to be in town, bring him by the house sometime. Or, let's have dinner. But nothing ever came of that. The kid was a hermit."

"Has anyone asked you questions about Rowan?" Collie asked. "Or Mandrake? Aside from us?"

Kieran smiled.

"I get — I mean, I got — a lot of 'what's with that guy?' about Ian. I get it about Joel, too. And the Embassy, come to think of it. Why does everyone think I would know what's wrong with these people?"

Anna wanted to say she couldn't fathom it, since Kieran was far too self-involved to really notice anyone else. But that wouldn't have been politic.

"It's a mystery," she said. "No one asked you anything strange or... nosy?"

"No. I'm not a front-line person, though. If someone came to town, a total stranger, and they wanted to find out about the occult crowd, they wouldn't come to me. They wouldn't know about me. Not unless they knew someone at the Embassy."

"Would they have gone directly to the Embassy?" Anna asked.

"Maybe," Kieran said thoughtfully. "They're reasonably well-known. It would probably be a natural place to start."

"Unless you didn't want to talk to the Embassy," Anna added.

Kieran raised his eyebrows as if that would never have occurred to him.

"I guess," he said, "Then you'd be stuck inquiring at the shops or something. Or... we have some people in town who advertise their services, so it's possible a stranger might knock on their doors. But really, you should ask the Embassy. And you might want to ask them what kind of work Rowan was doing for them."

"Anything else?" Collie asked. "Friends of Ian's, maybe? With whom did he hang out?"

Kieran pulled an embroidered pillow onto his lap and hugged it.

"You should know. I seem to remember you being at his last party. Specifically, I recall you being the one with the bright idea to port the smell away. What did you call it? Blowing the stank out?"

"I'm sorry!" Collie said, a shrill edge to her voice. "I said I was sorry!"

"One guy's eardrum actually burst," Kieran said in a wondering tone, as if he still couldn't believe the carnage Collie had wrought. Jerk.

"She didn't make Ian do anything," Anna said. "She made

a comment. If you think people have to obey her every word, I'm going to ask her to ask you to stick your head in the toilet and flush it."

Kieran opened his mouth, probably with the intention of saying something, but was wise enough to abandon the idea.

"Since you remember the party," Anna said, "you should know we didn't really have time to be introduced to anyone. So we'll take names if you have them."

Somewhere upstairs, a door slammed. After a moment, it slammed again. Kieran rubbed his eyes with the heels of his hands.

"I should probably go up there." He looked at them. "Ian didn't have many close friends. I'll email the list to you."

"Text me instead," Collie said. "We'll be out and about."

"Shame on you," Kieran joked, colouring a little as he met her eyes. Apparently it had sunk in that he might have been rude to her. "Okay. Did you want me to set up an appointment for you with the Embassy?"

"Actually," Collie said brightly, "they told us to get whatever we needed through you. So please do go ahead and see what they know about Rowan, and if anyone asked them about Rowan or Ian. We'll check in with you tomorrow about that."

"Fucking hell," Kieran muttered under his breath. Anna felt, strangely, a bit shocked. It wasn't like him to say such a thing.

"Excuse me?" Collie said.

"Sorry," Kieran said, smoothly polite again. "I'll take care of it. I just have a lot on my plate."

"So, tell the Embassy to pound sand," Anna said. Kieran waved a hand at the room.

"They fund the house," he said. "I'll tell them to pound sand if you evict the guests."

"They don't do charity, hey?" Collie said.

"Not really," Kieran said. "But this is about Ian, so it's worth doing. Is there anything else?"

Collie stood, then turned to smooth the blanket she'd been sitting on.

"That's it for now," she said as she worked. "Thank you."

"No problem," Kieran said, getting to his feet. He watched, without moving, as they went toward the foyer. It seemed he wasn't going to show them out.

"Oh," Collie said, looking at Kieran, "one more thing... wow, I feel like Columbo all of a sudden."

"You don't look like him," Kieran said, smiling.

"It's not about Ian. I was just thinking; Mrs. Karr has a point. If her husband cursed her, why does he get the house?"

"Not that it's any of your business," Kieran said, "but this isn't about fairness. The curse he put on her... did you notice her jacket didn't fit right?"

Collie nodded.

"It's changing her," Kieran said. "Except when she's in this house. We have certain... protections."

"Oh," Collie said. She'd been proven right about the house being warded. Somehow, she didn't sound happy about it.

"The Embassy will sort this and she will go home. But right now she has to stay here."

"Okay," Anna said, putting a hand on Collie's shoulder. "Thanks."

She steered Collie out the door and down the walk, not taking her hand away until she'd pushed Collie right into the Jeep's passenger seat. Collie didn't push back, didn't say a word.

As Anna rounded the front of the Jeep, she felt eyes on her and scanned the windows of the house. No one, as far as she could see. If recent events proved anything, though, it was that anyone could be watching, anytime.

At least Collie hadn't asked Kieran if he, too, had been visited by Mandrake's ghost.

THEY WERE NEARLY ACROSS the river when Collie spoke.

"Where are we headed?" she asked.

"Myth," Anna said. Urban Myth was an occult bookstore tucked into an unimpressive brick-and-glass building on an unremarkable street corner a few blocks from downtown. The shelves were jammed and indiscriminate. The most lurid and ridiculous of 1970s paperbacks and the most vapid of new age gift packages sat cheek by jowl with genuinely rare works by respected practitioners of the occult arts.

Not that Anna would know a respected practitioner if one put on a robe and drew a chalk circle around her, but the community seemed to think the little store was a treasure and she was told it had customers far beyond the city limits. Which made it exactly the sort of place a stranger would go for information.

"Yeah," Collie said. "Good."

Her voice was muffled by hair. Anna glanced at her to see Collie bent over her cell, laboriously poking at the miniature keyboard.

"Whatcha typing?" she asked in the chirpiest voice she could manage. Somewhere under the hair, Anna thought she saw green eyes flicker in her direction.

"Message to Kieran," she said. "I want the addresses of Ian's friends. He'll probably just assume we know where to find everyone because we saw them one time for five minutes."

Anna slipped into the right lane, wound her way onto a tricky and unnecessary one-way street and found a one-hour free parking spot less than a block from the store. Sometimes, she almost thought she was getting the hang of this Edmonton thing.

"I like this deal where we ask Kieran stuff and he has to tell us," Collie said as they walked to the Urban Myth's poster-covered front door. "Even if it is a pain in his keister. Have you noticed that Kieran is an I-E word and keister is an E-I word, but they're pronounced the same?"

"Keeps me up nights," Anna said. "I'm okay with whatever causes Kieran discomfort, but we should keep in mind that he can tell us the Embassy said pretty much anything. Doesn't necessarily make it true."

"I don't think he'd still be doing business in this town if he were given to that kind of behaviour," Collie said. "Unless you figure the Embassy for a bunch of gormless mooks. I don't."

"No, me neither," Anna agreed, tugging on the door. It stuck for a moment then popped open. It wasn't in any better shape than the rest of the place.

The store had a musty smell that was similar to the one Ian's suite had once had. In the store's case, it was forgivable. It was an occupational hazard of running a used bookshop.

The owner was behind his desk, head down over what looked to be an old-fashioned ledger. He didn't bother to look up as they entered. Probably had some kind of astral guard dog watching for shoplifters. Or maybe there were eyes following them from the portrait on the back wall.

Or, just possibly, the case was making Anna stupidly paranoid.

The owner, whose name Anna could never remember, had hair about as long as Collie's, though not nearly so thick. It made up for the lack of thickness by being a mare's nest of such frightening proportions that Anna thought the only real solution would be to chisel it off and start again.

"Hello, Matt," Collie said cheerfully. Right. Matt. Anna looked at the hair and tried to make a mnemonic of it.

"Hello," Matt said. He raised his head and looked at them impassively from behind glasses that seemed not only thick but runny too, the way glass was in hundred-year-old windows. If he knew them or didn't, if he was or was not surprised that Collie knew his name, he gave no sign.

"I'm Colette Kostyna. This is Anna Gareau. We met with Ian McLaren here a few times, in your back room."

"Mmm," Matt said. Maybe that rang a bell. Maybe he knew Ian was dead. Maybe not. Maybe Anna was going to haul off and smack him if they didn't get a reaction out of him soon.

"We're investigating Ian's death," Collie said bluntly. "Did you know he was dead?"

So she, too, was tired of talking to the Zen master. Matt nodded.

"I'm aware. I'm his landlord."

Collie's eyes widened.

"*Dude!* Seriously? Don't you mean slumlord?"

And thus was another potentially useful contact balled up and thrown into the trash. Except, proving that you never could tell with people, Matt actually smiled.

"I live upstairs. I used the basement for storage. Ian was helping me move some books one day and he asked if he could live there. He said he liked the feel of the place."

"Can't have liked the smell," Collie muttered. Matt didn't seem to hear her.

"So," Anna said, "were you there last night?"

Matt shook his head. Anna expected to see hair fly, but it stayed in place. Did he gel that mess?

"I was here. By the time I arrived home, the Embassy had sent a team in. They told me what had happened."

"Any thoughts about it?" Anna asked. "You must at least have some idea who went in and out of Ian's place."

"Most of his visitors didn't use the door," Matt said. "There was Rowan. He came by often. He used the door."

"Was he there last night?" Anna asked.

"I don't know," Matt said.

"Do you… what do you think happened?" Collie asked.

Matt looked at her for so long that Anna thought he might be having one of those quiet epileptic fits, the ones where people just stared off. She was about to ask if he was all right when he spoke again.

"Teleporter."

Collie sighed.

"Yeah. We concur. I think everyone does. But we were hoping maybe you'd have something more for us. Did Rowan say anything about people coming to get him? Did anyone come by asking questions about either Mandrake or Rowan?"

Matt shook his head.

"No."

"Have you seen anyone strange... I mean, new and strange," Collie added, "around town? Maybe around the store, or staking out your house?"

Matt's mouth moved and Anna realized it was his smile.

"No. A strange person could hang around my house for a year and it wouldn't matter. They wouldn't get in."

"Why not?" Anna asked.

"There's a ward."

Anna smiled back.

"We just went through the front door," she said. "Last night."

Matt looked puzzled. An expression. Anna counted it as a victory.

"Of course you did," he said. "You were on the guest list. If you aren't on the list, you're stopped at the door."

Oh. So he wasn't surprised that they'd walked in. He was surprised that she was dumb. Not a victory, unless she chose to be flattered that he had once considered her smarter than he did now.

"How good is your ward?" Collie asked. "I mean, we're dealing with magic types here, right? Could someone have broken it?"

Matt's smile, this time, would have been obvious to even a casual observer.

"No," he said.

"Oookay," Collie said, giving him a tight little smile in return. "Hey, do you know Kieran Gavril?"

Matt nodded. Collie gave it a beat, as if she actually thought he'd volunteer more information. Cockeyed fool.

"And you know about his place, right? The shelter?"

"Yes," Matt said.

"'Kay. It's warded. And we just walked right in. So, are we on the guest list there, too?"

"Why would I know?" Matt said. "Maybe. It's always different. I don't do wards."

Anna was going to protest that he had a ward, so obviously he did wards. But then she remembered she was in Edmonton, home of the urban sissy. Not that it was Toronto or anything, but people really did call professionals to boost their cars and change their tires and fix their leaky sinks. Sometimes, or so she'd heard, they hired goddamned shopping services. So why wouldn't he outsource his ward?

"Who does do wards?" Collie asked.

"A few people," Matt said. "I think. But I use Doris. She's the best."

Doris? Anna looked at Collie, who had a question mark on her face as well.

"We'll need to talk to her," Anna told Matt. Matt picked up a pen, flipped over one of the business cards on his counter and wrote a few lines. Collie put her hand out and he gave it to her.

"Thanks," Collie said. "Should we say hi from you?"

Matt's eyes widened. Was that an actual emotion? Anna was surprised enough that she felt her own eyes widen a bit in response.

"Please," Matt said. "No. She'll want... you'll have to say I told you where... tell her... I don't know."

"Is there something we should know about Doris?" Anna asked.

"No!" Matt said. "I don't talk about Doris. Tell her I don't talk about her."

"Will do," Collie said briskly, apparently trying to prevent a meltdown.

"Do you have the guest list, by the way?" Anna asked. Matt took a moment to process before shaking his head.

"Doris has it. Ian and I both added to it."

It didn't sound like first-rate home security to Anna, letting a renter — and known kook — put whomever they wanted on a guest list. But Collie was always saying she was mildly raving mad on the topic of security, so it was possible she wasn't the fairest judge.

"Oh," Collie said. "That downtown-looking woman. When you say you turned around and she was gone, do you mean... like... poof? Or did she use the door?"

"I heard the door," Matt said.

Of course the mysterious woman couldn't *be* the teleporting murderer. It couldn't be that simple.

"Thanks for your help," Collie said, reaching into her purse. "I'll give you our number, in case you think of anything else."

"I have your number," Matt said. "Ian had it."

"Ah!" Collie said, triumphantly producing a business card. "Here."

"I have it," Matt repeated. Anna bit the inside of her cheek, then said,

"Humour her."

Matt looked at her. She nodded. He looked at the card and took it.

"Thanks again," Anna said.

She waited until the door had shut behind them to say,

"Truly, I think he had it."

Collie glanced at her, looking confused.

"Huh?"

"Our number. I think he was not lying about that. I don't

think any of the last ten people who said they had our number were lying, either. Do you think they're all homeless and they need to sleep under a blanket of your business cards?"

"If they did, and if they had cell phones and could phone from the sidewalk, they might actually place a call," Collie said, unruffled. "One of the first things you learn in PR is that, if someone has to go anywhere to get a phone number, they will not make the phone call. The more cards I give out, the greater the chance that someone will have my card in their pocket when they're struck by the whim to call me."

Anna saw something dark in the corner of her eye and realized it was time to stop gawking at Collie and look at where she was going. She stopped and turned her head to see a tree trunk less than a foot away.

"You honestly think," Anna said as she corrected her trajectory, "that calling a detective with information about a murder investigation is something you do on a whim?"

"I honestly think," Collie said, "that most people could not be arsed to get our number from the next room even if they suddenly remembered seeing the murder, getting splattered with blood and taking photographs of the event. Because it's just. So. Far."

"Wow. Your faith in humanity is —"

"Justified," Collie said.

"You PR people are soulless," Anna said, pulling the Jeep keys from her jacket pocket.

"Not really," Collie told her. "We're just unhappily aware of what most people are like. If you wanted to open my door, like, today, that would be awesome."

Anna stopped midway to climbing into the Jeep and stared at Collie.

"You have your own key. Your own key, you have. Own key, you have, your. Key —"

"All right, all right." Collie dug through her purse again, and of course that was why she wanted Anna to open her door. It was the Marianas Trench of purses, deep and dark and liable to crush the incautious explorer.

Once Anna was seated and had the Jeep running, she looked to her right and saw Collie tugging on something inside her purse. Her keys were caught. Or they'd been eaten. Anna leaned over and tugged the lock open.

"Some days, I feel as if I'm driving a short bus," she said. Collie glared at her but got in anyway, apparently feeling that hostility wasn't enough to keep her warm. She pulled the door shut with feeling and tossed her purse onto the back seat.

"Gonna make it tough to reach that business card," Anna said. "Since I assume we're off to see the Doris."

Collie shut her eyes and leaned back, then rattled off an address in Oliver.

"It's an apartment," she added. "We can look up the suite number when we get there. Happy?"

"No," Anna said. "Why can't she live somewhere that I can park?"

"Because everyone wants you to be miserable," Collie said. "Why exactly are you so hell-bent on seeing this Doris person right away, anyhow? Weren't we planning to visit some other stores first?"

"I want to see Doris," Anna said, "because I want her opinion on whether someone could have broken into Ian's place. And because she probably has that guest list. I'd like to know who's on it."

Collie was grinning, eyes still shut.

"You want to ask a hot shot if she thinks someone else might be a hotter shot? That should go over well. Seriously, Anna, this is her business. What's she gonna say? That her services aren't that good?"

"We say it all the time," Anna pointed out.

"Spot," Collie said. Anna swung her head around, trying to find it.

"Details!" she said.

"Over there," Collie expanded, uselessly. Anna slammed on the brakes, earning a honk from somewhere behind them. Not close enough behind them that the person really ought to be honking, but that never seemed to stop anyone.

She looked at Collie, who was looking at her.

"You've gone past it," Collie informed her.

About half a block up, a minivan pulled away from the curb and drove off.

"That soccer mom just saved your life," Anna said, pulling into the vacancy. Collie was already halfway into the back seat, retrieving her purse.

Mere seconds after the ride had come to a complete stop, Collie was charging down the sidewalk, one hand under her purse, the other lost somewhere within, peering at its depths. Anna hurried to catch up and put her hands on Collie's shoulders, steering her.

"Ha!" Collie triumphantly pulled out the business card and held it up so Anna could see the apartment address over her shoulder. "I should have transferred it to an index card. Business cards are so fiddly."

Doris' building was a high rise, or something like it. Twelve, maybe fourteen floors. If the numbers of the suites bore any relation to the floors of the suites... and maybe they even did... Doris was living on the seventh floor. Her buzzer had no name beside it, but about half the buzzers were like that.

"People never stay in one place anymore," Collie commented, scanning the board.

"Or their heartless corporate landlords don't bother to tag their buzzers," Anna said. "Is this technically a high rise? I can't remember what the criteria are for that."

"I..." Collie looked up, her brow wrinkled, and jumped a

little when a tinny female voice came from the intercom.

"Yeah?"

"Doris?" Anna said.

"Who is this?"

"You don't know us," Anna said. "Matt sent us. From Urban Myth."

There was a pause so long that, if not for the crackling of the intercom, Anna would have thought Doris had shut them out. Then, a long sigh was followed by,

"Fine, come in. It's the eighth floor."

Of course 709 would be on the eighth floor. The buzzer sounded and Collie's hand shot out for the door handle, as if she were afraid to miss her chance. And fair enough, really. Anna wasn't sure Doris would ring them in again if they missed the door the first time.

The building looked to be from the 1970s, like a depressingly large number of buildings in Edmonton. Not a good year for a boom. Three elevators, husky light blue Otises and obviously plastic plants scattered among dingy couches with corduroy covers that might, at one point, have been crème.

"Funny," Collie said, pressing the elevator button. "I always think Oliver's going to be tonier than this. I guess the town-houses are."

"Location, location, loc –"

The opening doors of the elevator cut her off. They stepped inside and Collie stabbed the Close Doors button, which would have been rude if there'd been other people in the lobby. And Collie would have done it anyway.

"Seriously," Anna said, "it doesn't bother you that this woman freaks Matt out?"

Collie grinned at her.

"Makes me curious. Maybe she's normal and he just can't take it."

"That's likely it," Anna said. "Given her choice of career."

Collie patted her shoulder.

"Oh, Anna. You should know better. The career probably chose her."

There was nothing to say to that, so Anna said it, all the way to the door of 709.

The door opened to Anna's first knock, leaving her fist raised. Awkwardly, she pulled it back and down, trying not to stare at the person in the doorway.

She was Asian, maybe twenty-five or maybe thirty-five, five-foot-two at the most, and practically vibrating. She looked ready to go off in any direction, including straight up, at any moment. Her hair, getting in on that mood, was a wild dark circle around her head. She was about the furthest thing from a Doris that Anna had ever seen.

"What's the matter?" the woman asked. "Not what you expected?"

Her faint prairie accent was sharp-edged, and she leaned forward as she spoke, as if daring them to fight.

Collie shrugged. "No. I thought you'd be fifty, and round, and you'd have that yellowish white hair with the big curls. Like, curls the width of someone's arm."

The woman blinked and pulled her head back, the way a startled dog would.

"All that from my name? Your imagination runs *wild*, doesn't it? What's wrong with you?"

"Tons," Collie said. "I'm sure you can relate. May we come in?"

"That'd be funny, if I said no. After you came all the way up here."

"Hilarious," Anna said. "We only need a few minutes."

"Aw, stay all *day*," Doris said, stepping aside and waving her arm at the interior of her apartment. "I was just gonna hang myself. It can wait."

"Okay, then," Collie said, moving past her and crouching to remove her boots. Anna did the same, reluctantly. It was rude to leave her boots on, she knew, even though it was bone dry outside and all she'd been walking on was concrete. She hated, though, the feeling of not having her boots on. Especially in a strange place. What if she stepped in something? What if she wanted to leave in a rush? What if an anvil fell from nowhere, or she needed to kick something?

A lot of people would have said, "Don't worry about it. Leave them on." But Anna was already pretty sure that Doris was not a lot of people.

The apartment was small and plain, boasting few distinctions aside from a floor to ceiling window in the living room. Chairs, a loveseat and a table were placed in front of the window, all of them too delicate for Anna's comfort. They looked too high-end to be from IKEA, but they were similar in design – made for small urban apartments and the thin people who lived within.

From somewhere in the apartment, a woman with a low, bluesy voice was making threatening sounds over a sterile dance beat. Anna couldn't see a stereo. A Mac was sitting on a corner desk though. One of the big flat white ones, and the screen was showing a delicate fractal. It seemed a likely suspect.

Collie claimed the chair nearest the window, her jacket still on. The sight of outside was probably enough to make her cold, no matter how well sealed the window might be. Not that there was much of the outside world in the view, which was mostly of other apartment blocks.

Anna took her own jacket off and draped it over her arm. Doris made no indication as to where she might hang it up, so Anna proceeded to the living room and took over the loveseat. As long as she didn't make any sudden moves, she figured it might hold.

Doris claimed the remaining chair and looked from one of them to the other.

"So? You want a fruit candy?"

It was so disconnected that Anna couldn't think of a response and looked down instead, her eyes alighting helpfully on a small ceramic bowl in the middle of the coffee table. It was full of wrapped squares in pale colours. A spoon was sticking out of one corner. Anna had never acquired a taste for those candies, which reminded her of watered-down Mojos. She looked up.

"No. Thank you."

"If I eat one," Collie said, "do I have to stay here for six months?"

"What?" Doris asked, saving Anna the trouble.

"Never mind," Collie said. "Thank you."

She reached for a candy. As she was about to take one, Doris swatted Collie's hand away.

"Hey!" Collie and Doris said at once.

"Use the spoon!" Doris said, as if she were explaining the basics of table manners to a child who was small enough to have forgotten, but not too small to know better.

"They're wrapped," Collie protested. It never failed to blow Anna's mind when Collie argued with people about their house rules. Okay, so Doris was being a nut. But they were in her nuthatch, so Doris got to call the shots.

"Just use the spoon, would ya?" Doris said. Collie rolled her eyes, but took the spoon and carefully dropped a single candy into her hand. Anna had the feeling she'd just seen a catfight averted.

Collie barely had the wrapper in her pocket and the candy in her mouth when Doris spoke.

"Good, huh?"

Collie took a few deliberate chews then swallowed loudly.

"Phenomenal," she said. "So. You're planning to hang yourself?"

"Maybe I'll jump out of the window instead. You think that would be better? I'd have to go out and get rope."

"Lots of people use belts," Anna said. "But you don't have

exposed rafters, so it'll be tricky to find a way to affix them. Or is this just a cry for help?"

Doris snorted.

"Yeah, it's a cry for help. You gonna fix things for me? I have a business going around and around in the toilet."

"Because of Mandrake?" Collie asked. "I mean, Ian?"

Doris bounced in her chair, eyes wild.

"Sure, talk to everyone about it! You're going all over town telling people I did that ward? What'd you come here for, to rub it in?"

"It's good you're able to be rational about this," Anna said. "Of course we're not running around town talking about you. We didn't even know you existed until half an hour ago."

"If anyone's running around town gossiping," Collie said, "it's Matt."

The idea of Matt trotting across Edmonton engaging in hen parties was enough to make Anna smile. To Doris, who evidently knew Matt better, it was worth an outright laugh.

"Don't tell anyone," she said. "Reputation is everything in this business."

"Is it everything," Collie said, "or do you actually have to be good?"

"She's a PR person," Anna added quickly. "She's not trying to be rude."

Collie shot Anna an exasperated glance.

"I'm sure Doris understands," she said. "It can't come as a shock to anyone in this day and age that some businesses have purchased better reputations than they deserve."

"You can't have a good reputation for warding without being good," Doris said.

Collie pursed her lips and was still for a few moments. Then she said, "Let's back this up. It seems a little unfair to you that you don't know who we are, or exactly why we're here. And, you know, I'm not trying to be rude."

Doris laughed. It was loud, but raspy.

"I know who you are. She's that psychometrist, and you're the civilian. Believe me, you're known *all* over town."

"Is there any point in telling you our names?" Anna asked. "Or is that what you've decided to call us, regardless?"

"I don't need to know your names. You're supposed to be detectives, right?"

"We are supposed, by some, to be detectives," Anna allowed. Doris just blinked at her, seemingly unimpressed.

"So? That guy got killed last night and I had a ward on the house, so now I got detectives sitting here. Am I supposed to look shocked?" She spread her hands and framed her face with them, widened her eyes. Off Anna's glare, she dropped the pose and went back to staring at them impassively.

"But... don't you even want to know who we're working for?" Collie asked.

Doris shrugged.

"You gonna tell me?"

"No," Anna said.

"Look. I didn't... fuck up." She paused a little before dropping the f-bomb, as if concerned that a little old lady would pop up from behind the loveseat and shake a finger at her. "Did Matt say I did?"

"Yeah," Collie said. "It was a tirade. He went on for hours. Come on. I thought you knew the guy."

"Well, he probably thinks I did," Doris said.

"I doubt anyone will ever know what Matt thinks," Anna told her. "He and Ian probably understood each other."

Doris let out another raspy cough of a laugh.

"Whatever. Whatever."

She stretched the word out in the middle somehow, some play with the A and the E that made it sound like a heckle from the back of a comedy club.

"We're not saying you fucked up, per se," Collie said.

Bizarrely, Doris giggled.

"Per se."

"Look," Collie said, no longer remotely conciliatory, "I'm the civilian, right? So I don't know the first thing about warding. People say, 'He can't come in because my house is warded,' or, 'I don't lock the front door because it's warded,' and to me this is like... Voxcom for the strange. I am *not* assuming, if someone got through your ward that you screwed up. For all I know, you made a perfectly good lock and someone had an even better lock breaking kit. I do not know how this works. Please feel free to educate me."

"And me," Anna put in. "Psychowhatsis is all I know."

"Wow," Doris said. "You guys really are green."

"We're relatively unburdened by preconception," Collie said. "It's helpful in our work. What happens if someone tries to enter a place that has a ward?"

Doris shrugged.

"Depends. Are you asking me what happens when someone tries to go into Matt's house?"

"Sure," Anna said.

"Depends whether they're on the pass list. Matt gave me a list."

"Are we on it?" Collie asked.

Doris shrugged again and reached for a fruit chew, which she carefully extracted with the spoon.

"I dunno," she said, unwrapping the candy and popping it into her mouth.

"You don't know who's on the list?" Anna asked. How could that work?

"I don't know your names," Doris corrected. "Remember? Jeez."

"Okay," Collie said. "Okay. Let's leave that for now. Assume we are on the list. We try to go in, and... what happens?"

"You... go... in," Doris said.

"Does a little chime go off somewhere?" Collie asked. "Do you get a twinge? Is there some kind of mystic video camera that shows us entering?"

Doris was giggling again.

"A twinge? Twinge? Are you stupid?"

"Yes," Collie said, a knife-edge to her voice. "We are very, very fucking stupid. Are you saying nothing magical happens when people who are on the list enter or leave that house?"

"*Good*, Sherlock. You've got it."

"Terrific," Collie said. "And what if someone who isn't on the list tries to enter? Say, the meter reader?"

"Mmm," Doris said. She moved her jaw, presumably to flip the remaining candy to the other side of her mouth. "Matt or Ian could invite him in."

"Can anyone who's inside the house invite someone else in?" Anna asked. "Or is it just Matt or... ah... Matt?"

"Just Matt and Ian," Doris confirmed.

"Once you get invited in, can you come in anytime?" Collie asked.

"No," Doris said. "That would be stupid."

"Again, we are stupid," Collie said. "Make peace with it. What if I wasn't on the list and I wasn't invited in and I tried to go inside?"

"Matt's house?"

"No," Collie said. "The Alberta Legislature."

Doris rolled her eyes.

"You don't have to be rude about it. It's different depending on how you set it up."

"How did you set up Matt's house?" Anna asked, trying to keep her voice even. No sense stirring the crazy person up worse than she was stirred up already. "If someone who's not on the list tries to go inside, and they're not invited, what happens?"

"They don't go in," Doris said.

"What you do mean?" Collie asked. Doris rolled her eyes.

"They don't...go... in."

"Is there some kind of force field or something?" Collie asked. That, apparently, wasn't a painfully stupid question, since Doris managed not to sneer or giggle as she responded.

"No. You just don't. Go. In."

"You don't feel inclined?" Anna asked. Doris shrugged.

"Whatever. You think you forgot something, or you're late for something or... whatever."

"But wouldn't you go back later?" Collie asked. Doris shrugged again.

"You forget, or maybe you don't like the place. Cause you think it's *haunted*. Ooooh."

"So there's nothing that physically prevents someone from breaking in," Anna said.

"Well... *walls*," Doris said. "*Locks*. What do you have on your house? You just leave it open all the time? Do you have a whole wall missing, like a dollhouse?"

"We leave the door unlocked," Collie said, "but we have cobras loose inside. Are you saying some people get stopped by the wards but you have to hope a good deadbolt will stop the rest?"

Doris jumped up to crouch on the seat of her chair and proceeded to bounce there, eyes wide with horror.

"No! You can't tell people that! Who have you talked to?"

"We came here first," Collie said, with admirable patience. "With the proviso that we tell no one. Doris, is that the truth? Could some people just pick the lock and walk in?"

"No. I said I was good. What, you don't believe me?"

"No," Anna said. "We don't disbelieve you, either, but come on. There's stupid and then there's just believing you."

Doris stopped bouncing, but stayed in a crouch.

"Everyone stops, okay? And they don't come back."

"'Kay," Collie said. "Assuming that's true, then the only way to get in is to be on the list?"

"Yep."

"Matt said to ask you who was on the list," Anna said. "I'm not sure if he forgets, or if he doesn't know who Ian added. Did Ian add people without Matt knowing about it?"

"Yeah, he called me," Doris said. "Matt said it was okay."

"Do you want to call Matt to confirm that he said you should give us the list?" Collie asked.

Doris screwed her face up.

"I don't wanna talk to him. You can have the list."

She hopped off her chair and went to the computer, rudely awakening it with a darting swipe at the space bar.

"Oh," Collie said, "also, if there were changes to that list any time in the past few months – if anyone was added or removed – can you tell us that?"

Doris glanced at her.

"There's *one list*. Matt made it when he moved in. Ian added his people when he moved in. That's it."

It was a good thought, anyhow. Anna gave Collie an encouraging smile. It must not have sat right on her face, because Collie had to cough to cover a laugh.

Anna looked out the window again and saw a gap between the buildings. From the right angle, it might be possible to see the river. The house in Prince Albert where she'd spent most of her childhood had offered a similar river view, just a glimpse from the corner of an attic window. Only there, it had been spruce and not buildings in her way.

Doris brought over a few sheets of paper and gave them to Collie before taking her seat again. This time, she sat down in the conventional way.

"Yeah," Collie said after flipping through the pages, "we're on here. Toward the end."

"Anyone else we know?" Anna asked. Collie smiled, folded the papers and slipped them into her purse.

"The usual suspects."

She looked at Doris.

"How do you put people on this list?"

"I type," Doris said, waggling her fingers.

"I believe," Anna said, before Collie could respond, "that she was asking about how you make the ward let certain people through."

"I'm not gonna tell you that," Doris protested. "You want to put me out of business?"

"Increasingly," Collie muttered, softly enough that Anna barely heard her. Doris turned to her with a puzzled expression.

"Whaaaat?"

"Nothing," Collie said firmly. "Look. When someone is added to the list, do you have to do something to them or with them so that they can go in the house?"

"I didn't do anything to you," Doris said.

"Prior to today," Collie said, distinctly. Anna looked out the window, quickly, in the hopes that she wouldn't get caught smiling.

"Aw, you big baby," Doris answered. "Cause I said you were being stupid? You were. I just need the names."

"What if someone gave Ian a fake name?" Anna asked. "Or he was confused and got their name wrong?"

"Or someone spelled a name wrong," Collie added.

"Doesn't matter," Doris said. "It would be whoever was intended by the client."

"And you're not going to tell us how that works?" Collie asked. Doris raised her eyebrows so vigourously that Anna wouldn't have been surprised if Doris' hair had shot off her head from the impact.

"It's a trade secret. You're a civilian. That's two reasons why I wouldn't tell you. You're blabbing all over town. That's three reasons. You want more?"

"Three will do," Collie said. "Thank you."

Apparently she'd given up on correcting Doris' assumption

that they were hanging her dirty laundry out in public. That, or Collie intended to make the assumption accurate, as soon as possible.

"It must've been someone on that list," Doris said.

"We're planning to take a look at that theory," Anna said, "as it happens."

"Though you'd never have thought it from the way we came here specifically to get the list," Collie added.

"I'm just *saying*," Doris said, "nobody broke my ward. I don't brag. I'm good at this."

"Would you know if someone had broken your ward?" Anna asked. Doris grinned.

"Like, get a twinge?"

"Or whaaaatever," Anna said. With surprising speed, Doris grabbed the candy spoon, scooped up a candy and flicked it at her. It bounced off Anna's jacket sleeve and fell to the ground.

"Now you've messed the place up," Doris said. Anna just stared at her, waiting. Doris rolled her eyes.

"No. There's no twinge. I don't get a magic phone call. I just know because I'm good."

"And no one's good enough to break through?" Collie said. "Maybe someone from out of town?"

"No one I've ever met," Doris said mildly, all the nervous energy suddenly gone. If there was one thing that woman believed for more than five minutes at a stretch, this was it.

"Okay," Collie said. "Well. Thanks for your time, and for the list. I'll leave my card in case you think of anything you want to tell us."

"Oh, so I can confess?" Doris asked, grinning again. Because that was a real knee-slapper.

"Or if the murderer shows up here looking for that same list," Anna said, which wiped the damned grin off Doris' face.

"For example," Collie added, clearly enjoying the moment. "Not that you'd have time to make a call."

She pulled out a card and dropped it in the bowl of fruit candy, causing Doris to stiffen.

"You can't tell anyone you were here," Doris said. She stood and balanced herself as if getting ready to pounce on one or the other, about to dig her claws in. Anna, in an imitative mood, mimicked Doris' eye roll.

"We have other things to talk about," she said. "Don't worry about it."

"You'd better not tell," Doris said. Anna ignored her, stood, and headed for the door, relieved to hear Collie's footsteps behind her. They might actually get out of the apartment without a fight.

Doris said nothing as they put their boots on, and Anna felt a fresh surge of resentment at having had to take her boots off in the first place. How were they supposed to stalk out of a place with dignity if they had to cram into a tiny foyer and zip up boots?

Doris slipped past them, opened her door and held it.

"Don't want it to hit you in the ass," she explained as they passed her, but she smiled when she said it and Anna got the strange feeling that Doris didn't actually dislike them all that much.

They took the stairs to the ground, which wasn't Anna's idea. Collie apparently felt the need to work off some energy. Anna followed her about a half-flight behind, not hurrying. It wasn't as if Collie could go anywhere without her, since it would have meant actually digging for the Jeep keys.

As Collie started down the last flight her phone rang, echoing sharply in the concrete stairwell. Collie answered it but said nothing else before slipping through the door to the lobby. By the time Anna had caught up, Collie was putting her phone away. To Anna's shock, Collie was smiling.

"Ed McMahon just called to give you a million dollars?" Anna inquired.

"Better. My car's practically done."

"Practically?" Anna asked. Collie shrugged.

"There's one more small thing. He sounded encouraging. Can we go straight there?"

"Don't see why not," Anna said. "Is it the usual place?"

"Yeah."

They walked rapidly toward the Jeep, which Anna was pretty sure was in a two-hour parking zone. How long had they been in Doris' place, anyway?

Collie walked directly behind Anna. Anna turned to tell her to quit it, but Collie was looking at something on her cell's tiny screen. Likely following Anna with peripheral vision, using Anna as a guide dog to steer her away from trees and traffic. Anna was tempted to stop short, but quashed the urge. Collie was probably doing something productive.

"Got Kieran's list of Mandrake's friends," Collie said after a moment, confirming that theory. "This is good. We can cross-reference to Doris' list to see whom Mandrake probably added. Oh, and he put little asterisks beside the teleporters. That's adorable."

"It isn't," Anna hissed over her shoulder, "adorable. I don't know why you think everything that guy does is adorable. Also, here we are in public, so shut up."

Collie gave her an exasperated look, but dropped the phone into her pocket and left it there until they were back in the Jeep... which was not, to Anna's relief, sporting a bright blue ticket.

"He's being helpful," Collie said once both doors were shut. "I'm in a state of mind where I deeply appreciate that."

"A fair point," Anna conceded.

They drove in companionable silence for awhile, a voice from the stereo expressing the hope that, one day, laser beams would cure his sight.

Collie bounced in her seat.

"I just realized: I need to call Kieran."

"What for?" Anna asked. From the corner of her eye, she could see Collie smiling broadly.

"Oh, wait for it. This is gonna be great."

She fished out her phone and dialed. After quite a few rings, Anna heard Keiran's distant, irritated voice saying something that she assumed was hello.

"Hello," Collie said cheerfully. "Me again. I got the list, thanks. I just need one more thing."

She paused, tapping on the back of the phone with one finger as if twitting Kieran for having the nerve to speak.

"Yes, I know," she said. "But all you have to do is call the Embassy and set this up. It'll take five minutes."

Another pause. More tapping.

"Keep complaining and it'll take longer," Collie said. "Or you could just let me — fine. I need someone to test the wards on Ian's apartment. Well, Matt's whole house, I guess. What? No. That's it."

She shut her eyes, something she often did when frustrated during a phone call. Anna wondered if Collie did it when she was on the phone and driving.

"To see if they can get in. Or get someone else in. Whatever. It's — no, that's it. Just to see if the wards are tough to break."

A dramatic sigh, and then:

"I don't know. Tell them to get whoever's good. Or a bunch of people. Make a contest out of it. I'll buy the winner a cookie."

She probably would, too, thinking it appropriate compensation. Anna would have to remember to keep that from happening.

"Thanks."

"So, is that because you don't believe Doris," Anna asked as Collie put the phone away, "or because you think sending a bunch of raptors to test her electric fence will piss Doris off?"

"You're so linear," Collie said. "It doesn't have to be either/or.

Not that I don't believe her, but we'd be pretty dumb to assume no one could ever break in just because she says that's so."

"And it's no skin off our noses to sic people on the house," Anna said.

"*And* it will probably piss her off. Oh. My car's still inside. I was hoping it would be one more small thing they could, you know, adjust right out here."

"I don't think they ever do that," Anna said. She pulled in to the slot nearest the street.

Upon their arrival in Edmonton, Collie had somehow managed to find a mechanic who ran a quaint little filling station and fixed cars in a tiny shop. There were, as near as Anna could tell, no more than three people on staff, and there was no sign of a corporate overlord anywhere. She was pretty sure they had to travel through time when they went to the place.

Anna released her seatbelt and looked to her side in surprise when Collie spoke.

"No."

"No?"

"No," Collie repeated. "I mean, you can just wait here. I'll only be a few minutes."

"Afraid I'll embarrass you in front of the grease monkeys?" Anna asked in her most polite tone. Collie looked at the Jeep's dashboard as if it had spoken instead.

"It's just that you do all the talking when we go in there," she said.

"That's because you think a carburetor is what puts bubbles in pop," Anna pointed out. "Not that I'm much better, but you have a serious mental block in this area."

"I know, but I feel kind of... girly... when I can't get my own car fixed."

Anna paused for a moment, unsure which part to address first.

"I am a girl," she said finally.

"Yeah, I'm aware," Collie said. "I said I felt girly."

This from a woman who prided herself on intelligent language use. Anna stared at her.

"Are you hoping talking to a mechanic will make you feel manly?"

"Oh, as if you don't know what I'm talking about," Collie said. "As if you say nothing when you see some chick refuse to carry two grocery bags to her car, lest she break a precious pink nail."

You killed a man once, Anna thought. She didn't say that.

"I don't disrespect you," she said instead, "because you freak out when your car is in the shop. What is wrong with you? In general?"

"I just need to do this for myself," Collie said. "I swear it is nothing against you."

"Hey," Anna said, spreading her hands, "It wasn't gonna be the highlight of my week. I hope, anyway. You have fun."

"Huh," Collie said, and left the Jeep. Anna waited and wished she'd backed into her spot. She had the choice, here, of watching the wall in front of her or craning her neck to look at the building, which was only slightly more interesting. Or, she supposed, she could watch the street through the rear view mirror. But that seemed seedy, somehow.

She was about to start street-watching anyhow when Collie climbed back inside.

"I might get it back today," she said.

"Good," Anna said.

"They think there's one more little thing loose. Under the flavonoid. Next to the static guard. So they're gonna tighten that up."

"Wow," Anna said. "Either you have a really bad mechanic, or you weren't listening at all."

"The important thing," Collie said, "is that this procedure is supposed to take about forty-five minutes. Which is enough time for lunch."

"There's the African place," Anna said, pointing vaguely west. Collie took a deep breath.

"Do you think the waitress remembers me?"

Anna almost laughed. The last time they'd been there, Collie had praised the fine Ethiopian cuisine. Which turned out to be Eritrean. As did their waitress. It might have been a fine culinary distinction, but — as Collie had explained in a horrified whisper while they ate — it was a pretty raw political point. She'd miserably observed that there was likely spit on her food, and had eaten it anyway. Penance.

"She might not even be there today," Anna pointed out. Collie nodded.

"Except she totally will be. D'you wanna walk?"

"Usually," Anna said.

The area was quiet enough that they could walk side by side, though Anna regretted that as Collie's sharp elbows started hitting her arm. Anna turned her head and saw Collie pulling a handful of hair clips and elastics from her purse.

"Should we stop for a sec?" Anna asked. Collie shook her head and started shoving her hair back, pinning it as she went. Because if anyone were to recognize her, it would be due to all that hair.

"Would you rather eat somewhere else?" Anna offered. Collie didn't shake her head again, as it would have ruined her hard work.

"Nuh," she muttered instead, a hair clip between her teeth. "I liked that place. I don't want to, like, never eat there again just because I embarrassed myself there once. My god. The shrinking world I would live in if that were my policy."

"Fair point," Anna agreed. "Did you see anything interesting on that list?"

"Which one?" Collie asked. "The teleporter list or the ward list?"

"I don't know. Either."

Anna could hear Collie's grin as she spoke.

"Both would be a better answer. I don't know yet. We'll see."

Anna glanced at her watch as they arrived at the restaurant and noted with relief that it was only 11:30, which meant they'd probably get right in. One of the things she found irritating about Edmonton was the idea that waiting to get into a restaurant was not only normal but desirable. A line provided the confirmation most people wanted that they had made a popular choice.

Collie's eyes lit up as they opened the door to find that the only server on duty was a teenage boy. Unless the waitress had undergone not only a sex change but a damned good face lift since they'd last eaten there, Collie was safe.

To Anna's delight, they were the only patrons.

"Sometimes you win one," Anna murmured, earning a deliberate hit from Collie's elbow.

"Shut up," she said through the friendly smile she was directing at the waiter.

They were escorted to a booth toward the back of the restaurant, which widened Collie's smile. Anna smiled back. Collie loved booths on the reasonable grounds that they were cozier than tables, as well as the insane grounds that sitting in chairs allowed other diners to see your ass and judge whether you had any business eating at all.

"Sometimes you win two," Collie said, once the waiter had left.

"Is that the upper limit?" Anna asked. Collie hoisted her purse onto the table and lay it down on its side.

"Let's hope not," she said, already digging inside. Once she'd located the list, a pen and her phone, she put her purse on the floor and placed her prizes on the table.

"Corn holder," Anna said, on impulse. It was a game she'd started months earlier, in which she'd name random items and see if Collie happened to have them in her purse. Collie laughed.

"Not now, Monty Hall. We're working."

She unfolded the list and turned it sideways so they were equally inconvenienced when looking at it. Her phone's display was barely large enough for one person to peer at, so Collie kept that to herself.

"So," Collie said, picking up the pen, "these are the people Mandrake added. Probably. Unless Matt already had them listed."

She went down the list quickly, placing checks beside about two dozen names. Anna noticed their own names, and Kieran's. Not Joel's.

"This Adam Bennett," Collie said, circling a name. "Do you think it's the Adam from the Embassy?"

"Probably," Anna said. "Since he was Ian's boss. It doesn't matter, though, does it? If we know Ian was killed by a teleporter?"

Collie shrugged.

"It's just interesting. Okay... here are the teleporters. Jake Dysenko. Nadia Kuri. Sam Llewelyn. Sounds like a guy, a girl, and a question mark."

Clearly inspired by the Great Kieran, she put asterisks beside the names.

"Three's not a lot," she observed. "I mean, I guess it was four. But even so."

She said it with authority, as if she had a chart somewhere showing how many doctors, lawyers, and magical teleporters were required per million people.

"With a shortage like that," Anna said, "people might have to drive places, or mail things. Imagine living in a city where that went on."

Collie gave her an exasperated look.

"I'm just saying, I'm sure the Embassy keeps them all busy."

"Now the Embassy people might have to drive places and mail things."

"And now look who's calling them people," Collie pointed out. "Just lemme scroll down, in case I missed someone."

Collie proceeded to do that. Anna could never get it to scroll.

"Oh. That's funny."

"Have you ladies decided?" the waiter asked.

Anna hadn't heard him approach, and started a bit. Collie dropped her phone in surprise. Which was, really, a terrible reaction to a sudden burst of fear. Back off or I'll call 9-1… ah, never mind.

"I'm sorry," the waiter said quickly. "I didn't…"

"It's okay," Anna said. "Except we haven't looked at the menus."

"No one does," the waiter informed them. His British accent was beautiful and precise, the way British people's accents almost never were. Anna wondered where he'd picked it up. "If you can wait ten more minutes, we'll be bringing out a lunch buffet."

"That's perfect," Collie told him. "Thanks."

"Would you like coffee?" he asked. "Good coffee?"

Anna didn't normally drink coffee, but the waiter was right. Whatever was different about the coffee in this place, she liked it.

"Please," she said.

"Yes, please," Collie added. "Thank you."

"It's probably cat shit coffee," she said once the waiter was gone.

"What?" Anna said. Because she wanted Collie to elaborate? She shook her head and held up a hand, flat, like a police officer stopping traffic. "No. I didn't mean to say 'what.' You said something was funny?"

"Oh. Yeah." Collie picked up her phone and hit it with her thumb a few times, trying to wake it up. Eventually the screen flickered and glowed.

"There's a break at the end of the list," Collie said, "and then there's one more name. And Kieran's got a note here that says this is a teleporter, but not one of Ian's friends."

"Promising," Anna said. "The name?"

"Robin Hampshire. Doesn't say whether it's a guy or a girl."

Anna scanned Doris' list, twice.

"Not here," she said. "So much for promising."

"Unless Doris is overstating her ability," Collie said. "Which we should know fairly soon."

Anna snorted.

"And by 'fairly soon,' you mean that you have no idea how long it takes to test something like that, so it could be today or next week or six months from now."

"Probably not six months," Collie said, adding a "thank you" for the waiter, who had returned with the good coffee and a basket of injera.

"That's a shame," Anna said, "since we charge by the hour. Or is it by the day?"

Collie reddened a little.

"I never discussed it with Eric. Did you?"

"I've never spoken to him without you there. The converse is not true."

"Would that be the converse?" Collie asked. "I can never keep that stuff straight."

"Regardless," Anna said in the firmest tone she had available. Collie shrugged and took a sip of coffee, then quickly set the cup down.

"Hot! Hot hot hot!"

"Really? That's so unlike coffee," Anna said. "Am I right in thinking we have no formal financial agreement worked out with our client?"

The sound of metal clanging in a corner of the room drew Anna's attention. A pair of middle-aged women were filling the buffet trays. Neither looked to be their former waitress.

"We don't," Collie said, having apparently finished her ice cube. "But so what? He'll pay us or he won't. And I was thinking we'd charge by the day. Detectives do, don't they? PR would be more of an hourly thing."

"When they bring us the bill here, or when our rent comes due, are you thinking we'll either pay or we won't?" Anna inquired. "Because I don't think most people are as relaxed about that as you are."

Collie leaned back in her chair and let her breath out in an irritated huff.

"Where were you when that Adam guy said we wouldn't have to worry about money?"

"Ignoring him," Anna said, "as I ignore everyone who says ridiculous shit to me. Of course we have to worry about money."

"I bet we don't," Collie said. "I bet it's going to show up in our bank accounts. Or there'll be cash in my purse. Or it'll fall from the sky, in which case I'm hoping for folding currency."

"And you equate having to hope for the random appearance of unspecified amounts of money with not having to worry about money? And this is why you don't care whether our actual, aboveboard client ever pays us?"

Collie set her phone on the table.

"Would you like to call the Embassy and ask for details?"

"No," Anna said. "And I'm not calling Kieran, either."

"Then join me in hope," Collie said brightly. "What are the odds that both our clients will stiff us?"

"You and I are completely unequipped to run a business," Anna said. "I guess that's not really an important observation right now, but I wanted to put it out there."

"Duly noted," Collie said. "Anyway. Food."

Anna didn't even try to beat Collie to the buffet table. It wasn't going to happen. She wandered over at a dignified pace and took her time selecting food, as if it mattered. She had no idea what was in most of the brightly coloured stews. She just knew she liked them.

As she returned to her table, lunch patrons began to pour in. A fair number of them seemed to be from the same workplace, since they were talking and laughing loudly about an epic photocopier disaster. Anna didn't mind the volume. It made it less likely that anyone would overhear the conversation she and Collie were having.

"So," Collie said, vigourously chasing lentils around her plate as if the little bastards were trying to get away. "Next steps."

"We eat," Anna said. "We get your car out of hock. Your turn."

"See, that's just it," Collie said. "I don't know. The obvious thing is to investigate the teleporters, right?"

"Right," Anna said, not sure where this was heading.

"So... how are we gonna do that? Do you think we should go talk to them? Or will that lead to us getting shot in the backs of our heads?"

Anna considered that. It was a fair question, so she took her time with it, finishing her stews and sopping up the last of the sauce before answering. What would happen if they went to see the teleporters in person? What if they didn't? What if they just went around town asking questions about them?

"Okay, imagine you're a teleporter," she said. "And imagine you shot Ian."

Collie shut her eyes, which was going a bit far, but at least she was participating.

"'Kay. I'm imagining it. Are you checking to see if I'm psychic? Should I look in a mirror and see who I am?"

"Do whatever you want," Anna said. "Just... imagine you've killed a guy right here in town, who runs in your social circle."

"Business circle," Collie corrected. Anna shrugged, though it was wasted because Collie's eyes were still shut.

"The circles overlap," Anna said. "The point is, wouldn't you assume there'd be an investigation?"

"Probably," Collie said. "So?"

"So, you'd try to keep tabs on it, right? Like, maybe you'd check around and see if anyone's been asking questions about Ian's death. So, if you're halfway smart, how long will it take you to figure out who's investigating the crime?"

"Am I still a halfway smart person who can teleport?" Collie asked. "Because that's got to be great for the eavesdropping."

"Yes," Anna said. "You're still the murdering teleporter."

"A day or two," Collie said, opening her eyes. "At the outside."

"And, since you can teleport, it's not as if you're going to sit around your house thinking, 'I sure hope they come here to ask me questions so I can shoot them in the head and toss them off the High Level.'"

"No," Collie agreed. "I figure you would make your own opportunities, rather than sitting there waiting for victims to come to you."

"So I see no reason not to go talk to them," Anna said. "It won't be news to the murderer that we're investigating. If they think we're getting too close, they can kill us anytime, anywhere."

Collie let a piece of injera fall into her plate and showed no interest in retrieving it.

"This job sucks," she said, wide-eyed, as if the fact had just occurred to her. Anna nodded sympathetically.

"And we're not even sure we're getting paid."

ANNA TOOK CARE OF THE BILL while Collie headed back to the service station. Collie's plan was to settle up for her car, climb inside, and call Kieran to get phone numbers and addresses from him. That was assuming he had contact information for every teleporter in town. Really, though, given

Kieran's occupation, Anna figured he couldn't afford not to. Surely he had to get people out of the city in a hurry sometimes.

Anna didn't hurry on her way back, since it would take Collie awhile to go through the paperwork for her car and to get settled for the phone call.

There was no guarantee that the car would be ready, either. Collie might have found a mechanic from the 1950s, but apparently even 1950s mechanics could drag repairs out.

It was, anyhow, fall. Edmonton seemed to have heard her bitching about the endless summer and had responded with a perfect ten-degree day. Clear skies, bright colours, and just enough wind to keep people awake.

Anna liked fall. It felt fresh to her, the way spring felt to most people. It was notebooks that weren't torn yet, and a new desk that wasn't filled with ink from broken ballpoints and crumbs from Halloween cookies. When the air got the antiseptic bite of winter and the sidewalks got shiny with icy rain, Anna felt as though she were getting a new chance not to forget her math homework ever again.

Even these past few years, when it hadn't rained much and the air had been hot as in August, the kids had gone back to school and part of her had gone with them, hoping she could keep her record clean all the way to October.

She didn't like her chances this year.

She was relieved, upon reaching the block before the garage, to see Collie's red Tercel out front and Collie tucked happily into the driver's seat. It didn't hurt to have two vehicles when they were on a case, for one thing. For another, having the car back would put Collie into a vastly better mood. Anna was always a little afraid that the next repair on the aging car would be the one Collie deemed not worth it, setting off the horrors of selling her beloved ride, on the one hand, and dealing with car salespeople, on the other.

Anna didn't even want to think about the fact that one day, probably soon, her venerable Jeep would give up. As long as most of the gears still worked, Anna preferred to believe that everything would be all right.

She let herself into Collie's car, on the passenger side, and wrinkled her nose. It was an odd smell, not unpleasant... she looked at Collie, who was on the phone and nodding uselessly. No help there.

After a few deep inhalations, Anna placed it and nearly laughed. It was the indefinable but unmistakable new car smell. She'd heard it came in spray cans now, and it seemed that was true. Probably the mechanic's idea of a joke. She decided not to say anything about it, on the chance that Collie didn't think it was funny.

"Well," Collie told the phone, "there's probably no point talking to her anyway. Until we get the results back about the ward, we're assuming she's been eliminated."

There was an index card lying on the dash, close writing covering it, a pen carefully balanced beside it. Anna reached for the card and Collie slapped her hand, without so much as looking at her. Anna wondered, not for the first time, if Collie had extra eyes under all that hair. Like those frogs that had eyes at the tops of their heads and could see nearly everything that went on around them.

"Uh-huh," Collie said. "No, we should be good for now. But if you have anything else..."

She reached for the pen, paused, then slipped it into her purse.

"Okay. If we hit a dead end, we'll ca – what? No, repeat that."

Anna raised her brows at Collie, but Collie was busy giving her steering wheel a death glare.

"This isn't a fucking school assignment, like, if we don't do it ourselves, we won't *learn* anything. You're supposed to be helping. I would not call it 'spoon feeding.' Jesus."

Spoon feeding. Anna shook her head.

"Whatever. I'll most likely be calling you later."

Collie hung up and tossed the phone into her purse, not bothering to slip it into the little pocket where it was supposed to reside.

"You would think Kieran would just be happy to help," she said.

"*You* would think that," Anna said. "I mostly think he's a jerk. But, actually, I did think he'd be more cooperative. Since he liked Ian."

"You mostly think he's creepy," Collie corrected. "And, as a sideline, you think he's a jerk."

Anna smiled.

"True. Where are we headed?"

"124th," Collie said. "Thereabouts. That Nadia chick runs one of those little galleries with her husband."

"'Kay," Anna said. "Are we taking your car? Should I move the Jeep? We'll have to come get it later."

"Uh… we can take my car," Collie said. "And… yeah, you should move it. Unless you want to ask them to do a tune-up or something. As long as it's here."

"I'll pass," Anna said. It wasn't so much that the Jeep couldn't use a tune-up as that she didn't want mechanics digging around in there. They might mess with the delicate balance that was keeping it alive beyond its time.

"You're like a guy who doesn't want to go to the doctor because he's pretty sure he has colon cancer," Collie observed.

"It's more like rampant, carnivorous cancer of the every damned thing," Anna said. "There's no treating it. You're better off not knowing it's there. Follow me while I go spot hunting."

To Anna's surprise, it didn't take long to find a side street where she could stash the Jeep for an unlimited period of time. She wasn't one hundred percent sure she'd have hubcaps when she got back, but what the hell. She'd already lost two, anyhow.

As Collie turned toward downtown, Anna felt just a little proud of herself. She'd correctly guessed that 124th was the street, not the avenue. She even had a feeling, based on the gallery comment, that they'd be heading toward the south end of the north-of-the-river part of the street, since it was known as an art gallery area.

She'd discovered, upon moving to Edmonton, that the residents were involved in a massive cover-up. They all pretended the city had a reasonable grid system. Sure, it was full of places where three or four streets were skipped, or As and Bs were added to numbers, or entire chunks of the grid fell into deep ravines. Sure, a wide river wound like a giant "s" through the middle of town, dividing it into nearly equal north and south sides and making it possible for streets to vanish for a kilometre and then pick up again. And, yes, streets did sometimes run the wrong way and cross other streets.

But true Edmontonians opted to ignore those complications.

"It's a grid," one of Anna's co-workers at the clinic had happily told her when she'd asked for directions to a bank. She'd proceeded to explain that, for example, the address 11304 140th Street meant the second house from the corner of 113th Avenue and 140th Street.

"Or the corner of 112th or 114th Avenue," she'd added. "I always get that mixed up. And I don't know if that's a real address."

It might not be a "real address," Anna had realized upon reflection, because that location might hold picnic grounds, or an industrial park, or a ravine, or a railyard, or a bubble in space-time.

Worse still, people loved to give addresses without specifying street or avenue. They just figured she'd know. It had to be a street. If it were an avenue, the address wouldn't exist. Wasn't that obvious?

Sometimes Anna felt a nearly irresistible urge to pick up

some random Edmonton residents, dump them in the middle of a northern Saskatchewan forest and give them their latitude and longitude. You know where you are. You should be able to make it back to civilization. What? Ah, but the rich bastards would probably all have GPS.

"Why does everyone we want to talk to have to be in a business district?" Collie wanted to know. Anna blinked and realized they were downtown, circling the corner of 124th and Jasper. Which was a named street. But it was still a flawless, perfectly regular system.

"I'm just throwing this out there," Anna said, "but how about… because they run businesses?"

"I swear, "Collie said, "I am going to start investigating by transit. I'll only follow leads that are on bus routes. That's where most of the crime in this city happens anyhow."

It was an exaggeration but not, sadly, an entirely unfair comment.

"The city prefers to think of those incidents as bus-adjacent fatalities," Anna said. "There's a spot."

It was a short walk from their parking spot to the gallery in question, a narrow glass-fronted place with "Jeita" painted across the width of one tall pane. The glass was smoky, much too dark to see through, which seemed like a waste. Why have big windows if you weren't going to show off your wares?

There was no way to tell from the sidewalk whether there were lights on inside. The door had no sign indicating hours of operation.

"I hope this isn't one of those 'only open on equinoxes' shops," Collie said, and gave the door a tug.

To Anna's surprise, it opened. Not that she'd expected the place to only be open twice a year, but peculiar little shops did tend to keep peculiar little hours.

Upon entering, she could see the reason for the dark glass. Light would have spoiled the effect, which was of a glowing cavern filled with sculpture. The walls were dark. The individual pieces were bathed in jewel-toned lights. There was even a small fountain and pond in the centre of the room, quietly inflicting the punishment of Sisyphus on its chlorinated water.

"Pretty," Collie whispered, "but how can you tell how anything will look in your house?"

"Maybe they're recommending the whole design scheme," Anna whispered back.

"It is quite soothing," a woman's voice said from behind them. Anna turned quickly to see a tall woman with long dark hair standing behind what seemed at first glance to be a pile of rocks. A few more seconds of staring showed it to be a counter, with a few folders and a pen resting on the flat top behind its jagged front line.

"Totally unlike sneaking up on people," Collie pointed out. The woman laughed. She was broadly built and her laugh had some bass to it.

"I apologize. I was looking for something on the floor when you came in."

Which might have been true, but then again...

"Are you Nadia Kuri?" Anna asked.

"I am," she said. She stepped out from behind the counter with her hand outstretched. "And you are?"

"Anna Gareau," Anna said. "This is Colette Kostyna."

"A pleasure," Nadia said, shaking hands with each of them. Her grip was as warm and confident as her voice. "Are you truly concerned about what will fit in your home?"

"Not really," Collie admitted. "We're renting."

"And we're not here about art," Anna said.

"Is that so?" Nadia said, giving them a gracious smile that said, with kindness, that she had no trouble believing that was so. "Shall we have a seat?"

She gestured at a pair of benches toward the back of the room. Anna made her way there, carefully weaving between the presumably expensive lumps of clay. Her night vision had been getting worse every year since her late twenties and she wasn't sure how Nadia, who must have been in her forties at least, could navigate the room at all.

As the three of them settled in, Anna scanned Nadia's Holt Renfrew-y get-up and opalescent nails and the way her highlighted hair fell in perfect waves. She looked, yes, big, but also great, and Anna had mixed feelings about that. It was good to see a woman who wasn't a twig looking so unimpeachably attractive. But was the cost of that having the best clothes, always, and the finest haircuts and manicures and never, never a piece of lint anywhere? Collie just seemed happy to be in the presence of someone elegant. Not that she or Anna aspired to that, really, but it was a change from the usual.

"What would you be looking for, besides art?" Nadia asked. Anna realized she was feeling them out, trying to figure out if they were trying to hire her for that other service she offered. It was, trappings aside, very like the way prostitutes spoke to people who might or might not be cops.

"Advice, mostly," Collie said. Anna was relieved to hear it, because they'd never decided on an approach.

"But not about art."

"No. About teleportation."

"Certainly." Nadia's smile was less gracious now. "If you haven't got it, you haven't got it. Do not try to learn it from a spellbook or a wise old mentor. You will only lose your head, or something else of value. Was that all?"

"I wish," Collie said. "Life would be so much simpler. We're... ah... actually here about Ian McLaren."

"You want to know about teleportation and Ian McLaren?" Nadia seemed genuinely confused, which meant nothing. Anna knew quite a few people who could lie their asses off while looking just that puzzled.

"How well do you know Ian?" Collie asked. Her face said she

wasn't sure how uncomfortable she ought to be. Anna sympathized. Were they cruelly misleading one of Ian's close friends before breaking the news of his death? Somewhat less cruelly misleading a colleague and acquaintance of Ian's? Telling Ian's murderer a whole bunch of stuff she already knew? Emily Post did not cover supernatural murder investigation.

"Not well," Nadia said, relieving the tension. "We've worked together on a few projects. Would you mind telling me directly what this is about?"

"I'm sorry," Collie said. "Ian McLaren died last night."

Nadia looked from one to the other. It was difficult to tell with only coloured lights in the room, but her eyes seemed to be a pale, almost grey-green. Anna wondered if she was wearing those new colour contacts that could make eyes eerily light. Maybe that was why she saw so well in the dark.

"This is a strange way to break the news," she said.

"Yeah," Anna agreed. "That's not what we're here for."

"We're here because Ian was shot, in his home, in the back of his head," Collie said. "And there's reason to think a teleporter may have done it."

Nadia gave a bark of a laugh.

"And you are here to accuse me?"

"God, no," Collie said. "Haven't you ever played Clue? If you accuse someone too soon, you lose the game. We're trying to find out if anyone has your card."

Understandably, Nadia looked alarmed by the discovery that a murder investigation was in the hands of a crazy person. Anna decided to reassure her that there was at least one halfway sane person on the case.

"It's our understanding that it would not have been possible for someone to walk up behind Ian and shoot him, due to the nature of his abilities. It may, however, have been possible for someone to... ah... pop in behind him and shoot him. So, naturally, we're talking to all the teleporters in town."

Nadia shook her head. Her eyes had an amused gleam.

"That's a mad distinction."

"What is?" Anna asked.

"All the teleporters in town. Meaningless. If it's true, that he was killed by someone who could teleport, then it could have been anyone, anywhere. Not just in this town. That is the nature of this beast."

"Normally we'd agree," Collie said, "but Ian was in a warded house and — though we are investigating the possibility that someone broke the ward — it seems more likely that the teleporter was someone Ian knew."

"Certain people were on a guest list," Anna said, "and the ward didn't affect them."

"You are here because I was on this list?" Nadia said. She gave it the upsweep of a question. Collie nodded.

"Primarily. But also, to be honest, we do have some questions about teleportation in general. It's not a specialty of ours."

Nadia took in a long, deep breath through her long, straight nose.

"Would you care for tea?" she asked. "I have rooibos."

Anna reminded herself that "fuckin' A" was not an acceptable response to an offer of tea.

"I'm very fond of rooibos," she said instead. Collie gave the offer a polite pass.

Nadia nodded, rose, and vanished. No slow fade or *Star Trek* lights or sound effects. She was just gone.

"Huh," Collie said. "This never happened to Archie Goodwin. You figure she's coming back, or did we just lose our suspect?"

Anna smiled.

"Tough to say. I don't see a kitchenette in this place."

"I guess you wouldn't have to have one at the office," Collie said. "You could just pop home."

"You wouldn't have to keep anything at the office," Anna

pointed out. You wouldn't have, like, lip balm in your purse… and your desk… and your glove compartment… and your night stand… and the bathroom," Collie said. "You could just have one tube."

"I'm not sure most people have that many tubes of lip balm," Anna said.

"You wouldn't even need a car," Collie said. "What would you need a car for?"

"Sometimes I have passengers," Nadia said from somewhere behind them. Anna twitched with surprise and Collie jumped halfway out of her seat. Anna turned to see Nadia moving toward them, a tray in her hands instead of a gun.

Collie was still breathing hard when Nadia set the tray down on a little table a few feet away. Nadia either didn't notice or, more likely, was inured to that reaction, because she simply poured two cups of tea from a tall red carafe and returned to the seating area.

"You don't want sugar?" she said, another statement turned question. Anna shook her head and held out her hands.

"No, this is fine. Thanks."

It crossed her mind as she took the first sip that Nadia could have just as easily popped off to South America for some rare frog poison or something. Having tea with a suspect maybe wasn't the smartest thing. But, really, there were much easier ways for Nadia to kill them if she wanted to do so.

Anna laughed, suddenly, tea catching in her throat. Collie and Nadia looked at her with curiosity. Neither reached over to pat her back.

"I was just thinking," she said, "the main reason I trust people these days is that I figure I'd be dead already if they wanted to kill me."

"And that amused you?" Nadia inquired. Anna shrugged, careful not to spill the tea.

"Apparently. Did you say you needed a car for passengers?"

Nadia sat and took a sip of her own tea.

"Does that surprise you?"

"Not as much as having someone show up out of nowhere," Collie said, evidently getting good and tired of that. "But I would have thought you could just bring people with you wherever you go. Like you brought that tray."

Or a gun, Anna didn't say.

"I can only take what I can carry," Nadia said. She raised her chin at Collie. "You." Tilted her head at Anna. "Not you."

"You mean, what you physically are strong enough to carry," Collie asked, "or what you literally are carrying at moment? Like, I'd have to piggyback?"

"I must be carrying it. Lifted off the ground. I suppose you could piggyback, as you say."

Anna looked Nadia up and down, trying to decide if she'd be able to carry Rowan. Not if he were conscious and trying to kick her ass. But out cold and in a fireman's carry? It seemed possible.

"See," Collie said, "that's funny, because Mandrake – I mean, Ian – could take anything he wanted with him. I think he could, anyway. I saw him jump around with all kinds of stuff."

"Famously," Nadia said, "a room full of air."

"That's not exactly how it went down," Collie said, giving no indication that she cared to discuss how it had gone down. "But that is the kind of thing I mean."

"Well, I am not Ian," Nadia said, unnecessarily. Her hand wasn't glowing, after all. "I can do what I can do."

"So it differs," Anna said. Nadia smiled.

"Oh, yes."

"Is that something you're born with," Anna said, "or do you learn how to do different... aspects?"

"It can be some of both," Nadia said, "but I would recommend to anyone that they stay with the thing they were born with. Accidents can happen otherwise."

"Noted," Collie said, seemingly no more eager to hear about teleportation accidents than Anna was. "What if you were an insane teleporting cowboy, though? With no fear? Could you learn to do everything?"

"Not well," Nadia said. "Not reliably. And it would take decades. Even for those who acquire these skills by study, the skills naturally manifest themselves in individual ways."

Which meant, most likely, they weren't just looking for a teleporter. They were looking for a teleporter with the right chops.Not that she would have preferred to be cleaning cages, but there was a certain peace in knowing what to expect from your job. A cat who threw up in one corner? Not a problem. A big dog with the runs who panicked when stuck in a small space? A foretaste of hell.

With the investigation stuff, though, Anna was never entirely sure what was good news and what was bad, unless it was so spectacularly bad as to leave no room for uncertainty.

"Okay," Collie said. "So, you can only teleport yourself and stuff you're holding up off the ground. What about... ah... Sam Llewelyn? Have you ever worked with Sam?"

"Not worked with, no," Nadia said. "But we have been introduced. By Ian, if I recall correctly. At that club he likes."

Ah, the present tense. Anna was almost prepared to give a pass to anyone who used it, since they obviously thought of Ian as still being alive. Except that a really tricky murderer would probably use it on purpose.

"And Sam's specialty?" Collie asked.

"He opens portals," Nadia said. "Only little ones, I think. In fact, I believe the Embassy — you know the Embassy?"

"Yes," Anna said. "I don't think they'd care for you asking anyone that question, though."

Nadia looked puzzled, but Collie grinned.

"She's saying that the Embassy probably prefers that you don't bring them up at all unless you're sure the person you're talking to already knows about them. You know. But we do, so it's okay."

"And I don't stay up late worrying about what the Embassy prefers," Anna added, though it was more a wish than a fact.

Nadia sniffed, actually sniffed, like a pretentious person in a terrible comedy.

"Well. It's more pleasant here when they are in sympathy with you. And they pay quite well. I was only going to say I had heard they used Sam to distribute cheques."

Anna shot a look at Collie, who was glancing at her purse. Probably wondering if she'd had some guy's hand in there and never realized it.

"So, he makes some kind of hole in the air and shoves crap into it and that crap comes out someplace else?" Collie asked.

"I wouldn't put it that way," Nadia said, and Anna was quite sure she wouldn't. Possibly not even if you put a gun to her head and demanded that she do so. "But that is what appears to happen."

"Are appearances deceiving?" Anna asked. Nadia stood and, for a moment, Anna thought she might port away again. To Anna's infinite amusement, she even saw Collie's hand make an aborted grab for Nadia's skirt. As if that would help.

But Nadia was just going to the table to rid herself of her empty teacup which she, unlike Mr. Llewelyn, could not send back to the kitchen.

"I don't know," she said as she returned. "I don't choose to think about it. What matters is that things go where he intends with at least some regularity, and they arrive in acceptable condition."

"What do you mean, some regularity?" Collie asked.

"And acceptable condition?" Anna added.

"The things Sam teleports do not show up backwards or inside out. They are structurally intact. I don't know if he ever teleports living things. I assume you'll ask him about that."

"Yup," Collie said.

"The person who told me about Sam delivering cheques also said that he had lost a few cheques over the years, but that it was uncommon. They didn't say how uncommon."

"*Lost*, lost?" Collie said. "Forever? Or did they turn up under his sofa?"

"They were not seen again," Nadia said. She didn't have to add that this was another thing she chose not to think about.

"And the person who told you all of this was?" Anna asked. Nadia smiled.

"I expect she's on your list. Her name is Robin Hampshire."

Another gender question answered. They hadn't even had to ask, exactly.

"Mmm," Collie said. "Yeah. She's on our list. But would you happen to know where to find her? I don't have current contact information."

Nadia threw her head back and laughed. There was nothing classy about it. Anna thought this might be the first time they'd seen the real person under all that perfectly managed hair.

"Oh, dear," she said. "Oh... you're *working* for the Embassy, aren't you?"

"Didn't we say so?" Collie asked.

"Of course not. And it's fine. I don't mind assisting with their investigation. But I won't put you in touch with Robin Hampshire. If she wants to speak with you, I'm sure she'll have no trouble finding you."

"I guess we've got that to look forward to," Collie said. "Um... do you know anything about Jake Dysenko?"

"Nothing beyond the name," Nadia said. "And that he's in my line of work. More or less. I know I have received work, on occasion, because he wasn't available."

"Unavailable in some weird, 'he's disappeared and no one knows where he is' way?" Collie asked, sounding hopeful. She always seemed to find it encouraging when they dug up any kind of dirt, or even oddness, surrounding a murder suspect, regardless of whether it was remotely relevant.

"No," Nadia said. "Simply not available for work. As far as I know. Ladies, I have an appointment in a few minutes and this sort of conversation is not good for business. Did you need anything else?"

Anna suspected that talking about teleportation and murder in the back of an art gallery would be fabulously good for business. It would certainly get the place talked about, and wasn't that the first goal for any artist? She decided not to share her insight with Nadia on the grounds that Nadia hadn't been receptive to any of their insights so far.

Now Collie was smiling oddly, making Anna wonder if that was how her face had looked when she'd had her epiphany about trusting murder suspects. No wonder Nadia didn't take them seriously.

"I was just thinking," Collie said, "that I should ask you where you were when Ian was murdered. But I guess there would be no point to that."

"None at all," Nadia confirmed. "Please give my regards to Sam, and to Robin if you see her."

"When," Collie corrected with her cockiest grin. "When we see her, we will."

"LORD KNOWS, I could be wrong," Anna said once the door to Nadia's gallery had closed behind them, "but isn't Robin the extra teleporter? The one who wasn't on Kieran's list of Ian's friend, and wasn't on Doris' guest list?"

"That's our girl," Collie confirmed. "Or, I don't know... eighty-year-old woman. But at least we know she's a she."

"And Sam's a he," Anna said. "Not bad for a day's work."

"Did you get the sense that the reason Nadia won't put us in touch with Robin is that we're working for the Embassy?"

"That's my take," Anna agreed. "Should we decide where we're going before getting into your car, so we don't get honked at by everyone who goes by?"

"It won't be everyone," Collie said. "Just the ones looking for a parking space. And screw 'em."

There were times when Anna thought "screw 'em" might be Collie's last words. Or possibly, "fuck 'em if they can't take a joke."

They got into the car and, as predicted, the honking started within moments. Collie shrugged.

"We've got time on the meter. Anyway. Your thoughts on this Robin Hampshire thing?"

"It's not just that Nadia referenced the Embassy before telling us to pound sand," Anna said. "It's that she guessed we were working for the Embassy based on the fact that we didn't have Robin Hampshire's contact information. And, actually, that fact alone is pretty odd. I thought you were either with the Embassy or against 'em."

"If you're with 'em, they know how to find you," Collie added. "If you're agin 'em, you're either left dead in a ditch or you're run out of town."

"That is certainly the impression they wish to give," Anna agreed.

"Now," Collie said, "I am literally itching to talk with Robin Hampshire. I didn't misuse that word. I have hives."

"Sexy," Anna said. "Since we don't have Robin's contact information, we should probably go see Jake or Sam instead."

"Yeah," Collie said. "That'll be Sam. I only have a phone number for Jake."

"You need to stop at a Shopper's along the way, get some hydrocortisone cream?"

Collie grinned.

"Nah. I'll live."

After deliberately waiting out a yowling ape in a pickup

who'd been hovering behind their spot, Collie pulled into traffic and headed west.

"Is this a home or business address?" Anna asked.

"It's in The Mall," Collie said.

Capital T. Capital M. When it was said that way, with capitals and resignation, Edmontonians meant the *mall.* West. Ed. North America's largest, reputedly, and certainly Edmonton's damn loudest.

Anna thought The Mall would be vastly improved if people stood outside the doors and shot you before you could step inside. It would be merciful. But she had a feeling that Collie harboured a secret affection for the place, as she did for all things that were innocent of shame. The Mall was tacky in a way that Circus of the Stars could only envy, and Anna supposed there was something impressive about that.

"What does he do?" Anna asked. "Train sea lions? Conduct the merry-go-round? Man the bungee trampolines?"

"Oh!" Collie said. "The trampolines!"

"I was kidding," Anna said. "Please tell me he doesn't do that."

"No, no. But the trampolines reminded me of the water massage. I need to get one. Do you think we have time?"

"I don't think we're on a specific timeline," Anna said. "If you want to spend twenty bucks to get felt up by a waterbed. You freak."

"Ah, you'd love it if you only tried it," Collie said.

Anna suspected she wouldn't. She didn't know what went through people's minds when they were enclosed in those beds, but she had a sick feeling she'd know as soon as she put her hands on the controls. She didn't know if it would be worse to get a claustrophobic or someone who really, really liked it. A lot.

"So, what does Sammy do?" Anna asked, desperate for a change of subject.

"He manages a collectables shop. I imagine teleportation might help with that."

"It would make the collecting part easy," Anna said. "Assuming he's a thief."

"Or just that he has suppliers who know what he does," Collie said. "And the teleporting lets him avoid shipping costs. Sheesh. Always thinking the worst of people."

The only sensible response to that was to laugh out loud, so Anna did.

"Hell," Collie went on, talking right over the laugh, "if your buddy with the antique store had a teleporting friend, you and I might never have met."

"If things were different," Anna said, "cowshit would be butter."

Collie turned her head to look at Anna, eyes bright.

"The hell?"

Anna shrugged.

"Something my next-door neighbour used to say when I was growing up. She said it in German, but she translated it for me once."

"Ah," Collie said. "Accurate, but useless."

"Being German, she would have said accuracy was never useless."

Collie smiled.

"Holy ethnic stereotype, Batman."

"This from a woman who uses the term 'Mexican roadblock.'"

"What else are you gonna call it?" Collie protested. "Find me another expression for that and I'll use it."

"You could say you're pinned in by assholes," Anna suggested. "Or you could say you're too impatient to drive and should have your license taken away."

Collie rolled her eyes and flung a hand at the grey Explorer a few inches from the nose of her car. Neither of which did anything to improve her driving.

"Oh, and this guy going, like, forty isn't the problem? It's supposed to be sixty here. And you know what really gets me? I can't even tell if he *is* the problem, or if it's some jackass in front of him. Because I can see precisely fuck all. Because everyone in this town drives a vehicle that's taller than they are."

"My mistake," Anna said. "It's clear you're even-tempered and rational enough to be behind the wheel."

"Cram it," Collie said, by way of argument.

The traffic wasn't that bad, really, since it was still mid-afternoon. Collie darted into The Mall's sprawling lot near The Mall's largest theatre, drawing another laugh from Anna. Collie looked at her with narrowed eyes.

"What?"

"Nothing to do with you," Anna said. "I just had a dream about the theatre last night. And Rowan."

Collie pulled the parking brake with more force than was necessary.

"And you are just telling me this now."

"So?" Anna unlocked her door and reminded herself to shove it open with her arm, not by kicking it. Kicking doors open was a bad habit and people didn't appreciate it when she did it in their cars.

"Are you serious? You had one of your dreams."

They faced off across the top of the Tercel. Collie slammed her door with feeling.

"I can't believe you've been sitting on information."

"Col, I had a dream. You didn't report on your dreams either."

"I'm not a frickin' psychic!" Collie yelled. Her voice bounced wildly through the concrete parkade. Anna leaned over the car, hoping to bring down the volume of the conversation.

"Just," she hissed. "A. Cigar."

"Bullshit," Collie hissed back, then shook her head and

continued in a normal voice. "The last time we were on a murder case, you had dreams and they mattered. I have to assume they matter this time, too. Especially since you're dreaming about our missing person."

"And our client," Anna admitted. "Eric. But everyone dreams about stuff that's on their minds."

Collie threw her hands in the air.

"You are *so* not everyone. Come on. Walk and talk."

Anna matched Collie's brisk pace and they headed toward the nearest entrance. As they walked, she described her dream. Rowan. The dragon. Eric. The lake that came from nowhere.

"As you can see," Anna finished, "our case is solved."

"I refuse to believe there was no useful information in that dream," Collie said. "Even if it was just you processing. We'll understand it eventually."

They were inside, heading for the water park, which told Anna that Collie was serious about getting a massage. Unless Mr. Llewelyn's shop was also in the area.

"I'm sure you'll come up with an interpretation of that dream," Anna said. "One way or another. If you're really getting a massage, maybe you should do it after we talk to this Sam guy."

"I thought you said we weren't on a timeline."

"We're not," Anna said. "I just thought you might want to relax afterward, if the pattern holds."

"What huh?"

Anna steered around a group of teenage girls who had gathered for cell phone photos. She couldn't begin to imagine how many photos those girls had in their phones, all of the same six or eight people, pressed in so close that you couldn't even see where the shots had been taken. But, unless you took a picture, how could you prove the day had happened?

Once she was back at Collie's side, she said, "Everyone else we've talked with today has gotten on your nerves."

Collie grinned, still booting it toward the massage beds.

"Are you saying I'm testy?"

"No," Anna said, then reconsidered. "Yes. But people genuinely have been straining your patience, so I don't blame you."

Collie stopped dead. Anna had to back up a few steps.

"You could warn me when you're going to do that," she said. "Grab my arm. Pretend I'm trying to teleport away."

Collie laughed.

"Grab your arm. God, I can't believe I grabbed her arm. I am a dork. Um... yeah. Let's go see Sam. He's around here, anyway. Second floor."

"Ooh," Anna said. "Fancy."

It wasn't a hard and fast rule that shops on the second floor were pricier than those on the ground floor, but it was a pretty safe bet. It made little sense to her, since you had to go a bit out of your way to get to a second-floor shop. Wouldn't rent be higher on the ground floor? She made a note to ask Collie sometime, since Collie at least nominally cared about things promotional.

They picked an escalator and headed up, Anna close on Collie's heels since she didn't even know the name of the shop for which they were looking. Yet she was the one getting lectured about not sharing information.

"Ah. There it is."

Down a straight line from Collie's pointing finger, Anna could see a plain sign, black lettering on white, that read, "The Completist."

"It should be the Compleat Completist," Collie said. "How do you miss such an obvious opportunity?"

"Hard to imagine," Anna said, almost selling it. Collie elbowed her.

"You just don't appreciate my great ideas."

"That's true," Anna said, and sold it completely.

As they got closer she could see the inside of the store. It looked at first like a standard coins and cards shop, all glass counters and stacks of albums. Looking at the counters, though, she could see jewellery. Vinyl records. Toys. Dishes. Books. Ornaments. Everything was pretty, in its own way, but otherwise completely random. It didn't even seem to be organized into sections, unless blue-green and dark red were sections.

Behind the counter was a man in his thirties, maybe early forties, with short blond hair and features that Anna, having seen Collie's Björk albums lying around, thought of as Icelandic. Even though they were probably just Björkic.

Collie smiled and charged right up to the blond. Anna moved more slowly, wanting a closer look at the wares. They were a little less random up close than from a distance, if only in the sense that they were restricted to a certain time period. Late '60s, maybe, though mid-'80s.

It was hard to imagine mid-'80s items as vintage, but Anna was trying to accept it gracefully. More gracefully than Collie, at least, who had once demanded that a kid in a Sisters of Mercy t-shirt sing "This Corrosion" to her, and had become unruly when he admitted he didn't know it.

"I'm Colette Kostyna," Collie said, producing a business card from seemingly nowhere — a move that would surely have been impressive to any other audience. "This is Anna Gareau. Would you be Sam Llewelyn?"

"If you'd like," the blond said pleasantly, taking her card. His accent was what Anna considered the real deal: British English of indeterminate origin, perhaps Manchester mixed up with a few years in London and holidays in Scotland, then given a good shake by a decade or so in Canada. It was the sort of speech that might produce frage-ill rather than frage-ile, but would never ask for a twenny-dollar bill.

"It's all the same to me," Collie told him, "except that I need to talk to Sam Llewelyn."

Sam — if that was his name — smiled, making his thin lips

nearly disappear. Oddly, his narrow slash of a smile was engaging.

"Let's make this convenient, then, and say I'm him. What did you want to ask me?"

Collie glanced around the store, presumably to ensure that it was free of customers. It wasn't a big job, since the store was only slightly too wide for Anna to lie on the floor with her feet against one wall and her head against the other. Typical for a cards and coins shop, but it seemed a bit crowded – and, with its glass cases, more than a bit sterile – for a place that carried all kinds of vintage swag.

Apparently satisfied that no one was hiding behind the paint on the walls, Collie put her elbows on the counter and leaned toward Sam.

"We're here about Ian McLaren."

"Ah." Sam's smile went away. "That."

Anna hoped a day would never come when the mention of her name would make people look sad and say, "That."

"The Embassy sent us," Collie said. "We're looking into Ian's death."

Sam nodded. He flexed his fingers and Anna saw a chamois beneath them. She hadn't noticed it before. Then again, it might not have been there before.

"Good," Sam said, wiping the counter. A nervous habit, most likely, but at least it was a productive one. Glass counters could never get too much wiping. "Someone should be looking into it. There was no harm in Ian, you know?"

"He was pretty good to us," Collie said. It sounded concurrent, but wasn't, which was a nice trick. "I don't mean to distress you, but have you been told how Ian died?"

"It's not distressing," Sam told her. "It's just sad. I only heard that he had been shot. Is that right?"

"In his home," Collie said. "In the back of his head."

Anna felt a powerful urge to make a joke, a terrible Ian kind of joke, about Ian having been shot in two places. He was shot in the vestibule? That's always fatal!

She distracted herself by looking at the counter. A plastic necklace and bangles were scattered across the first Roxy Music album, the blue of the jewellery and the cover almost a match. Her friend Curtis, who ran an antique store on the west coast, would have dumped the jewellery in hot water and sniffed it, for whatever reason. He always did that with plastic jewellery, as if that somehow made it less ugly.

"That's odd, isn't it?" Sam said. "I wouldn't have thought that possible."

"Which part?" Collie asked. "Shooting him in his home, or shooting him at all?"

Anna looked up in time to see Sam's eyes widen.

"I... suppose both, actually. Are you familiar with Ian's panic button?"

Collie's mouth quirked upward.

"I can't say we knew him *that* well," she said.

Sam smiled in response. It wasn't a flirty smile, just a salute to a fellow smart-ass.

"Ian knew, somehow, when he was in some sort of trouble, and he'd teleport away. It was automatic. He'd suddenly find himself all sorts of funny places. But he never got hit by a car or conked on the head or the like. It was pretty unnerving, I might add, when you were standing next to Ian and he vanished. You wondered what was coming."

"I guess it would be," Collie said, sounding surprised that the thought hadn't occurred to her. "So, you're saying, if someone tried to shoot him, he would somehow sense it and pop off to... I don't know... Madagascar?"

"Yeah," Sam said. "That's about the size of it. But why do I have the feeling you've been told this before?"

"I wanted to hear you say it," Collie said. Sam raised his brows.

"Now, why would that be? Am I a suspect?"

"Could be I just like your accent," Collie told him. "Why are you surprised that Ian was shot in his house?"

"Stop me if I bore you," Sam said. "Since you probably know this as well. The house was warded, I believe. It wasn't Ian's house, either. It was Matt... ah... I can't recall his last name. But he's the shopkeeper at Urban Myth."

"So it was hard to sneak up on Ian," Collie said, "and doubly hard to sneak up on him in his living room."

"Make that impossible," Sam said, "and doubly impossible."

"Good," Collie said. "That leaves me with just four more things to believe before breakfast. Do you have any idea how someone might have gotten the drop on Ma — on Ian?"

"Oh, Mandrake, is it? Very nice. No. I've no idea. Didn't I just say it couldn't be done?"

"I'd find that a lot more convincing," Collie said, "if no one had done it. Anyway. How well did you know Ian?"

Sam shrugged, a twitch of his narrow shoulders.

"We both did some work for the Embassy. You know how that is, I'd imagine. Sometimes you get put on teams."

Anna couldn't recall a time when she and Collie had been put on a team, per se, but Collie nodded as if she understood.

"But why would they need to put you and Ian on the same team?" she asked. "Don't you — I mean, didn't you both do the same thing?"

Sam tilted his head to one side and sighed though his nose.

"Do we have to do it this way? I don't know who you've been talking to, but you obviously know these things and you're both brutal liars."

"Still just liking your accent," Collie said, unperturbed.

Sam put his hands flat on the counter. The chamois was gone. It was a shame, really, because he was getting fingerprints all over the place.

"Ian and I don't do the same thing. He teleported himself

wherever he wanted to go, and occasionally to places he did not intend to go. I teleport things. Small things. Smaller than a breadbox and, yes, I have measured a breadbox to be certain, since you hardly ever see them these days."

Collie looked at Anna, who spaced out a breadbox with her hands. Her father had kept one on the kitchen counter, next to the stove... an ugly avocado-coloured thing with a handle that was painted to look vaguely like tarnished brass.

"Huh," Collie said. Anna told herself that Collie was not trying to decide whether Rowan could fit through a space that small. She was not that spatially challenged. "Can you teleport living things?"

Anna looked at the counter again. Easy Bake? Cook Lite? Something like that. That's what Curtis had called that jewellery. Anna had said something plastic could hardly be antique, as she understood the term. Curtis had laughed and said nobody understood the term, which had struck Anna as a funny damned thing for an antique dealer to say.

Sam was taking his time with the answer, possibly because he was also wondering just what Collie had in mind. Finally he said, "I don't do that anymore."

"Why not?" Collie asked, as if she honestly couldn't imagine. Though Anna was pretty sure she could.

Sam stared at her in evident disbelief.

"Why *not*? Did you want me to describe it for you? It didn't *go* well, all right?"

"So," Collie said, "you took, like, a guinea pig and pointed at him and sent him somewhere and... what?"

Sam was gaping now, actually gaping. Jaw hanging slack.

"You do want me to describe it."

Collie breathed deep. Her shoulders and back straightened as she did so, as if she'd been taught all three moves in combination at some point in her life.

"Frankly, Sam, I could live without it. But this entire case may hinge on teleportation and I have to know exactly what it is you do. If you want me to ask around town instead of asking you, fine. But this is about Ian, when it gets right down to it, and I figured you might want to be helpful. Since there was no harm in him."

Sam's small, almond-shaped eyes narrowed, which made them nearly disappear.

"Don't you mean Mandrake?" he asked. Collie slammed an open hand on the counter. More fingerprints.

"My relationship with him isn't the point. If *you* were friendly with him and *you're* sorry he's dead, then *you* need to pony up."

Sam pursed his lips.

"I… they come out dead. I don't know why. I'm not a veterinarian. There wasn't an autopsy. They just came out dead, so I didn't do it anymore. And I don't point at things and pop them places. I open… sort of a window, and I push things through."

"So, you fold space or something?" Anna asked. Sam looked at her.

"You read *A Wrinkle in Time* as a girl, didn't you? Do I fold space, she says. Look… I have no idea what I do. You could go mad thinking about it. Does my window have a width? If… if I took this pencil," he said, producing a pencil, "and pushed it through, and my window was two millimetres thick, then we've got some pencil here and some there but that other two millimetres of pencil… where is it, exactly?"

He held up the pencil and waved his hand. As Anna watched, a black rectangle appeared between Sam's hand and Collie's wide eyes. He pushed the pencil forward and it began to disappear, as if he'd pushed it into a pool of ink. A similar rectangle appeared on the countertop and the pencil began to rise from it, straight up.

Anna remembered a movie she'd seen years ago, some comedy where a man was trying to escape a jail cell through this hidden trap door or that heating duct, except he kept popping back into the room from some other spot. Because, though you couldn't see it from inside the room, the whole thing was connected.

"Do you see the problem?" Sam asked. "You can't tell what's happening."

He gave the pencil a push and it popped out of the countertop. It stood on end for a moment, balanced, then fell to one side.

"How do I connect two places," Sam went on, "no matter how far apart? Why must it be the size of a breadbox, or smaller, but never larger? Why do living things die? Plants, too. I can't make sense of it."

"Where'd the pencil come from?" Collie asked. Her voice was distant, as if she had gone to the same place as the chamois. Wherever that was.

"You just saw," Sam said testily. Collie shook her head.

"No. Where'd it come from in the first place? You didn't have it when we came in."

"Didn't have a chamois, either," Anna added.

Sam picked the pencil up, looked at it, and flicked it over his shoulder to land on a cluttered desk.

"Came from the desk," he said. "If I know where something is — I mean, really know where it is — I can open a hole under it and it drops through."

"You'd be screwed without gravity," Collie observed. Sam stared at her for a moment, probably trying to figure out if she was making a joke. Anna wouldn't have been able to help him with that.

They would have been well advised, at that point, to end the conversation, or at least to move on to what Sam might know about the other teleporters in town. Sam wasn't the kind of teleporter they were looking for. But Anna was curious, couldn't help it, and she didn't figure Collie was done exploring the topic, either.

"Okay," Anna said. "What if we went on the internet and you looked at something on a webcam. Could you grab it?"

"Yeah," Sam said. "I've done that. Or if I remember where I saw something, or where I put something, I can grab it. As long as it's still there. Otherwise, nothing comes through."

"And when you push stuff?" Collie asked. "For example, I have reason to believe you've put a few cheques into my purse."

Sam smiled. His blue eyes did something Anna, were she not so adverse to the term, might have called "twinkling."

"Pushing's much simpler. I've just got to have the intention. Off you go, little cheque, into Colette Kostyna's purse. Never mind I haven't met you. Well, hadn't."

Collie's brow wrinkled.

"But... I have more than one purse."

She had, truth be told, more than ten purses. What she didn't have was the patience to transfer a metric tonne of crap from one purse to the next each morning, so Anna rarely saw her use anything but the big brown blob currently on her shoulder.

"Doesn't matter," Sam said. "It's all about intent. I intend to put it in whatever purse you're using, so there it goes. Did you ever meet Ian's friend Rowan?"

If Sam had asked if they'd ever met Queen Elizabeth II, Anna couldn't have been more surprised. She might have been less surprised, in fact, because it would have simply been a non sequitur instead of the last thing she'd expected him to say.

"Uh...we... did once," Collie said. "Why?"

"I assume you know he's an astral projector."

Anna looked at Collie. Collie was shaking her head.

"He never mentioned what he did."

Anna tried to recall if that was true and couldn't. Embarrassingly, she'd have to ask Collie after they left.

"Well, he would have said he was a remote viewer," Sam said. "That's how he was brought up – with a load of pseudoscientific claptrap. He'd lecture you on it if you let him. This whole thing about finding places without knowing where they were by following the intent of the questioner. I swear, it could bore you to tears, but it did seem very like the way my... ability... works."

"We're actually looking for Rowan," Collie said, doing an admirable job of sounding offhand. "We wanted to ask him some questions about Ian. Do you have any idea where we could find him?"

"No," Sam said. "I could send him something, but I couldn't find him for you. Ridiculous, isn't it? Did you want me to send him a note asking him to get in touch with you?"

Collie looked at Anna, eyebrows raised. Anna shrugged.

"Why not?" she said.

"Can't think of a reason," Collie agreed. She pulled an index card and pen from her purse. "Is it okay if I write on the counter?"

"Just a tick," Sam said. He turned around and pulled a battered notebook from his desk, set it on the counter in front of Collie. The cover featured Benji, whose face Anna hadn't seen in years. She was tempted to wave.

"There," Sam said.

She wrote quickly. Anna didn't look over her shoulder, having learned that Collie didn't appreciate it. Sometimes she phrased her failure to appreciate it in the form of an elbow to the gut.

"Okay," Collie said, handing the note to Sam. "Go ahead."

If it wasn't the downright strangest experience of Anna's life, it was certainly a contender. Sam opened another of those black rectangles, this one just a bit larger than the card itself. She peered at it, as if she'd see something other than black, maybe Rowan standing on the other side. They were, in a sense, standing right next to him. But she had no way of telling where he was.

She wondered what would happen if she touched the black

spot. And had Sam ever put a hand through? Even without Anna's quirk, you'd have to wonder what it *felt* like.

Sam pushed the note through without ceremony, seemingly untroubled by thoughts of where it might be going or how it got there. As if he'd spat out his worries for them and now they were gone from him, not to be considered again.

"Well," Collie said, trying for cheerfulness but sounding no less unnerved than Anna was. "Thanks for that. Um... we have to talk to Nadia Kuri and... ah... Jake Dysenko. Would you happen to know what kind of teleporting they do?"

Sam frowned in concentration.

"I'm fairly certain Nadia just ports Nadia. I believe Jake is a point and port, but you wouldn't want to take that to the bank. I've never met him, myself."

"Point and port?" Anna asked.

"Yeah," Sam said. He pointed at Anna with a long, thin finger. "And away you go."

"And away we go," Collie agreed. "Really, we should head. Thanks for your help."

"No worries," Sam said, though Anna thought he looked like a man with plenty of worries. At least one for every line on his forehead.

Collie didn't run from the place, but she didn't waste time, either. She went so far as to grab Anna's arm on her way past.

"Something bothering you?" Anna asked pleasantly, as Collie hauled her toward the escalator.

"Place gives me the creeps," Collie said.

"Huh," Anna said, eloquently. "I don't know. I kind of liked it. But it's weird in a mall."

Collie looked at Anna, still walking, apparently confident that anyone who saw how fast she was moving would get the hell out of her way.

"What do you mean?"

"Everything here is new," Anna said. "Brand new products

people have never owned before. There's no history anywhere. It's strange to walk into that place and see all the... time."

"And potential," Collie said. "Imagine if you handled the merchandise. Aren't you ever tempted to do that? It would be like having a time machine. You could see what the sixties were really like, you know? Oh – what if you went to a museum or something? What if you touched, like, a sarcophagus or something? You have to admit, that would be pretty amazing."

"Yeah. I could see people from the Middle Ages have stupid fights over nothing, or Victorian people stabbing each other. You forget, I nearly always get the suck eye view."

"I can't believe I never thought of this before," Collie said, either not listening or not caring. "You could be an amazing historian. You'd get the real flavour of the times. Like Max the 2000 Year Old Mouse. I know – I was *there*!"

"I'm not prepared to admit that I know who that stupid mouse is," Anna said. "So I'll restrict my comments to this: no."

"I can't believe how little curiosity you have," Collie said.

"I can't believe how short your damn memory is," Anna responded. "This shit does not make me happy. Remember? Picking up unpleasant garbage from the 1600s is not going to be a treat just because it's really old unpleasant garbage. It's like... it's like saying, 'drink this bucket of historic puke. Charles II himself horked it up.' Forget it."

"I'd be impressed if a bucket of puke lasted for hundreds of years," Collie said. "They didn't even have refrigeration back then."

"It would be a miracle," Anna agreed. "What did you put on that note to Rowan?"

"I just said that we needed to talk to him. It was actually a pointless exercise. I could have written a nursery rhyme on there and it would have been equally useful. I only went through with it because I wanted to watch Sam do it."

"Pointless how?" Anna asked. She suspected she knew, but

she wanted to know how Collie was looking at the situation.

"Well, he's one of three things, as near as I can tell. He's at liberty and keeping his head down for some reason – in which case, he's not going to call us. He's been kidnapped and has no ability to get in touch with anyone – in which case, he's not going to call us. Or he's dead – in which case, he's probably not going to call us, though I guess you never know."

"Or he has amnesia," Anna said. "He was hit on the head with a bowling ball. In which case, our note is his only clue to his real identity."

"And a confusing clue it would be," Collie said. "My name. A brief request that he call me as soon as possible. And let's not forget the part where it fell from the sky."

"He probably doesn't have amnesia, though," Anna said.

"Be great if he did, "Collie said. "He'd call. We'd get together with him. We'd hit him on the head with another bowling ball. Problem solved."

"Except Ian would still be dead."

"Oh, yeah," Collie said. "You've always got to rain on my parades."

"Do you think Sam actually sent that note to Rowan?" Anna asked.

"I don't know. He can't be our guy, because he can't pop in behind someone. I mean, if he and Nadia are both telling the truth about what he does, anyway. So I have to assume he wasn't involved with Rowan's kidnapping or whatever, either."

"So why not send the note to Rowan."

"It would be easy for Sam. That's provided he actually can send stuff to a person he's never met in a place he's never been. But, I have to say, we've always gotten our cheques."

Complications leapt to Anna's mind, as they often did. Was there a way to shield someone from teleporters? If someone who could work the magic system had Rowan, maybe it wasn't even possible to send him a note. But whether he got it and couldn't respond or didn't get it at all, the results were all the same from her end. No point bringing it up.

"Your chariot awaits," Anna said instead, pointing at the water massage pods. Three of them were open and unoccupied.

"Fantastic," Collie said. "While I'm in there, could you call Jake Dysenko and set up a meeting? His number's on the index card."

"Col..." Anna said, aware that her voice had taken on the faintest hint of a whine. "Come on. You know I hate cold calling."

"Don't think of it as calling a stranger," Collie said, already walking toward the massage tables. "Think of if as calling a potential murderer."

Anna took Collie's purse and found a bench near the entrance to the submarine rides.

She had to go through about ten index cards before finding the right one. It wasn't much of an organizational system, really, when you had things on a million index cards. No better than writing stuff on napkins.

"Okay," she told herself, setting Collie's cell phone on her lap. She was damned if she was going to use her own minutes. She placed the index card with the name and number beside the phone and tapped the digits in with the phone resting on her knee. It was easier than holding the phone in her hand and having to go back and forth.

Once it started ringing, she picked it up and toyed with the idea of saying "wrong number." In fact, she could tell Collie she'd dialed wrong and make Collie phone the guy. Except Collie would ask why, in the space of ten minutes, she couldn't have tried redialing. And Anna would say, "Hrm," or something equally clever, and Collie would probably elbow her again.

Better to just get it over with.

Four rings. Five. Six. Anna had once worked with a woman

who'd insisted there was a set number of polite rings, after which you were being rude and ought to hang up.

Seven. Eight. At which point, she had every right to just hang up and tell Collie, sorry. He wasn't ho –

"Yeah?"

Crap.

"Uh... hi."

And she had nothing. Because she'd spent the whole time the phone was ringing thinking about chickening out, rather than about what she was going to say.

"My name is Anna Gareau," she offered. It was one thing of which she was reasonably sure. "I'm a..." Oh, the hell with it. "I'm a private investigator."

"Huh. Really."

He said it not as if he didn't believe her, but as if he was often mildly amused by the things the world came up with, and this was a fine example.

"Really," Anna said. Not that she was licensed or trained or anything, but she was investigating something and she wasn't doing it for the police. What else were you supposed to call that kind of thing?

"Well, that's pretty cool, Anna Gareau," the voice said. It occurred to Anna for the first time that she wasn't sure whether this was Jake Dysenko or not. She wasn't even a hundred percent sure she had the right number.

"Not really," Anna said. "I'm looking for Jake Dysenko."

"This is him."

Jake Dysenko sounded young, laid-back, and possibly just the tiniest bit stoned.

"Okay. Good. I... would like to talk with you about a case I'm working on. Would it be possible for us to meet?"

"Anything's possible."

A lot of people said that, but this kid sounded as if he honestly meant it. And why not?

"Could we meet with you this evening?"

"Who's this we?"

"My associate and myself."

Now she sounded like a Mafioso. Smooth.

"Hey, *yeah*. I've got to get me some associates."

"Uh-huh," Anna said. "Would I be correct in thinking you're somewhere in the University area?"

"Little rich for my blood, dude. Look south. Look waaaaaay south. But if you buy my dinner, I'll meet you wherever you want."

If he really was smoking up as they talked, she didn't have to wonder what he might like to eat. Anna wondered if the Embassy, or Eric, would ask for itemized expense lists. She could picture herself stapling receipts for Twinkies and beer to the invoice.

It would probably be better if they bought him real food.

She picked a greasy spoon that she liked and Collie barely tolerated. There had to be some benefit to being the one making the awkward phone call. Jake agreed to meet them there at six PM. Provided Jake knew what time it was and what city he was in, they had a date.

"Looking forward to it," Jake told her. "Dinner with a PI and an associate. Cool beans."

"As you say," Anna said. "Cool beans."

She hung up and looked at the blank screen of Collie's phone. Why couldn't there just be a button labelled "press this button when you don't want to waste power but you still want to leave the phone sort of on so that you can take calls"? Probably because the label would be larger than the phone.

She pressed something that might have been correct, or might have activated a hotline to the Kremlin, and tossed the phone into Collie's purse, along with the index card.

Until Collie's ten minutes were up, there was little to do but watch people doing whatever people did. Kids in the food court were jumping up to split the arched fountains with their hands and watch the water fall straight down on either side. Tourists were taking each other's pictures by the replica of the Santa Maria, as if it were the real thing or even something seaworthy. And as if the damned Santa Maria had been a good thing anyhow.

Anna was watching model helicopters somewhere in the distance when Collie startled her by saying, "It's like a whole new back. And new shoulders."

Collie was standing beside the bench moving her shoulders with a slightly surprised expression.

"They don't hurt," Collie elaborated. "It doesn't hurt when I do this."

"Then do that?" Anna tried. The joke didn't work as well that way. Actually, it didn't work at all. "I talked to someone who claimed to be Jake Dysenko. We're meeting him at that place you don't like, by that Italian place you liked that shut down. Across from the vet clinic that was too good for me."

Collie nodded and Anna felt the tug of a bond. She couldn't think of anyone else who would have had the first clue what she was talking about.

"Jake has shitty taste," Collie observed.

"He's stoned," Anna said, more than willing to let Jake be blamed for the choice of venue.

"Well, at least he'll be tractable. What time are we meeting him?"

Anna told her, and Collie looked at her watch.

"We have time to go home first. Or to the office. Do we want to do that?"

Anna considered that.

"There's tracking down that Robin Hampshire chick, I guess. For all we know, Robin Hampshire is in the phone book," Anna pointed out. "It's not as if we looked. At some point, someone will ask if we ever looked, and we'll say no, and then we will look, and her name will be there, and we'll seem stupid."

"Whereas, if we look now, her name will not be there," Collie said. "So, if we really want to find her, we shouldn't look in the phone book until doing so would humiliate us." Off Anna's glare she said, "What? Reality goes out of its way to make us seem stupid. It's physics."

It wasn't the least plausible thing Anna had ever heard presented as physics, so she didn't argue.

"We could ask every freak in town whether our teleporters are accurately representing their abilities," she suggested.

"Why lie about it?" Collie said, "Considering that we could easily do what you just said?"

"Ah, but what if the murderer figured we'd figure they wouldn't lie, so we wouldn't check, and so they *did* lie? Or what if they figured we might check, but they took the risk because they had no real choice because otherwise we'd know they could have done it, thereby making them our prime suspect?"

Collie frowned at her.

"Do you believe any of that, or are you just messing with me for fun?"

"Mostly that last thing," Anna admitted. "We could check with Kieran."

Collie grinned.

"He will love that. Have you still got my phone?"

"I have no idea what you're talking about," Anna said. "I have my own phone. Why would I have used yours?"

"Because you are cheap and punitive. Do you have it?"

"It's in your purse," Anna said.

Not wanting to hear another half-conversation with Kieran, she wandered while Collie talked. Not far, just over to the glass wall of the water park. The park was huge, with waterslides at one end and a wave pool at the other. She'd seen some poor girl vomit into the wave pool once. The water had caught it and spread it out within seconds, as if the lumpy green stuff had never existed. Anna, who had been in the pool at the time, had tried her hardest not to think about what else might be in the water, or exactly how much chlorine it took to make puke vanish as if it had been hit by a phaser.

"Okay," Collie said from just below Anna's left shoulder. Again, Anna hadn't heard her approach, in spite of the fact that Collie's boots had high heels. "Kieran says, to the best of his knowledge, everything the teleporters have told us is accurate. He also agrees with your assessment of Jake Dysenko."

"I have an assessment of Jake Dysenko?" Anna asked.

"You suggested he had a connoisseur's appreciation for kind bud."

Anna smiled.

"Sounds as if Kieran's in a better mood."

Collie leaned forward to rest her arms on the glass.

"Weirdly, yes. I think he likes Jake. Also, he says, if Robin Hampshire's name ever shows up in any phone book, anywhere, he will eat said phone book."

"So naturally you're going to fake that with the whatchama. Adobe something-a-whosis."

"Yeah, eventually. I'll need the right paper. It's complicated. And we're a little busy at the moment."

"Are we?" Anna said. "I didn't think busy people stood around staring at the water park."

"We need to check the company bank account and see if the Embassy put money in there already."

"Because we're both buying new vehicles?"

Collie grinned.

"Maybe. But mainly this is because I want to spend some of that money on the case, only I don't think we'll get reimbursed for what I'm about to do if we expense it after the fact."

Anna looked between her feet for the stomach she'd felt drop out of her.

"Col?" she asked, piteously.

"It'll be fun," Collie said. Her tone suggested that comment was supposed to be reassuring, which showed how poorly she understood Anna sometimes. "C'mon. We need to go back to the office."

She pulled her phone out and used it as they hiked back to the car, weaving through the bank's voicemail system as adeptly as she steered around teenagers and tourists. As they reached the car, Collie smiled broadly and slapped the roof with an open hand.

"Goddamn."

Anna looked at her and Collie named a figure. It was ridiculous. It reminded Anna of high school, her algebra teacher rambling on about imaginary numbers.

"They're nuts," she diagnosed. Collie laughed.

"Who cares? This is going to be excellent."

Collie's enthusiasm for her mysterious idea showed in her driving. She upgraded her performance from driving like a maniac to driving like a maniac on PCP. Anna grabbed the "oh shit" handle and considered taking up a religion so she could pray. Collie bitched a little about traffic, since they were edging toward rush hour, and she had plenty to say about where overpasses and bridges ought to be built, but she sounded madly cheerful through all of it.

She barrelled into an empty spot across from the office at a speed best suited to the final lap of the Indy 500 and bolted from the car so quickly that Anna thought she must have dragged her seatbelt with her. Anna followed at a dignified pace and was unsurprised to find that Collie was already upstairs by the time she opened the building's front door.

"'Kay," Collie said the moment Anna had entered the office. Anna pushed the door shut and went to her desk.

"'Kay," she said, cautiously.

"'Member how Nadia said we'd find Robin when Robin

decided to find us?"

"'Member whole words?" Anna asked. "We have time for them."

Collie waved that aside.

"Yeah, yeah. Did you ever read that Spenser book – I forget which one – but he was looking for someone, so he put signs up all over town. 'Where's Warren?' Or was it 'Who's Warren?' Anyway, it was really embarrassing for someone, so they eventually came to tell him who Warren was. Or to beat him up or something. But either way, it worked."

Anna stared at her.

"Where to begin," she said. "Your brilliant idea is from some detective book you read? Your brilliant idea is only half-formed, if that, because you can't properly remember the book, or even which book it was? Or the idea itself, which, if I understand it correctly, is very likely to get us beat up? Where 'beat up' equals 'wished into the cornfield.'"

"Ha!" Collie said. "*Now* who's referencing their reading material?"

"Are you seriously –" Anna stopped. "No. You know what? I drop all charges related to you getting your ideas from mass-market paperbacks. Let's focus on the idea itself. You are planning to piss this woman off until she comes looking for us. Right?"

"Exactly," Collie said. She was beaming. Anna made a note of that for the commitment hearing. She was beaming when she said it, Your Honour.

"And you think this will be like putting flamingos on someone's lawn for their fortieth birthday? She'll be sort of mad, but in the end she'll appreciate the joke, and we'll all have a good laugh about it?"

"Ooh," Collie said. "Flamingos. I like it. Except maybe frogs or something instead. Those companies have frogs, don't they? Hoppy Birthday?"

"And then she said Hoppy Birthday, Your Honour," Anna said. Collie squinted at her, obviously confused.

"What?"

"Has it occurred to you that maybe the Embassy hasn't kicked Robin Hampshire out of town because they are not capable of doing so? Exactly what level of scary do you think that makes her?"

Collie smiled. It wasn't her broad, crazy smile. It was more thoughtful and, somehow, even more disturbing.

"I don't know," she said. "What have we actually seen the Embassy do? Maybe they're all talk. Wouldn't that be neat?"

"Neat," Anna echoed, not believing her ears.

"I'd be so impressed," Collie said. "I love a long con."

"I think it's a long shot, Col. I think instead they are badass. And she is badder. And you want to make her mad."

"Pshaw," Collie said. "Sure, she might get mad. But she'll be curious, too. Who are we? What do we want? What makes us think — this is the main thing — what makes us think we can get away with this? Following your logic, if the Embassy is scary and she's scarier and we're deliberately provoking her, doesn't that make us the scariest of all?"

"It makes you the scariest of all," Anna allowed. "From my perspective."

"It'll be fine," Collie said. "I swear. If she shows up with magical guns blazing, I'll tell her it was my idea."

There were a million things wrong with that offer, but Anna was too tired to get into any of them.

"Do what you want. At least we'll have interesting obituaries."

Collie was already ignoring her, plundering her desk drawers for something vital to her insane scheme.

Anna wandered over to the kitchenette and plugged the kettle in for tea. She'd pointed out to Collie at least seventy billion times that they could just heat water in the microwave, but Collie had some kind of problem with that and the kettle remained firmly in place. Anna supposed, if she brought the subject up again, Collie would tell her they couldn't use the microwave because it was haunted.

As she waited for the water to boil, Anna gave the microwave two soft taps with her fingers Two bits. The door stayed closed, but the light came on.

"Loose wire," she muttered.

"Hey... Deepti... it's Colette. How're you doing?"

Anna always found it interesting when Collie worked her contacts in Edmonton because, as near as Anna could tell, Collie wasn't actually friends with any of them. Occasionally they'd have lunch or dinner with one of Collie's old pals from school, or someone Collie used to work with, but by and large Collie seemed to have shoved her past behind an oaken door and bolted the thing shut.

Unless she needed something. Then it was old home week.

"I want to throw money at you, Deepti. *That's* why I'm calling."

Yep. Another heartwarming relationship. Anna turned to face Collie, carefully sitting on the edge of the microwave cart. There was a fair amount of stuff weighing the cart down, but Anna was willing to bet she could still tip it.

"I'm sending you an email right now," Collie said. She was, too. She was typing as she spoke. Anna would never understand how that was possible. "It'll have my requirements, and the budget. The thing about this job — and the budget takes this into account — is that it's ASA freakin' P. Huge rush on this. I mean, if you have time and if you want the job. You can let me know once you see the email."

A soft whistle, and steam hitting her between the shoulder blades, told Anna her water was ready. She turned, reluctantly, and made her tea in record time. She hated to miss even a second of Collie's facial expressions when Collie was doing this kind of thing.

"This is all about getting someone's attention," Collie said. "One specific person. When you see the budget you'll think that's crazy, but my client can afford it. Oh, and any paper trails should lead to me. Buy everything in my name, not your agency's."

That was followed by about a minute of Collie pressing her lips together and staring at the ceiling, obviously fighting the urge to interrupt. Even though she already knew what Deepti was going to say and even though it was pointless and even though people were forever wasting Collie's precious time telling her things that did not matter and things she already knew. All of which was frustrating as hell.

Anna lifted her mug and smiled behind it.

"I know," Collie said, the words exploding from her. "I'm sorry. I just – it doesn't matter if you get your agency discount. Honestly. The client won't care."

Collie actually set the phone down on her desk after that. She didn't hang up, just gently placed the phone in front of her. Anna could hear a faint buzzing that was probably Deepti asking what the hell Colette was doing and whether she was likely to go to jail for even discussing it.

When the buzzing stopped, Collie picked up the phone again.

"For your purposes, I'm the client," Collie said. "Liability, if it ever became applicable, would rest with me. I'll sign something to that effect if you – okay. Fine. I just said I would, didn't I? If you decide to take the job, I'll fax a statement to you."

Collie held the phone away from her ear, but didn't go so far as to set it down again, which told Anna she was planning to jump in the first time Deepti took a breath.

"Just read the email. Okay? Read it, and then call me and ask any other questions you have, and tell me if you want the job. Also, you're going to think you need more background or context or whatever, but you'll have to let that go, because either you don't need it or I don't have it."

Collie rolled her eyes.

"Deepti! Hand. Written. Liability. Statement. I will fax it to you and then mail you the original."

Anna sipped tea and frowned as the bag bumped against her lip. She hated the way that felt. The bag was always cold, somehow, no matter how hot the tea was, and felt like a dead thing in the water.

Deciding she hated that feeling more than she hated weak tea, she pulled the bag out and tossed it into the adorable little garbage can Collie had picked up at some home décor place. The point in making a garbage can adorable was lost on Anna, but Collie had assured her it gave the office some class.

Anna had said it was a damned good thing that something did.

"Chickie, you are going to be thanking me for this. It will be the easiest money you ever made. You might not even need to bring in a designer."

Interesting. Some women did not like being called "Chickie", even when another women was doing it. Apparently Deepti was objecting, either to that or to Collie's claims, because Collie was rolling her eyes again.

"Just get back to me fast, okay? Like, tonight. You'll have to call me on my cell, though, because I have a dinner engagement."

Anna snorted. That was probably the first time in history that anyone had ever claimed to have a "dinner engagement" at the restaurant to which they were headed.

Collie rattled off her cell number, then slammed her phone down on her desk.

"Jesu, Joy of Man's Desiring," she cussed. "They used to have to throw that girl out of exams because she would stay until the last second, just checking her answers over and over again. She's nuts."

"Wow," Anna said. "What's that thing from philosophy, about the donkey who can't pick a haystack to eat from because they're both equally good?"

"Buridan's ass," Collie said. "Though I believe it was a dog in Buridan's original version. And I think he got the idea from Aristotle."

"Dogs don't eat hay," Anna said. "Anyway, I can't pick a response to your comment about this Deepti chick being nuts. They're all equally incredulous. So, just... wow."

"I'll have to fax my liability statement after dinner," Collie said. "I can write it on the way, if you don't mind driving."

"Your car?" Anna asked.

"Or we can go up and down the street seeing if anyone left their keys in their vehicle," Collie said. "Is there a problem with my car?"

"Not if you're Billy Barty," Anna said.

Collie laughed.

"You should have said Verne Troyer. This is why the kids of today do not relate to you. We should really head if we're meeting the pothead at six."

"I can't believe you're taking a tone about someone's pot use," Anna said, setting her mug down. She should probably take the mug down the hall to the washroom to rinse it out, but Anna figured having a tea stained mug wouldn't be the death of her. Especially considering her current line of work.

"I wouldn't toke and drive," Collie said. Anna smiled.

"I think we can assume he doesn't drive."

"No, he just sends stuff – people – through space-time, breaking all known laws of physics. Well, except for those quarks that teleport. But that's totally subatomic. The point is, would you want someone who thinks Spongebob Squarepants is hilarious teleporting you around?"

"I would not want anyone doing it," Anna said. "Ever. Just so we're clear, if it should come up. And, god help us both, it might."

"I think I'd like to try it," Collie said. "I mean, lots of people seem to have been teleported without any problems. Nadia has, obviously. And I think Kieran has. And... I don't know. Probably all kinds of people we know. And Captain Kirk."

"It made his hair go all funny," Anna said. "In the long term."

Collie grinned.

"Is that what happened to his hair? It explains so much. C'mon."

She headed for the door and Anna followed, grabbing her jacket along the way. She was about to remind Collie to take some paper for the liability statement, but that would have meant assuming that Collie had no paper in her purse. A ridiculous assumption. Collie probably had a sawmill in her purse.

After a prolonged struggle with the seat controls, Anna managed to squeeze herself into the driver's seat of Collie's car. Collie wrote while Anna contorted, carefully looking away from anything that might cause her to make an ill-advised show of amusement.

"You could have done that in the office," Anna said, moving the rear view mirror. "It's not as if this guy is likely to be on time."

"People never are," Collie agreed. "Teleporters are probably the worst for that. Mandr – Ian was."

So now they were censoring themselves in private. Nice. Was Collie just trying to train herself out of using the nickname around other people? Or did she honestly think Ian was watching them from their microwave?

"I always figured Mandrake was late because he was a lousy teleporter," Anna said. "He kept going places he didn't intend to go. The rest of them are probably punctual. They'd never run out of gas or get stuck behind a train."

"I know," Collie said, "but the closer you are to an appointment, the more likely you are to be late. Studies have shown this. You get cocky and you figure you have all the time in the world, so you delay your departure. These guys probably figure they don't have to pause their video game or get off the toilet or whatever until five seconds before they have to be someplace, and then they remember they have to feed the cat and then they're late. It's basic psychology."

"I'm now going to assume every teleporter I meet has just gotten off the toilet and not washed their hands. Thanks very much."

"You're welcome."

"Also," Anna said, "Who the hell conducts studies of what makes people late for appointments? There are a lot of people in the world who need to be — what's that bullshit word you use? Repurpose. They need to be repurposed into building dams in developing countries."

"Dams aren't always a solution," Collie said absently. She was writing again. Anna decided to leave her to it.

The diner was a converted gas station, and Anna knew that was trite. She would have known it anyway, but Collie belaboured the point anytime they got near a place with bay doors opening on a patio, or an old gas pump sitting in the corner of the lot. What Collie seemed unable to grasp was that Anna didn't care. When she was a kid, her father would sometimes take her to a highway truck stop to split a giant cinnamon bun, and she'd loved that. She still loved the feel of those places, even when it was contrived.

"How are we going to recognize our guy?" Collie asked as they entered the diner and pulled up in front of the deliberately stained "Please Wait to be Seated" sign.

"If he just appears in the middle of the restaurant," Anna offered, "we'll be pretty sure it's him."

"And assuming he's not an idiot?" Collie asked sweetly.

"He's looking for a statuesque brunette and a redheaded dwarf," Anna said.

"That may work," Collie said thoughtfully, "but wouldn't it have been better to say, 'an annoying brunette who's wearing a whole bottle of ketchup'?"

Before Collie could follow that up with a ketchup attack, a skinny shadow of a guy slipped into the space between them and the sign.

"Tall brunette," he said. "Cute redhead."

Collie smirked. Anna sighed.

"Five seconds, Jake," she said, "and already you are in trouble with me."

"Huh?"

"You don't need to repeat everything you hear," Anna told him. Jake still looked puzzled, but he shrugged it off.

"I got us a table," he said. Anna glanced at Collie and mouthed "early" at her. Collie just kept smirking.

"That's not attractive," Anna informed her as they sat.

"On me it's cute," Collie said. She offered Jake a hand. "I'm Colette."

"Jake," he told her, shaking her hand.

Jake was a sketchy guy. Not that he seemed like a crook – it was more that he looked poorly drawn. He was all quick, harsh lines and unfinished motions. His hair was a washed-out brownish black and his eyebrows looked like impatient squiggles. Even the bright spots in his eyes looked like the white of the paper showing through.

"I'm Anna," Anna said, not offering a hand. "But you knew that."

"The PI," Jake said. He looked as though his amusement with that idea had not worn off.

"Sure," Anna said. "How long were you waiting for us?"

"I dunno. It's no big, though. I was early. Traffic was really good."

Collie raised her eyebrows.

"Was it now?"

"It's always good for me, man." Jake said. "I take the high road."

Collie laughed.

"That is what I hear."

Jake laughed back.

"I don't even wanna know who you've been talking to."

"Good," Collie said amiably. "I never reveal my sources."

She picked up the ketchup bottle and stared at the name brand label on the front, dulled by hundreds of damp wipes.

"It's not, you know," she said. "They buy cheap stuff and just pour it in the bottles."

"Yeah, but it's a glass bottle," Jake said. "You can hardly even get them anymore. Ketchup always tastes better when it comes out of a glass bottle."

Anna dropped her menu enough to see Jake's face on the other side.

"You're finding your way back into my good books," she told him. Jake grinned.

"I'm just gonna smile and say 'okay,' because your reactions to the stuff I do? Seem pretty random. So... okay."

"They're completely random," Collie said, setting the ketchup bottle down. "She's nuts."

On that note, they scanned the menus and gave their orders to a short woman who had a blonde ponytail sticking through her ballcap and a profound disinterest showing through her smile. She called Jake "Honey" and it would have been perfect, all of it, if the waitress had only been chewing gum. Anna was tempted to offer her a stick or two.

"So," Collie said. "Jake. I don't know if Anna told you, but we are investigating Ian McLaren's death. I should say, his murder."

Jake's eyes widened.

"Anna did not tell me *that*."

Collie glanced at Anna. Anna shrugged. Collie looked at Jake again.

"I'm sorry, if he was a friend of yours, and if you didn't know."

"Actually," Anna said, "we're also sorry if he was a friend of yours and if you did know."

"Well, of course we are," Collie said, "but what I meant, obviously, was that I'm sorry about breaking the news that way. As Anna well knows."

"Woah," Jake said. "Hey. Do you guys need to take this outside?"

"No," Collie told him. "This is nothing. Did you... were you aware of what happened to Ian?"

"Yeah, I heard," Jake said. "I figured that was why I got the supper invite. Not that the ladies don't ask me out all the time."

Collie smiled. It looked genuine.

"I'm sure they do," she said. "How well did you know Ian?"

"Aw," Jake said. "That fuckin' guy. I mostly stayed away from him."

Anna was running her fingers over her cutlery roll-up, the feel of the abrasive paper napkin reminding her of every restaurant, ever, until she'd moved away from home.

"I can't think of anyone else," she said, "who has even once referred to Ian as 'that fuckin' guy.'"

"I'm not making myself look too good, am I?" Jake said. What he looked, at that moment, was sheepish. "I didn't, like, hate him. He was just an idiot."

"This is going to sound like the kind of thing an idiot would ask," Collie said, "but what exactly do you mean by 'idiot'?"

Jake shrugged. His shoulder blades were so long and thin that Anna could see them moving against the booth. Unless he sat up perfectly straight, Jake probably never felt a chair along his back.

"He didn't think a whole lot about implications and shit. Like, I'm gonna do this, which is gonna make this happen, which is gonna lead to this shit down here, which is maybe not something I want to do. Everyone said he was accident prone, right, popping into the middle of the 401 or whatever…"

"Coquihalla," Anna murmured. Jake glanced at her.

"I said whatever. Point is, he was always going places he supposedly didn't intend to go. But you know, you gotta focus some to make this shit happen. On some level. Right?"

Anna would, at first glance, have pegged Jake at around nineteen. The same as Rowan. Now she was thinking older. Not a lot, but twenty-four or five, maybe. Those particular five years, for most people, came packed with experience. Only the first five years could compare.

"We don't really know," Collie said, her tone oddly gentle. "We're not even sure exactly what you do. Is it the same as what Ian did?"

"Wellllll," Jake drawled. "Technique. Mandrake pretty well left from wherever and showed up wherever, if you get me. I'm a little different. I've gotta go to the can."

Anna expected him to get up and do just that, but he stayed in his seat and looked at Collie as if he expected her to respond. Was he waiting for permission?

"If I say you can do that," Collie said, apparently thinking along the same lines, "are you gonna be like that Steve Martin character and make a straining face and then say 'thank you'? Because that would not be okay."

Jake shook his head.

"What?"

"If you have to go," Anna said, "then go. By which we mean, the washrooms are over there."

"I know where they are," Jake said. "That's how I got here. I told you. I have to use the can."

Collie stared at him so hard, it was as if she were trying to see through him.

"*What*?"

"It's just easier in, like, a universal sense. All public washrooms are the same. If I go into one, I go into all of them. Doesn't matter where I come out."

"Are you telling us," Anna said, "that you travel by going into a public washroom somewhere and then coming out in a different washroom somewhere else?"

"It's really all the same washroom," Jake said. "The doors are the same. The toilet paper holders are the same. The urinal pucks –"

"Okay, we're with you," Collie said. "So, you just think, 'I want to come out of that washroom' and it happens?'"

"See, you're not with me. But you totally could be. Do you wanna go somewhere? I'm not sayin' dine and dash, but after?"

"If it involves breaking the laws of physics, and me and Colette sneaking into the men's washroom in a crowded diner, I think I'll pass," Anna said. "Just walk us through this. How did you get here tonight?"

"I went to the gas station on the corner by my place," Jake said. "They've got a real nice standard-issue crap shack. No strange colours, no fancy sinks, just the basics. I mean, I can do it even if the washroom's a little off, but it's not as smooth a ride."

"What if the washroom were fancy?" Collie asked. "I mean, I'm assuming you can't use a home one because they're all kind of different, but what about a restaurant that has, like, a really nice restroom? Wood doors? Marble counters?"

"Well, first off," Jake said, "the men's can usually isn't half as nice as the ladies'. So you see less of that. But if it's too high-end, it doesn't work. It's gotta be consistent with the usual."

"So you went into a gas station washroom and thought, 'I want to come out in the diner'?"

The waitress did a drive-by with their drinks, dropping them without looking back. She got the right beverages to everyone, though. Clearly a veteran. If she'd heard any of their conversation, she didn't show it.

Jake traced the condensation on the outside of his Coke glass with one spindly finger.

"Nah. I think, okay, I'm heading to the diner. And then I leave the can and I'm wherever's closest. Like, tonight, it was here, which was awesome. But sometimes it's a block away or whatever. See, I figure most washrooms — like, public ones — are part of the great cosmic washroom. But some aren't. So I can't go to those."

"Can you use a ladies' washroom?" Collie asked. Jake shrugged and sipped his Coke.

"Yeah, sure. But it's kind of an ass pain because ladies' washrooms have, like potpourri or little wicker chairs and shit. Not always, but enough times. It's like, if I'm in an apartment building and all the bathrooms are the same, I can jump around, but I feel queasy because there's personal stuff all over. The more personal a washroom is, the more it's..."

"Not part of the cosmic washroom?" Anna asked. Jake smiled.

"Now you're with me."

"I beg you not to accuse me of that," Anna said, and knew the moment it left her mouth that it was uncalled for. She shut her eyes for moment, took a breath, and opened them. "I'm sorry. That was rude. I'm just finding this a little hard to wrap my head around."

"How the hell did you find out you could do this?" Collie asked. Jake grinned.

"I used to get lost when I was a kid."

Collie laughed, then coughed as her coffee went down the wrong pipe. Anna patted her back. Collie waved her off.

"I'm good. I... fucking bet you got lost. How did you get home?"

"I tried going back into the washroom, and it worked."

"Did you tell your parents?" Collie asked.

"Yeah," Jake said. "They took away my copy of *The Lion,*

The Witch and the Wardrobe. I never liked that book anyway. Stupid lion."

"So they didn't believe you?" Collie asked. Anna looked at her.

"What do you think?" she asked.

"Well," Collie said, "he could have showed them." She looked at Jake. "Right? You said you could take people with you."

"I can now," Jake said. "I couldn't when I was little. Like I said, about Mandrake, you've gotta exercise some kind of will. Same thing here. The first time, I really wanted to see my grandma in Toronto."

"What did your parents do when you kept talking about it?" Collie asked. Jake laughed. He had a hissing, rattling laugh. Not unpleasant, but maybe not healthy.

"Why would I have talked about it, dude? I'd already lost a book I didn't like. The next one might've been a book I did like. Oh, you know what I really dug? Those Three Investigators books. Those were sweet. One of the kids had an uncle or something who had a junkyard, and there was a mobile home or something in the yard, all covered in trash so you couldn't even see it. Except they had secret entrances and they used it for their headquarters. They could go in one entrance and come out another one. So, if washrooms are all one washroom — that one washroom is my secret headquarters. Which makes sense when you consider that going to the can is the great human equalizer."

"I thought that was death," Collie said.

"Okay, yeah," Jake allowed, "but you go to the can way more often than you die. Animals do it, too."

"Even educated fleas do it," Collie said. Jake grinned.

"Do they?"

"I'll have to look that up," Collie deadpanned.

"Now I see how you became so interested in detectives," Anna said. Jake laughed again.

"See, you *are* with me. You just don't want to admit it."

"I read those books," Anna admitted. It wasn't the admission Jake wanted, but it would have to do. "About Ian… you're saying he went to all those places… what? Accidentally on purpose?"

"Mandrake was a geek. Don't get me wrong here. I have nothing against the geeky. But the Embassy was all, 'Mandrake, Mandrake, you're our man. If you can't do it, no one can.' Real fucking affirming, you know? I'm guessing that never happened to him before. So, they said, 'Do this nasty shit no other teleporter in town will touch,' and he said, 'How high?' He was the best in town, aside from The Hampshire, but they still would've made him their right hand guy – no joke intended, there – even if he'd sucked completely. Because he loved them. He would've done anything for them."

It took Anna a second to process all of that, mainly because she was stuck on the "no joke intended" comment. Then she realized it was about Mandrake's glowing hand. Because that was a joke. Hell, it was the town joke. And Mandrake was a geek.

"Another fun fact about Mandrake," Jake said. "That cryptic bullshit way of talking he had? Actual bullshit. He thought it made him seem mysterious. I was standing behind him in the Safeway customer service line one time and he was completely coherent. See, this is how geeky he was. Talking like a parrot on acid is what he thought was cool. And you can bet the Embassy encouraged him. The less sense Mandrake made, the better they liked it."

"I heard you worked for the Embassy sometimes," Collie said. She didn't sound as if she were having fun anymore.

"Yeah, I do freelance sometimes. But I think about what I'm doing. I take maybe one job in ten. That's why my subconscious doesn't send me into the middle of a freeway at rush hour."

And with that comment, the conversation slammed on its brakes. Anna wouldn't have been surprised to see skid marks on the table. She looked at Collie, who was looking at the table, and at Jake, who was looking at both of them, and at Collie again, and then at the waitress who had, thank God, arrived with their meals.

"You need anything else here?" the waitress asked. "HP Sauce? Vinegar?"

A do-over on the last five minutes? They probably didn't have that.

"Vinegar," Anna said. "Thanks."

"Otherwise," Collie put in, "we're good."

Lies and damned lies.

Anna didn't wait for the vinegar to start on her fries, which had skins on and looked as though they'd been cut by a human being. They were hot, too. Almost too hot to touch.

"That's why forks were invented," Collie said, as Anna dropped a fry for the second time.

"I think forks predate fries," Anna said, but even as she said it she reconsidered. Did they? She knew nothing about history.

Jake was putting away a tuna melt with no evident concern about the mood at the table. Anna wondered if that "I don't care if I've offended you" attitude, which Lydia and Ian had shared as well, came from being able to leave in a heartbeat. Did they live their whole lives as if they were in an online chat room, so free of consequences that they couldn't resist being rude?

Not that Jake had, exactly, been rude. They'd asked what he thought and he'd told them. It wasn't Jake's fault they didn't like it.

"I guess we didn't know Mandrake very well," Collie said. She was picking her food apart, a bad habit she was just starting to drop. It came back in force when she was anxious or upset. "I mean, Ian."

"William Burroughs said you should watch whose money you pick up," Jake said.

"Oh," Collie said casually. "On that topic, do think that William Burroughs subconsciously intended to shoot his wife in the head?"

Jake stared at her, seemingly at a loss.

"Since accidents don't happen," Collie clarified.

"That many accidents?" Jake said. "To one guy? And you really, really have to want to go somewhere to make this thing work. Doesn't matter if you're me or Mandrake or Nadia or The Hampshire. Sam, he might be different, but the rest of us have to want it. That's how it goes."

The waitress dropped the vinegar on the table and ran. No, "How is everything?" No, "Is there anything else I can get for you?" Anna was starting to love her.

"Okay," Collie said. "Here you are suggesting that Ian had some subconscious death wish, but everyone else we've talked to says he had a panic button of some kind that took him out of dangerous situations."

"I never said he wasn't conflicted," Jake said. "Yeah, he was maybe a little precog. He knew something was going to happen maybe one, two seconds ahead and he got out of Dodge. But he always said he didn't *know* know, you know?"

"I do not know," Collie said.

"It wasn't like he thought, oops, piano falling, gotta split. He just went."

"Where did he go?" Anna asked. Jake looked at her. There was tuna on his lower lip. It was stuck on with melted cheese and, unless she or Collie said something, it was likely to be there awhile.

"He never said," Jake said. "At first, I figured it must be some safe place, like maybe his bedroom from when he was a kid. But then, sometimes he'd come back with mud on his clothes, or scratched up or something, so I dunno. Probably, knowing Mandrake, he went someplace that was less dangerous, right, but not undangerous."

"Couldn't you have followed him?" Collie asked. "Not that you'd want to, but the way you do things... can't you think, 'follow that teleporter' and come out of a bathroom somewhere near him?"

"Naw. I have to choose a location. I know a person kind of is a location, but I need a real, like, place."

"Somewhere you've been before?" Anna asked.

"No. I could go to the Taj Mahal if I wanted. Except I don't know what the bathrooms are like, so maybe not. But places I've heard of, yeah. If they're specific. I couldn't go to your house, right, because I don't know anything about it except it's your house and, for all I know, you live in, like, a yurt. But if you gave me an address, I could go. I'd probably wind up at a 7-Eleven or something."

"It's a two-storey yurt," Collie said, almost smiling. "Hot and cold running mare's milk."

"Sounds nice," Jake said. He probably meant it.

"Look," Anna said, "Jake... everyone is a little puzzled about how Man – Ian died."

"Really?" Jake swallowed the last of his tuna melt. "I heard he was shot."

"In the back of the head," Anna said. "So he didn't see it coming. But he wouldn't see a falling piano coming either, would he?"

"Hmm. True. Not that an actual piano ever came at him, but I hear what you're saying."

"People are saying someone teleported in behind him and shot him," Collie said. "But wouldn't he have felt that coming and... popped out of the way?"

"Apparently not," Jake said. "I'm not trying to act like I think this is a joke, because I think it's pretty serious and, besides, there's a difference between thinking a guy is a dweeb and thinking he should get shot in the head. But what can I say? It doesn't make total sense, okay, but someone shot him in the head. Therefore, it was possible to shoot him in the head."

"*Quot erat duckonstrandum,*" Collie muttered. Jake didn't even blink. He was probably used to people saying weird things in, or around, Latin.

"It's probably that teleportation isn't Newtonian," Jake said. "Or, I guess... Einsteinian? You know how people ask, how far is Calgary, and we're all, 'three hours,' because that's how long it takes to drive there on the usual road at the usual speed, so we say that like it's a constant? Like it's the same as what goes up comes down? But it's not really three hours, right, because you could take a plane. Or that bullet train, if they ever put that in. Or you could walk. My thing is kind of like that."

Collie looked at her hand, which was holding a small, almost unrecognizable piece of her chicken burger. She let it fall to the plate and looked at it sadly, as if wishing it were an apple.

"'Splain," she said. Jake smiled.

"It's not three hours to Calgary for me. It's not, like, three seconds, either. It's no time. Time isn't involved. I take the time out of the space-time continuum. Oh! Hey! That's good. I should put that on my business cards. If I had any."

Anna stared at him. He really did seem proud of himself, as if he'd thought of something intensely clever. Hi! I mess with the only thing holding this planet together and keeping all of us on its surface! Here's my card!

She wondered if, someday, physics would get tired of all the scofflaws and just quit.

"So," Collie said, "if Ian got a two-second warning on impending doom, that wouldn't apply to a teleporter coming in behind him."

"But it would," Anna said, "because there's the two seconds before the teleporter leaves. Also, it takes time for a trigger to be pulled. Not two seconds, but not *no* time."

"He couldn't have dodged a bullet from right behind him," Jake said. "He wasn't that fast. And he wouldn't jump until something actually happened, not just when someone was thinking about doing something. If he, like, took off when someone was thinking about punching him in the face, I would never have finished a conversation with him. He would've been gone."

Collie's eyes narrowed.

"You know we're investigating his murder, right? Trying to figure out who might have wanted him dead?"

Jake's eyes, just to be contrary, widened.

"Hey, come on...you know it wasn't me, because he didn't get shot outside a washroom."

"Fair enough," Anna told him, "but if not you, who? Who do you think would have wanted to kill him?"

"You say that like I'm your best suspect," Jake said. "He annoyed me, okay? You guys seem pretty annoyed with me and I'm not dead yet. Don't you have someone who had a grudge against him for real?"

"We're asking you," Anna said.

Jake thought about it. While he did, Anna finished her fries. Still warm, and not even that soggy from the vinegar. Life didn't get much better.

"You should talk to the Embassy," he said finally. "Whatever happened, it was probably because of something they asked him to do."

"Do you know a guy named Rowan Bell?" Anna asked. Jake brought a skinny leg up and hugged it to his chest, foot planted on the seat in front of him. Watching him was like watching a subtle contortionist working a very small crowd.

"Yeah. Yeah. Why do I know that name?"

"Still asking you," Collie pointed out.

"Was he that kid Mandrake was always hanging around with? What was up with that? I would've thought they were dating or something, except the kid was way too hot for him."

"We're not sure what was up with that," Anna admitted. "I

think they were just friends. I take it no one else has asked you about Rowan?"

"Why would they?" Jake asked. He looked at Collie. "Seriously, why would they? Am I supposed to know something?"

Collie smiled.

"No."

"We're asking this of everyone," Anna explained.

"Do you think that kid killed him?"

"I don't think he teleports," Anna said.

Jake made a face.

"No — not because... you don't think some teleporter did this, like, spontaneously, because he was sick of Mandrake's fuckin' orange hand, do you? I thought it was probably that someone hired someone to shoot him. For whatever reason."

"Having to do with the Embassy," Collie said.

"Whatever he stepped in," Jake said, "It's their fault he stepped in it. Guaranteed."

"And how do you think Rowan fits into that?" Collie asked.

"I don't know. Maybe the kid was working for someone who had it in for them. Or maybe... oh, hey — maybe Mandrake was, like, a bodyguard or something. He could have whisked the kid out of harm's way. He could take people with him."

"To the Coquihalla," Anna said. Jake grinned.

"See, that's another reason why I figure his subconscious was doing it on purpose. He never pulled that shit when he had a passenger. Never."

"Maybe he never misfired at all," Collie said. "Maybe he made it up to get attention."

"Lady," Jake said, sitting up straight and pointing a fork at her, "now you are talking my language."

"Blows your subconscious guilt theory out of the water," Collie said. Jake scowled and put the fork down.

"Whatever."

"Whatever," Anna said. "Exactly. What this boils down to is

that none of us think Ian got shot because he was Ian. He got shot because of something he did for the Embassy, or maybe something to do with Rowan Bell. Or both. Okay? So discussing Ian's character or supposed lack thereof is not productive. Jake, can you think of any *specific* reason why someone would have shot Ian?"

Jake shook his head. Anna waited, but he didn't say anything. Just looked at her.

"Fine," Anna said. "Leaving aside motive, Jake, who do you think could have popped in behind Ian? Obviously you couldn't, unless you're lying to us."

"I'm not. You'll have to ask around about me, I guess. I dunno. Nadia could have. Not Sam. He just does milk chutes."

Anna almost laughed. Where would a kid his age have even heard of milk chutes? You never could tell what people were going to come out with.

"And The Hampshire could have done it. But why are you all about the locals? If you think about it, man, you can get a teleporter from anywhere."

"I guess one can," Anna said. "In theory. I wouldn't know where to look. But, in this case, the teleporter probably had to be local because the house was warded. The only teleporters on the guest list were from Edmonton."

Jake's eyebrows rose, cutting into his forehead.

"I was on the guest list?"

Anna nodded.

"You. Nadia. Sam."

Jake grinned.

"Not The Hampshire?"

Anna shook her head.

"No. What can you tell us about Robin Hampshire?"

Jake was gnawing on a dill pickle. He set it down.

"Why? If you're only interested in people who were on that, uh, guest list, that leaves her out. Right? Not right?"

"Right," Collie said, "provided the ward was unbreakable. Though I don't know if anything's really unbreakable."

Jake giggled.

"Ask Anton Cagel. Or Mandrake's hand."

"What?" Collie said.

"This Cagel guy, around 1930, created a book of unbreakable spells. That's what happened to Mandrake's hand. Cagel's Spell of Luminescent Flesh. But I don't think Cagel wrote any wards. Who warded it?"

"Doris... something," Collie said. "We never caught a last name."

"Ooh, Doris," Jake said. "Shit, it might as well have been Cageled."

"She's that good?" Anna asked.

"She's as good as she thinks she is," Jake said. Collie laughed.

"Aw," Jake said, "I didn't mean that the way it sounded. She knows what she can do, okay? If she says a place is locked up tight, that's good enough for me."

"Yeah," Collie said. "Not for us. But we're looking into it. In the meantime, we really do want to talk to Robin Hampshire."

"No you don't," Jake advised. "I hear she lit a guy on fire once because he bumped into her on the sidewalk."

Oh, terrific. This was the person they were going out of their way to annoy. Anna was tempted to ask Jake for the first bathroom out of town.

"She carried a lighter and hair spray in case of emergencies?" Collie asked. Jake looked exasperated.

"Dude. No. She did it with her mind."

He decorated that statement by waving his fingers in their direction. Collie swatted them away.

"Ridiculous. It's bad PR. The Embassy would run her out of town."

"You'd think so," Jake agreed.

Bad PR. Collie was probably just trying to look at it from

the Embassy's point of view, in which killing someone was one thing — one forgivable thing — but drawing unwanted attention to them was quite another. Still, there was something ghoulish about even being *able* to look at things from the Embassy's point of view.

Possibly more disturbing was Jake's easy acceptance of Collie's reasoning.

"So why is she still here?" Collie asked. "Assuming she is. Because everyone talks as if she's unquestionably in town, and yet no one seems to have the first clue as to how to get in touch with her."

Jake's response was to grab the little flip chart dessert menu and start tossing sheets over. Collie tilted her head.

"I like dessert as much as the next person..." she said.

"I'm the next person," Anna reminded her.

"I like dessert at least ten times more than the next person," Collie amended, "but can I ask what the hell you're doing?"

"Getting dessert," Jake said. "We're gonna be here awhile."

Collie seemed to see the wisdom in that, because she tugged at the corner of the chart until it was centred between her and Jake.

"People make these for a living," she said softly as she gave a speculative eye to an improbably tall piece of carrot cake. "These little displays. They're called menu rolls. I know a graphic designer who just does menus and stuff."

She sounded wistful, as if writing puns about onion blossoms, day after day, were looking more appealing all the time.

Anna caught a glimpse of an apple crisp as the sheets flew back and forth and decided it was something a diner would probably do well. Not that they likely had anything to do with their desserts, apart from signing for them when they arrived at the back door, and maybe popping them in the microwave. She kept seeing the same six desserts on menus all over town.

Their pro of a waitress swooped in for their plates and

dessert orders mere seconds after they'd all decided. She didn't ask how their meals had been. The food was gone. What more did she need to know?

Anna planned to tip huge.

"Okay," Collie said. "Food's coming. Talk."

"First thing," Jake said, "you have to let go of this whole 'in town, not in town' dichotomy. That's like... if I made a big deal over whether you lived in your kitchen or your living room. You live in your house. Yurt. Whatever."

"So you're saying she, what, eats in Edmonton and sleeps in Halifax?" Collie asked. Jake shrugged.

"I hear she has a house in Salem. She thinks it's funny."

"Salem, Massachusetts?" Anna asked. Jake looked at her.

"Is there another one?"

"At least one," Collie said. "In Oregon."

"Oh," Jake said. "It's got to be Massachusetts, anyway. It wouldn't be funny otherwise, right?"

"I guess," Collie said. She didn't sound convinced, though Anna couldn't say whether she thought it would be funny regardless, or whether it just wasn't funny at all. "So we could look her up in the Salem phone book?"

"Hey, hey," Jake said, raising his hands. "Just a rumour. Don't know if it's true."

"Do you know The Hamp —" Collie stopped. "Robin. Robin Hampshire. Jesus. Why do you call her that?"

"Dunno," Jake said. "I was gonna say it's because she's, like a force of nature. But hurricanes have names. I guess it's because she kind of looms for me, you know? In my head, she's a hundred feet tall. She keeps telling the Embassy to fuck themselves and she is still around."

"But didn't you say around was relative?" Collie asked. "I mean, I was at an outdoor Spirit of the West concert once where the crowd was moshing and the bouncers kept throwing them out and it was ridiculous because they'd get thrown out one side of the stage area and come back in the other. Wouldn't it be the same thing if you threw a teleporter out of town?"

"You were at a Spirit of the West concert?" Anna inquired.

"The crowd was moshing?" Jake asked. Collie glared at them.

"My point," she said, "is that there's not really any getting rid of people who can just blink and be in another city, and then wiggle their noses and come back."

"Yeah," Jake said. "Well. That's what other teleporters are for. They can eliminate that kind of problem."

They all chewed on that thought for a few long, silent moments, until their desserts arrived and gave them something else on which to chew.

"So," Collie said after her first tiny bite of cheesecake. "The Embassy hires teleporters to... um... eliminate other teleporters?"

"And to be clear," Anna said, "we're talking about killing them, yes? Not just scaring them off?"

Jake nodded.

"I've never done it. But the offer's been on the table."

"For Mandrake?" Anna asked, startled.

"No. I wouldn't have been a good choice. Washrooms, remember? They called me when they wanted to get rid of a chick who hung out at a mall. And another time, there was a guy who worked in a convenience store. Don't ask me why they wanted him gone. Anyway, yeah. I said, thanks but no thanks and it's always gonna be no thanks so take me off your list. And I guess they did because they never called me for that kind of thing, after those two times."

It came to Anna with dizzying suddenness that they were in a restaurant, a public place, and here they were nattering about contract killings and, well, teleportation, for that matter. She wasn't sure which was worse. She sat up straight and tried to see what her fellow diners were doing. Were they engaged in their own conversations, or sitting perfectly still and canting slightly toward them?

Jake laughed, more quietly than usual.

"Are you doing what I think you're doing?"

"Incredibly stupid question," Collie said. "How is she supposed to know what you think she's doing?"

"It doesn't matter," Jake said to Anna, ignoring Collie. He kept his voice low. "Seriously. I talk about this shit all the time. People think I'm going on about a D&D game or something. If they're really staring, I start talking about dice rolls."

"I'd say it's a little late to be locking the barn doors," Collie said. "Regardless."

"I could save versus unwelcome attention," Jake offered. He raised his voice a little. "I have, like, a plus five for that."

"Oookay," Collie said. Anna said nothing. She didn't know what Jake was talking about, but wasn't about to provoke an explanation.

"So," Anna said, "getting back to Robin Hampshire."

"Yeah," Jake said. "I don't know. I don't know how she gets away with going her own way, and I'm not about to ask her."

"We asked if you knew her," Anna reminded him.

"Right," Jake said. "I do, kind of. I mean, I've met her."

Collie sat up so quickly, the booth's vinyl squeaked a little beneath her.

"You can describe her?"

"Sure," Jake said. "Real tall – not a hundred feet, okay, but maybe, like five-ten or something. Like you," he added, gesturing at Anna. "And she's totally hot."

"Hair colour?" Anna asked. Her voice came out as tired as she felt. "Eye colour? Distinguishing marks?"

"Aside from hotness?" Collie put in.

"Dark hair. Curly, kind of like yours. Only not red."

"Yeah," Collie said. "Got that from the dark hair part. Eyes?"

"Dunno," Jake said. "Blue, maybe? Green?"

Collie laughed. Anna looked at her.

"I miss something?"

"Aw, it's this old Frantics bit," Collie said. "This guy's writing a poem about his ex-girlfriend's eyes and he can't remember what colour they were and finally he's all, 'Okay, I remember her tits.'"

"Huh," Anna said. She looked at Jake. "Anything special about her tits?"

Beside her, Collie spat out whipped cream.

"Jesus," she said, still laughing. "Warn me."

"Standard-issue," Jake said. "I liked 'em."

"So we're looking for a tall brunette with curly hair," Anna said, "and no distinguishing marks that you can recall."

"Oh – one thing. She has the fakest English accent ever. It, like, roams the countryside."

"Noted," Anna said. "Thank you."

"No big," Jake said.

"How did you meet her?" Collie asked.

"Um, two times," Jake said. "Actually. I was at Verflücht and Kieran pointed her out to me."

"Kieran Gavril?" Anna asked.

"Yeah," Jake said. "Instead of all those other Kierans you probably know. Okay, so, that. I went up and said hi, hear you're a 'porter, me too, we should totally take a long romantic walk on a beach in Australia and have dinner in Paris."

"How'd that work out for you?" Collie asked.

"She cut my balls off," Jake said. "Oh – not literally. I guess I should be happy she didn't. Anyway, yeah. She said, 'I've heard of you. You're the Potty-porta.'"

For those last few words, Jake had switched into an English accent that bobbed and weaved through the words, never quite landing on any earthly location. Collie grinned in response.

"I guess you can't take anything too hard when someone says it like that."

Jake grinned back at her.

"I found it hot. I have a whole problem where this lady is concerned. Okay, right, so I met her again one time at Myth. Just bumped into her."

"Except not literally," Collie said. "Or you'd be on fire."

Jake pointed a finger at her.

"Good one. Yeah. No. I just saw her there and I nodded and she rolled her eyes and looked away."

"You find that hot, too?" Anna asked.

"Hell, yeah."

"You like bad girls," Collie said, in a commiserative tone. Anna resisted the urge to step on her foot.

"Just this one," Jake said. "Doesn't matter. It's not like she gave me her phone number."

"Doesn't seem like she gives anyone her phone number," Anna said.

"Though it may be in the Salem book," Collie said. Which had to be a joke, because there was no way Collie could seriously think this chick would be listed.

"So you're around town a lot," Anna said. "In the sense that I'm in my living room a lot."

"Yeah," Jake said. "Why?"

"You haven't seen her except those two times?"

"Nah, but I hear about her because people bug me, you know? Saw your girlfriend. So I know she's around. I don't think she goes to Verflücht anymore."

Anna nodded. She could commiserate with that, because she didn't go to that club anymore either. They'd been dicks about Colette, for one thing, not letting her in until Anna and Kieran had insisted. For another, a room full of magical types made Anna only slightly less nervous than a room full of angry cobras. It was no place she wanted to hang out, have a drink and bust a move. If the kids were even busting moves these days.

"About how old is she?" Collie said, suddenly.

"I dunno," Jake said. "About your age, I guess."

"Are you saying that like a guy who goes up to a clerk in a lingerie store and says 'she's about your size'?" Collie asked. "Or is she really about my age?"

"I don't want to get into guessing your age," Jake said. "Okay? Let me rephrase that. She's not twenty. I don't think she's forty. So she's in there. Probably in the middle of there. Maybe a little on the high side."

"Thirty-five-ish?" Anna asked. Jake shrugged.

"Considering how much she likes me, you think I was gonna ask?"

"She might have liked it better than a knee-jerk proposition," Collie said. Jake blinked at her.

"What?"

"Yeah," Collie said. "Of course you don't know what I'm talking about. Shocker. Never mind."

Anna patted Collie's arm. Collie looked at her.

"Yes?"

"Good girl," Anna said. "Not doing the shocker gesture."

Collie pulled her arm away.

"Jake," she said, "do you think Robin could get into a house that Doris had warded?"

Jake shook his head.

"Not even The Hampshire," he said.

"Wow," Collie said. "What did Doris do to earn her reputation?"

Jake shrugged.

"She knows her job, and she never screws up."

"That is pretty impressive," Anna said. "Regardless of the profession."

"You don't see a lot of it at the Sev," Collie agreed.

Anna snorted.

"I'd love to see you working at the Sev. You wouldn't last ten minutes."

"I get that impression myself," Jake said.

Collie set her fork down with what looked like finality.

"And once again, something that has nothing to do with me becomes all about me. Are we done here?"

"Done talking about how you're kind of a princess?" Jake asked. "Or done in general?"

"Both," Collie said. She didn't open her mouth all the way to say it.

"I think we're done," Anna said.

"I'm done eating," Jake said. "Which is what I came for."

"Then we're done," Collie confirmed. "Jake, thank you for your candour."

So much nicer than "thank you for being a jackass and prick." This was why Anna was not the one in PR.

"Thanks for the food," Jake said, already halfway out of the booth. Collie watched, silently, as Jake left through the restaurant's front door.

"Looking for a gas station," she surmised. Anna realized she was still holding her own fork. She set it down on her plate.

"Or going to Whyte to get piss-drunk."

"And then teleport home from a gas station washroom," Collie put in. At that moment, their excellent waitress dropped the bill at Anna's elbow and spirited herself away, not giving a damn what they were talking about. Anna pulled out her wallet as Collie went on. "One hopes he does that unseen, or only in front of other drunk people."

"Since it hasn't made the papers," Anna said, picking up the bill, "we can assume he's discreet."

"Maybe," Collie said, sounding as if she could think of several other possibilities and wasn't inclined to name them. "You thinking fifteen? Fast, got the orders right, but nothing special?"

Anna shook her head.

"No chitchat. She didn't push the specials. I'm going over twenty."

Collie was pulling her coat on. Anna was surprised she'd waited until the end of the meal. Usually she was shivering by the time the main course had arrived.

"Most people like chitchat," Collie said.

"Then most people can tip for it," Anna responded. Move the decimal point, times two, round up, add a little bit. "Are we keeping the receipt?"

"It's an expense," Collie said, then smiled. "Hey, it's an expense. Tip whatever you want."

ONCE THEY WERE IN THE CAR, Anna tucked the receipt into Collie's purse.

"It's in the outside pocket," she said.

Collie nodded. She was looking over her shoulder, watching two rusting and dented '70s boats as they fought to be first out of the lot. Anna wondered if they'd elevate the battle to a shoving match. Neither had much to lose.

"So we can report it all legal-like," Anna said. "Along with our income from the Embassy."

"Okay," Collie said. Her throat was slightly constricted from the way her head was turned.

"Since I assume we're reporting that income," Anna added.

"It's sitting in our business account," Collie pointed out. "I think we had better."

"But it's a stupid amount, right? Aren't we going to look kind of Al Capone-y?"

The scrap pile had finally cleared. Collie backed out quickly, heedless of what other frustrated driver might be doing the same thing. Anna held her breath until they were on the road. Collie, oblivious to their good fortune in being alive, rattled on happily.

"I wouldn't call reporting income Al Capone-y. Ish? Anyway, that's the last thing I'd call it. We're planning to be completely honest. I'll probably cheat less than my mom does."

Anna glanced at Collie, startled that she'd actually mentioned her mother. Probably best not to make a big deal of it. Anna looked out the window.

"We're gonna get audited," she said. Collie shrugged.

"Let 'em. We made that money fair and sq – aw, Jesus. Can you get that?"

Anna fished Collie's phone from her purse, hit talk, and handed Collie the phone.

"Yello," Collie said, switching lanes and earning honks by it. A deliberate and pathetic display. Look what a *bad* driver I am when I have to talk on the phone at the same time. *You* should have answered it.

"Oh, that's great! When – uh-huh... yeah... what frequency is that?" Collie put the phone against her shoulder. "Anna, I need 105.3 FM."

That kind of thing was easier said than done on Collie's archaic car stereo. It didn't have automatic tracking or a digital display. It barely had buttons. Anna popped the tape and plowed through static and clutter until she found The Hip hovering at an appropriate spot on the dial. Collie lifted the phone.

"'Twist My Arm'?" she inquired, then rolled her eyes. "That's what they're playing. I don't have a very good dial display. Is this the right station?"

Collie put the phone to her shoulder again.

"She's checking."

Anna nodded, mouthing the staccato chant of the song. *Martyrs don't do much for me...* She hadn't even known she knew the words, but she guessed she'd heard them enough times.

"Okay, thanks." Collie said. "I'll call you back when it's over."

"What, the song?" Anna asked as Collie handed her the phone. Collie grinned.

"Nope. Our ad."

"Our what now?"

"Our ad. We've got a live spot coming up. They're going to ask Robin Hampshire to call the office."

Oh, for fuck's sake.

"For fuck's sake," Anna said. "You're happy about this? We're going to have every yahoo in town call —"

"Shh!"

"I don't want to give anyone the wrong idea," the announcer said, tromping over the last few bars of music. "We don't normally do missing person announcements here. But this one's a paid advertisement. Apparently someone wants to find a Ms. Robin Hampshire pretty badly, so, Robin, if you're out there — or if you know where Robin can be found — give a call to..."

Anna crossed her arms on the dash and put her head down as their office number was read aloud. Twice.

"Oh, get over it," Collie laughed once the ad was over. "Haven't you been saying it was stupid to have a landline in the office anyway? Once we get Robin, we can get a new number, or get a business cell."

"Every yahoo in town," Anna repeated, not lifting her head. She heard the beeps of Collie dialling her phone.

"Hey — just heard it. Definite grabber. How many slots do we have?"

Anna sat up and looked out the side window while Collie got the details from her media buyer. The words "share" and "sister station" and "voice tracking" were flying around. Anna wished she could duck them. As if she wouldn't get stuck going through their voice mail for hours because of Collie's stupid idea. And that, actually, was the best scenario she could picture.

"Hee."

From the corner of her eye, Anna could see Collie tossing the phone into her purse.

"I love this."

"I can tell that you do," Anna said. "Personally, I —"

"Could get that?" Collie asked, inclining her head toward the purse in which her phone was, once again, making an annoying noise. Anna pulled the phone out, turned it on, and handed it to Collie.

"Commence speaking," Collie told it. Anna was always surprised that more people didn't hang up on her. "Oh. Hey. What's up?"

There wasn't much Anna could get from Collie's side of the conversation. About a half-minute in, Collie started heading in a different direction from that of their home, so that likely had something to do with whatever she was talking about. And whoever she was talking about it with.

Collie turned the phone off and tossed it back into her purse.

"Interesting," she said.

"What was?" Anna asked. Collie smiled.

"If you'd wanted to know, you could have answered the damn phone."

Anna nodded.

"Later tonight, maybe we can fill your car with sand and fight over plastic dumptrucks."

"Okay," Collie said. "But we're going to Mandrake's place first."

Anna stared at her.

"Because... we're stumped, and you're hoping someone will return to the scene of the crime?"

"Because Kieran's got a three-ring circus out there trying to break the ward and he thought we might want to see it."

Anna noticed the tape was still sticking out of the stereo, the radio still playing. She pushed the tape back in. Brian Molko started bitching about something, and Anna turned it down. She wasn't in the mood.

"What's the point in seeing it? Has someone managed to get in?"

Collie shrugged.

"He didn't say. He just said it was worth seeing."

"You think it's an actual circus?" Anna asked. "Maybe they break wards as a sideline."

"Nothing would surprise me," Collie said.

Seconds later, parked across the street from Matt and Mandrake's house, Collie shook her head and slapped the steering wheel.

"Spoke too soon," she admitted.

"Uh-huh."

Around twenty people were gathered in front of the house, some waving wands, some chanting, some kneeling before fires and coloured sand. Some were dressed in street clothes, others in robes and one, mostly hidden by the others, didn't seem to be wearing a damned thing. One was dancing with lottery tickets in his hands and an elephant mask on his face.

None of that, however, was what had made Collie retract her statement. The surprise was in the form of Doris, who was sitting atop what looked to be a tennis ref's chair, taunting and jeering, a box of Laura Secord mints carefully balanced on her knees.

"Where the fuck did she get that chair?" Collie asked, just loud enough for Anna to hear.

"They're practising for the buskers' fair," someone said from beside Anna's elbow. "I asked."

She looked down to see a girl, maybe eight years old, feet planted on either side of her hot pink bike.

"Yeah?" Anna asked. "Free show?"

"It's not very good," the girl said. She cranked the front wheel around, jumped to stand on the pedals, and rolled away.

"I beg to differ," Collie said. "This is the best thing I've seen in weeks."

"Shake it!" Doris yelled to the elephant-masked dancer. "Shake it, baby! Lemme see your trunk!"

"It's pretty good," Anna conceded. They crossed the street to the foot of Doris' chair.

"How's it going?" Collie asked, tilting her head far back.

"Great. Weeeeeell... not so great for *them*..." Doris said, gesturing toward the masses at her feet. "Losers."

"No breakthroughs yet?" Collie asked. Doris made a face.

"You think they'd all still be here? They're getting nowhere. Someone made a big window in the wall a few hours ago. So fine — walk through it. You can't. A window is not a door."

"Knowing that could save me some facial lacerations," Collie said. "Thanks."

"Anytime," Doris said expansively. She opened the box of chocolates on her lap, carefully sliding the ribbon to one side. She took out a single square and put the ribbon back on the box before putting the chocolate in her mouth. "Mmmmph."

"I had an aunt who used to love those," Collie said. "She — holy shit! Was that thunder?"

Anna had always had trouble with low noises. Was it thunder, or a trainyard, or combines crashing in the demolition derby at the fair? At least two of the three were seasonal, which usually helped to narrow things down.

"It's cold for thunder," Anna said. The temperature had dropped while they were in the restaurant and was now, at her best guess, just above zero.

"That was thunder," Doris said. She was looking at the sky anxiously, probably wondering whether she ought to climb down from her perch. The magicians around them had stopped chanting and sanding and were also looking at the sky, which was as clear as it had been that afternoon.

"It can happen," Collie said. She was distracted, looking to the west. "Middle of winter, even. It's just really rare."

A flash of lightning, somewhere to the west, and Collie started to count.

"One one thousand. Two one thousand. Three one thousand."

Doris' eyes widened and she scrambled to the ground, chocolates safely tucked under one arm.

"Okay, people, I'm calling it," she told the magicians.

"Nine one thousand, ten one thousand —"

And thunder, again.

"What is that?" a woman in a dark blue robe asked. "Two miles?"

"Does that include distance up, or just out?" the elephant dancer asked.

"I don't know," Collie said. "I heard under ten was bad."

"I heard under thirty was bad."

This came from a white-haired man who was carrying a set of bongos and hastily shoving his bare feet into a pair of green Crocs. Aside from the third eye tattooed on his forehead, he might have been an elementary school music teacher. It was possible that, by day, and with the help of some pancake makeup, he even was.

"We can discuss this in the car," Anna said, grabbing Collie's arm. "Come on."

"You need a lift, Doris?" Collie asked. Doris shook her head. She was stuffing the chocolate box under her windbreaker.

"Naw, I'm covered. Thanks."

There was more lightning seconds after they'd shut the car doors, and Collie squinted through the windshield.

"No rain," she said.

"No clouds," Anna said. "Can we go home before frogs start falling?"

"Huh," Collie said, pulling away from the curb with a cautious eye on the scattering magicians. "Frogs. You know they find them encased in stone sometimes, still alive?"

"And that's all for this week's episode," Anna said, "of *Ripley's Believe It Or Not!*"

Collie grinned.

"I always loved that name. Believe it or not. See if I care. It's not my problem."

As they drove, Anna watched the houses, the faces at the

windows. People were pulling their curtains back and looking upwards, puzzled. At least she wasn't alone in thinking this was strange.

COLLIE KEPT ON MOVING once she was inside, barely pausing at the door to shed her coat and purse before running to drawers and shelves to bring out every candle and match she could find. Anna glanced at the closet shelf to be certain the flashlight was still there, then took a seat in the living room and watched Collie scurry around.

"Appreciate the help," Collie said from the kitchen.

"Least I could do," Anna told her. "The power's not out, you know."

"Wait for it. The last time we had lightning this late in the year, the power was out all night."

Anna could have pointed out that it wasn't windy or raining or sleeting or doing anything that, outside of a direct lightning strike on a power station, would likely cause a rerun of that event... but she didn't think rational conversation about the weather was in line with Collie's mood.

"Unless someone finds a way into that house, Robin's starting to look like our only possibility," Anna said, raising her voice to reach the kitchen. They kept candles in the kitchen? Anna couldn't recall ever having seen one there.

"I guess someone could be lying about their abilities," Collie said, "but it seems as if the other teleporters would know. Just from working together."

"Yeah. Are we having a film shoot or something if the power goes out? Because I think we'll be able to see by the fifty candles you've got now."

So much for not getting rational about Collie's behaviour. To Anna's relief, Collie decided to sit down across from the couch.

"I'm just antsy," she said. "I don't know why."

"It's probably the weather."

The thin, sharp-edged voice came from the archway into the dining area. Anna looked up and saw a tall woman, maybe even as tall as Anna was, with long, dark brown curls and an aura of smugness. She was dressed casually in jeans and a red silk shirt, leaning against one wall of the archway as if she were a guest who'd just gone into the kitchen for a glass of water.

Apparently they had located the Hampshire.

"First our office," Collie said distinctly, "and now our house. Anna, how much do you suppose it costs to hire Doris?"

Robin Hampshire snorted.

"I doubt you could. It's not the amount. It's the currency."

"I think what she's saying is that you could have knocked," Anna said. Robin stopped leaning against the wall and stood straight, the top of her head nearly touching the top of the archway. Her hair was taller than Anna's.

"I suppose this *was* rude. Next time I'll put your names all over the radio instead of quietly breaking into your home."

"Yeah," Collie said. "Okay, fair enough. Sorry about that, but we needed to talk with you. Can I get you anything? Tea? Coffee?"

"I'm fine, thanks," Robin said.

Collie nodded.

"If you hang on a sec, I can call my agency and have the ads stopped."

"No need," Robin said. She smiled, and it was nasty, like an ape bearing its teeth. "Oddly, lightning has struck all the local transmission towers."

"You made lightning strike transmission towers? You can do that?" Collie's eyes were huge. Robin tilted her head in a way she probably thought was cute.

"Did I say that? I said it was odd. Strange weather and a

strange coincidence. Now. What the fuck did you want to see me about?"

Anna could hear it now, what Jake had said about the accent. It was British, but every kind of British, with no regard for the unique sound of one place or another. Not that Anna was an expert, but it was really all the worse if even she could tell.

"I'm surprised you haven't guessed," Collie said. "Have you heard about Ian McLaren?"

Robin's eyebrows shot up until they'd disappeared under a fringe of curls.

"Mandrake? Yes. I heard someone shot him. What does this have to do with me?"

"We're trying to find out who did it," Collie said. "For the Embassy."

Robin shook her head. She looked as if a headache had suddenly come on.

"I should have known, if my evening was being ruined, that they were somehow the cause of it. They told you to investigate me, did they? That's bloody typical, isn't it?"

"I wouldn't know," Collie said evenly, "but it doesn't matter, because they didn't say anything about you. We're just talking to every teleporter in town."

Now Robin looked amused. Her moods changed so quickly, so effortlessly, that it seemed unlikely any of them were real.

"For God's sake, why? You can't be enjoying it. They're a load of ineffectual cowards."

Collie gave Robin a half smile that was as fake as Robin's sudden good humour.

"Jake mentioned you were fond of him. We're talking to teleporters because there's a good chance Mandrake was killed by a local teleporter."

Robin waved a hand at one of the chairs in the dining nook and it obediently slid forward until it was at her side. She sat down, legs wide, and put her hands on her knees.

"And? I'm not one of the local crowd. I don't even live here, really."

"We're just being thorough," Collie said. "Did you know Mandrake?"

"Certainly. I knew enough to avoid him. He was a disaster area. Though I can't imagine, actually, why someone would kill him. Was it one of his ridiculous accidents, do you suppose?"

Collie glanced at Anna, as if Anna must somehow know what to say to the crazy witch lady. Anna leaned forward and put her elbows on her knees.

"A friend of Mandrake's was kidnapped that evening. We think it was connected."

Robin looked from Anna to Collie, something that looked like genuine amusement playing with the corners of her mouth.

"Not Rowan Bell?"

"You've heard of him?" Collie asked. Robin laughed. It was too sharp and too full at once, like a handbell choir.

"I kidnapped him," she said.

Collie was halfway out of her chair before she seemed to think better of it and lowered herself to her seat again.

"You... what?"

"I kidnapped him. It was the night Mandrake was shot. Just outside the house, in fact, before he could get to the door. I'm familiar with Doris' wards. Don't tell me the Embassy is interested in that — I can't imagine why they would be."

"And Rowan is where the fuck now?" Collie inquired sweetly. Robin smiled, just as sweetly.

"Not a clue. Honestly, the Embassy didn't ask about Rowan, did they?"

"I think they're mostly interested in what happened to Mandrake," Anna said. "But I'm not an expert on what interests them. Would you mind telling us why you kidnapped a nineteen-year-old kid outside his friend's house?"

Robin shrugged.

"I was hired to do it. Is that all you wanted?"

"Noooo," Collie said. "We would also like to know the whereabouts of Rowan Bell."

"I told you," Robin protested. "I don't know. I handed him over to my client and that was that. Why do you care, anyhow, if you were just hired about Mandrake?"

"We have other interests," Anna said. Robin looked at her, puzzled, then her dark blue eyes went almost black.

"Oh, balls," she said. "You're not working for Eric Quinlan, are you? I'd heard he was working with someone local, but I thought it would be mundanes. God. It is you, isn't it? Excuse me."

She stood. Anna stood, for no reason that made any sense. What was she going to do, stop the lightning-summoning teleporter? Maybe tackle her to keep her from leaving?

"I'm just getting a drink," Robin said, holding up a hand. "I assume you have beer."

"Fridge," Collie said. "Third shelf."

Robin returned after a moment with three bottle of Keith's and set two of them on the coffee table. Collie picked one up. Anna let the other sit, slowly dripping onto the wood.

"Okay, here's what," Robin said, then took a swig of beer and wiped her mouth with the back of her hand. "Tell Mr. Quinlan that I took Rowan Bell on behalf of Varanus, who hired me to do this one thing for them. It was a contract. I am not on their payroll. Possibly you should write this down."

"Mind like a steel trap," Collie said, tapping her beer bottle against her temple. "Keep going."

"I ported with him to Fort McMurray. I offered to take him anywhere they liked, but they said I might be traced and they'd rather fly him out from Fort Mac. I said fine, I'll port him to the Edmonton airport, but they said Quinlan would check flights from there as soon as he found out Rowan was missing. I assume they picked Fort McMurray because it has quite a busy airport, what with all the oil workers flying in and out. They must have thought Quinlan wouldn't think to check it. Really, honestly, are you getting this? I don't want him to have any questions for me."

"I think he will anyway," Anna said. She had a feeling Eric's questions would start with, "what the hell kind of person kidnaps a teenager and dumps him with evil magicians in Fort McMurray?" She opted not to share that thought with Robin.

"Well," Robin said after another swig of beer, "that won't do. What else might he want to know? I don't know who hired me — it was done over the phone. I left him in the Fort McMurray bus station. They paid me with money that was hidden in a public place. Quite untraceable. And, as I say, I don't know where they took Rowan from there. So there is no need for Mr. Quinlan to speak with me."

Collie swallowed beer, set the bottle down, and smiled.

"Wow. He really scares the pants off you."

Far from taking the bait, Robin simply nodded.

"Of course. I can't believe you're willing to work for him. Mind you, you're a mundane," she said, waving her bottle at Collie, "and you're close enough to it." A wave of the bottle at Anna. "He's not likely to decide he doesn't believe in you. Still, it's not as if he only does his number on magical types."

"What are you talking about?" Collie asked. "Seriously. I've talked to him a few times and he's a little brusque, but he's a hell of a lot less creepy than... I don't know... you. So what's the problem?"

Robin was surprised enough that she let her beer arm drop, spilling a few drops on the hardwood before she pulled the bottle to her mouth again.

"You really don't know," she said.

"We're as dumb as you think we are," Collie said. "What. The. Hell?"

Robin frowned.

"Let me tell you a story. It's about a woman named Clara who'd been around for a long, long time. She was working for Varanus – she was on their payroll – and she was in a bit of a tussle with Eric Quinlan, who had broken into a Varanus facility. She tried to bite his neck, as she was apt to do, and he couldn't quite believe that, because he doesn't believe in vampires. Nor dragons, famously. So he looked at her and she just faded away. Vanished."

"He made her disappear?" Collie said. Robin laughed. It was not as merry as the handbells, but it sounded more genuine.

"From what I hear, he told people afterward that she was never really there. She was a projection – some kind of complicated visual effect, all done with mirrors and technology. I'm told," Robin said, leaning forward, "that someone went back the next day and found projectors in place."

"So she was an illusion all along?" Anna asked. Robin looked at her.

"I – suppose she was," Robin said. Her voice sounded odd. Not smug at all. "Look. I don't like to be bothered, so please do tell him everything I've told you. And give my love to the Embassy. I'm sure they miss me."

"How can we rea –"

Collie stopped, because Robin was gone. No fancy lights or sound effects, just gone. The beer bottle, nowhere in sight, had apparently gone with her.

"– ch you," Collie said. "Provided we don't want to take out more radio ads. Once they've repaired the towers. Which will probably take a few days, I would imagine. Wouldn't you think? Anna? Am I babbling?"

"You could do it at the Olympics, if it ever became an event. You want me to put that other beer in the fridge?"

Collie shook her head.

"No. I'll get around to it."

In the meantime, she stared at the bottle as if it had been

smack talking her all night. Anna was about to remove it anyway, if only to keep Collie's glare from curdling it, when Collie said, "Would you buy any of that for a dollar?"

Anna shrugged.

"Not that I trust that woman, but I actually don't see why she'd lie about this stuff."

"But that would mean someone killed Mandrake for the purpose of killing Mandrake."

"Yeah," Anna said. "It would."

"That's nuts, right? Who would do that?"

It wasn't fair to the beer to let it sit there without anyone drinking it. Anna snagged the bottle and opened it.

"Who knows? He worked for the Embassy. He saw the wrong thing or he rubbed someone the wrong way. Or he was rude to the paperboy and the kid finally got tired of it. I hear people shoot each other for no damned reason these days."

"Might have been an argument over James Brown's height," Collie agreed. "I don't know. I don't know what to think."

A noise came from the top of the stairs, something that rattled falling in the hall. Anna looked at Collie, who was holding her beer to the side of her face.

"I have a people-breaking-into-my-house headache," she said. "It's like a tension headache, only it's triggered by people breaking into my *fucking house!*"

This last was directed up the stairs, presumably in the hope that whoever was up there would fear her rage and leave.

"Why don't I go check on that?" Anna asked.

"Yeah, why not?" Collie said. "It's not as if we're investigating a teleporting murderer."

"Who could as easily have come down here," Anna pointed out. She stood, set her bottle on the table, and went up the stairs, squinting into the darkness. Why their townhouse had been designed without a light switch at the bottom of the stairs was beyond her.

It was like playing hide and go seek as a kid, moving slowly in the dark, half-excited and half-terrified by the prospect of finding someone. Hoping she'd know, somehow, that someone was behind a door before she opened it. It had always knocked her legs out from under her to open a door and unexpectedly find someone there, not leaping out or trying to scare her, just standing quietly and calmly in what should have been empty space.

As she neared the top of the stairs, she held her breath and listened for someone else's breathing.

Nothing. None of the "someone's watching" feeling. Just silence and the dark.

At the top, she turned, looked down, and had to stop in her tracks to keep from disturbing two rows of Scrabble tiles, pressed firmly into place on the dull brown carpet. They had been picked from the rest of the tiles, which were scattered around, some still lying in the box. The box was lying where it had apparently fallen (been pushed?) from its usual place in the linen closet.

The tiles read, "Believe her."

"THIS DOESN'T HELP US with your case, Ian."

Collie was sitting next to the tiles, flipping a blank tile over and over in her fingers. Anna took a seat on the stairs and watched, sipping beer. When she finished the beer, she brought the bottle downstairs, put it in the recycling and extinguished the candles. No matter what else happened to them, at least the house wouldn't burn down. She made sure their front and back doors were locked. That would solve the last of their problems. No way was anyone getting past their landlord's ten-dollar deadbolts. Yup. Safe and secure.

Then she climbed most of the stairs and said, "If that was Ian, that's probably as much as we're getting from him. For tonight, anyway."

She stayed a few steps from the top as she spoke, in case Collie objected to the suggestion that they give up and over-reacted, maybe threw the lone Q at her head. Which would leave Mandrake in a bind if he wanted to call someone a quisling.

Instead, Collie flipped the tile and flipped the tile and flipped the tile and took a deep breath.

"Go to bed. I'll stay up for awhile. In case."

"Suit yourself," Anna told her, and carefully climbed over both Collie and the tiles to reach the bedroom on the other side. "Good night."

"Not so far," Collie said. "Oh, I called Deepti, by the way, just in case... you know. Anyway, she's fine. She thinks I cancelled the ads earlier. Robin must have done something."

"And it didn't involve lightning," Anna said. "Lucky Deepti."

Anna shut the bedroom door, in case Collie decided to start chanting or howling at the moon. She changed into a t-shirt and pyjama bottoms and crawled into bed, which was every bit as good as she'd remembered it being. There were times when she really wasn't happy being anywhere else. She got up in the mornings thinking she just had to make it through the day and she'd be able, as a reward, to get into bed again.

This was a bigger problem now that she had decent linen and good pillows, but she'd loved even ill-clad and lumpy beds in her time.

It did occur to her, just as she was falling asleep, that Collie had probably sent her to bed in the hopes that she would have helpful and informative dreams. The thought did not quite piss her off enough to keep her awake.

The chair is so comfortable that, at first, she mistakes it for her bed.

"It's like a dentist's chair," she comments to Rowan, who is in the chair next to hers. "One of the really good ones."

Except dentist's chairs are usually horrible colours, yellow-lime or cantaloupe. Not black. And not leather.

"I never went to see a dentist," he says. He's on his back, with his eyes shut. "They brought everyone in to me. But the chairs looked kind of the same, on TV."

"It is like TV?" Anna asks. She doesn't know what she's asking, but Rowan doesn't seem confused. Just distracted, focused on something else.

"Is yours?" he asks.

"No," she says.

"No," he says. "I asked them once to put stars on the ceiling. They wouldn't."

She looks toward the ceiling and can't make it out. The room is dark and could be any size, for all she could see of it. The soft light lets her make out herself, and Rowan. And the chairs.

It's warm, though, and the sound of their voices is almost swallowed by the walls. She thinks maybe she could touch the walls, if she reached for them.

"You know what this is?"

He's holding up an off-white ball, flattened on one side. His eyes are still closed.

"No," Anna says. She does, though. She has seen it somewhere before.

Rowan sets the ball down on his stomach.

"There's a Judaic belief that everyone has an indestructible bone called a luz. It might be at the base of the skull, or the base of the spine. It doesn't decompose along with the rest of your bones." He takes a deep breath, the movement bouncing the ball on his stomach. "The soul hovers above it. If God wants to resurrect you and recreate your body, he works from the luz."

The off-white now looks bone white, pitted and rough.

"Is that a luz?" Anna asks. Rowan laughs and reaches up a hand to catch the ball before it falls.

"No."

"That's just a story," Anna tells him. Rowan tosses the ball toward the ceiling, where it disappears into the dark. It doesn't come back down.

"I might not have one, anyway," he says.

Anna doesn't care about the luz. It isn't her job to care about the luz. She's supposed to find Rowan.

"Where are you?" she asks.

"I don't know," he says. "Sometimes they just give me a code number and say, go there."

"No, where are you?"

Rowan smiles a little.

"If two people know something, it's not a secret. Tell Eric it's a secret. And tell him..."

"To go home?" Anna asks. Rowan's eyes open. The room's lights go on and Anna sees that it isn't the plain, sterile space she'd imagined, but instead a hotel room, cheap and ugly. Orange and brown patterned wallpaper and curtains that looked like dyed burlap. No beds — the chairs are in their place. A scuffed dresser along one wall and, between their chairs, a nightstand bearing a bulbous drip-glazed lamp.

Rowan turns his head to look at her, but he can't be seeing her. His eyes are the dull black of chalkboards, white numbers scrawled across them in a hurried hand.

"No," he says. "Never there."

WHEN ANNA ARRIVED at the kitchen table, breakfast was already on it. The seven-grain bread she particularly liked, even though they were currently on a loaf of rye and Collie would have had to truck herself down to the basement freezer for it, not to mention opening a new loaf before the old one was gone.

And cherry jam, which was her favourite and which she was not having at the moment because they were sharing that lemon stuff Collie liked. So something else had been opened out of turn.

And tea, Earl Grey.

And an orange, peeled and in sections, because Anna didn't like peeling them and getting rind under her nails.

The whole thing couldn't have been more obvious if Collie had set out one of those seating cards, a little gold-lettered piece on creamy paper propped carefully beside her plate and bearing the word, "Talk."

"Sorry," Anna said, before Collie could greet her. "I've got nothing."

"No dreams?" Collie asked. Amazing. She didn't look ashamed to have been caught out, just disappointed.

"Nothing useful," Anna said. Collie frowned.

"So you did have a dream."

"Nothing useful," Anna repeated.

"See, you say that, but —"

"But I mean it?"

"I'm sure you do," Collie said, "except you might be missing something. You tend to downplay this stuff."

Anna spread jam on toast, aware that one or both might be punitively taken away at any moment.

"There is nothing to downplay."

"In the great annals of self-defeating statements," Collie said, "that one comes in just under 'I am not being defensive.'"

"What if you're not?" Anna asked. Collie shook her head.

"Can you just humour me and tell me about your dream? It would be, what, five minutes of your time?"

"In theory," Anna said, pouring tea, "yes. But, in practice, you're going to grill me about every second of the dream for the next few hours. And then it'll be at least another hour of 'Do you think the naked dog catcher was a symbol for our client?'"

"Naked dog catcher?" Collie asked. She even straightened a bit in her chair.

"I made that up," Anna said. "Are we still meeting Eric this morning?"

"Why wouldn't we be?" Collie asked.

Anna shrugged.

"Things change. At ten? At the office?"

"Yeah," Collie said. "You can tell me about your dream on the way."

THE BRIGHT SIDE of reciting her dream in the car was that they'd head straight in to see Eric, and Collie wouldn't be able to start with the questions until after their meeting was done. Maybe she'd even have lost interest by that time. Even if she hadn't, she'd stop nagging once she got all the information, and would never stop nagging if Anna simply refused to tell her about the dream.

Anna was rationalizing like a fiend, but it was better than admitting she had a stupid but unshakeable fear of actually missing something important.

"That's interesting," Collie said as she circled for a parking spot. "Do you remember what numbers were in his eyes?"

"I did not have a pad and pencil," Anna said.

"Ooh!" Collie was nearly vibrating. "Did you see a notepad? Or a matchbook? Something with the hotel's name on it?"

Anna stared at her.

"You think Rowan is locked in a cheap hotel room."

"You're doing that side," Collie said, pointing at Anna's side of the road. "Stop looking at me."

"That's ridiculous," Anna said. "Spo – sorry. Loading zone."

"I need a commercial vehicle license," Collie said. "Then you get the half hour or whatever, instead of five minutes. Maybe I could just put a business name on the side of the car."

"Cheating Bint Limited?" Anna suggested. Collie giggled.

"Aw... bint. I haven't heard that in ye-oh! I can do it! I can do it!"

Anna doubted it, but it wasn't her car and, besides, she'd been wrong before. She closed her eyes and waited until she heard the car shut off.

They carefully half-opened their doors and slipped into the narrow spaces between the Tercel and the SUVs on either side.

"We could get you hypnotized," Collie said, "to get all the details from your dreams."

"We could get you hypnotized," Anna said, "and take you back to the first time you suggested that, and I said hell, no."

"I will never understand you," Collie said. She actually sounded sad about it. "Seriously, do you think they've got Rowan in a hotel room somewhere? Or... because, you were in those chairs, so maybe it was the place where he does... whatever he does."

"You already know what I think," Anna said. "I think it was a dream. Until I have some reason to think otherwise, I'm assuming it's just some weird shit my brain cooked up, like all the other weird shit my brain cooks up while I'm sleeping."

"What about the luz?" Collie asked. Anna frowned.

"What about it?"

"Had you heard of that before? I know you've worked a lot of jobs, but I don't think you were a Kabbalist at any point."

"Depends what you call a cabal, I guess," Anna said. She pulled her coat closed with one hand, trying to shut out the sharp wind. Frustrated by having a coat thrown in its face, it settled for biting her knuckles instead.

Collie laughed.

"Okay, my *point,*" she said. "Not cabal. Kabbalah. Ooh, though... I bet that's the origin of the word. What do you want to bet?"

"Five bucks," Anna said. It was the standard amount she was prepared to bet when she knew Collie was just guessing.

"Done." With her hands jammed deep in her coat pockets, Collie did not offer to shake on it. "Anyway, Kabbalah is Jewish mysticism. A Kabbalist is the kind of person who would know what a luz was. In other words, not you. So, assuming a luz is a real thing and not something you just made up because you were staring at Scrabble tiles before bed —"

"That was mostly you," Anna pointed out.

"— your brain has to have picked the information up somewhere. You dream stuff you have never heard of. Real stuff. That's not just random neurons firing. You are getting the 411 from somewhere."

"It's impressive when you use ten-year-old street jargon," Anna said. "It makes other people want to be you."

Collie ignored her and pulled a glove from her pocket. Instead of putting it on, she wrapped it around the handle to their office building's front door. Because touching cold metal was uncomfortable. And putting a glove on was too much work. Or maybe Collie was thinking she'd just have to take the glove right off again, so what would be the point?

"Five bucks," Collie said, "says Eric's waiting for us in the office."

"No bet," Anna said. Which was a good thing, because, as they climbed the stairs, she could see the office lights through the cracks around the door.

Collie had to use her keys on the door, which wasn't a surprise given Eric's level of paranoia. Provided it was Eric in their office.

"I have huge news for you," Collie said as she stepped through the door. "It would be a shame if your finger twitched and you never got to hear it."

Ah. Eric was waving a gun around again, obviously. And Collie, with a gun on her, was making jokes. As usual.

As Anna entered the office, Eric was putting his gun away. She stopped, not because of the gun, but because there was another man sitting next to Eric, stiff-backed and antsy. He had curly white hair and a young face. She would have thought him an albino if not for his light blue eyes.

Perhaps more annoying than Eric breaking into their office for a second time, pointing a gun at them, and bringing an uninvited guest, was the fact that said guest was sitting on Anna's chair. It was understandable, in a way, because there were only three chairs in the office and the one behind Collie's desk was hard to move, but that didn't give Anna a place to sit.

Anna wasn't suited, physically or temperamentally, to perching on the corner of Collie's desk, so she opted for leaning against the wall instead. Next to the door, which she pushed closed with enough force to make Collie wince. Collie hated, beyond reason, the sound of slamming doors. She'd never told Anna why.

"You're still incautious," Eric told them, as if that were news. Collie smiled.

"And you love it," she said seductively. Eric looked baffled, but the non-albino laughed.

"That was a joke," he said, placing a hand on Eric's shoulder and giving him a gentle shove. Eric glared at him.

"Does any of this strike you as a joking matter?" he asked. Anna sympathized, to some extent, but she also had trouble imagining what Eric *would* consider a joking matter. She could picture him in the front row of a comedy club, arms folded and scowling while people laughed themselves to tears around him. Now, if Collie had declared something to not be a joking matter, that might have carried some weight.

To his credit, the non-albino gave Eric a shrug and a smile.

"That was still a joke," he said.

Eric stopped glaring at him and glared at Collie instead.

"This is Michael Orslin," he said. "Michael used to do the same work for Varanus that Rowan did."

"Basically," Michael said. He looked a little uncomfortable.

"You were a remote viewer?" Collie asked. "Oh — I'm Colette Kostyna, by the way."

"I know," Michael said. "I was briefed. Yes, I was a remote viewer."

Why Eric thought they needed to talk to a remote viewer was beyond Anna's grasp. She couldn't imagine what good it would do, unless the kid knew something about Varanus that might help. Either way, telling Eric about Robin had to be their first priority.

"Okay," Anna said, "that's interesting, but we —"

"Did you use long reclining chairs?" Collie asked. "Like dentist's chairs?"

Sometimes Anna thought it was preferable, really, when Collie did nothing but crack jokes.

"Col," she said, "I think we have better things to talk about here."

"Yes," Michael said, ignoring Anna. "Are you familiar with remote viewing?"

"Not really," Collie said. "It was a kind of hunch. What kinds of rooms did you work in? Did you ever work out of hotel rooms?"

Michael looked puzzled. Eric didn't look anything, but it didn't mean he wasn't equally puzzled.

"No," Michael said. "Physically, we never left the Varanus site."

"Wait," Anna said. "You worked on the Varanus site? So you know where they are?"

Michael and Eric looked at each other.

“Varanus has multiple locations,” Eric said. “The site where Michael worked is no longer in use.”

“He got me out,” Michael said. “Everyone else had abandoned the place. They took their records and all of the other viewers, and left me locked up there.”

“They probably learned I was closing in on that location and decided to abandon it. Why Michael was left behind is a mystery, but it’s fortunate for me. He taught me a great deal about the organization.”

Michael shrugged.

“I didn’t know that much,” he said. “It’s more fortunate for me that Eric came along. I didn’t have any food in my room.”

“But you can travel places, right?” Collie said. “Like, project yourself? Couldn’t you have told someone you needed help?”

Michael shook his head.

“I’m a remote viewer,” he said. “We take information in, but we don’t send it out.”

Eric looked at Michael. The slightly surprised look on his face was probably a sign that he was utterly shocked.

“Rowan can be seen,” he said. “When he wants to be.”

Anna shut her eyes for a moment, remembering the way Rowan and Eric had met. When she opened her eyes, Collie was looking at her with concern.

“He can,” Anna said softly. Eric didn’t seem to notice.

“Michael?”

“That’s why I said basically,” Michael said, looking at Collie. “Rowan’s different.” He turned to Eric. “That’s what he and I talked about when you brought him to visit me. We were comparing notes. He’s not like any remote viewer I ever met.”

“So, you and Rowan didn’t work together?” Anna asked.

“No,” Michael said. “Eric found Rowan about a year after he found me.”

“I used information Michael had given me to find some other Varanus locations,” Eric said. “Michael, you never told me there was anything unusual about Rowan."

"I thought he would have told you himself," Michael said. He paused, as if uncertain he wanted to go on, then added, "If he wanted you to know."

"Everyone's entitled to their secrets," Eric said. Anna had heard more convincing lies from preschoolers, but she said nothing. Collie, for once, seemed to be taking the same approach.

"You have to keep some cards back," Michael said. He sounded apologetic. Eric didn't look at him.

"You," he said to Anna, "seemed to have something you wanted to tell me."

"Yeah," Anna said. "That's true. Well. We were proceeding on the assumption that whoever had killed Mandrake – ah, Ian McLaren – had also kidnapped Rowan."

"Yes," Eric said. "And?"

"That's not the case," Anna said.

Eric tilted his head as if he were a dog trying to hear her better.

"How do you know this?"

"Because Rowan's kidnapper stopped by our house last night," Anna said.

Eric was half out of his chair when he apparently thought better of it and sat again. It was a good thing he'd thought better of whatever he meant to do, because Anna had barely had time to realize he was coming her way and had no idea what she would have done had he arrived.

"She said she shot the sheriff," Collie said, "but not the deputy."

Eric looked at her. He did not, for once, look calm. His eyes were wide and his brow was creased with frustration.

"*What?*"

Anna almost smiled, in spite of everything. She knew the feeling.

"The woman who kidnapped Rowan," she said, "told us she was hired to kidnap Rowan and that's what she did – outside Ian McLaren's home, at some point before Ian was shot. She and Rowan were gone by the time Ian's killer arrived."

"Do you know this woman's name?" Eric asked.

"Yessss," Collie said, "but there's a kind of disclaimer we're supposed to give you."

Eric leaned forward and grasped the edge of Collie's desk.

"What?" he said again, his voice lower, but making up for it by being a great deal more menacing.

"She said to tell you that she's given us all the information she has – which I'm going to give to you," Collie added quickly, "because she doesn't want you to have a reason to come after her."

Eric tilted his head the other way.

"Is she insane?"

"That's really a legal term," Collie said. "A person can be completely –"

Eric's fingers tightened on the edge of the desk. Anna wondered what his next move would be – push the desk forward? Flip it over? Launch himself over it? Maybe he'd scratch the varnish, which would actually be more annoying in the long run.

"Just. Tell. Me."

"She said Varanus hired her over the phone. They told her to kidnap Rowan and bring him to Fort McMurray, where she was to leave him in the bus station for pick up by Varanus agents. She assumes they meant to fly him out of town, but she doesn't know for sure. She teleported him to Fort Mac from here. The bus station is the last place she saw him."

"And her name?" Eric asked. He was back to sounding almost rational, which was somehow the most frightening tone he'd taken yet.

"Robin Hampshire," Collie said.

Eric frowned.

"Should I know that name?"

"I don't know," Collie said. "Probably not. She's not a Varanus person, just a freelancer."

"Ronin without honour," Eric said darkly.

"Rebel without a cause," Collie said. "Though, for all I know, she might have a cause."

"And honour," Anna said. Eric scowled at her.

"No one who would willingly work for those people has honour. She kidnapped a teenaged boy."

"Yeah," Collie said. "That wasn't good. But the important thing is, we've given you a lead."

"Robin Hampshire," Eric repeated.

"No!" Collie said. "Fort McMurray. Jesus! Did I not just tell you that there's no reason to go after Robin Hampshire?"

"You're taking a kidnapper at her word?" Eric asked. "Is there some reason for you to support her desire for privacy?"

"Hells yes," Collie said. "I fear her. More than I fear you."

That was sensible, but Anna couldn't help wondering where Collie's fear of Robin had been while Collie cooked up the "let's annoy the piss out of her" plan.

"I'm sitting here right now," Eric said. Collie laughed.

"Oh my God. Was that the 'you should fear me more because I'm the one currently in your face' threat? Okay, this lady teleports and throws lightning around, so proximity is not giving you an edge. Seriously, man, you can't go after Robin. She will take it out on us. And possibly on you."

Eric released his death grip on Collie's desk.

"Intimidation tactics," he said. "These people make a lot of claims. You are naïve if you believe them."

"Okay," Collie said. "I'm naïve. I totally believe them. Could you just… go to Fort Mac first, check it out, and if you think you still need to see Robin then… whatever. Fort Mac really is the lead. It's where I'd go."

"Unless it's a trap," Eric said.

Collie rolled her eyes.

"Not unless you're an eighteen-year-old moron who goes up there to work the rigs and winds up spending all his money on drugs. Look, I think Robin Hampshire was on the level. She told us as much as she knew and told us to pass it on because she doesn't want to talk to you. You give her the willies."

Eric frowned.

"You fear her, and you think I should fear her, and you believe she throws lightning around... but you think I give her the willies?"

Collie shrugged.

"She basically said so."

Eric leaned back in his chair.

"Is that so?"

Anna shut her eyes and let her head hit the wall behind her. No question about it — Eric was fascinated. He wanted to know how, exactly, he was putting the fear into this putative badass. No way was he going to stay away from Robin now.

"You have a mystique," Collie said. "People seem to wonder how you've stayed alive so long. She's probably assuming you must be trouble if you've shut down a few Varanus locations and they haven't killed you yet."

Anna opened her eyes to get a look at Collie's face. It was instructive, looking for tells when she knew Collie was lying. Why Collie was lying, Anna didn't know. Maybe she'd decided she'd said more than enough already. Which she had.

"Mystique," Eric said. He sounded as if he'd been told he had a pink tutu and a glittering wand. "I'll ask her when I see her. After I get back from Fort McMurray."

"Thank you," Collie said. Eric actually slouched a bit in his chair.

"Nothing to do with you," Eric said. "I'm following my best lead. I am going to find Rowan."

"I think you will," Collie said. "If it helps any. Is there anything you need us to do?"

Eric shook his head, then stopped and sat up straight.

"Actually — one thing. Two things."

He reached into his pocket and put the steel ball — the luz, Anna thought — onto Collie's desk. Then he reached into the pocket on the other side of his jacket and produced Rowan's toy duck, which he placed next to the luz.

"I may be getting into some trouble," Eric said. "If I get into more trouble than I can handle, I want you to give those to Rowan."

Collie looked at the ball and the duck.

"Excuse me?"

"I'm saying that I want to keep you on this job until Rowan is located, either by me... or by you. The duck's his, and I want that artificial joint to go to him. I'll call in once a day until I find him, or until I don't. If you miss a call, it's time for you to start looking for him. I'll make arrangements for you to be paid in the case of —"

"That's not what's worrying me," Collie interrupted. "You hired us because of our local connections and those aren't needed anymore. Maybe you should put some actual detectives on retainer."

"No," Eric said. "I'll stick with you. I believe you have some interest in finding Rowan. You have motivation."

"We'd like to find him," Anna admitted. She hoped Eric didn't ask why, because she couldn't really say. But it was true.

Eric nodded.

"I would, too. I told him he would never have to go back to that place."

It was about the most human thing Anna had heard Eric say, and it startled her. Collie, too, looked surprised.

"Oh... man... are you beating yourself up about this? Because you told him you were going to look after him, or whatever?"

Eric looked at Collie and Anna didn't think he was going to answer the question, but he surprised her again by saying,

"Something like that."

Collie leaned forward.

"Eric... I don't know how you lived this long without figuring this out, but when we say shit like 'I won't let anything happen to you' or 'I'll take care of you'... it's just good intentions. I mean, there are earthquakes and stuff, you know? You can't actually promise anyone that you'll make things okay for them. You just mean, 'I will if I can,' or 'I would if I could.' Dude. Honestly. I'm sure Rowan knows that."

Eric looked as if he'd just swallowed something painfully sour.

"We have yet to see what I can or can't do," he said, and got to his feet. Michael, who had been so quiet that Anna had nearly forgotten him, stayed in his chair, looking confused.

"What's the second thing?" Anna asked. Eric turned to her.

"What?"

"You said you wanted two things from us."

"Oh," Eric said, seeming dazed. Anna wondered if she should grab her phone and snap a picture. Eric seeming dazed had to be one of those Halley's Comet, catch it now or wait a lifetime events. Eric drew in a quick, deep breath, and his gaze sharpened.

"Right. Michael asked me to introduce him to you because he would like to move to Edmonton."

"Really?" Collie said. "I mean, nothing against this town, but the politics are..."

"That's why I wanted to meet you," Michael said. "I need someone to help me meet the Embassy and ask if it would be okay."

Anna wanted to say that it wouldn't be okay, regardless of what the Embassy said, because it's never okay to live in a city where you have to ask someone's damned permission to get an apartment and a job. But she had a feeling that would only start an argument and she was, suddenly, too tired for that.

"I guess… we can take you to see Kieran," Collie told Michael. "He handles a lot of things for the Embassy. We need to see him anyway."

"Remember about the joint," Eric said. He'd moved until he was standing right next to the door. Anna had barely registered the motion, intent as she was on looking at Michael's face and wondering why he would want to live under the Embassy's thumb.

Anna looked at Collie, who seemed to be wondering when Eric had slipped her a joint. Anna lifted her chin toward the steel ball and Collie's expression cleared. Oh. Right. *That* joint.

"Got it," Collie said, grabbing the joint and throwing it into one coat pocket. The duck went into the other pocket. It was just as Eric had carried them, though Anna didn't know whether Collie had copied him on purpose. "I guess we'll… expect your calls?"

"Hope so," Eric said, and slipped out the door, pulling it shut behind him.

"So," Collie said, looking at Michael. "Is he always this easy-going?"

Michael smiled a little.

"He's worried, I guess. But he's… yeah. Like this."

"Okay," Collie said. "Good to know. Let's go talk to Kieran."

IT CROSSED ANNA'S MIND, as she and Collie walked Michael to the car, that Eric was a near-stranger, and an odd one at that. One that Robin, who Anna truly believed could teleport and throw lightning around, seemed to find terrifying. It also crossed her mind that the person tagging along to see Kieran was even closer to being a complete stranger, and one they'd only met through their strange, scary client. He was going to ride in their car, and probably in the back, because Anna was too damn tall to ride in the back, and they would have to turn their backs to him and trust that there was no harm in him.

That, even more than believing Robin's story, seemed a little naïve.

Not that there seemed to be any harm in the quiet kid loping beside them, his off-white curls bouncing with every step. He seemed reasonable enough, aside from wanting to move to Edmonton, and he was even polite — at least, by Anna's recently revised standards of politeness, which included not teleporting into her living room and not clawing at Collie's furniture.

Anna wondered about him as they walked. Had he, like Rowan, spent more or all of his life in a Varanus facility? What was he doing, now that he was living in the outside world? What exactly did remote viewers do, anyway? Why was Rowan different?

But she wasn't about to ask him as they wandered down the sidewalk, even if most of the neighbourhood seemed to be at work or school, well away from the rows of brightly painted character homes on either side of the street.

Michael kept his head down, watching his feet, as if he'd otherwise trip on a crack. Maybe he would. Maybe he wasn't used to walking on anything besides linoleum. Or maybe he was just shy.

When they arrived at the car, Collie held her keys up to Anna.

"Did you want to drive?"

Oh. There was a solution Anna hadn't considered. She could drive, and Collie could squeeze her relatively tiny self into the back seat. But that was a solution for, say, being afraid someone would pull a gun on you, or try to strangle you with a seatbelt, neither of which she could really imagine this kid doing.

"It's okay," Anna said. Collie raised her brows, not in a disagreeing way so much as a "but are you totally sure?" way. Anna shrugged. Collie shrugged back and they piled into the car, Michael opening the door the few inches allowed by Collie's parking spot, then ducking and folding until he'd found a place between the backs of the bucket seats.

"Do we need to pull our seats forward?" Collie asked.

"It's okay," Michael said, which added to Anna's impression that he was, at heart, a decent guy.

"Well, good," Collie said, "because I'm not sure we actually could pull them forward. The slidey things aren't working very well."

Michael nodded sympathetically and did not recommend shopping for a car that had been made after the fall of the Roman Empire, which sealed the deal for Anna. He was beyond polite. He was angelic.

"So," Collie said as they pulled out of the spot, "Michael, you look to be about nineteen or twenty. In my experience, guys that age are always hungry. Did you want us to buy you breakfast or something? We don't have to go straight to Kieran's."

Michael opened his mouth, then hesitated. Collie, keeping half an eye on him in the rear view mirror, smiled.

"It's no skin off us," she said. "We'll just bill Eric."

Michael shook his head.

"I'm okay."

"Okay," Collie said. "Well. Do you mind if we stop and chat with you for a few minutes, anyway?"

"I guess," Michael said, though he looked less than thrilled with the idea. Collie followed a steep road down to a riverside park and parked, with the car running, at the far end of the parking lot. The park was empty aside from their car, at least as far as Anna could see. There might have been joggers or cyclists in the bushes surrounding them, but a weekday morning with grey skies and a bite to the air wasn't a popular time to hang out in a park.

Anna heard a clink as Collie dropped her car keys into her pocket, the same one that held the joint. She was surprised, because usually Collie let the car idle while they sat in it. Maybe the stickers all over town that shamed people who left their cars running were having a subconscious effect.

"I just want to know a few things," Collie said, taking off her seatbelt and turning to face Michael. "I don't mean to freak you out or anything. It's just that we don't know a lot about what you and Rowan do. Or, did."

"I still do it," Michael said. "I just don't work for Varanus anymore. I thought maybe I could work for the Embassy."

"You probably could," Collie allowed, "but you might not want to. They keep a pretty tight lock on this city. It's their way or the highway."

"I'm used to that," Michael said. Collie nodded.

"That doesn't mean it's the best thing for you. I'm just saying. Anyway. What exactly is it that you and Rowan do?"

"We're different," Michael said. "I'm a remote viewer. I lie in a dark room and someone gives me coordinates – kind of a code – and I go to the place or whatever that's indicated by those coordinates and look around. It's like being invisible and flying around, looking at things. But I can't touch things or move stuff."

"By coordinates, do you mean longitude and latitude?" Anna asked. "Or something like GPS?"

Michael shook his head. He'd taken his own seatbelt off and was sitting cross-legged on the back seat, something Anna could have done if she'd had all her leg bones removed.

"No... they're not real coordinates. They just take numbers and assign them to people or places or things, so we don't know what we're looking for. We search for whatever's associated with the number. I guess it's so they can tell whether we're really getting good information, or whether we're imagining things. Or making things up."

"How do fake numbers help with that?" Collie asked. "You'd be free to make shit up, wouldn't you?"

"Yes," Michael said, "but, if you knew you were supposed to be going to a place in Russia, you could say, there's snow or... something that sounded real. When you just have the numbers, you don't know what would sound reasonable, so you can't fool them by making up stuff that sounds right. You might say you saw a jungle instead, and they'd know you didn't have good information."

"Couldn't you be reading their minds?" Collie asked. "I know that sounds asinine, but a lot of people would say mind reading and... clairvoyance, I suppose... are equally impossible."

"I don't know," Michael said. "I never thought about it. But we got good information, at least sometimes. I know because they went to places and found things we said would be there."

"So," Collie said, "what's the difference between remote viewing and clairvoyance?"

"Remote viewing's real," Michael said. "People just imagine they're clairvoyant."

Collie's lips twitched.

"Really?"

Even Anna, loving the paranormal as she didn't, had to admit the kid's response sounded like hair-splitting. At best.

"Doesn't clairvoyant mean seeing stuff that's too far away to see?" Anna said. "Or behind a wall, or something?"

"Basically," Collie said, still looking amused.

"So, what is the difference?" Anna asked Michael. He was plucking at a loose thread on his jeans, watching his fingers move.

"Remote viewing is controlled," he said. He sounded as if he were reading from a script. "The conditions are controlled and information received is recorded and objectively assigned value. Remote viewers do not choose their own targets, nor are they aware of the nature of their targets."

"So it's controlled clairvoyance?" Collie said. Michael raised his head, quickly, and Collie raised a hand in response. "Sorry. Never mind. It doesn't matter."

"What about Rowan?" Anna asked. Michael looked at her.

"He was different," he repeated.

"Did that have something to do with Rowan growing up on-site?" Collie asked. Michael frowned.

"I did too. Most of us were born there and grew up there. They had a way of making people become remote viewers."

Anna glanced at Collie, who was looking steadily at Michael and not betraying her emotions, whatever they might have been.

"Do you mean, through training?" Collie asked. "Or was it something you were born with?"

Michael shrugged.

"They never said. They just said we were special."

"And Rowan was particularly special," Anna said.

Michael looked out the window. Anna followed his gaze and saw a sparrow on a nearby stand of caragana. Neither the sparrow nor the caragana were anything worth staring at, not on an Alberta riverbank. But Michael kept staring.

"He's... he can choose to appear places, instead of being invisible. And I think he can maybe move stuff around, but he didn't say for sure about that."

"Is he like a hologram?" Collie asked. "Like, you could put your hand through him? Or could you grab his arm?"

Michael kept looking at the sparrow, which was jumping from one branch to another as if looking for some special branch that would be different from all the others.

"I don't know," he said. "I never saw him do it."

"Okay," Collie said. "It's probably not important. We're mostly just curious. And, on that topic... you never actually said why you wanted to move to Edmonton."

Michael shrugged, but not in the sullen way that most kids did it. He just looked lost, reminding Anna of Rowan.

"Varanus usually stays away from here," he said. "And things are under control. And there's lots of work."

"I'll concede the third point," Collie said, "but I hope recent events have been an eye-opener for you regarding how safe and quiet this town really is."

Michael looked at her, eyes wide.

"It's worse other places," he said.

Collie looked at Anna. Anna looked at Michael.

"We wouldn't really know," she said.

Michael shrugged again. Slowly, as if her joints ached, Collie turned around, pulled her seatbelt on and put her hand in her pocket for her keys.

Anna was about to face the front of the car when two things happened. Collie made a surprised sound and pulled her hand from her pocket, as if something had nipped her. And Michael disappeared.

"WHAT THE SHIT?!" Collie yelped. Anna had to look at her face to see that she was looking into the backseat, and not reacting to whatever had happened in her pocket. "Where did he go?"

"I don't know," Anna said. Stupidly, she looked around at the parking lot and the bushes, as if he'd somehow slipped out of the seat in a nanosecond and made for the hills, opening and closing the door before they saw or heard him. Because he was The Flash. She shut her eyes and forced herself to think for a moment. The kid was a remote viewer. Like Rowan, kind of.

"Maybe he was never here," Anna said. "Did you touch him, ever? Did you see him move anything? Maybe he was lying when he said he couldn't project himself places."

"He opened the car door," Collie said, distractedly. "He put on a seatbelt."

Anna couldn't imagine what could be distracting her from the sudden disappearance of the kid in the backseat, but Collie was definitely thinking about something else.

"Oh, for Christ's sake," Anna said. "What?"

In answer, Collie pulled something from her pocket and showed it to Anna. It was a ball, flat on one end, off-white in colour, the same size as the steel joint but pitted and mottled, like bone.

"Where did you get that?" Anna asked, but she knew. It was the joint, no longer artificial. No longer steel. It was the luz, and it never broke down, and Collie had been carrying it ever since she'd dropped it into her pocket at the office. It was what Eric had been carrying most of his life.

"It changed," Collie said.

Anna thought that wasn't quite right, either, unless Collie had meant that it had changed before they ever saw it. It had been in disguise. She knew that, for no good reason, and decided not to say it because she didn't want to say that she just knew. She never liked to say that.

"I don't get it," Collie said softly, turning the luz over and over in her hand. She sounded wounded by that, her feelings hurt. As if someone had played a prank on her and she couldn't quite see the joke.

"Things change," Anna said, not really knowing why she was saying it. It was like the way she talked when she was having a vision, words making their own way out of her mouth without even a nod to her.

Collie shot her a suspicious look.

"Are you visioning?"

"No," Anna said firmly, giving her head a shake. "Why do you think Michael and the lu – the joint went weird at the same time?"

"Is that our new expression for 'completely changed its physical state and/or vanished off the face of the Earth'?" Collie asked. "'Went weird?'"

"It's more succinct," Anna said. "Your thoughts?"

"I don't want to oversell what's going on in my head by calling it thinking," Collie told her. She set the luz into one of the front cup holders. "Do you think Michael's okay?"

"How the hell would I know?" Anna asked. "I hope so."

"Nothing we can do about it if he's not," Collie said.

"Probably not," Anna agreed.

"Maybe Eric would know," Collie said. She was already reaching for her purse as she spoke. Anna retrieved the purse from the floor on the passenger side and put it in Collie's hands.

"Couldn't hurt to ask," she said.

Collie took out her phone and tapped the screen three or four times. She had evidently added Eric to her Contact list.

After no more than two rings, the colour left Collie's face.

"Who is this?" she said, sounding as if she knew and was just hoping she'd be surprised by a different answer, better than the one she was expecting.

Apparently she didn't get one, because her next move was to throw her phone onto the dashboard and stare at it with a mixture of fear and disgust.

She hadn't hung up. Anna realized, to her dismay, that she was actually curious enough to pick up the phone. After a moment, she did. Collie didn't stop her.

"Hello?" Anna said.

"Oh, hello, Anna," a pseudo-British voice chirped in her ear. "Colette doesn't want to speak to me. Should my feelings be hurt?"

There were a lot of smart-ass comments Anna could have made but, somehow, none seemed appealing. Instead she said, "What are you doing with Eric's phone?"

Robin sighed.

"That is beneath you. You know what must have happened if I have his mobile. I was asked, if possible, to eliminate Eric Quinlan, which I considered a public service and might have done even if I weren't being paid. So there you are."

Anna tried not to think about the timing of it. That they'd met with Eric, in their office, and then Robin had found him. She tried to convince herself that he'd lied about going to Fort McMurray first and had, instead, gone looking for Robin. That Robin hadn't found Eric because she'd known where to look for him, and that she hadn't known where to look because Anna and Collie had let on that he was their client. That Eric's death was in no way their bad.

It was a hard sell.

"You there?" Robin asked. "Is there anything else? I don't have all day."

"Sure," Anna said. "You have people to murder."

Robin laughed.

"Oh, stop it. I have no reason to kill either of you. And, despite what you may have heard, I don't do this sort of thing for no reason."

Now we have to find Rowan, Anna thought.

"Anna? Hello?"

"Fu —" Anna started, but the phone was grabbed from her hand by thin, icy fingers.

"When did he die?" Collie demanded. She was holding the phone so tightly that Anna thought it might crack. "When did Eric die?"

A few moments of silence. Collie's eyes narrowed.

"I don't know, bitch," she said. "Maybe I want it for the coroner's report. What do you care?"

From her seat, Anna could hear Robin laughing. When the laughter stopped, she must have said something, because Collie listened and her lips tightened and finally she took a deep breath.

“That’s none of your goddamned business,” Collie said. “And fuck you.”

Collie turned off the phone and, once again, tossed it onto the dashboard.

“Sorry about cutting you off,” she said, not looking at Anna.

“I was only going to say ‘fuck you’,” Anna said.

“She killed Eric a few minutes ago,” Collie said. “She shot him. She said, ‘He believed in guns.’”

“So did Charlton Heston,” Anna said, irritated. “So what?”

“She asked if anything weird happened when Eric died,” Collie said.

Oh. Anna thought of Michael, and the luz. Her stomach hurt.

“None of her goddamned business?” Anna asked.

“That was my feeling.”

Neither said anything for a few minutes, or a few centuries. The sparrow looked at them, unconcerned. He’d probably seen a lot of cars in his urban, exhaust-coated life.

“Is that why you asked?” Anna said. “About when he died?”

Collie shrugged, but it was enough of an answer. They sat some more. It got cold, even for Anna. Collie did not turn the car on.

“We should still see Kieran,” Anna pointed out. Collie took the keys from her pocket and started the car.

“I guess,” she said, “we might as well.”

THEY DIDN’T TALK on the way to Kieran’s house. It wasn’t far, for one thing – just a few blocks. And there wasn’t anything Anna felt like saying. She suspected Collie felt the same way.

They parked in front of the house and were somewhat surprised to see a young woman with a vivid purple mohawk on the front stoop, crying. As Anna got out of the car, she could hear the tone of the sobbing – it was the deep, inconsolable kind that seemed to go on forever. The woman wasn't covering her face, just staring straight at the road and not seeming to see it. She didn't look at them, or even blink, as Anna and Collie started up the walk.

As they got closer to the house, they could see vomit in the shrub beside the front door. It was probably the woman's, though Anna wasn't about to ask her about it. She looked away before she could recognize anything specific in the mess, which would have put her off that particular food for a good long time.

They went around the woman, careful to avoid both her and the shrub, and gave the open door a push.

"Hello?" Collie said, sticking her head into the foyer.

"Not a great time," Kieran's voice said from somewhere inside.

"And yet..." Collie said.

There was a pause, then,

"All right. Come in."

They went into the living room, not bothering to take their boots off, and found Kieran kneeling in front of the longest couch. Joel was sitting on the couch, looking at Kieran. Kieran had a hand on his leg and looked profoundly miserable.

"I know it wasn't on purpose," Kieran was saying. "I never said it was on purpose."

"Everything wants to get away from itself," Joel said. Collie backed up a step, into Anna, and Anna realized it was the first time they'd heard him speak. Joel looked up at the sound and gave Collie a slow, formal nod.

"Detectives." he said. "Can I help? About Mandrake?"

Anna had forgotten that Joel had given them his phone number. It seemed as if it had happened in a past life. Collie shook her head.

"I don't think so," she said, in the soft voice she used for children. "We're here to see Kieran."

Anna had a sense that something was off about the room and took a careful look around. One. Two. Three.

"Kieran," she said. "Didn't there used to be four couches?"

"Sat on a cat," Joel said. Apparently entranced by the sound of it, the rhyme, he began to repeat the words, drumming on his thighs with his open hands. "Sat on a cat. Sat on a cat."

"Okay." Kieran patted Joel's leg. "Upstairs. We can work this out later."

"Like an arrow," Joel said, and left the room. Anna could hear the stairs creaking under his feet. Kieran sat on the couch and rubbed his eyes.

"It's not even noon," he said. "Well. What can I do for you?"

"I'm not sure," Collie said. "We have something for you."

Kieran took his hands from his eyes and looked at them.

"Is it Advil?"

"We know who kidnapped Rowan Bell," Collie said.

"I don't really care," Kieran said. "Not to sound heartless, but I have my own problems."

"Yeah," Collie said, "except we were assuming whoever kidnapped Rowan Bell had killed Mandrake, remember?"

"I don't know if I was assuming that," Kieran said. "I said it was a good possibility. So?"

Collie shook her head.

"She didn't kill Ian. It was Robin Hampshire, and all she did was kidnap Rowan. She was hired to do it. She didn't even take him from Ian's house."

Kieran frowned.

"How did you find this out?"

Collie twitched a little, seemed uncomfortable in her skin.

"From Robin," she admitted. "But she was very upfront with us, believe me. She doesn't seem to feel she has to lie about anything."

"Yeah," Kieran said grimly. "She doesn't."

"So," Collie said, "we're at a loss for a motive. It was probably because of something to do with the Embassy, and we're not privy to his work for them."

"Also," Anna said, "Robin killed Eric Quinlan."

Kieran looked at her.

"Who?"

"Never mind," Anna said. "But you can tell the Embassy. They know who he is. Was."

"Okay," Kieran said. "Write down the name for me and I'll tell them. Anything else?"

"We've been talking to teleporters," Collie said. "There were three on Ian's guest list and one not on Ian's guest list – that would be Robin Hampshire. Of the three on the list, Sam and Jake are pretty much out, because Sam only opens small portals and Jake can only teleport from one bathroom to a very similar bathroom, so..."

She stopped and looked at Anna.

"Jesus. We never eliminated Nadia."

"No," Anna said, thinking back. "We had to talk to Robin first."

"And then there was all the shit with the Scrabble tiles and with Eric and... Jesus. We forgot about Nadia."

"Nadia Kuri?" Kieran asked. "Are you saying she's the one who killed Mandrake?"

"Well," Collie said, "it's – she was on the guest list. She could have gone into the house, carrying a gun. She could even have gone in there carrying a smaller person on her back. She says she can take anything she can carry. Jesus."

Anna felt as if she were back in church, dragged there by her mother's parents. She hadn't heard Jesus mentioned so often in decades.

"We should have known," she admitted. "When we eliminated Robin, we should have known."

"We did know," Collie said. "We just didn't know we knew. We're idiots."

"We were doing two things at once," Anna reminded her. "We were thinking about Rowan."

"I guess the motive is irrelevant," Collie said. "You can convict someone in court without motive. They always say means, motive and opportunity, but actually you don't need to prove all three as long as you can prove that someone must have done it. There have been cases —"

"Babbling," Anna said simply. Collie nodded and shut her mouth.

"Um," Kieran said, "That's good work, actually. You probably should have called last night, but Ian isn't getting any dead — oh. Forget I said that. That was terrible. I meant to say the delay hasn't caused any harm. I'll let the Embassy know that they should bring Nadia in for questioning."

"Yeah?" Collie said, an odd look on her face. "How's that done?"

"What, questioning?" Kieran said. He looked even sadder than he had when they'd walked in. "They'll ask and she'll answer. It'll be like her idea. I... you know, I never had any problems with Nadia."

"She seemed nice," Collie said.

"Never can tell," Anna offered. Kieran looked at her.

"Sometimes you can."

Collie reached into her purse, took out a card and handed it to Kieran.

"What's this?" Kieran said, not looking at it. Normally Collie would have bit someone's head off for that, but this time she just answered him.

"Eric Quinlan's name. To give to the Embassy. We're not happy about what Robin did."

"People often aren't," Kieran said, putting the card in his pocket. "I have to ask you to leave now. It's not you — I just have things to look after."

"Understood," Anna said, though she didn't actually

understand in the sense of knowing what he meant. She just had the impression that something was supremely fucked up in Kieran's world. Worse even than in hers and Collie's.

They moved carefully through the foyer and out the door, neither willing to step on the spot where the fourth couch had been.

The purple-haired woman was still crying on the stoop as they left.

"ONE CLIENT'S DEAD," Collie said, "and I think the other one just fired us."

"Well, we solved the case," Anna said. "And we're still supposed to find Rowan."

They were by the University again, parked at the top of the riverbank.

"Yeah," Collie said. "I feel competent to do that. You?"

"I feel as though tying my shoes is beyond me," Anna said. "I can't believe we missed that, about Nadia."

"Feels funny, though," Collie said. "I can't picture it, you know? Her?"

"You never can tell," Anna repeated, trying to convince herself. It was easier to think you could tell. It was a scary world if you couldn't.

Collie had the car running. She was switching things up, throwing curveballs. Anna was losing the ability to predict her every move.

"You know what else bothers me?" Collie said. Anna smiled.

"I could write a book," she said.

"Ha," Collie declared. "Look. I've been thinking about Mandrake's alarm system. I know we've been assuming it just wasn't fast enough to get him out of the way of a bullet. I mean, getting hit by a bullet and getting hit by a truck, those things happen at different speeds."

"Were things different, I would never cross against the light again," Anna said.

"You don't now," Collie said. "But... it's all the same thing, right? Mandrake jumped when something was going to hit him. Truck or bullet, the only difference would be the speed. And didn't Jake say something about taking the time out of space-time? If what Mandrake did was instantaneous – faster than instantaneous, if there is such a thing – what difference would the speed of the projectile make?"

The stereo was running, a woman with a clear, warm voice singing about pieces of a whale flashing in the light, just above the water. Hit a whale in the heart and the whole ocean turns red.

"All the difference," Anna said. "Apparently."

"Yeah," Collie said. "Apparently."

Anna reached for the luz, wanting to feel the roughness of its surface. Her hand closed around it.

And she's on a dirt road, sneezing because there's ash in her nose. Burned out buildings line the street on either side of her, blurry through her watering eyes. A crunch in the dirt, and she turns her head to find Rowan there, the luz in his hand.

"Flesh and bone," he says. "See this road?"

Anna looks at her feet, and the dirty grey earth beneath them. It's warm enough that she feels the heat through the soles of her boots. Pieces of glass are scattered around. Windows, she thinks. Got too hot for the windows.

"They could have put it anywhere," Rowan says. "But they ran it right down the line."

They did. The road is always warm, not just because of the fire. It's always been warm. The road is a tracing of a line.

"People call them ley lines," Rowan says. "And other things. Varanus needed this place. Eric could only have been born here.

Do you get that?"

"Did they really send a dragon?" she asks. She can see it for a moment, flying low, breathing heavy with the exertion of flying from somewhere far away. Maybe China. Maybe farther.

It pants, and the fire goes everywhere.

Anna ducks. The dragon disappears as she raises her hands toward her face.

Rowan laughs.

"Only Saint George can prevent forest fires," he says.

He holds up the luz and Anna watches as it turns to steel in Rowan's hand.

"See?" he says. "No such thing."

"Eric did that?" Anna asks. "Eric can change that?"

Rowan leans against her shoulder and speaks softly at her ear.

"Sometimes," he says, "I think, before that fire, people saw dragons all the time."

"No such thing," Anna repeats. Rowan stands up straight.

"If you say so," he says. And is gone.

The luz falls to the earth.

It marks the spot.

"HOT DAMN!"

Anna blinked and her hand came into focus. It was empty and she was opening and closing it as if that would change things. Beyond her hand, on the coffee-stained floor mat, she could see bone white. She leaned forward and took the luz again. Collie breathed sharply. Anna set the luz back in the cup holder.

"You totally had a vision," Collie said. "You did, didn't you? Unless you had a stroke or something."

Anna looked at her. Collie squinted and leaned forward, staring into her eyes.

"Pupils are the same size."

Anna looked at the luz again. It wasn't asking anything of her.

The stereo was playing something different, now. It must have been awhile that she'd been in Grayling Cross, breathing ashes. *You're still missing something,* someone sang.

"So?" Collie said. "What'd you get?"

Still missing something.

"Are you okay?" Collie asked. Anna looked at her.

"I think I know where Ro —"

Collie's phone rang.

"Shit," Collie said mildly, and grabbed the phone from the dashboard. Her eyebrows rose and she answered it.

"Miss Doris," she said, sounding as surprised as Anna felt. Collie listened for a few moments, then said, "Okay. Give us fifteen."

The phone went back into Collie's purse, not onto the dashboard. She's forgiven it, Anna thought. She'd been mad at it. Because a good phone would never have let her call Robin Hampshire, even unintentionally. You had to blame something, didn't you?

"Doris says to meet her at Mandrake's," Collie said. "Pronto. She actually said pronto."

"Weird," Anna offered. She leaned back and looked out the window. The scenery spun dizzyingly as Collie swung them around to face the nearest bridge. The tires screamed. Anna knew the feeling. She closed her eyes and waited for something to be over.

DORIS WAS STANDING outside the house when they arrived. Anna thought that standing might not have been the right term, though, since Doris did not seem, at any point, to have both feet on the ground at the same time. She was bouncing from one foot to the other, playing some hopscotch game that valued repetition over distance and was only sketched out in her mind.

She gave them a deadly glare as they got out of the car.

"Why did you take so long to get here?"

"Oh," Collie said, "air friction. Curvature of the Earth. What's up?"

"I am going to fix this," Doris said. She'd stopped bouncing, but it was clearly through an immense effort of will. "Okay? I know you're gonna have to tell people about this, but I am going to fix it."

"Fix what?" Anna said.

"The *loophole,*" Doris said in a "what else have we been talking about for the last three hours?" tone.

"Loophole?" Collie said, glancing at Anna and seemingly wondering if maybe Anna had, somehow, been discussing loopholes with Doris for hours. Anna spread her hands.

"Ask the jumping bean," Anna recommended. Collie looked at Doris.

"Loophole?"

Doris rolled her eyes.

"*Yeah*. How they *shot* that guy."

"We... uh," Collie said.

"Already know that," Anna said. "There was a teleporter on the guest list and she could carry a smaller person inside, so —"

"*No!*" Doris said, waving a hand at Anna's face. Anna was pretty sure that, had she been standing closer, Doris would actually have slapped her.

"Yes?" Collie said, tilting her head.

"You're not gonna go — if someone tries to carry you in, you're just not gonna go. You're not gonna walk in the front door, but you'll get someone to carry you in? Forget about it."

"Well," Anna said, "okay, she might have shot him herself."

Not that she could see Nadia doing that, not for love or money, but she didn't know Nadia well. In truth, she couldn't say she knew Nadia at all.

"You don't want to go in," Doris said.

"True that," Collie said, glancing at the house and undoubtedly thinking of what they'd found the last time they'd gone inside.

"Shut up," Doris said. "I'm talking."

Collie raised her hands and Doris nodded.

"You don't go in because you don't wanna go in, remember? That's how the ward works. It makes you not wanna go in. But if you don't wanna or not wanna go in, you could go in anytime."

"Is this a koan or something?" Collie asked. Doris gaped at her.

"That is so racist!"

"What?" Collie said, her voice rising to a squeak. "I – what?"

"Doris," Anna said, "what is your point?"

Doris rolled her eyes again, obviously frustrated by having to deal with such obtuse people. She looked at the lawn and started to walk around, bent over, eyes on the ground. Anna watched in amazement as Doris made her way to the neighbour's lawn, still staring down. She would have offered to help, maybe, if she'd had the first idea what Doris was doing.

Doris went straight for a flower bed and started picking at something, though there was now a hedge blocking Anna's view and she couldn't make out what Doris was doing at ground level.

"Do you..." Collie began, but then Doris straightened and returned to them, a fair-sized rock in one hand.

"This!" Doris said, and, without further comment, pitched the rock through the living room window.

The window shattered and Anna could, for a moment, see fire racing up the street, windows everywhere spitting glass onto the dirt road. And then it was just a city street, where some punk had thrown a rock through the window of an ordinary house.

Collie was staring at the window, as pale as she'd been when Michael disappeared.

"It went in," she said. Under other circumstances, that would have been a stupid comment and Anna would have ribbed her for it, but Anna had nearly said the same thing herself. It went in. It did not bounce off a force field. It did not stop at the glass and hover there, or simply fall to the ground. Instead, it had behaved like any other rock going through any other window. Because it was a rock, and it didn't know any better.

"You could shoot someone," Collie said. Anna thought of Sam's portals, how he couldn't put anything sentient through them, nothing alive, even. But anything else could go.

"Through a portal," Anna said, and Collie nodded.

"Because a bullet doesn't want anything," she said. "It doesn't want to go in or not want to go in."

"Is that a koan?" Doris inquired. Collie didn't look at her.

"Thanks," Anna said to Doris. Doris shrugged. She didn't seem remotely bouncy anymore.

"Tell Matt I'll pay for the window," she said. "I don't know what I should pay him for the tenant. Lost revenue?"

It wasn't disrespect for Ian, that comment. Anna could tell. Doris was simply, and profoundly, unhappy with herself. There was nothing like feeling you'd gotten someone killed to take the spring out of your step.

"You didn't shoot him." Anna said. "And there's no such thing as a perfect security system."

"I'm going to fix it," Doris repeated.

"I know," Anna told her, and meant it.

Collie had her cell to her ear and was tapping the ground impatiently with the heel of one boot.

"Come on, Kieran. This is important. Answer the phone, prick..."

She hung up, hit a different number, and began showering abuse on some other ringing phone.

"Fucking answer..."

Collie hung up and threw the phone into her purse.

"Doris, don't be so fucking hard on yourself. You broke the case. Anna, come on."

"We going somewhere?" Anna inquired.

"Yeah," Collie said. She was halfway to the car and not looking back. "The Embassy."

Collie slammed her door and shoved her seatbelt into place and punched her keys into the ignition with a closed fist. She barely waited until Anna was inside the car before she peeled out, laying rubber. Until they rounded the corner, Anna watched Doris watching them drive away.

"SHE FEELS GUILTY," Anna said. Collie rubbed the steering wheel with the palms of her hands.

"Don't we all."

They were speeding, certainly, though Anna wasn't sure by how much. You couldn't go by the speed of other drivers, not in Edmonton. You had to assume everyone else was speeding, too. She considered glancing at the speedometer, but decided she'd be happier not knowing.

"Maybe that's true in general," Anna said. Collie shot a quick look at her before concentrating on her dangerous driving.

"What, that we feel guilty?"

"No," Anna said, "that I'd be happier not knowing things. Sorry. I was talking to myself."

"People talk a lot about ignorance being bliss," Collie said. She was stressed, talking fast. "Maybe it is, but it's not realistic. It's not human nature. We want to know. All primates want to know. We're curious animals."

"I'll say," Anna said.

"Secrets are like... like fame. Probably thousands of famous people have said it sucks, and we all still want to be famous."

Anna didn't want to be famous and, what's more, hadn't followed that leap, but it didn't matter. Collie was just talking.

She was panicking and she was talking. It was to be expected.

"It could still have been Nadia," Collie said.

"I know," Anna said. "It could even have been some random person who's not on the guest list at all, if you think about it. Opening a portal isn't the same as going in."

"A window is not a door," Collie said. "I know. But Nadia..."

"When I had that coughing fit," Anna said, "she patted my back."

That didn't prove anything. Anna knew that. But it had been thoughtful and kind and had seemed very Nadia, in a way that murder did not.

"Yeah," Collie said. "I know. I think maybe the reason we didn't think of her last night was that it didn't feel right. Back there, when I thought about Sam opening a portal for someone..."

"It felt right," Anna said. Collie nodded.

"Why, though? I like – I mean, I liked Sam."

Anna shrugged.

"Maybe he's a good actor. Or maybe we're just wrong again."

Collie was silent, presumably thinking that over as she wove into every Tercel-sized space the traffic gave her.

"It's still stupid that Mandrake didn't jump," she said. "Death wish," Anna reminded her. "Jake said he had a death wish."

"Never stopped him from jumping before," Collie said. The car swerved, sickeningly, and Anna felt a slight tearing as the "oh shit" handle pulled from the ceiling vinyl. To her amazement, Collie pulled over on a side street, in front of a neat little blue house, and threw the car into park.

"Could it have been Jake?" Collie said, looking Anna in the eye. "Is there any way?"

"Not unless the fact that a cat had pissed in Mandrake's apartment made it a washroom," Anna said. Collie gave her a twitch of a smile.

“Is something art just because you hang it on a wall? I just thought, Jake said time wasn’t a factor in what he did. Maybe that’s the trick. Mandrake didn’t jump because there was no time to jump. Because he got shot in no time.”

Anna shook her head.

“I think Jake meant time wasn’t a factor in teleporting,” she said. “In general. And there’s always… the bullet had to leave the portal and enter Mandrake’s head. Even if the portal was right up against him, the bullet had to go through his skull. That would take time.”

“Everything takes time,” Collie said absently. “Curvature of the Earth. Gravity. Friction. Everything’s a time suck.”

“Including this conversation,” Anna said. “Col, look… whatever kept Mandrake from jumping, he didn’t jump. *Quot erat duck*. It’s not our job to figure out the why on that.”

Collie looked at her.

“You said something.”

“A few things,” Anna said.

“No. Something important.”

“Mark your calendar,” Anna suggested with a glare. Collie shook her head in annoyance. She was thinking. Anything Anna said now would just be random numbers shouted out while Collie tried to count.

A tall woman walked by with a brown and white Papillon on a leash, the tiny dog rushing to keep up with the woman’s easy pace. Anna felt sorry for Papillons. All they wanted was to be taken seriously. It wasn’t their fault they were the size of guinea pigs on stilts.

“Check your purse,” Collie said as the woman and dog passed the car. Anna looked her.

“For?”

“No,” Collie said. “I don’t mean check your purse. I mean, remember? Ian said that to me when I asked him where our cheque was. The last time we saw him.”

"Okay," Anna said. "If you say so."

"And the cheque was in there. Which it wasn't, when we walked in, because I had just been through my purse looking for my phone. No cheque."

"I'm not sure you can be sure of that," Anna told her. "Your purse has a lot of —"

"I know what's in my purse," Collie said. "The cheque went in there while we were sitting next to Mandrake. I assumed he'd ported it in there, but, when we talked to Sam, he said he was the one who delivered cheques."

Anna leaned back. In the rear view mirror, she could see the woman and dog walking away. If she hurried, maybe she could catch up. Pet the dog. Dogs rarely said pointless shit to her when she was already having a bad day.

"So?" she asked.

"So, how did that happen?" Collie said. "Mandrake didn't call Sam. He could have popped over to Sam's place and told him to deliver the cheque, but we would have noticed that he was missing."

"Or maybe he's telepathic," Anna said.

"Sure," Collie said, "right, except I picture Mandrake sitting there and thinking he should get us our cheque, because we are sometimes bitchy about late cheques —"

"In equations where we equals you," Anna said. "Yes. Go on."

"...and where does he go to find Sam? That junk shop where Sam works. And they stand there, surrounded by old stuff in bags and boxes, most of which looks kind of new, if you think about it. Maybe Sam doesn't just do things to space. Maybe he does them to ti —"

"Are things not complicated enough for you?" Anna demanded. "Why are you throwing another wrench in?"

Collie just looked at her, face calm.

"It's not any weirder than him being a teleporter. And it would explain why Ian didn't jump, if time was all funny."

"And it would explain Sam's holographic buddy, Al," Anna said. Collie grinned.

"Exactly. No, seriously... why not? He works with vintage stuff. It makes everything make more sense. And we're already dealing with people who do impossible things."

"Its —" Anna stopped. "It doesn't matter. Okay? Think what you want. Because, like I said, it's not our job."

"Okay," Collie said. "Let's go tell the Embassy what's news. Here's hoping they haven't bothered Nadia yet."

IT TYPIFIED "easier said than done" to make their way to the Embassy, though it wasn't really so far as the crow flew. Or the raven, if ravens were creepier.

"Fuck," Collie said. She was hitting the steering wheel, open-handed, as she waited to get into a lane. "All we do is go over fucking bridges. Back and forth."

"We need a hovercar," Anna agreed.

"Or a secret underwater tunnel," Collie said.

"Or an amphibious vehicle," Anna finished.

"That would solve everything," Collie agreed.

Anna looked at the river as they crossed. Something about it, maybe the high banks, always made her think of mountain streams — those icy, rocky things that looked like spilled antifreeze.

"We should go to Jasper," Anna said once they'd reached the south side. Collie, waiting at a light, took the opportunity to look askance at her.

"What, now?"

"Just sometime," Anna said.

"Maybe now would be good," Collie said, but she went southeast instead of northwest, so obviously she hadn't meant it.

By the time they were half a block away from the Embassy, Anna could see that a scene was in progress. People were gathered on the stoop, with shoving and yelling and... she turned off the stereo and listened. Yes, crying.

"No wonder they weren't answering their phone," Anna commented.

"I have a sick feeling that we caused this," Collie said. "You figure?"

"These guys?" Anna said. "It might not be about our case. Could be anything."

It wasn't, though. As Collie pulled up outside the house, Anna could see that the crying was coming from Nadia. She wasn't trying to escape, as Anna would have expected, but was instead clinging to the redheaded woman they'd met on their visit to the Embassy office.

"You can't think it was me," Nadia was choking out between sobs. "I would never do that to you!"

Anna stepped onto the sidewalk and heard the redhead's softer voice.

"I know you didn't do it, Nadia. I know. Just... go home now."

"Don't make me leave you!" Nadia wailed. She sounded like a three year old clinging to her mother's skirts. It was the last thing Anna could have imagined hearing from that dignified, self-possessed woman.

A short, delicate brunet was attempting to gently pry Nadia from the redhead, but it wasn't going well. At one point, Nadia elbowed him and he fell backward into the railing.

"Don't do that," the redhead said, and Nadia looked stricken.

"I'm so sorry," she said – to the redhead, not the man she'd pushed. Anna tasted something sour at the back of her throat.

"Col? Maybe this is not a good time."

Collie said nothing. Anna turned to find her staring at the redhead, eyes dark, her face bearing the same combination of slackness and desperation that Anna could see on Nadia. Yes, Collie inexplicably thought that the redheaded skank looked like a million bucks, but that didn't explain the way she was looking at said skank. Anna had sat next to Collie through a raft of Jennifer Connelly movies and knew for a fact that Colette did not look at anyone, *anyone* quite the way she was looking at the redhead now.

"You know," the short man told the redhead, "this little knack of yours is getting to be more fucking trouble than it's worth. If you ask me. Which no one ever does."

"Oh, that's a lot of help," the redhead spat at him. "Can we not discuss this later?"

From the corner of her eye, Anna could see Collie moving past her, toward the door. She grabbed Collie's arm and pulled her back, careful to stay well away from her elbows.

"Colette," Anna said. Collie ignored her and kept trying to get to the door. Anna shoved her toward the car.

"Hey!" Collie said, sparing her a glance.

"Get in the damned car," Anna instructed.

"Get in the house!" the short man said. Anna suspected it wasn't directed at her or at Collie. She kept shoving.

"Let me *go!*" Collie demanded. Anna shoved her.

"You are getting in the car or I am putting you in the car," she said. "You will thank me later." With another shove, she added, "Profusely."

To Anna's relief, she heard the front door of the house slam. Nadia wailed, but Collie blinked and stopped shoving. She looked confused, but at least someone was at home behind her eyes.

"Get in the car," Anna repeated, looking her in the eye. Collie nodded.

"Getting," she said simply, and got.

Anna faced the house again and saw Nadia trying to pull open the door. The man was watching, exasperation on his young, handsome face. His light, almost rosewood brown hair was tied back in a ponytail and he was wearing a t-shirt that graphically proclaimed the superiority of Mario on mushrooms to Mario not on mushrooms.

"Nadia," he said, not unkindly. She didn't bother to look at him. He sighed. "Please, just go."

Anna stepped forward, thinking maybe she could do something, maybe slap the poor woman. Before she reached the foot of the stoop, though, the man raised his hands and flicked them in Nadia's direction. She made a surprised sound and fell back from the door, as if someone had given her a hard push in the stomach. She would have landed on her ass and fallen down the stairs, but the man waved his hands again and she instead drifted just above the steps until she was sitting on the grass near Anna's feet. She seemed surprised enough, for the moment, to have forgotten her desperate need to get inside the house.

The man looked at Anna and pointed at the door with his chin. Anna ran up the steps as the man opened the door, and they both dashed inside. The man shut the door behind them and locked it, throwing the deadbolt for good measure.

"Sorry," he told Anna. "That was kind of messy."

"That's one adjective," Anna told him. "I need to see Adam."

"Yeah?" the man said. "Come back later."

"Nope," Anna said. "I need to see him now."

The man smiled with one side of his mouth.

"That's fairly impossible. Can anyone else help you?"

Anna leaned against the door and tried to think of a way around what she had to say next. The man shook his head a little.

"I don't have all day," he said. "I have to find someone to knock Nadia out and take her home."

"Nice," Anna commented.

"Beats leaving her there," the man said. "So? Can someone else help you?"

"Yeah," Anna admitted. "I guess I'll talk to the redhead."

THE MAN WENT DOWN A HALL and through a door and, a few seconds later, the redhead came through that same door and walked down the hall to stand in front of Anna.

"You wanted to talk to me?" she asked. Anna shrugged.

"Not like Nadia does, but yeah."

The redhead looked irritated. It probably was irritating, when you broke a perfectly functional person and then said person refused to take her weeping carcass off your front lawn. Anna put her hands in her pockets and reminded herself that she needed to conduct some business with the skank. Punching her arch, plasticky face would probably not make things go more smoothly.

"I just put a..." the redhead rubbed her fingertips together, feeling for the word, "whammy on her. She'll get over it."

"Whammy," Anna said. The redhead exhaled, hard, through her thin, sharp nose.

"Whatever you'd like to call it," the redhead said. "I notice it doesn't affect you. That's actually kind of refreshing."

"Well, gee. I'm happy you're happy," Anna offered. "Look – I think we were wrong about Nadia."

"You must have been," the redhead agreed. "If she'd done it, she would have told me."

"We just found out there's a way through Doris' ward."

Perfectly plucked eyebrows rose. The woman's brow did not wrinkle. Anna wanted to hold an acetylene torch near her and see if she'd melt.

"Really?"

"We were assuming someone had to have gone in and shot Mandr – Ian, because we thought someone kidnapped Rowan at the same time. But last night we found out that Rowan's kidnapping was unrelated to Ian's shooting. A few minutes ago, we found out that inanimate objects can be propelled through the ward, as long as no one tries to go with them. With that in mind –"

"Someone opened a portal," the redhead finished.

"Could have been anyone," Anna said. "Technically, I don't think it would have had to be someone on the guest list, if all they did was open a portal. But now we're looking at someone who wanted to kill Ian, personally... so I'm going to guess the killer was not a stranger to him."

"We called all the porters in town today," the redhead said. She'd backed up against a wall and was leaning against it, knees bent a little. Taking the pressure off her high heels. Who wore heels in their own house? Even if someone did, if their feet hurt badly enough for them to need the wall-leaning dodge, wouldn't they take the damned things off?

"Um," Anna said, forcing her brain back on track, "and?"

"Sam Llewelyn did not answer or return our calls. At the time, I didn't care because we were focused on Nadia, but... now I wonder."

"We like him ourselves," Anna said. "As a suspect, I mean. He —" Oh, damn it. If she didn't share Collie's crackpot theory and Collie found out about it, there'd be hell to pay. "Ah... do you think maybe he does anything besides teleporting? Because we're thinking, if he could travel in time, that would... it's just that Ian didn't jump out of the way of the bullet. So another factor would explain that."

The redhead's face was perfectly still as she regarded Anna. It really did look plastic, seamless and utterly inhuman.

"Sam is likeable," the redhead said, not confirming whether she meant as a suspect or otherwise. "Adam and I have speculated about his potential for time travel. If he can do that, and he might well be able to, he's cagey about it."

"Sometimes things aren't your business," Anna said, without thinking. To her relief, the redhead smiled.

"So I've heard. Look, Anna. I need to talk to Sam, obviously, but he's ducking me and teleporters and time travellers are the worst people to have to find. He might come to visit you if you asked. Maybe at your house."

"So you can make him cry on our lawn?" Anna said. "No thanks. Your friend Adam said we had to bring you a name and then we were out."

"He may have killed Ian," the redhead pointed out. "He probably did."

"That's a point," Anna admitted. "But I still don't want you pulling that whammy shit at my house. Not around my friend, in particular."

"We can send someone to pick him up," the redhead said.

"I'll think about it," Anna said. "While I'm thinking, did Kieran tell you that Robin Hampshire kidnapped Rowan Bell and murdered Eric Quinlan?"

The redhead shrugged. Her shoulder was narrow and her green silk shirt rose to an awkward point.

"That's Robin's business," she said. "We wish she wouldn't do business in Edmonton, but you try to stop her."

Anna stared at her. She hadn't thought the woman a saint, but hadn't she and Adam said something about Eric being one of the good guys?

"Didn't you and Adam say you didn't want to have to kill Eric?"

"It's like that thing Stewie said about his mother on *Family Guy*," the redhead told her. "What was it – something about, I don't want to kill her; I just don't want her to be alive anymore. We really didn't want to have to kill him."

Anna was gawking now, she knew. She couldn't stop herself.

"Did you just quote a cartoon show to me? By way of saying that you don't care that a man was murdered this morning for no fucking good reason? For *money*?"

"I'm saying it's not our concern," the redhead said coolly. "Unlike Ian. And Sam."

Forget the acetylene torch. Anna wanted to dump water over her, see if that would make her melt.

"Let's see," she said slowly, "if I can change your views on that."

The redhead looked amused.

"Oookay..."

"Before our client was murdered by a hired gun working freely in your supposedly peaceful city," Anna said, "he asked us to find his friend Rowan for him, should anything happen to him. I believe I know where Rowan is."

"Great," the redhead said. She stood up, grimacing as all ninety-seven pounds of her landed on her feet. "Mission accomplished."

"No," Anna said, "because we are supposed to get him out of there, and that is beyond us. So you're going to have to rescue him instead."

The redhead put a hand on her hip, not seeming to realize that she needed a 1940s wave and a dressing gown to sell that pose. That, and a hip.

"Why would we do that?"

"Because, if you do that, we will help you out with Sam."

The redhead's green eyes shut and it was at that moment, oddly, that Anna realized her eyes were perfectly matched to her shirt. Did she bring a mirror with her when she went shopping and hold fabrics up to her face? Maybe she got them specially dyed.

"Where do you think Rowan Bell is?"

"In the Varanus facility," Anna said, "that I'm pretty sure is hidden in the old mine at Grayling Cross. The one Varanus supposedly built and abandoned. Grayling Cross is near Fort Chip."

"I know where it is. We told you, remember?" The green eyes were open again, wider than Anna had seen them before. "God. You're probably right. Why did we never think to look for a facility there?"

Anna was struck by the comment, by how similar it was to the things people must have said when they walked away from Ian and Matt's house. I don't know why I didn't go in. I don't know why I didn't try to sell them a vacuum cleaner. I just don't know.

"They seem pretty good at keeping things on the down low," she offered. "So. Do we have a deal?"

"Go home," the redhead said. Any languor in her manner was gone. "Draw Sam in. Call us once you've got him. We'll get Rowan Bell for you."

"Fine," Anna said. "Forgive me if I don't shake hands."

She turned her back on the redhead and left.

"I DON'T FEEL HUMILIATED in the least," Collie said as Anna got into the car. "If you were wondering."

"Good," Anna said. She gestured at the lawn, which was now bereft of weeping teleporters. "What happened to Nadia?"

"Some guy came out and touched her forehead and it put her right out. He put her in the back of a blue Cavalier and drove away. I thought about following him." She looked at Anna. "Do you think I should have followed him?"

"No," Anna said. "That guy who was on the stoop said he was going to have someone take her home."

Collie nodded.

"Good. I'm glad I didn't watch some serial killer driving her off to a gravel pit."

"Gravel pit?" Anna started at her. "Never mind. Anyway, I still say that redhead is skanky."

"Ha," Collie said. She didn't laugh, just said the word. "Can we leave?"

"In a sec," Anna said. She took out her own cell phone, causing Collie's eyes to widen.

"What the hell has provoked *you* to make a call?"

"You got Sam's number?"

Collie went through her purse by feel, keeping her eyes on Anna.

"Yeah, but –"

"I have to ask him to meet us at our house."

Collie stopped searching her purse.

"What?"

"I told the Embassy we'd set him up," Anna said, "in exchange for them rescuing Rowan from the Varanus facility at Grayling Cross."

"Uh – oh," Collie said. "You... um... there's a Varanus facility at Grayling Cross?"

"It's a vision thing," Anna said, not adding that Rowan hadn't actually said where he was, or that she had no explicit reason to even think Varanus had built a facility in the old mine site. It just made enough sense to Anna that she was willing to go with it.

"You mean, that mine they dug, that Eric said they'd abandoned?" Collie asked.

"I'm thinking maybe they didn't."

Collie looked surprised.

"Maybe they didn't," she said slowly. "No kidding. Wow. We should have thought of that."

"Eric should have thought of that," Anna pointed out. "Varanus probably has a Doris, you know?"

"Oh. I guess they would," Collie agreed. "So, we're asking a murderer to meet us at our place?"

It was the same tone she might have used to confirm a dinner date, or to check that it was skim milk she was to pick up after work, and not 2%.

"That's right," Anna said. "Provided he did it."

"I guess the redhead will find that out," Collie said. She sounded nauseated. "I mean, the other redhead. Not me."

"I guess so," Anna agreed.

"And we're not asking him to meet us at our office because?"

"We're not sure where Robin killed Eric," Anna said. "I don't think we should go near our office right now."

"Right." Collie now sounded as if she had actual bile in her mouth. "Good point."

Anna put a hand on her arm.

"Number?"

Collie pulled her arm away and took out her own phone, read the number off from there. Anna dialed as Collie spoke. Anna didn't know what she was going to say to Sam, not exactly, but she figured sounding flustered could work to her advantage.

"Hello, Ms. Gareau," Sam's voice said, cutting off the first ring. Anna jumped a little.

"Uh — hi. You must have been sitting right next to the phone."

"I've been expecting your call. I'd like to meet with you and Colette, if I could."

It couldn't be that easy, could it? Anna looked at her phone, but it didn't flash an answer on its tiny screen. It never did.

"Well... we'd like that, too," she said. "Could you come by our house? Our office is a little complicated right now."

"A complicated office," Sam said, sounding amused. "That is a difficulty. Your home would be fine."

"Great," Anna said, and gave him the address. "We can meet you there in... half an hour?"

"Done," Sam told her. "I'll see you then."

Anna put her phone away and looked at Collie.

"We have a date," she said. Collie started the car.

"A date. Why am I thinking we won't get dinner before we get fucked?"

"SO," COLLIE SAID. "Not to get bitchy here, but offering to trap Sam was a pretty big decision to make all by your lonesome."

"I was by my lonesome," Anna pointed out.

Collie was, apparently, too dispirited to comment as they drove over a bridge again. She didn't even speed as they traced Groat Road's inviting curves. Anna wanted to say that the redhead obviously put her "whammy" on all kinds of people, even magical types. And that Nadia was going to be okay, most likely. And that Sam probably didn't intend to kill them. But she didn't think Collie wanted to talk about any of those things.

The stereo's contribution to the silence was a deep-voiced man insisting that walking away now would start a war.

The one thing she could think to say that Collie would want to hear was:

"The Embassy likes your stupid time traveller theory. They've been wondering about it themselves."

It was an indication of how far Collie's spirits had fallen that she simply nodded, and said nothing.

Their townhouse was still standing when they pulled up, a little scruffy but basically undamaged, midway through two blocks of identical row housing.

They went in the front and didn't, at first, notice anything. It wasn't until they were rid of boots and coats and heading into the living room that they saw Sam Llewelyn sitting halfway up the stairs.

"Jesus fuck!" Collie shrieked. "Oh, man, what is *wrong* with you people? Do any of you knock?"

"I'm sorry," Sam said, sounding genuinely sheepish. "Outside isn't a good place for me right now, or I'd be on your porch. I had a friend finesse your lock. It's your business, of course, but perhaps you should consider getting Doris to put a ward on your home."

"Worked so well for Ian," Anna commented. Sam took a few breaths and said nothing. He didn't look much happier than Collie did.

"Please," Sam said at last, "sit down. I have something to say and you won't like it."

Anna went to her usual spot and Collie did the same. Murderer on the stairs? Sky falling? At least they were sitting in the right chairs.

"I suspect you know this," Sam said once they were settled, "but you only know the bare bones of it. I want... I would like to tell you why I did what I did to Ian McLaren."

"To be clear," Anna said, "you..."

"Shot him," Sam said. "Through a portal. I'm sorry. I am sorry."

"Well," Collie said. "Since you've apologized."

"I know that changes nothing for you, or for Ian. Selfishly, I suppose, I wanted to say that I am sorry, and that I did not want to do it."

"Someone made you do it?" Collie asked. Sam gave her a sad smile.

"I wish I had that sort of excuse. All I can tell you is that I knew something about Ian that other people didn't. He was a dangerous person."

"Oh, come on," Collie said. "Ian? He was going to make a play for world domination or something? Get off it."

"He wasn't going to do anything on purpose," Sam said. "But you may have noticed that he had a self-destructive impulse, at war with his better instincts. There was going to be an incident in which Ian accidentally, or at the urging of his subconscious, was going to cause a disaster. A notable disaster."

"*Ha!*" Collie said. "You do jump around in time! Don't you?"

Sam stared at her, brow so deeply furrowed that Anna figured she could successfully plant things in it.

"Where did you hear that?"

"And *when!*" Collie said. "Don't forget when. We forgot when for awhile and it completely misled us."

Sam rubbed his brow, dislodging Anna's imaginary seeds.

"It's not important how you know," he said. "Yes, I can open portals in time as well as space. This means that I can know quite a bit about the future. I know Ian was going to cause something… unsupportable. It's the reason I came here in the first place. I've been trying to find a way to stop it."

"Your Honour," Anna said, "I happened to know he was going to shout and start an avalanche, so I had to kill him now."

"You're taking the piss," Sam said, "but that's how it was. Or was going to be, until I shot him. Which I wouldn't undo, but I do regret."

"You couldn't have just told him not to go around yelling on mountaintops?" Collie asked. She sounded as if her throat hurt.

"I tried that," Sam said. "I've tried a lot of things. I've been down this road many times."

Anna pictured him on the road through Grayling Cross, walking from one end of the town to the other and then finding himself at the beginning again.

"Maybe not enough times," she said. "Or maybe you could have tried some other road."

Sam shook his head.

"Even without being able to look through time," he said, "I would have known Ian was dangerous. You can't have that kind of power and be as unbalanced and dissociative as he was."

"Oh, really?" Collie said. "Because, Exhibit A: this entire city."

"Ian was different," Sam insisted. "He didn't have the capacity for control. Ladies, do you suppose I like to kill people?"

"Wouldn't know," Anna said, though actually she thought she did know. She thought he probably didn't like it. Not that it would have made a substantive difference to Ian.

"I don't," Sam said. "I tried everything else. I did. I suppose… you've probably got the Embassy out there, waiting for me?"

No, since Anna hadn't expected Sam to be waiting on the stairs when they got home. Neither she nor Collie had made the call. But she wasn't saying so. Not to a guy who'd killed at least one person and who could, she expected, open a portal the size of a bread box directly below one of her legs.

"Rotten trick," she said. "I know."

Sam looked her in the eye.

"Like shooting someone through a portal," he said. "I don't feel well. May I use your loo for a moment?"

Collie waved a hand at the top of the stairs.

"Go ahead."

Anna shut her eyes and leaned back in her chair, then suddenly sat upright and opened her eyes again. Shit. Shit, shit, shit.

"What?" Collie asked. Anna didn't waste time answering, just bolted up the stairs and knocked on the bathroom door.

"Sam? Say something if you're in there!"

She heard Collie tearing up the stairs behind her.

"Anna?"

Anna turned to find Collie directly behind her. She took a step back, fetching up against the door.

"Jake," she said. "The way he talked about Ian. And the bathroom."

Collie's eyes were huge.

"Fuck," she said.

"Shit," Anna agreed.

"But it's a private bathroom," Collie protested. She reached past Anna and rapped on the door. "Damn it, Sam!"

"He said he could use private ones sometimes," Anna said. Collie's brow furrowed with thought.

"If they weren't too... unusual."

Anna turned around and slammed her fist against the door. She didn't expect an answer. She said,

"Every fucking house on this block."

"Oh, Christ."

Collie took off down the stairs. Anna followed. Collie

stepped into loafers at the door and kept going, not bothering to grab a coat. Anna slipped into low-heeled mules and stayed right behind her.

Collie looked from one side of the street to the other, hair flying as she whipped her head around.

"There!"

She was pointing, and now running, north, toward the shopping mall at the end of the block. Sure enough, Sam and Jake were at the end of row houses, hauling ass to the back of the mall.

"Food court," Collie called over her shoulder, still running.

The food court entrance was at the back of the mall and it was, indeed, Sam and Jake's most likely destination. Washrooms didn't get more generic than the ones attached to mall food courts.

Anna overtook Collie halfway up the block, thanks solely to her relatively long legs. Neither had much time or patience for gyms and jogging, so they weren't breaking records on this run. Happily, Jake didn't seem to be much of a runner either. Twice, Anna saw Sam slow his pace to let Jake catch up.

By the time Jake and Sam had made it to the food court doors, Anna was only a few metres behind them. She noticed, from the corner of her eye, that the usual smoking teenage punks outside the doors were actually standing out of the way, which marked the first time she had ever seen them move for anyone. Apparently they'd sussed that these peculiar grown-ups wouldn't hesitate to bowl them over.

She made a sharp right and skidded into the food court, where she could see Jake and Sam leaving a trail of resentment as they wove around tables and strollers and shopping bags on their way to the washrooms. Anna dove into their wake and found herself confronted with yelling people who weren't about to be shoved a second time. Some deliberately jumped into her path. She was relieved when Collie caught up to her a second or two later. Collie had no problem using her sharp elbows to clear the way.

On the other side of the tables, Anna could see the washroom entrances. Sam and Jake were going into the men's. Of course.

Anna was actually sufficiently conditioned by that particular taboo that she slowed for a moment before charging into no woman's land.

The washroom doorway was doorless, just an open space slightly larger than a regular door. She dimly noticed, as she crossed the invisible line, that there were other people in the washroom. She couldn't have said exactly how many, though, or what they looked like. She was focused on the two men directly in front of her, trying to squeeze into a single stall. She lunged forward, grabbed the back of Sam's kicky little vintage leather jacket – which was probably smaller than a breadbox if you folded it right – and yanked him toward her.

She thought she heard people saying something, yelling, maybe, but she didn't feel anyone moving closer. Fine. They could yell all they wanted. As a woman, she guessed she'd be left alone to wail on Sam all she wanted. Never mind that she had a few inches and about thirty pounds on the guy. No one in that washroom was likely to be up for punching some chick.

She turned as she pulled Sam back, flipping him into the washroom wall, next to the entry space. The lights flickered and she realized with clarity, as if nothing could be more important, than he must have bounced against the light switch, turning the lights off and then on again before they'd had a chance to go out completely.

Sam made a noise of protest and, Anna liked to think, surprise. Didn't open a portal on this shit now, did he?

Behind her, Anna heard a stall door slam. Jake, making good his escape. Nothing to be done about that. She kept her focus on Sam.

He looked about to say something and it occurred to her

that she didn't remember how his power worked exactly. Did he gesture? Was it something he said? The image of a portal opening beneath her came to her again, and she wasn't having that. She pulled him back and shoved him again. To her astonishment, he sagged and went to his knees, raising a hand to his bleeding nose. She let him go and he turned until he was sitting on the floor, a dark tile that was doing a decent job of hiding all that blood.

She raised her hands and took a step back. She glanced at the doorway and saw Collie standing there, phone to her ear, giving directions to the washroom.

"I wouldn't try anything," she told Sam. "They're just up the street."

She looked at Anna.

"They were on their way to stake our place out."

Anna nodded and moved her shoulder in a small circle. She'd probably pulled something, yanking Sam around. If so, she couldn't feel it yet.

Collie stepped away from the washroom for a moment and Anna heard her thanking someone. For the phone, Anna realized. Because Collie had left hers in the house.

"I'm not going to do anything to you," Sam said. Between his accent and his bleeding nose, it took an effort to understand him. "I never was."

Anna shrugged. Still no pain.

"I didn't know what you were going to do."

Sam gave a sharp nod, wincing as he did so.

"My point," he said. A thin, balding man in a waffle-textured grey golf shirt took a careful step forward and held paper towel toward Sam. Sam took it without looking at his benefactor.

"My point," he repeated, in case Anna hadn't caught it the first time. Now Anna's chest hurt, though she doubted it had anything to do with her arm.

"Fuck you," she said distinctly, "would be mine."

"YOUR ARM OKAY?" Collie asked. They were walking back to the house, having left Sam in the tender care of the Embassy's goon squad. Anna had been surprised to see the young man with the ponytail and Mario t-shirt among their number. He'd given her a rueful smile and commented that it was shaping up to be a hell of a day. She had not argued.

"It's fine right now," Anna said. "But I think I'll be feeling it come winter."

"Hell of a performance," Collie said. "You bar brawler. It's too bad you didn't have a beer bottle."

"You blame me?" Anna asked, glancing at Collie. It wasn't a sarcastic question. Anna had no idea whether she blamed herself.

"No," Collie said. "That guy... he could maybe open a portal right inside someone. You ever think of that?"

Anna's stomach flipped over.

"No," she said. "I didn't. But thank you for the image."

"Communicating ideas," Collie said. "It's what I do."

They walked the rest of the way to the house in silence. Neither said anything about Sam's reason for the murder. Neither said anything about how many times Anna had been planning to bash a man's face into a bathroom wall. Neither said thing one about time travel, and Anna assumed that was because it gave Collie as bad a headache as it gave her. Predestination. Changing fate. Goddamn it. Sam could explain it all to the Embassy, and they were welcome to him.

Once they were inside, Collie spoke.

"At least we don't have to worry about Rowan. We held up our end."

Anna nodded. The last they'd seen of the Embassy, they'd been cheerfully bundling an unconscious Sam into their vehicle while the little girl and boy she'd met on her first visit to the Embassy scrawled chalk drawings on the sidewalk outside the food court doors.

"Don't step on my flowers," the girl had warned as Anna passed by. "They're forget-me's."

Indeed, everyone from the Embassy had carefully sidestepped the flowers.

"Little bit of PR work," one of the goons had told Collie with a wink. "Damage control."

"They have Sam," Anna said, "and they did their damage control, so I can't see them having anything to complain about. Except Jake."

"Yeah," Collie said. "Well. They don't seem too concerned about him. I guess it's their problem, anyway. Maybe he's on their list, right after Rowan."

"You'd think they'd want to find Rowan for their own reasons," Anna said, "since he's a remote —"

She stopped. She felt dizzy from the sensation of her mind going in circles, over and over the facts, over and over her memories.

The jacket.

She went up the stairs, not in a rush. She wasn't sure she wanted to know. She had to, though, because the Embassy would not appreciate being sent on a fool's errand. Provided they still meant to go.

She opened the linen closet door and started lifting towels and bedding, peeking underneath them. What had Collie said, exactly? That she'd stashed it under a sheet? Anna was about to give up and ask when the backs of her fingers brushed leather and she pushed the sheet aside to see Rowan's jacket, right where Collie had left it.

"Way ahead of you," Collie said, and Anna realized Collie had come up the stairs behind her. She turned and saw that Collie was holding Rowan's rubber duck in her hand. "I thought, maybe Rowan was... you know. One of Eric's imaginary friends. Like, I guess... like Michael was. So I checked just before we got home before, when Sam was here. I forgot to tell you."

"I guess he's a real boy," Anna said.

"Seems so," Collie agreed.

IT WAS PAST LUNCHTIME. They pulled leftovers from the fridge and ate. They didn't say much. Collie had called the Embassy to confirm about Rowan and the Embassy had said yes, a deal was a deal. And that they liked remote viewers. And they didn't like Varanus much.

So that was it. Anna was relieved, but it left them with little to do or say until the Embassy got back to them. Not unless they wanted to call and apologize to Nadia for fingering her, but Anna figured that could wait for a day or two. Possibly forever.

"What now?" Collie asked, apparently doing a similar inventory in her own head. Anna let the remains of her sandwich fall to her plate.

"I don't know."

"Maybe you should do a hot bath or something," Collie said. "For your shoulder. Just in case."

"It's not the worst idea I've heard all day," Anna told her. Not high praise, on that day, but still true.

A few minutes later, running the water, she thought it was probably madness to think the bath would do any good. After all, it wasn't as if the water would come anywhere near her shoulders.

Anna couldn't understand why, as people had become taller and taller through the years, bathtubs had gotten smaller and smaller. Not the fancy round ones with marble and jets that heavily mortgaged people had in their en suites. Those were a good size, mostly. But the normal ones that normal people had in their normal homes... they'd become little better than sinks with ambitions. Nothing like the clawfoots you could still find in farmhouse and character homes.

She poured bubble bath into the water. She didn't care overmuch what her bathwater smelled of. That wasn't the idea. She just felt that having to look at herself, pale and outsized with inconvenient hairs popping up... it spoiled an otherwise nice bath. Before moving in with Collie, she'd bought the cheapest bath foam she could find and had often emerged from the tub with a faint scent of grape or bubble gum clinging to her skin. Collie, upon discovering this habit, had rolled her eyes and insisted that Anna share whatever she brought home. And so Anna used what she supposed was the good stuff, now. She found that the bubbles looked exactly the same.

By stuffing a facecloth into the overflow drain, she managed to collect enough water to at least spread the soothing heat up her back. She stared, unfocused, at the glass jar of bath salts Collie kept at one end of the tub. She'd never seen the level of salts change. It was like those little trays of guest soaps people kept, the same soaps, unused for years. They probably had to be dusted when the washroom was cleaned.

Oh, people were crazy. Everything was crazy. Anna considered going crazy, to stay in step.

And then it seemed her plan had decided to implement itself, because the jar of bath salts began to move slightly. It tilted, as if awkwardly grasped, and the tight lid twisted a bit before popping off and falling into the water, quickly disappearing beneath the bubbles.

Anna sat up, pulling back from the lid. Because the lid, obviously that was her problem.

"Ian?" she asked, keeping her voice low. She didn't want to panic Collie and, besides, she felt dumb as hell saying it out loud. "Is that you?"

The jar tilted and bath salts spread onto the damp floor beside the tub. They'd had a bath mat for awhile, but it had never quite dried out and they'd finally decided it was less pleasant than a wet floor.

Before the salts could dissolve, letters were traced in them. Anna watched, stunned, as the words "Stop Them" appeared.

"Stop who?" she asked. The last word was rubbed away and fresh salts were poured.

"Embassy," it read. More salts. "Joel."

"Stop them from what?" Anna asked. She couldn't imagine that Mandrake would object to Rowan's being rescued. They'd been friends, after all.

More salts, the last in the jar.

"Kieran knows."

Anna realized, suddenly, that she was in the altogether. It wasn't a state in which she would ever have been happy to greet Ian. She got out of the tub, hurriedly, and pulled towels from the rack. Two towels did the job, mostly. Underneath them, she pulled her clothes on.

"Knows what? Ian... they're just going to rescue Rowan. I'm not going to keep them from doing that."

The water in the tub started to slosh, spilling past the useless drain and onto the bare floor, washing the salts away. It looked for all the world as if someone were throwing a tantrum in the water.

"Jesus, settle down!" Anna said. Instead, she watched in horror as the empty salt jar flew at the small, frosted window above the tub. Upon impact, the jar shattered and the window cracked.

"Anna?" Collie yelled from downstairs. "Are you okay?"

"Yeah," Anna said. She thought she was, anyway. Nothing was flying at her head and she wasn't likely to drown in a puddle.

"What the hell was that?" Collie wanted to know.

"Just a sec," Anna called back. Then she lowered her voice and spoke in the direction of the window. "We'll see Kieran. Okay? Good enough?"

There was no answer. Anna pulled on the last of her clothes and dropped her towels to the rose-scented floor.

"Was that our *window*?" Collie wanted to know.

"I think," she called, opening the door, "we'd better go talk to Kieran."

"THAT IS FUCKED UP," Collie said, but in a way that suggested she was bitter about having missed it. "That was some fucked-up shit."

They were in the Tercel, heading for the nearest bridge. Anna's hair was damp and she smelled strongly of whatever Collie's bath foam was supposed to smell like. She usually rinsed off in the shower after taking a bath, but it hadn't been worth the bother of cleaning broken glass out of the tub.

"I don't know," Anna said. "Seems in keeping with the Scrabble tiles. What really bothers me is that we're never going to get our damage deposit back."

"Why do you think Mandrake wants us to talk to Kieran?"

"I've been thinking about that," Anna said. "I've thought about it a lot, and I've come to the conclusion that I have no idea. I have a corollary, if you want to hear it."

"Wouldn't miss it," Collie said with a sideways smile.

"I think we should talk to Kieran."

"Ah," Collie said, nodding. "Well reasoned."

"Thank you."

They didn't talk about anything else on the way to Kieran's house. No need, really. None of the things they urgently wanted to know could be discovered through conversation with each other.

The purple-mohawked woman was no longer on the stoop when they arrived. Anna was relieved to see it. She wouldn't have said she'd expected, exactly, to find someone still crying, or puking, hours after she'd last seen them doing so... but it wouldn't have shocked her senseless, either.

"Guess she bucked up," Collie said. Anna nodded. She

thought about suggesting that maybe someone from the Embassy had knocked her out and driven her home, but it wouldn't have made Collie happy or solved a damned thing, so she said nothing.

The door was ajar, which made twice in one day that they'd found it that way, and twice in one day that Collie had been too distracted to comment upon how it had been a door just moments earlier. Anna gave it a gentle shove.

"Hello?"

She couldn't hear anything in the house. Usually there were sounds, muffled, from the upstairs rooms or the kitchen. And conversation, in the living room.

"Hello?" Collie added, looking past Anna's shoulder.

They looked at each other, then carefully proceeded toward the living room. To Anna's surprise, Kieran was there, a ball curled tightly and neatly on the couch farthest from the door.

"Um... everything okay?" Collie asked. Slowly, seemingly unsurprised that they were there, Kieran unrolled himself and fixed red-rimmed eyes on Collie's face.

"Dandy," he snarled. "What do the two of you want?"

His voice was rough and, for the first time since Anna had met him, he wasn't even trying for civility.

"Would you believe," Collie said, "that Mandrake told us to talk to you?"

"I beg your goatsucking pardon?" Kieran said. Anna blinked a few times, making sure it was really Kieran sitting there asking for her goatsucking anything.

"We think we're being haunted," she said carefully, "and we were given a message that said we should talk to you. Specifically, about Joel and the Embassy. Something about stopping them."

The rattiness that had, if nothing else, made Kieran seem self-confident gave way to weak confusion. Anna was almost sorry she'd said it. She'd liked mean Kieran better.

"Don't suppose," Kieran said, "he said how to stop them."

"So there is something going on with Joel and the Embassy?" Collie asked. Kieran looked at the living room ceiling. Whether he was doing a slow eye roll or praying for guidance – or salvation – Anna couldn't say.

"If you want to discuss this," Kieran informed the ceiling, "I am going to have to tell you a few unpleasant facts of life."

"It's not as if you're going to ruin our day," Collie said. "It has not been a world-beater so far."

"No," Kieran agreed. "It has not. Sit down."

Not "please sit down" or "have a seat" or "make yourselves comfortable," so Kieran still wasn't exactly himself. Anna felt relieved. She took a seat on the left hand couch, nearest the door. Collie sat beside her. Kieran shut his eyes.

"The reason the other couch is missing," he said, "is that Joel sat on a cat. It was under a blanket and it scared him when it moved, so he turned on it and it... Joel would say that it wanted to get away from itself. He says everything does, which is true in a sense. Joel believes in the expansion of the universe."

"Don't most people?" Collie asked.

"Joel doesn't believe it – he believes *in* it. And it seems to believe in him."

"This isn't clarifying anything for me," Collie said. "I'm sorry."

"Oh," Kieran said, "no. I'm sorry. I should have been clearer. Joel makes things disintegrate. He used to do it by accident all the time, which made him an unfeasible monster. So the Embassy gave him to me."

Collie had made a gagging sound somewhere around the word "disintegrate." Anna didn't blame her. Anna's stomach wasn't doing much better. How many times had they sat or stood next to Joel? How many times had Joel looked at them, thought something or other about them? How long did it take for someone to get something in his eye and blink the wrong way an accidentally disintegrate you?

"I take it," Anna said, her throat tight, "that it's not something anyone can fix? When he does that?"

Kieran snorted.

"It's time's arrow," he said. "That's what they call it. You can tell that time has a direction to it because things move from together to apart. Whole to broken. That's how we know time flows. Because broken things don't come back together."

"Some things flow backward," Collie said grimly, but she didn't get into details.

"Why would the Embassy give you a… an unfeasible monster?" Anna asked. "It seems like kind of a big responsibility, if he could have… he could have…"

"Anything," Kieran said. "He could have done pretty much anything. To anything. But, you see, it's difficult for people to do unfeasible things around me. Or unlikely things. Or unusual things. I'm the enemy of the un, I am."

"Excuse me?" Collie said. She was rolling her purse strap between her fingers, which was a fidget Anna had not seen from her before. It was always good to see someone exhibit personal growth.

Kieran opened his eyes and looked at them.

"Anna, have you ever tried to use your psychometry around me?"

"Mostly I try not to use it," Anna said. Kieran smiled and it was ugly. It made his face look scarred.

"Then you should like me more," he said. "Because I suppress it. I suppress magical powers or psychic abilities or whatever people want to call these things. It's not impossible to play tricks around me, but it's harder. And it's easier, see, if you're someone who doesn't want to have accidents. Because you really have to push to make anything happen."

Anna remembered something she'd seen on one of Collie's favourite DVDs, a character who called someone a constipator.

"You mess with my shit," he'd said, and the same could evidently be said of Kieran. She decided it would not be a good time to share that notion with him.

"So you were supposed to keep Joel from accidentally destroying things?" Anna asked. Kieran gave her that same nasty smile.

"That's what they said," he said. "So that's what I did. It was more palatable to all of us monsters than locking him up for being a monster. Or putting him down. And it was going very well, you know. When Joel was in a talking phase, he and I used to say that he was now a hopeful monster, because there was some hope for him after all. That was our hysterical joke. You don't know what a hopeful monster is, do you?"

Anna looked at Collie, who raised her shoulders in a "got me."

"Sorry," Anna said. Kieran laughed softly.

"Of course you don't. Why *would* you? It doesn't matter. Turns out it was all humbuggery. Or, unasked-for buggery. Joel's not here, by the way."

"I was getting that sense," Anna said. "Is anyone here?"

"They decided to give me some alone time," Kieran said. "Everyone here is allowed to throw things and break things and yell things, except for me."

"Sucks being the only grown-up," Collie said. "Where is Joel?"

"I don't know for sure," Kieran said. "I didn't need to know. I was the last person they would have sent along."

"Kieran..." Collie started.

"Seems someone," he said, cutting her off, "gave the Embassy a tip about a Varanus facility and they thought, 'wouldn't it be great if we could destroy that place?' And then they remembered that they had an actual weapon of mass destruction sitting a few blocks away. So they sent the goddamned siren over here to give Joel his marching orders. She had a private talk with him and then she left, and then he got a coat and put his shoes on, and then he left. I tried to talk to him, but I'm not a redheaded witch, so he wasn't interested."

"Oh," Collie said quietly. Kieran was looking at his hands, now, instead of at them. Anywhere but at them.

"I thought people couldn't do things like that around you," Anna said.

Kieran shook his head.

"You don't listen. I said it was more difficult. The siren has enough power to disregard my field."

Anna didn't ask how much power that was. She waited for Kieran to go on.

"Joel left in a cab," Kieran said after a moment. "I guess all the Embassy's teleporters are gone, or dead. It must drive them craz — even crazier, having to take cabs and planes like puny mortals."

"They didn't leave together?" Anna asked, ignoring the bit about mortals, which she hoped was just angry hyperbole. "Joel and the redhead? I think he has to be with people, or her love potion wears off."

"Depends on whether she does it as hard as she can," Kieran said. "Sometimes it takes months to wear off. Sometimes people don't make it that long and they cut their throats on the lawn of the Embassy and I'm surprised, frankly, that you don't know this. Because it is very, very bad PR."

"They must have handled it somehow," Collie said. "Do you really think I would have taken that kind of job?"

Kieran looked at her. His eyes were redder and Anna realized he'd looked down so he could cry. Couldn't be seen doing that. It wouldn't be manly.

"What kind of job?" he asked. "Are you sure you can tell the kinds of jobs apart?"

Collie said nothing. Her purse strap was starting to show wear, tiny cracks in the leather.

"We know where Joel went," Anna said.

"Bully for you," Kieran said. She waited for him to say more, but apparently he felt that was all that was required.

"We know someone who's inside that facility," she said. "We need to keep Joel from destroying it."

Kieran laughed, loud and sharp.

"Oh, you know someone in there. That makes it bad. *That* makes it very bad. Otherwise the receptionist and the people they've kidnapped and the cleaning staff and the cafeteria workers, they'd have it coming. Don't you think?"

"Shut up," Collie said. "I sympathize with you, Kieran. Do not make a smart comment about that, either. Just shut up. I sympathize and I know why you're being like this, but your pity party is loud and I need to hear myself think."

Kieran looked surprised and, after a few heartbeats, put his head down again. Anna kept still. She didn't have any thoughts worth mentioning and, if Collie did, she was more than willing to give Collie all the quiet she needed.

There was a clock that ticked, ticked, ticked on the wall across from Anna. She watched it for just under two minutes, until Collie's voice startled her.

"I need the internet," she told Kieran. Without looking up, he waved a hand at a desk crammed into the small enclosed sunroom leading off the living room.

"It's up," he said. Collie went into the other room. Anna stayed put, in case Kieran... she didn't know exactly what, but she stayed anyway.

A few minutes later, Collie came back into the living room. Her cheeks were bright red, the way she got when she was feverish or under a tight deadline.

"How long ago did he leave?" she asked. Kieran looked at her.

"A few hours."

Collie didn't look happy about that, but she didn't say so. She just pulled her phone from her purse and dialed.

"We need something from you," she said a moment later, as she returned to her place on the couch. "You will like it, because you will be pissing all over their cornflakes."

She paused, presumably for a response, and Anna watched Kieran to see if he seemed to be listening. He didn't. He seemed to be somewhere else. Maybe with Joel, wherever he imagined Joel to be.

"Good," Collie said. "Where can we meet you?" A second and a shaky breath. Collie was jumpy, though her voice was calm. "Now. There's no point in anything later than now." Collie looked at Kieran and her breathing evened out. She'd made some kind of decision. She always got calmer when she'd started making decisions, when the variables started to get nailed down. "Here will be fine," she said. "But I think we'll have to meet you out front."

COLLIE SAID NOTHING to Kieran in the way of goodbyes or thank-yous. She hightailed it out the door. Anna lagged and looked at Kieran, was surprised to find him looking at her.

"You going to kill him?" Kieran asked.

"Whatever the plan is," Anna said. "It's her plan. I don't know what she's got in mind."

"It's not his fault," Kieran said. "I know... I do know ... if a nuclear reactor goes off, you still have to bury it."

"We prefer not to bury anyone," Anna said. "We prefer not to throw stones."

"That's nice," Kieran said. "Very civilized. Someone forgot to tell you that you'd signed up for dodgeball."

Anna had nothing to say to that. Kieran tried for a smile.

"Bring him back here, please," he said. "We'll disappear. We won't make you sorry."

"Do my best," Anna told him, and went to join Collie.

She found Collie pacing on the sidewalk, from one end of the lawn to the other.

"See," Collie said once Anna had fallen into step beside her, "he's got a head start, and I have to assume they threw money at this and chartered a plane, and you can go Edmonton to Fort Chip in a couple hours from City Centre, and they do have car rentals there — well, truck rentals, probably — and it's just a few klicks away and I know you're not going to like this, but —"

She didn't say what Anna wasn't going to like. She didn't have to. It was walking up the street toward them, dark curls bouncing, high-heeled boots clicking on the pavement, smiling as if this were the finest part of a particularly fine day.

"Jesus," Anna said under her breath. "Col..."

"I know," Collie said, and stepped forward to meet their visitor. "Glad you could make it, Robin."

"AND TO THINK you were calling me 'bitch' just a few hours ago," Robin said cheerily. "How the wheel turns."

"You're still a bitch," Collie said flatly. "The wheel is never going to turn that far. But that doesn't change the fact that there's something you can do for us. With the understanding that, really, you'll be doing it for you."

"It's nice to be understood," Robin said. "What will I be doing, then, and why will I be doing it?"

"I'll take the second part first," Collie said. Anna was transfixed by the conversation, but she managed to tear her eyes from Collie long enough to glance at the window and make sure Kieran had not rejoined the world and stepped forward to watch this. It was hard to tell, through the thick gauze of the sunroom curtains, but she didn't think he was there.

"You're going to thwart the destruction of a Varanus facility," Collie was saying. "Which will make you look very good to your client. And, since the Embassy is behind this, you'll be ruining their plans."

"That does sound good," Robin said. "What do I have to do to experience these benefits?"

"Just give us a lift," Collie said. "Turns out you're the last damned train to Clarksville, and we are in something of a rush."

Robin looked genuinely amused. Pleased. Fond, even. Anna couldn't keep herself from shuddering under her heavy coat.

"A lift?" Robin said. "That's all?"

"In and out," Collie said. "With an extra passenger on the return trip. And you'll maybe have to knock him out. I assume you can do that?"

"A snap," Robin confirmed. She snapped her fingers and Anna jumped, expecting something. Unconsciousness, maybe. Or dead birds falling from the trees. "And where am I taking you ladies today?"

Collie pulled a piece of paper from her pocket and unfolded it. Anna realized that Collie must have printed it out in the sunroom.

"Here," Collie said, the opaline nail of her pinky finger tracing the line that ran through Grayling Cross.

ANNA HAD NEVER intended to be teleported anywhere. Not ever. She recalled having said as much to Collie, somewhere in the whirlwind of the past few days. She'd seen teleporter accidents on *Star Trek* and she'd thought about it, off and on, and she didn't know how it worked with the magical types, but it couldn't be good. It couldn't be right. It couldn't even really be you on the other side, could it? Not by any laws she could figure out.

She wanted to pussy out, but Kieran... that son of a bitch had shamed her. It had been self-serving and self-pitying and selfish, but it didn't change the fact that she hadn't spared a moment's thought for the people working on the Death Star, and she didn't like herself much for that.

Also, on a more personal note, she was fucking certain that Collie was going to go, whether Anna went with her or not.

"Grayling Cross it is," Anna said. Robin clapped her hands, once.

"Lovely. I'll need you both to take my hands, and there's a chant..."

Anna kept her hands at her sides and looked at Robin. Collie spoke for both of them.

"Fuck you, bitch."

Robin laughed happily.

"Fine. Close your eyes."

ANNA CLOSED HER EYES and, like that, the ground was warm beneath her feet. Not as warm as on the road through town, but still warm enough to rise through the soles of her boots. She breathed lake water and pine. And Jake was wrong, plain wrong, because he didn't take the time out of space-time. You couldn't.

It took no time, she thought. And where there was no time, there could be no space. They lived in each other's pockets.

That was how it was done.

She opened her eyes.

They were at the edge of a clearing, back far enough to be hidden by the venerable pines around them. Old-growth forest. Beautiful and airy and easy to walk through. Always a lightning strike away from burning to stumps and dirt. Anna was amazed that any of it had survived the dragon.

Joel was ahead of them, ten metres or so, fixated on what looked like an overgrown, abandoned mine. Beside her, Anna heard a gasp. She turned to see Robin gaping at Joel, not looking remotely cool or ironic or detached.

"You never said it was him," she hissed.

"So?" Collie asked. She was on Anna's other side, watching Joel as she spoke, just above a whisper.

"So, I'm not going to 'knock him out,' as you say. He's doing his bit, isn't he? I'm not going to draw his attention."

"I thought it was a snap," Collie said, finally glaring at Robin. "Cow. Boy. Up."

"Forget it," Robin said. "He is... look at him!"

They did. In front of Joel, grass was going to seed, blurring, stuttering into pixels and dust. Brush and trees were distorting the way things did on a blazing summer day, when mirages poured water on dry pavement. Anna felt motion sick with fear, nauseated and going numb.

"I'm leaving," Robin added.

"No, you're not," Collie said. "Or you'd already be gone. You want to see what the fuck we do now."

Robin shrugged.

"I don't have anywhere to be."

They stood and stared. Brush scattered. The air felt odd, charged with something.

"What do we do now?" Collie asked.

Anna looked around and saw a piece of heavy wood, about half the length of her arm. She picked it up, careful to be quiet about it. There was, when all else failed, an old-fashioned way to get the same job done. Even if they didn't have a bowling ball.

She looked at Collie and saw that Collie was watching her, eyes wide with disbelief. Anna smiled.

"He seem distracted to you?" she asked.

"You can't do that," Collie breathed.

"I think there's a good chance I can," Anna said. "The guy is a known space cadet." She moved her arm up and down, liking the heft of the branch. "Wish me luck."

"Luck," Collie repeated. "Luck."

Anna took a step forward and felt a hand on her arm. She turned to look at Collie.

"Hey, dude?" Collie said. "I, uh... would if I could."

Anna was puzzled for a moment, then remembered. She smiled.

"Right back at you."

It took about forever to creep across the grass, but Anna didn't mind. It was peaceful, somehow. She was going to get to him and clobber him, or he was going to turn around and she'd be done. There was nothing now but to put one foot in front of the other and see which it would be.

This was, then, the serenity Collie felt as spinning coins fell and points of decision disappeared.

She didn't watch what Joel was doing. She only had to see the back of his head, black hair ruffling in the light breeze.

Then it was an arm's length away, and less. And she swung.

He fell hard, forward, taking the energy of her swing with him to the ground. She saw blood, a little, under the black hair. She might have killed him. Twice in one day, she was wondering about someone she'd hit, trying to figure out if they were taking it worse than she'd meant. Or how badly she had, honestly, meant it.

It occurred to her, no matter what she'd said to Kieran... maybe she should take another swing. If she even needed to. Maybe it would have been right for Joel, who had to live with having accidents, and Kieran, who though himself responsible, and everyone who was around when Joel went off.

Hell, no.

Before Anna could kneel to check Joel's pulse, Joel vanished. She looked back where she'd come from, hoping Collie had seen what happened and could explain it to her, and was relieved to see Joel beside Robin and Collie, Robin touching long fingers to his eyes. Robin looked at her and Anna was there, looking down at Joel.

"No telling when they'll wake up when you clock them," Robin said. "It's surer my way."

"Thanks for stepping up," Collie said. She was going for sarcasm, but Anna could hear a faint note of sincerity.

"So?" Robin said. "Back to Evil E? Slit this boy's throat before he sneezes and turns the planet to dust? Thoughts?"

Collie looked at Anna.

"We're not killing him," she said, forcefully, as if expecting an argument.

Anna nodded

"I was wondering what you had in mind. I don't really want to kill him either," she said. "Not for things he might or might not do."

Collie looked as if Anna had slapped her.

"You thought I might want to kill him?"

"Oh, you people are pathetic," Robin said. "You'd get on with the Embassy. Truly. You think you can just play nice and everything will work out, and if it doesn't, well, it's not on you, is it?"

"What would it take to get you to bring him back to Edmonton and leave him with Kieran?" Anna asked. Robin smiled.

"Just a chit, I suppose. You can owe me. If that's really what you want."

"In this best of all possible worlds," Anna said. "Yeah. That is really what I want."

"What we want," Collie said.

Robin shrugged.

"Sometimes you can get what you want," she said. "I'll let you know when I need my favour."

And then she was gone, and Joel with her. Collie broke the sudden silence.

"I would never have killed him. Not just… on spec."

"Okay," Anna said.

"Okay," Collie said.

"I thought about it," Anna admitted.

"I didn't," Collie said. "It just wasn't his fault. Being that way. People are born different ways."

"Fault isn't everything," Anna said.

Collie was about to say something when a twig snapped behind them. It might have been a deer or a rabbit. From the way Anna and Collie reacted, it might as easily have been the Viet Cong.

A slim figure emerged from behind the wide trunk of a tree and it was neither animal nor enemy forces. It was just Rowan Bell.

"SCARE THE HELL OUT OF US why don't you," Collie said. Rowan grinned. He was wearing a t-shirt and jeans. Not enough for autumn in a place so close to the sixtieth parallel, but he didn't look uncomfortable.

"Sorry," he said. "Didn't mean to."

"It's okay," Collie said. "Are you okay?"

"I'm good," Rowan said. "Thank you for that. I was scared he was going to wipe the whole place off the map."

"It's already off the map," Anna pointed out. "Are you in there, right now? In the facility?"

Collie looked surprised, then looked Rowan up and down with narrowed eyes, as if trying to see through him.

"No," Rowan said. "I should tell you something, right off. You're gonna be mad."

"You mean my mood will get worse?" Anna asked. "I'm almost curious as to how."

"I got away from them the same night they took me," Rowan said. "They don't know where I am."

Anna had to give him points for accuracy. She was mad, all right. And she didn't even have to look at Collie to know that Collie was white hot at that little revelation.

"You what? You have been at liberty since this all started

and you didn't call Eric? You didn't get in touch with anyone? Do you have any idea what has been going on? What is wrong with you?"

"See, yeah," Rowan said. "That's why I haven't called anyone. Oh, I did get your note."

He reached into his pocket and produced the note Collie had scrawled in Sam's shop.

"I've been trying to find something out, so I couldn't call you. And, actually, I do have some idea what's been going on. I told you to believe Robin, didn't I? I told you about Joel."

Collie had sudden tears in her eyes. Anna felt more stupid than sad. Eric and Michael... whatever Michael had been... had both said Rowan could move things. Like jars of bath salts, say. But they'd convinced themselves it had been Ian. That Ian wasn't really, completely, gone.

In their defence, any sensible person would have assumed that Rowan's messages would be different, if he were free to send them. I'm here. I'm okay. Don't look for me. Eric, go home. There's a witch after you. There's a price on your head. Go home.

Maybe he hadn't known about the witch.

"Look," Rowan said, "I don't want to get into it, but I had some reason to... I really needed to know about my past. I needed to know what Varanus had in their records about me, and my mother. And I really, *really* couldn't have Eric around while I was looking into it. That could have, uh, changed everything."

Anna said nothing. She knew exactly what he was really, *really* saying, but didn't feel like saying so. She felt like letting it lie.

Rowan gestured at the mine.

"If that place had been destroyed, I would have had to find another Varanus facility to get a look at their records. Not to mention, there are probably people like me in there. It's, like, not always your idea to be working for them."

"So we've heard," Anna said. "You, have any luck remote viewing in there?"

Rowan shook his head.

"They have people guarding the... there's a kind of space I travel in, and they have guards there. I've been looking for a way around them. No luck so far."

"Maybe you won't have to," Collie said. Her voice was a little high, a little girly. It was misleading, when her pitch rose. It made her seem inconsequential, when in fact it meant that her throat was painfully tight and she was angry, raging, almost beyond words. "Where are you, Rowan? Really?"

"Fort Mac," he said, grinning. "Never crossed their minds that I might just stay in town. I am in the shittiest hotel room."

"I've seen worse," Anna said. That threw him, but he didn't have a chance to say so, because Collie had taken something from her pocket and was holding it toward him.

"Oh..." Rowan said. "Shit... where did you get that?" He took the duck in his hand and turned it over, smiling a little.

"Eric said you needed it," Collie said. "He said you couldn't get by without it."

Rowan nodded, still looking at the duck.

"I used to be like that. I never told him I'd gotten over it." He looked at Collie. "I just liked having a few secrets, you know? I never did before."

"Why not?" Collie said evenly. "Teenagers like that. Secrets and angst. I don't know who I am. I don't know what's real. My college buddies and me, we're gonna pour a half cup of sugar in our cups of coffee and we're going to talk and talk and talk about it. Everyone does that, Rowan. Then we grow up. We are or we aren't and we do what we do and at best, kid, we try not to be complete shits to other people."

Rowan couldn't have looked more puzzled if Collie had spat in his face, out of the blue. He drew his head back and frowned at her.

"Hey... lady... what?"

Collie took the luz from her other pocket and held it out on her flat palm.

"Look familiar?" she asked. Rowan peered at it.

"I..."

"It's the dragon joint," Collie said. "Take it."

Rowan took it, his face seeming older with the lines of confusion everywhere. He rubbed it between his palms.

"It turned to bone," Collie said, "it changed, the same time one of Eric's imaginary friends disappeared. When Eric got killed, looking for you."

Rowan stared at her. He was horrified, beyond speech. Anna felt miserable, just looking at him, but Collie didn't soften.

"Happy birthday, Pinocchio," she said and finally, finally, her voice broke. She didn't cry, but the tears were thick in the last word.

Rowan's head dropped and he looked at the luz in his hands as if it could be the salvation of something, be the seed of a person, the way the mystical ones were. Anna watched him and, before her eyes, the trees became visible through his face and shirt and jeans, and then the trees were the only things she could see.

"You think he went to Fort McMurray?" Anna asked. "Or...?"

"I don't know," Collie said. She was soft now, still teary "I know that was mean."

"It was fucking mean," Anna said, not with malice.

"He was just so stupid. He can't be stupid like that. He won't survive being stupid."

"That's your right," Anna said, "when you're nineteen."

"Not when you're like him," Collie said.

Not, Anna thought, when you're playing dodgeball with all the stone throwers.

"You'd think the luz would have dropped when he left," she said. "I didn't think he could take things with him."

Collie shrugged.

"Why have expectations?" she said. Then she looked toward the ruins of the town, though there was no reason for her to know where they were. She wasn't the one who'd been there before.

"Is that the road up there?" she asked. "Do you think Joel rented a truck?"

"Truck or boat," Anna said. "That would be about the only way to get here from town. Barring magic."

They walked toward the ashes of Grayling Cross, the ground warming with every step.

"WHERE DO YOU THINK she took Joel?" Collie asked as the town came into sight. "Do you think she really took him to Kieran?"

"Yeah," Anna said. "I think she wants that favour from us. She might even have something in mind. That'll keep me up nights."

"Tell me about it," Collie agreed.

They rounded a corner and Collie laughed. Anna was shocked to hear it. She looked at Collie to see if she'd lost her mind, was wearing a rictus like the Joker's. She looked very much herself, though, so Anna followed her gaze and almost laughed, too.

Her Jeep was parked in the middle of the road.

Not her Jeep, obviously. That was, she suddenly realized, still at the garage where they'd left it. But it was the same age, same colour, even dented in a few of the same places.

"Incredible," Collie said. "Joel rented your damned Jeep."

"Alberta plates," Anna said, thinking out loud. They were the reason the Jeep looked strange to her.

"Oh," Collie said, "Yeah. God, Anna, you have got to switch your plates over. Your Saskie insurance won't cover you if anything happens, and —"

"I know that," Anna said wearily. "I couldn't afford to fix the Jeep, remember? No out of province inspection, no insurance, no registration."

They reached the side of the Jeep. The driver's door was unlocked and the keys were on the seat. At least one thing was going to be easier than it had any right to be.

"You could get it fixed now," Collie said. "We have all that money in the bank. You could get all the guts replaced if you want. Or you could get a new one. Whatever you want."

"And get my Alberta plates," Anna said.

"Well, yeah," Collie said. But she didn't sound so certain.

"And back to Edmonton," Anna said. "That's where we're going. Next flight out of here. Back to them."

The Jeep started easily. By Anna's lights, anyway. It had a first gear.

"Fort Chip flights go to Fort Mac," Collie said. "Mostly."

"Fort Mac flights go all over," Anna said. "Robin said so."

"She doesn't lie much," Collie said. "You think maybe we should look at our options?"

"We're rich," Anna said. "World's our oyster."

Not that they were truly rich. Not by rich people's standards. But they didn't have to work for awhile, at least. And they could afford to move.

She barely had to steer. The Jeep knew where to go, like a trail horse used to the paths it took every day.

"What are we going to do?" Collie asked. Anna looked at the dark green trees against the bright blue sky and thought about that.

"At best," she said finally, "we'll try not to be complete shits to other people. And we'll see how that goes."

Thanks to: Ryan, Val and Iain, Mom and Dad, Anne, Wong, Shep, Beck, Heather, Jill, Lori and Dwight, Cori, Tyler, the 3-Day gang, Audrey's and Greenwoods, the Corp Comm that was, Andrew the editor, and everyone else I should have thanked (and hope I thanked in person).

The multi-talented Gayleen Froese is a novelist, musician, and communications professional. She has also worked as a radio writer and talk show host, an advertising creative director, and a communications officer.

Froese was featured on Canadian Learning Television's *A Total Write Off!* and was the overall winner of BookTelevision's *3-Day Novel Contest,* filmed over three days in 2007 at an Edmonton Chapters bookstore. She was also shortlisted in the overall 2007 International 3-Day Novel Contest. Her nonfiction and humour writing has appeared in publications including *SEE Magazine, The Rat Creek Press,* and *The Session*.

Gayleen Froese's first novel, *Touch,* is part of the NeWest Nunatak First Fiction Series.